KT-382-640

# UNFORGOTTEN

Clare Francis is the author of ten international bestsellers, including *Deceit*, *Betrayal*, *A Dark Devotion* and, most recently, *Homeland*. She lives in London.

### Praise for *Unforgotten*

'An expertly rendered tale with psychological tension, pyrotechnics, courtroom drama, good old-fashioned detection and some well-deployed red herrings'  *Guardian*

'Francis skilfully constructs a slow burning thriller that derives its impact from a firm grounding in the processes of the legal system and the dynamics of happy and unhappy families'  *Spectator*

'Francis draws you in and keeps you guessing'  *Woman & Home*

'Both murder mystery and domestic drama'  *Financial Times*

'The plot intricate and the solution ingenious. A very good read'  *Scotsman*

# CLARE FRANCIS

# UNFORGOTTEN

PAN BOOKS

First published 2008 by Macmillan

This edition published 2008 by Pan Books
an imprint of Pan Macmillan Ltd
Pan Macmillan, 20 New Wharf Road, London N1 9RR
Basingstoke and Oxford
Associated companies throughout the world
www.panmacmillan.com

ISBN 987-0-330-48406-0

Copyright © Clare Francis 2008

The right of Clare Francis to be identified as the
author of this work has been asserted by her in accordance
with the Copyright, Designs and Patents Act 1988.

All rights reserved. No part of this publication may be
reproduced, stored in or introduced into a retrieval system, or
transmitted, in any form, or by any means (electronic, mechanical,
photocopying, recording or otherwise) without the prior written
permission of the publisher. Any person who does any unauthorized
act in relation to this publication may be liable to criminal
prosecution and civil claims for damages.

5 7 9 8 6 4

A CIP catalogue record for this book is available from
the British Library.

Typeset by Set Systems Ltd, Saffron Walden, Essex
Printed and bound in the UK by
CPI Mackays, Chatham ME5 8TD

This book is sold subject to the condition that it shall not,
by way of trade or otherwise, be lent, re-sold, hired out,
or otherwise circulated without the publisher's prior consent
in any form of binding or cover other than that in which
it is published and without a similar condition including this
condition being imposed on the subsequent purchaser.

Visit www.panmacmillan.com to read more about all our books
and to buy them. You will also find features, author interviews and
news of any author events, and you can sign up for e-newsletters
so that you're always first to hear about our new releases.

for O. H.

# ONE

Hugh Gwynne arrived at the Royal Courts of Justice soon after nine thirty and made a quick inspection of the noticeboard and the location of Court 12 before stationing himself to one side of the Great Hall to wait for the rest of the team. The hall was more church than law, a vast Gothic cathedral of soaring arches and high stained-glass windows, designed to overawe. As clumps of people formed and dissolved, he shifted a little to maintain a clear view of the entrance, where a stream of barristers, solicitors and officials hurried in only to bunch impatiently at the security check. There was still plenty of time, but that didn't prevent him from feeling a nudge of anxiety in case one of the team should get held up, a tension heightened by the rarity of his trips to London and the unfamiliar surroundings of the Royal Courts. There had already been a scare late on Saturday evening when it looked as if their key witness Dr Ainsley might be delayed by a snowstorm in Chicago. Then Hugh's client Tom Deacon had called last night to insist on a case conference before court resumed, on a subject he refused to reveal in advance. The conference was meant to happen at ten, the hearing to resume at ten thirty, so when no one had appeared by five to ten Hugh allowed himself a more serious twinge of concern. Where had they all got to?

A minute later Hugh spotted Desmond Riley's round figure approaching at a leisurely pace, his gown draped over one arm, his briefcase swinging lazily at his side, and, close behind, Sanjay, dragging a wheeled case, his free arm full of documents. Leading and junior counsel, and no mistaking which was which.

'Oh, hello, Hugh,' said Desmond with a show of mild surprise, as if they'd bumped into each other by chance. 'Well, here we are again.' His tone, like his walk, was deliberately casual, almost off-hand, an affectation which Hugh had found disconcerting in the early days of the hearing, until he realised it was less a vanity than a disguise for the anticipation Desmond felt at the prospect of a stimulating day in court.

Sanjay smiled. 'Hi, Hugh.'

Hugh was on the point of asking after the latest addition to Sanjay's family, which had been imminent when they'd last met, when Desmond came in with: 'All set?'

Hugh said, 'We're just waiting for Tom.'

'Ah.' Desmond's face took on a distracted expression, as if clients, essential though they were, could be something of an unwelcome complication.

Hugh said, 'I'm sure he won't be long.'

Desmond made a show of looking at his watch. 'But do we really need a confab now? Can't it wait till lunchtime?'

'He was anxious to go through a few points.'

'Points?' Desmond echoed dubiously.

'I think he's been going over some of the witness statements.'

'Ahh.' Desmond managed to instil the sound with a breadth of meaning. 'He gave no indication of what these points might be?'

'No.'

There was a pause while they pondered the intricacies of dealing with Tom Deacon. For Hugh, who could never think of his client without a stab of sympathy intensified by a reflexive guilt at his own good fortune, Tom's wilder ideas and strange inconsequential obsessions demanded respect and attention, if, ultimately, firmness. The fact that Tom no longer trusted Hugh with his ideas, stubbornly guarding them for Desmond's scrutiny, was just another manifestation of the man's psychological injury, which was, after all, why they were here in the first place.

'It's nothing *urgent* though?' Desmond asked hopefully. 'Nothing that concerns this morning's business?'

'He didn't say.'

'Nothing in the way of new instructions as such?' Desmond persevered.

'Not that I'm aware of, no.'

Desmond glanced towards the doors, as if to emphasise Tom's non-appearance.

'He must have got held up,' Hugh said lamely.

'In that case, I think we'll go on ahead,' Desmond declared with a brisk smile. 'Perhaps when Tom arrives . . .' He passed this thought to Hugh with a lift of his eyebrows.

'I'll bring him straight up.'

'And if there's no time for the confab we'll hold it

over till lunchtime, shall we?' Abandoning any last pretence of languor, Desmond moved rapidly away.

As Sanjay started to follow, Hugh asked quickly,
'Boy or girl?'

Sanjay gave a happy grin. 'Boy.'

'Wonderful news. Congratulations.'

Sanjay tilted his head in thanks and hurried off,
only to turn back with an air of having forgotten his
manners. 'And your son – did he get that university
place?'

As with so many matters concerning Charlie there
was no simple answer to this, and after a moment's
hesitation Hugh called, 'Near enough anyway,' adding a baffled shrug, which Sanjay took as a show of
fatherly modesty, but which caused Hugh a darting
sense of disloyalty, as though he had damned Charlie's
achievement with faint praise.

Finally, Hugh's trainee Isabel Mazzara came into
sight with Derek, the firm's outdoor clerk, wheeling a
porter's trolley of boxed documents.

'The traffic,' Isabel breathed, with residual anxiety.
'I knew London was bad, but . . .'

'Lots of time,' Hugh assured her.

'What's the news on—' Isabel broke off with a deep
spluttering cough. 'Sorry.' She scrabbled for a tissue
and blew her nose. 'Thought I'd shaken this off . . .'

Isabel was a health and yoga devotee, who in her
eighteen months at Dimmock Marsh had tried with
gentle fervour to encourage Hugh into healthier lunch-
ing habits. Seeing her watery eyes and reddened nostrils,
Hugh offered a sympathetic wince. 'Bad luck.'

Her naturally grave face, accentuated by a wide,
slightly startled gaze, creased into an expression of

concern. 'Just hope I don't give it to everyone else.' She snuffled into her handkerchief again. 'Did Ainsley's flight get in all right?'

'Yesterday morning. He said he'd be here by ten fifteen.'

He could see Isabel mentally assembling the documents that would need to be on hand for Ainsley's evidence. When she had ticked everything off to her satisfaction, her expression, always a mirror to her thoughts, registered the fact with a small gleam of relief. 'And Hugh – what do you want me to do once I've got things set up? Do you want me to come back and wait for Tom?'

'No.' It was unthinkable that anyone else should wait for Tom. 'No. If you'd just keep an eye out for Dr Ainsley. In case I miss him in the crowd.'

Needing no encouragement to get up to the courtroom and work out how best to arrange the documents, Isabel picked up her briefcase, only to set it down again and root hastily through her handbag.

Derek took a step forward. 'How are you, Mr Gwynne?'

'All right, thanks, Derek.'

'Mrs Gwynne keeping well?'

'She is indeed.'

'Still working for the Citizens Advice?'

'Yes. Keeps her pretty busy.'

'And the rest of the family?'

'Thriving.'

Having a good idea of what was coming next, rather hoping to avoid it, Hugh made a point of looking away towards the entrance. But Derek had served thirty years in the Bristol police before coming to work for Dimmock Marsh and took a fussy proprietorial interest in events that impinged on his former territory.

'No further news?' he asked in a confidential murmur.

'Sorry?'

'From the local force?'

'It was only a broken window, Derek.'

'And fifty pounds in cash,' Derek corrected him, in the manner of someone who likes to get the facts rights. 'And some jewellery.'

'It was costume jewellery, worth very little.'

'You haven't found other items missing subsequently?'

They'd had this conversation several times in the last two weeks, but going over old ground had never been a problem for Derek.

'Nothing, no.'

Departing from his usual script, Derek declared, 'Likely an addict then. They're the ones that go for the cash.'

Hugh cast him a sharp look, wondering if he knew about Charlie's problem but was too polite to mention it.

But Derek's bland transparent face was void of pretence as he said, 'Likely as not someone known to the local lads if they'd bothered to take prints.'

'They issued me with an incident number, Derek. That's all you can expect nowadays.'

Derek's doleful expression suggested that things had gone steeply downhill since his time on the force. 'Well, if there's anything I can do, Mr Gwynne, you know where to find me.'

'Thanks, Derek.'

With a small exclamation, Isabel finally extracted a small packet from her handbag. 'Here, Hugh, take one of these every two hours. They're the best thing for warding off colds. They've got vitamin C and zinc and—'

'No, you keep them, Isabel.'

'But I can get some more at lunchtime.' Conscientious to a fault, she would go without eating to scour the neighbourhood.

Hugh shook his head. 'Really. I'll have some extra chips instead.'

The cold or the stress had made her slow, she gazed at him in puzzlement.

'Spuds are good for vitamin C, aren't they?'

'But chips aren't—' Then, catching his expression, she coloured slightly. 'Here,' she said, thrusting the packet forward. 'Have one for now.'

Hugh took the pastille dutifully and, as Isabel set off with Derek to find Court 12, slipped it into his pocket.

Resuming his scrutiny of the entrance, Hugh searched for Tom Deacon's taut discordant figure, his characteristic staccato stride. At ten twenty he decided Tom must have got lost on the Underground or badly misjudged the travelling time. Tom had talked vaguely about staying with friends somewhere beyond Putney, as if there was some region of south-west London yet to acquire a proper name. Though it was more than twenty years since Hugh had been articled to a firm of solicitors in Westminster, returning each evening to a cramped flat-share in Fulham, he was familiar enough with the layout of the suburbs to know that the rail links were few and far between. Tom had probably underestimated the time it would take to reach the nearest station, and the number of changes necessary, and the likelihood of delays due to points failures, bomb scares, and driver no-shows. Hugh only hoped he wasn't suffering a full-blown panic attack.

To know Tom Deacon was to worry about him. In the four years since Hugh had taken on Tom's personal injury claim, through all the setbacks and delays, the hagglings and manoeuvrings with the other side, not to mention the numerous crises in Tom's health and personal life, it seemed to Hugh that he had spent more time worrying about Tom than all his other clients put together.

Hugh called Tom's mobile, knowing it would be switched off on the advice of his therapist, who insisted he pick up messages no more than twice a day. Hugh left a message anyway, reminding Tom they were in Court 12, saying he might have to go on ahead.

A moment later his phone beeped, but the text wasn't from Tom, it was from Annaliese, Hugh's PA, to say she would be dropping off some urgent mail at his house that evening.

Hugh left it as long as he dared, then, two minutes before court was due to begin, started up the stone steps at a run, diverting briefly to the first-floor balcony to take a last glance into the Great Hall below. He was veering away when a familiar figure caught his eye. It was Tom, standing in the queue for the security check. Even in the shadows at the end of the hall he was unmistakable, the bony head, the hunch of the sharp shoulders, the ill-fitting jacket cut by the straps of his rucksack.

Hugh hurried down again and, overcome by affection and relief, strode across the hall to meet him. 'You've made it! Well done!'

Tom was too busy casting around the hall to notice his outstretched hand, so by way of a greeting Hugh touched his sleeve instead.

'Problems on the Underground?'

'Where's Desmond?'

'He had to go on ahead.'

Focusing properly on Hugh for the first time, Tom's eyes flickered with agitation. 'What about the conference?'

'It'll have to wait till lunchtime.'

'But I need to talk to him.'

'Court's just starting, Tom. It's ten thirty.'

Tom's frown contained puzzlement but also what looked like a more general confusion, and Hugh wondered whether he'd overdone his medication. It had happened a couple of times before, most notably on the second day of the hearing when Tom, giving evidence, had found it so hard to form even the most basic sentence that the judge suggested he step down till another day.

'You all right, old friend?' Hugh asked, noticing the pallor of his skin where it stretched over the sharp cheekbones, and the sheen of dampness that clung to his forehead.

'Yeah . . .' Tom murmured distractedly. 'Yeah . . .'

'Anything you need?'

'No, I . . . just didn't sleep too well . . .'

'Always difficult in a strange bed,' Hugh said, knowing that Tom hadn't managed a good night's sleep in five years, ever since the road accident when, unable to free his four-year-old daughter from the overturned car, he had been forced to watch her burn to death. 'Look, do you want to go for a coffee first? Take a few minutes to—'

'No,' said Tom with sudden urgency, as if he'd finally understood how late it was. 'No, we should get up there!'

They moved off, Tom walking in long jerky strides, his eyes fixed doggedly on the floor ahead. 'What I've got to tell Desmond,' he said, 'it's very important.'

'Okay,' Hugh said. 'Why don't you tell me what it is, then I can pass him a note?'

But Tom was wearing the stubborn, harried expression that suggested he had other plans. 'It's . . . too complicated. I'll have to write it out.'

'Fine. So long as I can see it first.' Then, because this had sounded peremptory, never the best approach with Tom, Hugh added, 'You know how it is, Tom. Procedure.'

'I know the procedure.'

'Yes, of course,' Hugh said easily, as they started up the steps.

'It hasn't been *that* long.'

It had in fact been five weeks since the hearing had overrun its time allocation at Bristol High Court and been adjourned until the next gap in the judge's peripatetic schedule. This week, the first available, had found the judge sitting here at the Royal Courts, so like a band of gypsies they had struck camp and brought the caravan of lawyers, documents and witnesses to London.

'I've been working on the case non-stop,' Tom went on, with a hint of rebuke.

'I know you have, Tom.' And Hugh had batches of his typed notes to prove it, in duplicate, a set for him and a set for Desmond on which Hugh had exercised a certain discretion, either editing them heavily or omitting to forward them. More recently Tom had taken to calling Hugh in the evenings, sometimes quite late, to go over points they had covered a dozen times before.

Tom climbed the last few steps at the double.

Hugh said, 'We shouldn't have missed too much, you know. There's bound to be some preliminary stuff before they call the first witness—'

'*Price*,' Tom breathed derisively. 'Bloody *Price*.' Price, a former army comrade of Tom's, was giving evidence for the other side.

'It's not Price on first, Tom. It's Dr Ainsley. Price won't be on till this afternoon at the very earliest.'

Tom halted. 'But you said it was going to be Price.' The lack of sleep or the medication had lent his voice a childish whine.

'What I said, Tom, was that Price *could* be on first if Ainsley got delayed. But Ainsley's made it okay, so we're back to the original schedule.'

'For God's sake . . .'

'I said I'd phone if there was a change.'

'You said it was going to be Price,' he repeated reproachfully.

Tom had these little frets from time to time when events were crowding in on him and he was struggling to retain a sense of control. Hugh said reassuringly, 'Much better to start the week with a key witness for our side. That way we get to restate our case before Price gets into the witness box.'

Tom moved forward again, but cautiously, as if the day still had the power to spring further unpleasant surprises on him. 'When will I be giving evidence?'

They had been through this on the phone as well, but Hugh answered as though for the first time, 'I'm not sure, Tom.'

'Tomorrow?'

'Umm . . . Desmond thinks, unlikely.'

'But as soon as Price has finished.'

'You know how Desmond is – he likes to see how things go.'

Stopping again, Tom said hoarsely, 'But you promised.'

'No, Tom. What I promised was that I'd put your request to Desmond – which I did. I told him you were keen to counter Price's evidence in person. Which he already knew from his last meeting with you. He's really very clear about what you want. But at the end of the day we have to let him decide. He's the advocate. He's the expert. He knows how to play it.'

Tom tipped his head back and held it there for a second or two before relenting with a slow expressive closing of his eyes, as if further argument would simply cost him too much in terms of nervous energy.

At times like this, Hugh felt the impossibility of comprehending what Tom's life was like, not just the battle to get through the day with its flashbacks and panic attacks, nor the nights with their jolting nightmares, but the fact that he was having to endure it alone. Two years after the tragedy Tom's wife had left him, taking the two remaining children with her, and now lived seventy miles away with a new partner. To have lost his wife was bad enough, but to be separated from his children seemed unimaginable to Hugh.

'Okay?' he asked.

Tom sucked in a long breath. 'Yeah.'

As they walked on, Tom returned to an old grievance. 'I suppose there'll be a whole lot more crap from the other side.'

'Ainsley's going to be a strong witness. I don't think they'll manage to beat him down.'

'But they tied Munro up in knots, didn't they?'

It was partly true. Munro, a psychotherapist who'd treated Tom with cognitive behavioural therapy, had produced an excellent written statement, but under cross-examination had through inexperience or lack of confidence hedged his comments with so many ifs and buts that he'd appeared ponderous and uncertain.

'His evidence stood up okay,' said Hugh firmly. 'But we always knew the other side was going to throw a lot of mud, didn't we? It doesn't mean it's going to stick.'

'But that's all the judge gets to hear – crap.'

Like many people encountering the adversarial system for the first time, Tom kept taking it personally. The opposition's attempts to show that his troubles had started long before he witnessed his daughter's death, that he'd been suffering depression and undiagnosed post-traumatic stress disorder since his military service in Bosnia, never failed to unnerve him.

At the doors to the court Tom unhitched his rucksack and paused to straighten his shoulders and take a series of deep, snatched breaths, like someone who's been taught relaxation exercises but hasn't quite got the hang of them.

'You realise Price may be sitting in court,' Hugh said.

Tom gave a tight nod.

'Well, play it cool, eh? Don't give him the satisfaction of letting him get to you.'

'Sure,' Tom murmured. Then, allowing the idea more room in his mind, rallying to this vision of himself as a man in control, he gave a more definite nod. 'Yeah. Sod him.'

His gaze had turned hard, his voice flat and unreadable, and for a moment he might have been the Tom Deacon of four years ago, sitting in Hugh's office, asking him to take his case.


It was the time immediately after Hugh's old firm Dimmock Warrington had merged with the up-and-coming Marsh & Co. While Hugh hadn't opposed the merger, he hadn't seen much point in it either and had been judged behind the times for saying so. According to the forward thinkers, standing still was no longer an option; the firm had to grow or die. In the old set-up it had never been thought necessary to have a corporate objective; it was taken for granted that the firm would do the best possible job for its clients while providing a decent living for its partners and employees. But the newly formed Dimmock Marsh was made of more ambitious stuff and had rapidly acquired a mission statement, to become the top firm in Bristol and the West, or as the slogan-writers had it, The Best in the West. Specialisation and expertise were the new watchwords. Generalisation was regarded as a necessary but unprofitable sideline. Of the nineteen partners in the merged firm Hugh was one of only three not to answer the call to specialise, preferring to stick to the traditional hotchpotch of conveyancing, wills, probate, and contract: what he liked to call high street law, but which was now termed private client work. Under the new regime Annaliese was required to ask potential clients the nature of their business in advance so they could be directed to the appropriate specialist. But Tom Deacon had refused to disclose his reasons for coming to see Hugh, so, on welcoming him into his office that first day, Hugh was expecting to hear about some kind of dispute, with a neighbour perhaps, or a business associate, because in his experience it was confrontation that made people secretive; that or shame.

Tom Deacon was about forty and painfully thin, his neck scrawny inside the over-large collar, his jacket swimming on jagged shoulders. But most striking at first sight was his face, the skin so tight over the bones that the course of the veins and sinews was visible beneath, while a sharp groove had formed under each cheekbone, as though the flesh had been sucked inwards and held firm by some invisible claw. When Hugh got to know Tom better, he wasn't surprised to find he was a heavy smoker and hard drinker who ate little and badly. But his immediate impression was of a man being consumed from within, as if by some voracious parasite.

Deacon sat down stiffly and, though the pristine steel-and-glass decor shouted of a rigidly enforced no-smoking policy, he pulled out a cigarette. 'Okay, is it?' he asked, very much as an afterthought.

'Sure. I'll find an ashtray . . .' For lack of anything

better Hugh emptied the papers out of his wastebin and placed it next to Deacon's chair.

Lighting up, Deacon fixed his intense gaze on Hugh. 'I was recommended to you.'

'Oh? Can I ask who by?'

But Deacon wasn't about to be drawn. 'A couple of people,' he said vaguely.

'Well . . . I'll try to live up to expectations. So what can I do for you, Mr Deacon?'

Deacon stared at Hugh a while longer, as if making up his mind about him, before beginning to speak in the dull monotone Hugh would come to know so well. Until last year he'd had a good life, he said: a wife, two boys of six and three, a daughter of four called Holly, and a regular job as a joiner and cabinet-maker. Then one day when he was driving Holly back from a birthday party a car came round a bend on the wrong side of the road and crashed into them, sending their car down a steep slope where it landed on its roof. Knocked unconscious, he came round to the sound of Holly's cries. He managed to unfasten his seatbelt and get out – the driver's door had been thrown open – but as he went to free Holly the car burst into flames. The rear door was jammed tight, he couldn't open it. By the time he got back to the driver's door the interior was an inferno, he was beaten back by the flames. He was in hospital for several weeks, he couldn't remember how long exactly. He had bad burns and a broken leg. When he eventually tried to get back to work he couldn't hold down a job. The other driver, an eighty-year-old farmer, had suffered a heart attack just before the crash, and died as a result of one or both. The insurance company had offered Deacon thirty thousand pounds in settlement, but if he couldn't work again then it wasn't going to be enough. He wanted to know if he could get more.

He told his story without obvious emotion, gazing at Hugh in an unfocused way, as if looking through him to some distant world. Only when it came to the money question did his eyes sharpen again.

Hugh said, with considerable feeling, 'My condolences on your terrible loss, Mr Deacon.'

Deacon gave a brief nod of acknowledgement.

In a tone of sympathy Hugh explained why he couldn't take the case. It required an expert, and he was a generalist without experience in personal injury. The man Deacon should see was Martin Sachs, a senior partner at Dimmock Marsh who was highly respected in the field and could advise him on the best way forward.

While Hugh was speaking, Deacon's expression darkened. With a shudder of tension or irritation, he stated bluntly that he'd come to Hugh on the recommendation of friends, that he'd chosen the man not the firm, and – showing a spark of the flint within – that he wasn't about to be shunted sideways on to someone else.

Hugh knew he shouldn't hesitate to turn the case down. Quite apart from the gaps in his knowledge, which would need a crash course to fill, a case like this would carry a huge weight of responsibility. It was one thing to guide clients through the mundane transactions of life, when the collapse of a house sale was considered a major setback, and quite another to deal with the aftermath of tragedy, when you had the one shot at getting the compensation right. There was something else that bothered him, something he couldn't quite put his finger on until he was showing Deacon out of the office. As they waited for the lift, Deacon said, 'All I want is to get my life back.'

Hugh should have pointed out there and then that the law wasn't in the business of restoring lives, that all it could offer was money, and then generally far less than you were expecting. But something made him hold back, probably the same thing that had made him go against his earlier intentions and agree to consider taking the case after all. At home that evening, trying to explain it to Lizzie, he said he felt a duty to protect Deacon from the sharks who infested the personal injury pool, firms that promised the earth, took a fat fee, and delivered a rubbish job. He wanted to save him from Martin Sachs as well, for while his revered partner couldn't be classified as a shark he had an aggressive bulldog style, all bark and worse bite, which would have been quite wrong for someone like Deacon, who would need support at every stage along the way.

'So what's worrying you?' Lizzie asked.

'Whether I'm up to it.'

'Why wouldn't you be?'

'Lack of experience. Lack of speed. Having to fumble around in the dark . . .'

'Would you do a worse job than Martin Sachs?'

'No . . . No, I'd make sure I didn't.'

'There you are then,' Lizzie said.

'I'm still not sure . . .'

'Why?'

'Partly Deacon's expectations . . . wanting his life back. The responsibility of the case. And . . .' It came to Hugh then, the concern he hadn't been able to name. 'The feeling that Deacon's holding on to his sanity by his fingertips.'

Hugh got a rough ride at the next partners' meeting. Martin Sachs, sitting on a very high horse indeed, asked what point there was in having specialists if their expertise was ignored. Not only was it amateurish to use a non-specialist, but there was a considerable risk of mistakes being made, mistakes which, he hardly needed to remind everyone, could bring the firm's name into disrepute. The chairman, an arbitrator by trade, suggested that Martin might act as an éminence grise for Hugh, guiding the case from behind the scenes, factoring his time into the fees equation. But Martin wasn't having any of that. It would result in a dangerous blurring of responsibilities, he declared, and was therefore unworkable. There the matter might have rested if Ray Wheatcroft hadn't come to the rescue. Ray, whose history stretched back as far as Hugh's, to the old firm and beyond, and who had become his closest ally in the combative climate of the new regime, pointed out that it was surely better to have won the job on less-than-ideal terms than not to have won it at all, particularly when it was such an unusual case which was bound to create widespread interest.

Hugh wasn't convinced about the widespread interest argument, but it was enough to carry the day and permanently sour his relations with Martin Sachs, whose blood pressure rose visibly at every mention of the case, and didn't get any lower when two psychiatrists confirmed that Tom Deacon was suffering from post-traumatic stress disorder, thus propelling the claim into a different financial ballpark, confirmed when Desmond Riley advised them to turn down an offer of three hundred thousand pounds and enter a fresh claim.

So here they were, four years down the line, starting the last week of the hearing that would decide whether Tom was entitled to the full eight hundred and ninety thousand pounds he was claiming for injury and loss of earnings following the car accident and tragic death of his daughter. Passing through the second set of doors, the courtroom hush closed softly around them, barely disturbed by the voice of Edward Bavistock QC, leading counsel for the defendants – nominally the estate of the eighty-year-old farmer, but effectively his insurers – who admitted negligence but were contesting both the timing and extent of Tom's psychological injuries.

The court wasn't crowded. As always in such cases, the judge sat alone without a jury, while the two legal teams barely filled the first two tiers of benched seats. In the third row was one man Hugh hadn't seen before, but going by Tom's lack of reaction it obviously wasn't Price. They slid into the bench beside Isabel, who shot Hugh a relieved smile. The judge registered their arrival with a mild glance before returning his attention to Bavistock, who was making some kind of procedural application. Before Hugh had time to grasp what it was about, the matter was decided and the first witness called.

Dr Ainsley looked every inch the eminent consultant psychiatrist. His finely drawn features, thick silver hair, well-cut grey suit and bow tie, slim pair of reading glasses which he perched on the end of his nose to read the oath, proclaimed distinction and authority.

Desmond Riley stood up. 'Dr Ainsley, you will find your witness statement on page fifteen in the bundle in front of you.' A pause while Ainsley found his place. 'However, as some months have passed since you made your statement, I would like to ask you a few questions about the intervening period.'

Hugh noticed with relief that Tom seemed to have given up on the idea of writing Desmond a note. Having pulled a pad and pen out of his rucksack and written the date in large block capitals, he put the pad on the table in front of him and sat back in his seat, a fist pressed against his mouth, watching Ainsley.

'Dr Ainsley,' Desmond said, 'you made your statement on the seventeenth of June of this year. In it you said you had last examined Mr Deacon one week beforehand, namely on the tenth. Have you seen Mr Deacon since that date?'

'I have. On the ninth of October.'

'That is . . . three weeks ago?'

'Yes.'

'As a result of that consultation have you had any reason to alter your opinion of Mr Deacon's condition?'

'No.'

'Would you summarise your diagnosis for the court, please?'

'In my opinion Tom Deacon is suffering from PTSD – post-traumatic stress disorder.'

'And has the seriousness of his condition changed, in your opinion?'

'No. I would say it has remained the same.'

'Which is?'

'Severe.'

'And his symptoms – are they the same?'

'Essentially, yes. I found he was still suffering vivid flashbacks of his daughter's death, sometimes as often as once an hour, as well as debilitating panic attacks, insomnia, nightmares, acute anxiety, headaches and a fear of strangers which amounted to paranoia.'

'And during this period had any of these symptoms altered in severity?'

'Well, some had got a bit worse – the flashbacks, for example, while some had improved a little – the insomnia. But fluctuating symptoms are to be expected in this sort of case.'

'And these symptoms had persisted despite continued medication?'

'Correct.'

Desmond turned the pages of his notes. 'Dr Ainsley, in your statement you say that Mr Deacon didn't appear to have suffered any adverse effects from his army service. Would you say that is still the case?'

'Yes.'

'No indication that he contracted any sort of stress-related illness as a result of his service?'

'None.'

'How have you come to that opinion?'

'For one thing, Mr Deacon himself doesn't see his army service as a problem. He never even thinks about the Bosnian War until something reminds him – a news item, or a film. Or when he hears a sudden noise – a firework or a motorbike backfiring. For another thing, he shows no signs of anxiety or distress or memory-avoidance when asked about it.'

'Is it possible that his experiences in the conflict could be having a subconscious effect on him?'

'You mean, in a damaging sense?'

'Yes.'

'I would say, unlikely. No, in my judgement Tom Deacon seems to have dealt with his war experiences in a mature, healthy way.'

At Hugh's side Tom gave an emphatic nod.

'And the trauma of watching his daughter die – that couldn't have activated a long-delayed traumatic response to his war experiences?'

'Extremely unlikely, in my opinion. Because, as I've said, there's no indication of any trauma from that time.'

Desmond found another place in his notes, whose edges supported a rainbow of Post-it stickers. 'Dr Ainsley, in the period between June and October did your prognosis of Mr Deacon's condition change at all?'

'No.'

'So the outlook remains poor?'

'Well, he made some progress after he first came to me, of course, when I recommended he undergo cognitive behavioural therapy with Dr Jack Munro. But since then there's been little discernible improvement in my opinion. And, as things stand at the moment, I can't see the prospect of any more, no.'

'When you say there was some initial progress – this would be between three and four years ago?'

'Yes.'

'And could you indicate the degree of improvement? Was it small? Moderate? How would you rate it?'

'I would say the improvement was significant. But not enough to make him anything like a well man. We were of course starting from a low base, after Mr

Deacon had suffered a severe breakdown with suicidal tendencies.'

The judge, who was writing steadily, murmured without looking up, 'Mr Riley, surely this period is covered by the witness statement?'

'My Lord,' Desmond conceded with a nod. 'So, Dr Ainsley . . . you say you can't see any prospect of improvement? Has your opinion changed since June?'

'My opinion hasn't changed, no. I can't see any chance of improvement while Mr Deacon's life remains as it is now, basically in ruins, without anything to occupy his mind, living on benefits in a damp cottage. It gives him no chance at all.'

'What *would* give him a chance in your opinion?'

'Two things. Firstly, a conclusion to this case, which should give him some degree of closure. Secondly, practical changes. If he could have a proper workshop to do his woodwork, a decent place to live, and some freedom from financial worries, then – well, I can't make any firm predictions, I can only say that such changes would offer the best environment for, if not improvement, then at least stability. It would make his condition more bearable.'

Bavistock clambered to his feet. 'My Lord, surely this is speculation, and therefore beyond the bounds of medical opinion.'

The judge flexed his eyebrows. 'I'm not sure I follow, Mr Bavistock. I think the medical profession can be allowed to speculate on the outcome of its treatments and interventions.'

'With respect, my Lord, Dr Ainsley is commenting on a change of lifestyle not a medical treatment.'

'I would have thought that a change of lifestyle

would constitute a treatment, Mr Bavistock, especially in the field of psychiatry.' The judge turned to Ainsley. 'Would that be correct, Dr Ainsley? You might, on occasion, advise a change of lifestyle as a form of treatment?'

'Very much so, your lordship.'

The judge cast Bavistock an eloquent look.

'As your lordship pleases.' Bavistock sank back into his seat.

Tom, his head low, slid Hugh a look of avid satisfaction, as if they had just won a significant point instead of a routine legal challenge.

Desmond resumed, 'Dr Ainsley, you have stated that you think it highly unlikely that Tom Deacon will ever be able to hold down a job again. Has your opinion in that regard altered at all?'

'No, it hasn't.'

'And if his circumstances were to change in the way you recommend, would that improve his prospects of finding work?'

'At best he might be able to make a few pieces of furniture, but only at his own pace in his own time. In my opinion, he'll never be able to hold down a full-time job again.'

'You also stated that you think he'll never be able to lead anything approaching a full life. Is that still the case?'

'Yes.'

'He will always be prone to flashbacks and panic attacks?'

'Correct.'

'He will always need treatment?'

'Yes. But medication can only achieve so much. It

can only dull the patient's symptoms to a limited extent. And of course the amount of medication has to be balanced against the patient's ability to function. There's no point in making the patient so drowsy that his remaining quality of life is impaired.'

'Thank you, Dr Ainsley.'

As Desmond dropped down into his seat, Tom put his mouth to Hugh's ear and hissed, 'Is that all?'

Hugh nodded, and Tom's expression dipped in frustration. For him, the written statements which the court used as its main source of evidence were a poor substitute for evidence delivered in person from the witness box.

Bavistock stood up and began to go through Ainsley's statement point by point, starting with Ainsley's qualifications, career, and experience, dwelling for some time on the fact that he now spent a significant amount of time lecturing and appearing as an expert witness.

'So, you do very little clinical work as such, Dr Ainsley?'

'I try to see long-standing patients whenever I can.'

'But new patients – you simply assess them? You don't treat them?'

'New patients, yes.'

'And you assess them for medico-forensic purposes, as an expert witness?'

'Not always. Sometimes I'm simply called in to give a second opinion.'

'Perhaps I could rephrase it then – the majority of your work is medico-forensic?'

'Correct.'

'Now, there are different descriptions of post-traumatic stress disorder in current use, are there not? Perhaps you could take us through them?'

As Ainsley launched into a detailed explanation, Tom sank lower in his seat and finding a pencil began to sketch on his pad. He drew quickly and confidently. Looking across, Hugh saw a desk taking shape, traditional in design, with pedestals and drawers, shown corner on, with the effortless perspective of a true draughtsman, and was reminded of a summer day some three years ago when Tom had drawn something similar at the lunch table at Meadowcroft. It was shortly after Tom's wife had left him, and thus a time of particular concern for his well-being. It had been Lizzie's idea to invite him for Sunday lunch. Tom bicycled over, arriving an hour early, so Hugh suggested a walk. Tom had only one walking speed, which was fast. Spurning the footpaths as too crowded, though there was only a single dog-walker visible in the far distance, Tom struck out across country, leading the way over fences, ditches and boggy pastures, Hugh following as best he could, breathlessly, with the occasional unscheduled halt to extricate himself from barbed wire. After half an hour at the same furious speed Hugh pleaded an arthritic knee and they returned at an easier pace, though Tom had a job keeping to it, often surging ahead without thinking, slowing with an effort. They talked about serious walking, which for Tom was hill walking, the steeper the better, while Hugh told of his early childhood in Llandeilo, close to the Black Mountains, with his schoolteacher parents and two sisters, and moving to Swansea when he was ten, where he had missed the mountains, the sight of them, and the summer walks. Tom preferred winter walks, he said; not so many people and less chance of getting overheated. Then, darting Hugh a faint smile, he declared, 'It was you being Welsh that swung it.'

'What?'

'When I came to see you that first time. You keeping your accent, not having ditched it for something snotty. I thought you'd probably be okay.'

Hugh laughed, wondering at the slender thread by which the decision had hung. 'It's a poor Welshman who ditches his accent.'

'That's what I mean.'

They had drinks on the terrace. Tom downed his first beer at the same rate he did his walking, seriously fast, but the alcohol did little to lift his mood, which had plunged for no apparent reason, leaving him morose and uncommunicative. Even Lizzie, who had a rare talent for drawing people out, struggled to get more than two words out of him. Nor did the appearance of Lou, in all her freshness and serenity, rouse him; if anything he seemed to retreat further into his shell. It was Charlie of all people who saved the day. Charlie had got home at ten to four that morning; Hugh knew to the minute because he'd heard the voices, the slam of a car door, and had fretted miserably over who was driving and how stoned or otherwise off their heads they'd been. Now, having slept through the best part of the day, Charlie had dragged himself out of bed at the third time of asking and arrived at the lunch table pale, unkempt, eyes screwed up against the light. Perhaps Tom recognised a fellow traveller, perhaps he sympathised all too readily when the crash of a pan lid caused Charlie to flinch, but after a while the two of them exchanged a few words, and when Hugh next broke off from his conversation with Lou and Lizzie it was to hear them discussing cabinet-making, how much more it was than mere carpentry, how much artistry was involved, and how there was a big demand for bespoke pieces if you could only break into the market. Producing a notepad from his pocket Tom sketched out a couple of designs for tables and chairs, drawing quickly, skilfully, while Charlie made appreciative noises. Hearing him say, 'Hey, that's cool,' Hugh felt a pang, not just for the paucity of Charlie's vocabulary – everything was cool when it wasn't a drag – but for the transience of his enthusiasms, which, with the notable exception of dope, came and went with bewildering speed.

After Tom left, Lizzie said, 'He looks like he's on the edge.'

'Yes.'

'What support is he getting?'

'As much as humanly possible. But short of hiring someone to watch over him . . .' And for a split second, in a confusing flight of fancy, Hugh might have been talking about Charlie instead of Tom Deacon.


The definitions of post-traumatic stress disorder having been established to Bavistock's satisfaction, he moved on. 'So, in the definition you prefer, Dr Ainsley, the symptoms include flashbacks, panic attacks, depression, guilt, chronic anxiety, insomnia, mood swings, phobias, lack of concentration, stress avoidance. Would you expect to find all of these symptoms in every case?'

'No. But I would expect to find a good number of

them, particularly flashbacks, mood swings and stress avoidance strategies. They're central to any diagnosis of PTSD.'

'Would it be true to say that the more symptoms present, the more confident you would be of your diagnosis?'

'No. The nature and severity of the main symptoms would be the most important consideration.'

'Now, Dr Ainsley, could you tell us how it was that Mr Deacon came to consult you in the first instance?'

It had always been unrealistic to hope that this issue wouldn't be explored in open court. Hugh's error, so easily made at the time, so obviously wrong in retrospect, was already there in the evidence bundle for all parties to see. It would be an inept defence that didn't bring it more fully to the judge's attention. The only question now was how much salt Bavistock would rub into the wound.

Ainsley replied, 'I got a letter from Tom Deacon's solicitors, asking if I would give an opinion as to his condition.'

Tom whispered fretfully in Hugh's ear, 'What's this got to do with anything?'

Non-essential conversation was discouraged in court and Hugh automatically glanced at the judge before scribbling, *My error in original letter*. Tom read it and shrugged before crossing his arms tightly across his chest.

Bavistock was saying, 'Didn't they go further than that? Didn't Messrs Dimmock Marsh say in their letter, I quote, "We fear Mr Deacon is suffering from an acute post-traumatic stress disorder and would be grateful for an opinion"?'

'You may be right – it's four years ago now.'

'If I could refer you to page thirteen in the evidence bundle, perhaps you would like to refresh your memory.'

Hugh didn't need to look at his copy of the letter to see it clearly in his mind, complete with offending phrase and his signature at the bottom.

When Ainsley had read the letter, Bavistock said, 'So having received this letter you were in no doubt as to the diagnosis they wanted?'

Desmond got to his feet. 'My Lord, could it be noted that the letter also asked Dr Ainsley for advice on treatment and rehabilitation?'

The judge nodded. 'It is noted, Mr Riley.'

It was a loyal effort on Desmond's part, but there was no escaping the basic mistake. Bavistock hammered it home. 'It was clear what they were hoping for in the way of a diagnosis?'

'Given the nature of Mr Deacon's experience, such a diagnosis would always be a possibility. That said, I would never be influenced by what people were hoping for,' Ainsley said with a puff of self-importance, 'only by what I find.'

'Indeed,' Bavistock said with a fleeting mechanical smile. 'But of course post-traumatic stress disorder is actionable under the law, while a grief reaction, however intense, is not. When the patient is aware that grief alone won't be sufficient to win him compensation, that only PTSD will do, could that not influence him, consciously or subconsciously, into emphasising certain symptoms that would improve his chances of getting the more advantageous diagnosis?'

Ainsley paused before saying with obvious reluctance,

'In theory it's possible, yes. But I don't believe that happened in this case.'

At Hugh's side Tom was rubbing his forehead in harsh repetitive movements, the tension radiating from him like a heat.

'And is it also possible that a patient who has learnt about the symptoms of PTSD might persuade himself he has new symptoms that weren't there before?'

'Again, it might be possible in theory. But in my opinion it didn't happen in this case.'

'Oh? And why would that be?'

'The descriptions he gave of his symptoms were too spontaneous, too vivid.'

Bavistock looked doubtful. 'How would that rule out the possibility of exaggeration or amplification?'

'Well, it would have required an extraordinary degree of imagination on his part to describe the symptoms with such accuracy.'

'What, even if he'd studied such symptoms in depth?'

'I would say so, yes.'

Bavistock raised his eyebrows slightly. 'Now, you have described Mr Deacon's symptoms in your statement – if I can refer you to page seventeen, paragraph three.' When Ainsley had found his place, Bavistock went on, 'Mr Deacon seems to have every possible symptom of PTSD. Nothing missing at all. What you might call a textbook case. Would you agree?'

'Well . . . In simple terms, yes.'

'In any terms, surely?'

For the first time Ainsley showed faint irritation. 'Yes,' he said shortly.

'Isn't it odd that one person should have such a comprehensive list of symptoms?'

'Not at all.'

'But you've just told us that you wouldn't expect to find the full range of symptoms in every case.'

Ainsley seemed to falter, and for a moment Hugh thought he was going the same way as the cognitive behavioural therapist Munro. But then Ainsley straightened his back and said crisply, 'I meant only that it was uncommon. I didn't mean it was impossible.'

'You didn't think it strange at the time?'

'No.'

'It didn't occur to you that Mr Deacon might have imagined a fuller range of symptoms than he actually had?'

'As I've said, I think it unlikely.'

Adopting one of his coping strategies, Tom hunched forward over the table and, resting his forehead on his fingertips, screwed his eyes tight shut, as if to blank everything out.

Moving on, Bavistock leafed through his notes. 'Now, you have diagnosed Mr Deacon as having severe PTSD. Could you tell us what other degrees of severity there are?'

'After severe, there's moderately severe, moderate, and minor.'

'Could you define the moderate category for us, please?'

Ainsley thought he must have misheard. 'Moderate?'

'Yes, moderate.'

'This is when the injured person has largely recovered, and any continuing effects are not grossly disabling.'

'Not grossly disabling?' Bavistock echoed.

'Correct.'

'So a moderate case could be more difficult to diagnose?'

'It could be. But the critical factor is the exposure of the patient to a traumatic event that falls outside the normal range of human experience. If the patient's condition can be traced back to that, then they can said to be suffering from PTSD.'

'But if this link isn't spotted, if the patient himself doesn't realise why he's unwell – or indeed is in denial about it – then a moderate case might well go undiagnosed?'

A minute hesitation. 'It's possible, yes.'

'Could indeed be misdiagnosed?'

'That's possible too.'

'It might be diagnosed as depression, for example?'

Ainsley had the wary look of someone who realises he's being backed into a corner. 'It's just possible, yes.'

'Only "just possible"? Surely if a diagnosis of post-traumatic stress disorder is missed, then depression would be the obvious alternative?'

'Depression is only one of several alternatives.'

'Name a few, if you would.'

With the confidence of someone returning to safe ground, Ainsley went briskly through his list. 'Adjustment disorder, acute stress disorder, obsessive-compulsive disorder, conversion disorder – not to mention any number of psychosomatic disorders.'

'But these are diagnoses that would only be made by a specialist like yourself, would they not? An ordinary GP would not be qualified to give such diagnoses?'

Ainsley was forced to agree.

Behind the spread of his hands Tom still had his

eyes squeezed tight shut, but the dampness had reappeared on his temples and his jaw muscles were flickering angrily. Hugh signalled to Isabel for water and, touching Tom's arm, put the glass by his elbow, but if he noticed he gave no sign.

Bavistock was saying, 'If the patient doesn't get as far as a psychiatrist, if he only gets to see his GP, then depression would be the most likely diagnosis, would it not?'

'It might be.' Then, relenting, Ainsley added, 'Yes, it would be the most likely.'

'Now, in the annals of medical history, PTSD is a fairly recent condition, is it not?'

'The term itself is relatively recent, yes. But medically, the condition has been recognised for a long time, since the nineteenth century in fact, but under different names.'

'Indeed . . . And what sort of names would have been most common?'

'Well . . . shell shock . . . neurasthenia . . . war neurosis . . . battle stress . . . nervous shock . . . survivor syndrome . . .'

'It was seen, then, as a condition that arose mainly from combat situations?'

'War was certainly accepted as one of the most likely causes of the condition. But it was recognised in civilian life too, in mining accidents, train accidents, and so on, and then it was known as nervous shock or fright neurosis, among other things.'

'But shell shock, combat stress, combat neurosis were the most common terms. I put it to you that the medical community has long recognised, whether under the old names or the new, that PTSD is most commonly seen in people exposed to the horrors of war.'

'I couldn't say most commonly. The statistics would be hard to establish.'

'Well – frequently, then? Would you agree that the condition was, and still is, *frequently* seen in people exposed to the horrors of war?'

Ainsley paused, distrusting the semantics. 'I would only say that it's seen *regularly* in combatants.'

'Did Mr Deacon mention that he'd been treated for depression at various times in the eight years after leaving the Army and before the accident that killed his daughter?'

Tom sucked in his breath with an audible hiss and shook his head.

'He said he'd found it difficult to adjust to civilian life. And yes, he mentioned taking anti-depressants.'

'He didn't say what precisely was depressing him?'

'Well, adjusting to civilian life, as I've just said.'

'But what was it about civilian life that was giving him difficulty?'

'He wasn't specific.'

Hugh had a good idea where this was leading and hoped that Ainsley did too.

'Isn't that surprising?' Bavistock suggested. 'Wouldn't you expect him to talk about what exactly had been worrying him at that time?'

'Not necessarily.' Then, forgetting the golden rule of the expert witness, Ainsley volunteered additional information. 'People with depression often can't identify anything in particular that's getting them down.'

'So he may have *thought* it was his difficulty in

adjusting to civilian life that was causing his depression when in fact it was something else altogether?'

Too late, Ainsley saw the trap. He said tersely, 'Well, it's virtually impossible to separate depression from life events. Cause and effect feed off each other. So depression might cause someone to lose his job, then the loss of the job itself triggers further depression.'

'And Mr Deacon certainly lost his job on several occasions in the period after leaving the Army and before the accident. Did he mention that to you?'

'He mentioned losing at least one job.'

'But not several?'

'I don't recall him telling me that, no.'

'Did he mention that he'd been a heavy drinker at that time?'

'He said he'd had periods of heavy drinking.'

'Did he mention that, by his own admission, he was a regular cannabis user?'

Ainsley thought for a moment. 'That didn't come up, no.'

'Or that his marriage had experienced difficulties?'

'He talked about ups and downs in his marriage, yes.'

'No more detail than that?'

'Not concerning the period you mention, no.'

Making his point, Bavistock said, 'So the period of Mr Deacon's life between leaving the Army and the car accident effectively went unexamined by you.'

'With the exceptions I've already mentioned, the subject simply never arose.'

'But you see what I'm suggesting, don't you, Dr

Ainsley? That the difficulties and depression Mr Deacon had in this eight-year period could have stemmed from post-traumatic stress related to his active service, and that you would have been unaware of the fact.'

'I can only report on what I find, and as I've already stated he gave no indication of pre-existing PTSD.'

In the pause that followed, the judge suggested it might be a convenient time to rise for lunch. Emerging slowly from his self-imposed trance, Tom got up and went down into the body of the court to see Ainsley, who greeted him with a smile and an upturning of both palms which he converted into a handshake, his left hand laid over Tom's, so that Hugh was reminded of a priest giving benediction.

Desmond turned to Hugh and murmured, 'A couple of points we could have done without, but no serious damage.'

'Will you re-examine?'

Desmond plucked the wig off his head and stuffed it into his tote bag. 'I would say so, yes. But let's see what the afternoon brings.' Then, because he liked his food, he said keenly, 'How about lunch? There's a nice little place over the road.'

'And the conference with Tom?'

'Oh, while we eat, don't you think?'

Aware that the opposition were still in court, Hugh kept his voice very low. 'It's Price he wants to discuss with you.'

'I rather thought it might be.'

'He wants to tell the judge his side of the story.'

'A perfectly natural impulse.' Desmond's gaze travelled across to Tom. 'But one that is probably best resisted.'

'More harm than good?'

'There has to be a risk, doesn't there?' Desmond glanced at the clock. 'I don't mean to rush you, but we should get going if we want a table.'

Hugh went down into the body of the court, meaning to keep out of earshot, only to hear Tom say in a tight voice, 'But then I can't get to sleep again . . .'

Looking up, Ainsley narrowed his eyes at Hugh, as if to confirm he wasn't going to be much longer, then bending his head, touching a light hand to Tom's arm, spoke to him in a soothing voice. Tom gave a series of sharp nods, then as they moved apart turned towards Hugh with a look of unguarded distress.

Ainsley had made his own plans for lunch, and they left him at the doors to the courts. Desmond, walking at a cracking pace, led the team to a busy wine bar in a narrow lane off the Strand. It was a dark place with wood panelling, frugal lighting and a menu that tested Isabel's health convictions to the limit, a fusion of chips, pasta, and pies which catered to the boyish appetites of its clientele. The five of them squeezed round a table designed for four next to the window and ordered from an Estonian waitress called Anna, whose name Desmond enunciated with an elaborate flourish, as if to endow it with the authentic pronunciation.

In the confusion of examining menus, breaking off and reclaiming conversations, Hugh didn't hear what the others ordered, so that when some red wine appeared immediately in front of him he thought at first it must be Desmond's, who always had a glass of claret at lunch. But Desmond, sitting diagonally opposite, was already clasping his wine, while to Hugh's right Isabel and Sanjay were sipping mineral water. Which left Tom, immediately across the table, who was meant to be on the wagon.

Desmond was singing Ainsley's praises. 'A robust witness. Just the right amount of bloody-mindedness. Enough to irritate the other side, but not the judge.'

'You'll re-examine?' asked Tom, who knew all the jargon.

'Very probably,' declared Desmond with a growl of a laugh.

'That stuff about me making up symptoms?'

'We'd certainly cover that, yes.'

'And the depression thing?'

'We'll see . . .' murmured Desmond, with a quick smile, clearly not intending to go down that particular route. 'But the prognosis is certainly worth revisiting. We must press home the fact that your chances of recovery are extremely poor.'

'Yeah,' said Tom, looking blithely into the darkness of his own future.

'But overall, a satisfactory morning!' Desmond raised his glass in salute before swinging it smoothly to his lips. It was rare for Desmond to show anything as unguarded as optimism and Sanjay greeted this departure with a lift of his eyebrows and a quick amused glance at Hugh, while Isabel, blowing her nose, looked rapidly from one to the other with round, red-rimmed eyes. Tom, oblivious to these exchanges, was staring intently at Desmond, quietly noting and storing. When his gaze finally swung towards the table, he saw the unclaimed wine and picked it up.

Catching Hugh's eye, he said, 'I'm allowed some lunch and evening.'

'Great.' Hugh smiled to show that he'd intended no criticism, while wondering just what form this permission could have taken when Tom's GP had told him he had a serious drink problem. 'Your doctor must be pleased with you then.'

Before Tom could reply, Desmond swung his attention away from Sanjay and said brightly, 'Now, Tom, what do we need to discuss by way of a confab?'

Tom reached for the folder he had ready on the table beside him. 'Yeah . . . It's Price's stuff. I think I've found a couple of things we missed.' Then, out of respect for Desmond, he modified this to, '. . . could've missed.' He drew out a copy of Price's statement and handed it to Desmond.

The food arrived and Desmond, peering at the boldly annotated and underlined statement over his steak and chips, led Tom through each query with a deft blend of argument, explanation and reassurance. Nothing had been missed, Desmond managed to convey; it was a matter of going for the points most likely to succeed and avoiding the weaker points that might not look so good on re-examination by the other side. Tom listened with fierce concentration, barely eating but gulping his wine, reaching for his glass even after it was empty, interjecting now and again to repeat his arguments about Price.

'But that's a lie,' he said at one point. 'I can prove it.'

'Proof can be an elusive thing, Tom. It doesn't always turn out to be quite as straightforward as one hopes.'

'But the fact that he's always had it in for me – that must count.'

Desmond said, 'Yes, indeed. And we'll certainly bring that into play.'

'But if I could just tell the judge how it was,' said Tom in a relentless tone. 'If I could just tell him why Price is saying this stuff.'

Desmond took a mouthful of chips and chewed thoughtfully. 'I'm not ruling it out, Tom. But I don't think it's actually going to be necessary. And I'll tell you why – because our best bet, our primary objective if you like, is to make Price look unreliable, to encourage him to trip himself up, to show himself in a bad light. If we can achieve that, get him to reveal himself in his true colours, then the details of your falling out needn't concern us. Price's evidence will be discredited anyway. You see what I'm getting at?'

Tom said uncertainly, 'Yeah . . .'

'The fact that you fell out over a girl – well, everyone knows that story, don't they? No need to spell it out in detail. Not even for the judge.' Desmond glanced at Hugh, briefly sharing the joke. 'Best to keep it simple.' He made an expressive sweep of his fork, a signing off.

Tom began to nod slowly. 'If you think so, Desmond.'

'I do, Tom.'

Not looking entirely convinced, Tom turned distractedly to his food and began to eat without enthusiasm.

As the conversation drifted, Sanjay and Isabel went into a huddle over some pictures. Peering over Isabel's shoulder, Hugh saw Sanjay and his wife in the pose of proud parents, the new-born baby in his father's arms.

'A hands-on father, eh?' Hugh said.

'Oh, I'm not so good in the middle of the night,' Sanjay admitted, with a diffident smile.

'Were you there at the birth?' Isabel asked.

Sanjay beamed. 'I was, yes. It was . . . it was . . .' He searched fruitlessly for a word that would do justice to the experience and fell back on, '*astonishing*'. He added, 'My family were horrified, of course. These things simply aren't done, you know. Husbands are meant to keep away.'

Isabel passed the picture to Hugh. Sanjay's wife was serene and long-haired, flushed with the beauty of motherhood, but it was Sanjay's face that drew the attention, his expression of wonder as he gazed at his son. Hugh felt pleased for him, but with the pleasure came the old nudge of regret and curiosity, which, despite the long years of adoptive fatherhood, had never quite left him.

Sanjay asked, 'What about you, Hugh? Were you a hands-on father?'

'Oh, I'd like to think so. But really I stuck to the easy bits. It was Lizzie who did all the hard work.'

'And were you there for the birth of your children?'

'No . . .' Hugh passed the picture back. 'I didn't have the opportunity, sadly.'

'Bad luck. Not work, I hope.'

'No . . .' It was always a finely balanced decision, whether to tell people that Charlie and Lou were adopted, though with Lou it was obvious once they got to meet her. Hugh had always held the belief that the two children should not be defined by their adoption but by the kind of people they were, though given the world's love of labels it was a battle doomed to be lost. 'No,' he said, 'neither Lizzie nor I were there. We got Charlie when he was one, Louise when she was six months.'

Confusion came over Sanjay's face, then sympathy. He was about to speak when Tom's voice cut in.

'I saw two of mine born.'

Breaking the silence that followed, Hugh said, 'Well, two out of three's pretty good.'

The unasked question hovered over the table. Was it the birth of Holly, the beloved dead daughter, that Tom had missed? Or one of the two sons who lived in Devon with his estranged wife?

Tom said, 'But being at the birth doesn't matter, does it? It's being there for them afterwards that counts.' Bleak reflections, with their melancholy undercurrents, were a feature of conversations with Tom, to be given due consideration and gently worked through. But today, unusually, it was Tom himself who broke the mood by announcing, 'Had my boys for half term.'

'Did you?' said Hugh in open surprise, both because it was the first he'd heard about it, and because Tom's estranged wife Linda usually made access to the children so difficult as to be virtually impossible.

'Took 'em to the Brecon Beacons. Rained every day. Blew like stink. Toughened 'em up pretty quick, I can tell you.'

Hugh thought of the younger boy, who was only eight, and hoped it hadn't been too much of an ordeal for him. 'You went walking, did you?'

'Yeah. And orienteering. Got stuck in thick fog. But the boys, they worked out how to get us down. Got the nous, they have. Both of 'em.' In his face was all the thwarted love and pride he felt for his sons.

'Orienteering . . .' mused Desmond, who'd been paying scant attention. 'One day you must tell me what it involves, Tom. It sounds extremely useful.'

'It's about finding your way over difficult terrain, up mountains and over rivers and stuff like that.' Then, with a glance around the table, playing to his audience, Tom added, 'And nowhere to buy a glass of red wine, Desmond.'

They all laughed, as much with pleasure at the lightness of Tom's mood as at the idea of Desmond roughing it on a Welsh mountain.

Walking back to court, Hugh fell in beside Tom. 'I'm so glad you had the boys for half term, Tom. That's wonderful news. Things are better with Linda, are they?'

'Yeah. She doesn't put the phone down on me like she used to.' Tom spoke in a matter-of-fact way, without his usual bitterness. 'That's because she's having another brat, and she's glad to get the boys off her hands.'

'Another baby? Good God. I thought she'd only just had one.' But Hugh had lost track of time. It was eighteen months since Linda had left Tom for the third and last time, and moved to Devon with her new boyfriend.

'Lover-boy's out of work,' Tom said. 'They've got money troubles. Suddenly she doesn't mind talking to me again. Funny, that.'

'Well, so long as you can see the boys.'

'Yeah. Even better . . .' There was reticence in Tom's voice, but also a note of suppressed excitement. 'She's saying I can have the boys full time.'

Hugh stared at him in astonishment. 'You mean . . . custody?'

'Yeah. With access for her.'

Hugh hardly knew what to say. 'Tom . . . I'm so

pleased . . . That's wonderful . . . And the boys? Is that
what they want, to live with you?'

''Course,' said Tom, a touch defensively. 'They've
always wanted to live with me.'

'Well, in that case . . .'

They paused at a pedestrian crossing, a bus thun-
dered past, while Hugh thought of all the reasons why
it would surely be impossible for Tom to have full care
and control of his children. His illness for a start, the
poor prognosis and depressive episodes. His drink
problem, which flared up at regular intervals. The tiny
rented cottage, riddled with damp, with no prospect of
getting anything better till he was awarded his damages. The chances of Linda changing her mind.

'You'll go back to the family court for a new order,
will you?' Hugh asked.

In one of his rapid changes of mood, Tom seemed
to withdraw abruptly. 'Yeah . . . But it won't be a big
deal. Not when Linda's thrown in the towel.'

Tom's divorce had been heard in Exeter where to
save on costs he'd hired a local solicitor called Emma
Deeds. Hugh only hoped she hadn't raised Tom's
expectations too high. 'Well . . .' he said. 'I wish you
the very best of luck, Tom.'

'Yeah . . .' Tom murmured. 'Thanks.'

The afternoon began with the examination of
delayed onset in post-traumatic stress disorder. Bavistock suggested that a year after exposure to trauma
was the internationally accepted maximum period for
symptoms to appear, while Ainsley argued that there
were no hard and fast rules. For almost an hour
Bavistock took Ainsley through the various scientific

papers on the subject, trying to get him to agree that exceptions were so rare as to be insignificant. Finally, Bavistock came to his point.

'Now, in Tom Deacon's case it was *over* a year before he claims to have come down with PTSD. Fourteen months, in fact. That, you must agree, is almost unheard of?'

'An exceptional person might try to struggle on for a long time before seeking help.'

'But he sought help from his GP at regular intervals during those fourteen months – for depression. And according to his GP he never mentioned having flash-backs or panic attacks or an unusual fear of strangers. How do you account for that?'

'I can't comment.'

'Why not?'

'Because I didn't assess him at the time.'

'But you accept the GP's notes, surely?'

'Yes. But most GPs have only fifteen minutes to see each patient. That isn't long enough to investigate the symptoms of PTSD.'

'What, even when flashbacks are a universal feature of PTSD, and panic attacks a close second? Surely if someone was going through such frightening experi-ences, he would feel compelled to mention them?'

'As I have said, a brave man might deny his symp-toms for a long time, out of shame or pride or both.'

The debate meandered on until, with a symbolic closing of his file, Bavistock said, 'If I may summarise, Dr Ainsley . . . I put it to you that at the time of the car accident Mr Deacon was already suffering a stress-related illness from his time in the Bosnian War, but that subsequent to the death of his daughter his main problem was, very understandably, a severe grief reaction.' He raised his eyebrows to make a question of it.

'I disagree. In my opinion it was and is a clear case of PTSD.'

'Surely, the one thing we have agreed on is that it is *not* a clear case?'

Ainsley turned his gaze on Tom and said in measured terms, 'Tom Deacon watched his daughter die in the most appalling circumstances, a trauma that no man of any sensitivity could survive unscathed. Since then, he's been forced to relive the scene continuously in dreams and flashbacks. Irrespective of any bouts of depression he may have suffered in the past, or of any grief reaction, I repeat that he has one of the clearest cases of severe post-traumatic stress disorder that I've ever come across.' Ainsley looked back at Bavistock with a cool stare, as if to say, beat that.

There was a heavy pause in which Bavistock adjusted to the fact that he'd been outmanoeuvred, and the judge gazed thoughtfully at Tom, who had lowered his head to conceal a fierce grin. Isabel, leaning forward, saw the grin and exchanged an uncertain glance with Hugh.

For the next ten minutes Bavistock tried to extract some concessions from Ainsley on Tom's long-term prognosis – the impossibility of predicting he would never recover, the wide range of circumstances that might bring about a return to reasonable health – but the points were minor and hard-won, and there was a sense of relief when Bavistock finally sat down and Desmond began his re-examination.

Tom, his hand covering his mouth, was still concealing a recurrent smile forty minutes later when Ainsley finished his evidence and court rose for the day. As soon as the door had closed behind the judge Tom grinned openly and went to shake Ainsley's hand and pat him on the shoulder. Then, coming back to Desmond, he demanded excitedly, 'We did all right on that one, didn't we, boss?'

Excitement was something Desmond actively discouraged. Looking stern, he said, 'Not *too* bad, Tom. Not too bad. But we still have one or two bridges to cross, you know.'

'Sure! But it went okay. I mean, we scored some good points?'

Desmond made an equivocal gesture, a lifting of one hand that was partly a postponement of the question, partly a farewell wave as he made for the door with Sanjay in his wake.

Still desperate for his answer, Tom looked to Hugh and Isabel for confirmation.

Hugh said, 'It seemed to go all right, Tom.'

'Yeah?'

Isabel said earnestly, 'I thought so too.'

Taking comfort from this, Tom's exuberance returned, and as they made their way down into the main hall he said to Hugh, 'Hey, how about a jar? My treat.'

'I'd love to, Tom, I really would, but I'm hoping to catch the five fifteen.'

Tom looked surprised. 'You heading back to Bristol tonight?'

'Yes, I like to get home if I can. But you'll be all right, will you, Tom?'

'Sure,' he said on a tense note.

Isabel, anxious as ever, said in a voice heavy with the effects of her cold, 'I'd be happy to have a quick drink, Tom, if you'd like to.'

Tom shook his head rapidly. 'No . . .'

'Okay to get back to where you're staying?' Hugh asked.

'Yeah. Might take the train this time.'

'Do you want me to come to the station with you?'

'No.' He gave a hard smile. 'I'll think of it like orienteering, but with people as the enemy.'

# TWO

A steady drizzle was falling as Hugh drove out of the station car park; he negotiated the traffic through a blur of streaked lights. The approach to the motorway was solid, but once clear of it and into the north-eastern suburbs the traffic ran freely and then he was only fifteen minutes from home. Lizzie had called to say her meeting was overrunning and she wouldn't be back till eight thirty. He would use the time to have a bath. There was something about the London grime that seemed to lie heavily on his flesh, almost to chafe at it, so that he longed to scrub it away. Then he would soak for a while, a glass of Merlot in hand, and mull over the day while he listened for Lizzie's arrival, the clunk of the front door, the faint clatter of her keys as she dropped them into the dish on the hall table, her familiar call, a long hello sung on a rising note. Having called back, he'd wait for the sound of her steps on the stairs, which, if not actually audible from the echoing bathroom, would resound strongly enough in his imagination. Then the real thing, footfalls on the bed-room carpet, soft but distinct, and the squeeze of happiness he would feel as she appeared in the open doorway. She would bend down to kiss him, then, having stolen a sip of his drink, she would sit on the

chair at the end of the bath while they got the measure
of each other's day.

In the long years of their marriage such visions
of homecoming had never palled for him. He loved
Meadowcroft, the house where they had lived for the
past fifteen years, and he loved the pattern of their
evenings, the preparations for supper, the exchange of
news over the table, the discussions about the children,
Lou now halfway across India on her gap year, Charlie
at IT college in Birmingham, and their shifting plans
for weekends and holidays. But most of all, he loved
coming home to Lizzie. This was the miracle of his
existence, that the woman he loved was also his wife,
that he'd never been interested in any other.

They lived in what had been a small village until the
mid-nineties when the first of a series of utilitarian
housing developments had advanced into the surround-
ing fields, ultimately trebling the population. Now cars
clogged the main road and buses ran into the city every
hour and noisy teenagers caused trouble on Saturday
nights. But they had been lucky, their side of the village
was protected by the deep cut of a small river and, half
a mile away, the steep rise of the Cotswold Hills. From
Meadowcroft's upper floor you could see rolling fields
dotted with sheep and against the skyline the tiny dots
of walkers on the ridge path.

If the house with its odd proportions and pebble-
dash exterior had few pretensions to beauty, its plain-
ness was thoroughly redeemed by a rambling garden
of almost an acre, framed by a ring of magnificent
trees, ash and beech with a lone lightning-scorched
oak. While several of the partners at Dimmock Marsh
had migrated to handsome eighteenth-century honey-

stone farmhouses in the country proper, complete with stables and tennis courts and four-by-fours, Lizzie and he had never had aspirations to that sort of life. They were content to stay in their solid house in its unfashionable village, perhaps because they had always been happy there.

The rain intensified as he drove through the village and made his turn. The lane that led to Meadowcroft and six other houses narrowed into a single-track road that wandered back in a half circle towards the west and was therefore little used. Hugh accelerated up a slight rise to the first bend, then steadied his speed as the road straightened out. On either side, dripping shrubs and hedgerows gleamed and sparkled in the headlights, until a patch of darkness to the left marked the gates of a house. Another twenty yards and the porch light of his immediate neighbour twinkled briefly through a tangle of shrubs to the right. Then he was rounding the last curve and coasting towards the gates to Meadowcroft. Some ten years ago, following what the local paper had described as a spate of burglaries, they had installed a burglar alarm and a security light operated by a motion sensor. The spate of burglaries turned out to number just three, the thief was caught soon after, and it wasn't long before they began to set the alarm erratically, leaving it off altogether in the school holidays when Charlie and Lou and their friends were in and out the whole time. But since the break-in two weeks ago they had started to set it whenever the house was empty, even for half an hour, and last Saturday morning Hugh had propped a ladder against the corner of the house and climbed up to the light to turn up the sensitivity of the sensor. Tonight, however, he was glad of the security light for a rather different reason, because it stayed on for over five minutes after it had been activated and, by looking for the telltale flicker of light through the hedge, he could tell if Lizzie had got home just ahead of him after all. But despite peering in the direction of the house several times he saw no sign of the light and resigned himself to returning to an empty house. Evening meetings were a recent development in Lizzie's volunteer work with the Citizens Advice, a mark of added responsibility, even if she was too modest to admit it, so his immediate disappointment was balanced by a more general pride.

The curves and kinks of the lane, the rises and undulations of the surface, the glimpses of entrances and porch lights served as subliminal way marks for course and speed. If he thought actively about his progress down the lane it was only in terms of his closeness to home, or occasionally to take a fleeting pleasure in his car, which he enjoyed driving more than any he'd owned before, though it was neither particularly smart nor fast. In every other respect his actions were mechanical. Now, as he turned in through the gate, his mind was partly on the Deacon case and partly inside the house, planning his progress across the hall to the central-heating thermostat to notch up some extra warmth, to the kitchen to open the wine and check the answering machine, then upstairs to run his bath.

At first he registered the indistinct shape that showed palely against the greater darkness of the garden as a trick of the wet, the refraction and bounce of raindrops and light beams off distant leaves. This impression seemed to be confirmed when in the next instant it vanished. As the headlights continued their sweep across the garden his mind nevertheless tried to make sense of the blurred form, which had been small and vaguely crescent-shaped and close, even attached, to the trunk of a tall ash tree. Too high above the ground to be animal, too low to be another addition to Lizzie's collection of nesting boxes. Then, as the headlights settled on the house and reflected darkly off the windows, the shape mutated again in his mind's eye and took on a form that made his pulse leap and his foot stamp on the brake. As the car halted in a scrunch of gravel he was already leaning across the passenger seat to peer out through the streaming side window. Jerking upright again, he looked over his shoulder through the back passenger window into the glittering red curtains thrown out by the brake lights, then, craning further round, peered out through the rear window. Nothing. In his mind's eye he re-examined the shape. He saw the face again, half turned towards him, the cheek partly hidden by the tree trunk or something dark like a hood. He saw it pull back behind the tree. He was sure it was a face, and yet . . . The shape, whatever it was, had been some distance away and very blurred. Looking again through the side and rear windows, images were two a penny in the kaleidoscopic flashes of refracted light and shifting shadows. He must have been mistaken. Persuading himself to this idea, he straightened in his seat and prepared to drive on. As he put his foot on the accelerator he automatically glanced in the rear-view mirror.

There was no mistake this time: a shadowy figure

was loping away through the gates, hood up, a pale sliver of face visible in the rear lights as the youth cast a furtive eye back over his shoulder.

Hugh jammed the brakes on and, flinging the door open, came out running. The youth must have started sprinting the moment he heard the brakes because by the time Hugh got into the lane he was well ahead, racing away in the direction of the village, his white trainers bobbing like rabbit tails as they faded rapidly into the night. Fired by the heat of the chase, Hugh ran a full thirty yards before pulling up short. He hadn't the shoes, he hadn't the breath, and in the pitch dark and splattering rain he hadn't a cat-in-hell's chance of spotting anything, let alone a canny youth who was probably hiding in a nearby garden till the coast was clear, or, most likely, jogging away at a leisurely pace in the certain knowledge that Hugh, hampered by age and unfitness, would never be able to catch him.

Nursing a childish exasperation, Hugh tramped back. The rain had soaked his trousers, there seemed to be a leak in his right shoe, and by the time he reached the car a trickle of water had found its way inside his collar. At the house he parked quickly and, unlocking the door, took reassurance from the steady buzz of the alarm's entry tone, signalling that no one had managed to get in, and from the fact that the security light hadn't been activated until his own arrival. Either the youth hadn't had time to get close to the house or he'd been hanging around on the off-chance, hoping for an unlocked door and easy pickings.

Hugh stooped to pick up an envelope from the mat and, seeing the Dimmock Marsh logo in the top corner and his name written in Annaliese's bold handwriting, chucked it onto the hall table. Then, turning on lights, he went from room to room, checking windows and doors. When he was sure that nothing had been disturbed he drifted back to the kitchen and stood indecisively in the middle of the room, replaying the scene at the gates with a rather more glorious ending in which he caught the youth by the scruff of the neck and twisted his arm up his back until name, address, and purpose of visit had been extracted. Intent was impossible to prove, of course. Trespass wasn't even a crime. If he'd called the police they would have told him he was wasting their time. In the topsy-turvy world of political correctness, the only thing that would rouse them into action was a complaint by the youth, who would of course be fully familiar with his rights. A couple of years ago a farmer client of Hugh's had tackled a lad he'd caught breaking into one of his barns and held him till the police arrived, only to find himself charged with assault, unlawful arrest and false imprisonment, and the youth let off without so much as a caution. The charges were eventually dropped, but not before the farmer had been consumed by worry.

Hugh thought of opening some wine, but instead wandered over to the bay window with its breakfast table and curved window seat, and stared again at the left-hand window. A smudge of putty was the only evidence that the glass had been replaced recently, along with a dribble of watery paint from the glazier's cursory retouching job. Lizzie had discovered the break-in on her return from work one afternoon. When she'd called to tell Hugh, she'd made light of the whole thing, calling the thief a complete amateur because almost nothing had been taken, apart from the fifty pounds she'd left out for the cleaning lady Mrs Bishop, and some costume jewellery from the bedroom. When he got back that evening they had searched the house together just to be sure, but all the obvious things were still there, the computers and televisions, the clocks and silver christening spoons, the semi-precious objects they had accumulated over the years. The only jewellery of any value, two rings and a necklace, were safe in their hiding place in a bathroom cupboard. The loss of the costume jewellery was a nuisance of course, but also a bit of a blessing, Lizzie insisted, because it would force her to go out and buy something a bit more up to date. There was no question of claiming on the insurance. For one thing the amount of the claim would barely cover the policy excess. For another, there was the matter of the burglar alarm. When Lizzie had failed to mention it on the phone, Hugh guessed she had forgotten to set it and decided to maintain a diplomatic silence. But when they had finished their search she asked him to sit down. She would have told him before, she said, but she'd been hoping there might be some obvious explanation. The fact was, she had set the alarm that morning but it had failed to go off. They went through the limited range of possibilities: the thief had contrived by some extraordinary gymnastic feat to evade the beams that covered the dining room and hall; the alarm had gone off on cue but somehow managed to re-set itself; Mrs Bishop had been passing and had come in to switch it off, an idea quickly dispelled by Mrs Bishop herself when she came in next morning. With a sense of postponing the inevitable they called out the maintenance firm to chcck the alarm, though they shared an implicit understanding that no fault would be found. Finally they faced the explanation they had been hoping to avoid from the beginning, that the break-in was somehow connected to the bad old days with Charlie, that while Charlie might be away at college starting a new drug-free life, some of his former friends still had drug habits that required regular financing, friends who might have come to the house and watched Charlie tap the code into the key pad.

They changed the code on the alarm and, in case of further trouble, reported the break-in to the police, who mustered just enough interest to issue them with an incident number. Then, telling themselves no harm had been done, they put the event to the back of their minds.

But was the figure in the garden the same joker, back for another bite of the cherry? He certainly had every appearance of one of Charlie's less appetising friends, young, hooded, forever hanging around on the lookout for easy money. The media would have you believe these kids were all the same, feral children from dysfunctional single-parent families, who scorned all notions of responsibility, embraced victimhood with the righteousness of the oppressed, and blamed their addictions on bad parenting, bad schooling, society as a whole, anyone and anything but themselves, so that by a convenient twist of logic even the thieving wasn't their fault, simply a means of surviving in a cruel, un-feeling world. Trudging upstairs to peel off his wet clothes, Hugh almost wished he could buy into this rant and feel something as simple as contempt. But these kids weren't all the same, far from it, and to despise them was to allow for the unthinkable possibility of despising his own son, who, despite a stable home and loving family, a good education and constant support, had struggled with drugs from the age of fifteen. Fragile, impressionable Charlie, who didn't need the contempt of others when he directed more than enough against himself.

Hugh hung his suit jacket and trousers on separate hangers to dry and, with his mood long broken, abandoned the idea of a bath in favour of a shower. As he ducked his head under the streaming water he pondered, as he had pondered so many times before, the unanswerable questions about Charlie, why twenty years of nurture had been unable to override the disadvantages of his birth, why the receiving of family love had failed to translate itself into self-love. Had his first twelve months with his natural mother been so irretrievably damaging? Would everything have been different if they'd been able to adopt him immediately after birth? Or had the tendency to insecurity and lack of self-worth been ingrained in him from the start, set hard in some immutable genetic amber? Was the physiology of addiction itself genetic, as some scientists liked to claim, inherited just as surely as blue eyes or red hair? In which case Charlie would be battling the odds for the rest of his life, only ever a spliff away from falling over the next precipice.

Above the din of the water he heard Lizzie's voice and turned to see her blurred outline through the shower door. The familiar happiness bobbed up in him only to be overtaken by an acute, nameless anxiety, a sense of dangers padding up around them like wolves, and he came out hurriedly, with a clang of the door. Lizzie was holding up a towel to him.

'Hello, you,' she said.

'Hello.'

As he wrapped the towel round his waist she craned forward to kiss him without getting wet. He kissed her with equal care, then, forgetting caution, pulled her into a damp all-enveloping hug.

She gave a small muffled laugh and tilted her head back to give him a questioning look. 'All right?'

'All right.'

They embraced silently, swaying very slightly as if to some half-remembered dance music. When they finally drew apart he looked into her gentle honest eyes and followed the outline of her beautiful smile, and felt his anxiety slip away.

'How did it go today?' she asked.

'Okay. Well, I think so. Desmond Riley seemed pleased anyway.'

'And Tom?'

'One of his fretful days.'

'Well, he'll always find something to fret about, won't he?' she said sympathetically. 'No point in you fretting too.'

'I can't help it. I always think that if anything's going to go wrong, it'll go wrong for Tom.'

'But you've done everything you can, darling. It's out of your hands now.'

This was another reason he loved her, because she brought him back to earth, she made him see things in proportion.

'And you?' he asked. 'Lots of happy customers?'

She made a so-so movement of her head. 'Never as many as I'd like.' Kissing him lightly, she made for the door. 'It's pasta and salad, if that's all right.'

It was a family joke that he would eat anything put in front of him. 'Pasta and salad sounds all right to me.'

She called from the bedroom, 'What happened to your suit?'

'I got caught in the rain.'

A short silence while she puzzled over this. Then: 'How did you manage that?'

'Being in the wrong place.'

'An umbrella problem?'

'A stupidity problem.'

She laughed, then after a minute or two he heard the radio come on in the kitchen.

It had so nearly not happened, their getting together. He could never remember quite how close it had been without a shiver of relief. He had been in his second year's training in London when he'd come back to Bristol for a party. The party had been hot and noisy and overcrowded. The next morning, hoarse from the shouting and the smoke and too much rough wine, four of them had gone into the country for lunch. It was Andy, an old university friend of Hugh's, who'd suggested the pub high on the Quantock Hills, and a friend of Andy's called Sam who'd insisted on a full roast lunch in the dining room because he was bloody hungry, but it was Hugh alone, taking his first conscious decision of the day, who'd left the others to their food and gone outside for some air. The day was cold, with a fierce biting wind, the terrace deserted except for a hardy couple hunched over a table at the far end. Hugh went to the railing and, gazing out over the sweep of the flood plain to the hazy line of the coast, let the wind chill his skin and sharpen his brain. After a minute or so the couple got up from the table. Hugh had an impression of a striking-looking girl with a curtain of hair blowing across her face, and a man a generation older. Only when the man gave Hugh a smile of recognition and came forward to greet him did Hugh realise it was his old public law tutor, Professor Askew. As the professor asked after Hugh's progress, Hugh glanced towards the waiting girl with her flying hair and dark eyes. Something made him keep looking – the honest gaze, the lovely smile – and he found himself smiling back, it was impossible not to. Afterwards, he always maintained that everything was decided there and then. In fact it was a moment later, when Peter Askew took him over and introduced her as his daughter Lizzie. As they shook hands it struck Hugh with absolute clarity that this was the one, the search was over, he need look no further. Lizzie liked to say it took her quite a bit longer, at least five minutes, because she didn't want to seem fast. The reality was a little less straightforward. There was a boyfriend on the scene, and Hugh had the disadvantage of living in London. It took five weekends and a lot of rail travel to see the boyfriend off, and another three months before Lizzie agreed to marry him. Then, his training over, he landed the job at Dimmocks and they set up home together in a flat in Clifton.

Why had he chosen that particular moment to go out onto the terrace? Ten minutes earlier and Lizzie and her father would still have been in the bar, finishing their coffee. Five minutes later and they'd have been in their car driving away. He didn't believe in fate or any of that stuff, but he believed in luck, and, most important of all, in being thankful when it came his way.

When he got downstairs Lizzie was at the hob, tipping ingredients into a pan. She said, 'I thought we might text Charlie tonight.'

'Yes?' He pulled some Merlot from the rack and set two glasses on the worktop.

'But I couldn't decide what to say.'

Keeping in touch with Charlie was a delicate balance. Too many messages and there was a risk he might feel suffocated; too few and his confidence, always brittle, might falter at a critical moment, such as when he was being offered a joint, which for him was only ever one puff away from all the other so-called recreational drugs that sent him off the rails.

'What about his plans for the Christmas holidays?' Hugh said.

'Well, he'll be here most of the time.'

He put her glass on the worktop beside her. 'News then?'

She threw him an amused look. 'Since when did we have any news that was remotely interesting to the children?'

He went through a little pantomime of the thinking man perplexed, brow furrowed, eyes hunting around as if for ideas. 'Parents planning New Year break in sun?'

She laughed. 'Like I said – *nothing* that would be of the slightest interest.'

Hugh thought fleetingly of the hooded figure in the garden. That was news all right, but not the kind that Charlie needed just at the moment. 'How about asking how the NA meetings are going?' Charlie was meant to attend Narcotics Anonymous every day and counselling twice a week.

Reaching for her wine, Lizzie leant back against the counter. 'You don't think he'd see that as a lack of trust?'

'But it's meant to be part of the deal, Lizzie. That we're open about these things, that we don't do any more pussy-footing around.' This lesson had been drummed into them at the rehab centre's family sessions, along with the importance of rules and honesty and tough love.

She was nodding slowly, as if to persuade herself to his point of view. 'How would we word it though?'

'Just ask him how the meetings are going.'

She said proudly, 'He's done so well to get this far.'

'He's done very well.'

'It's almost six months now.'

'Well, there's your message, isn't it?' Hugh raised his glass to the idea. 'Let's congratulate him on however many days it is.'

'You don't think that would make him feel pressurised?'

She was right, of course. It would sound as though they were ticking off the days on a huge wall calendar. 'I know,' he said. 'What about, *Is it six months yet? We want to celebrate with you.*'

'Mmm. I'm not sure celebrate's quite the right word . . . And I think we should get away from questions that need answers.'

'Okay. What about *So proud of you?*'

She wasn't convinced.

'What's wrong with that?'

'It sounds a bit . . . I don't know, as though he'd won a marathon or something.'

'But he has, hasn't he? Well, not *won* exactly, but on the way to winning.'

'Mmm.'

'What about . . . *How's things? With you all the way, love Mum and Dad*?'

She gave her wide smile. 'Perfect!' She dug her mobile phone out of her bag and held it up. 'Shall I go for it then?'

Since Lizzie was a master of texting and Hugh was still struggling with the basics of abbreviation, he waved her on enthusiastically.

'If you could just keep an eye on the sauce . . .'

The sauce contained meat, onion, and tomato, to which he added random quantities of herbs and chopped garlic, though from the smell he suspected there was quite a bit of garlic in there already. Garlic was meant to be good for colds, he vaguely remembered from one of Isabel's strictures, its bug-defying properties enhanced, he supposed, by its ability to keep people at a distance.

Lizzie declared, 'There! Done.'

She took charge of the sauce again while Hugh began to make the salad dressing, which was always his department.

'I was thinking,' Lizzie said, 'that Charlie should have a counsellor in the holidays, someone fairly local.'

'You don't think he'll manage without?'

'Oh, I'm sure he will. But there's no harm in knowing he has support close at hand if he wants it. A sort of safety net.'

Lizzie often floated ideas like this, variations on the

theme of how best to support Charlie. In her volunteer work at the Citizens Advice she helped people tackle a wide range of problems, from debts and benefit claims to housing and legal disputes. She was trained to cover every angle, though when it came to Charlie Hugh suspected that her industriousness owed as much to the need to feel useful as to any practical help she might be able to give.

Hugh said, 'But Charlie would have to decide, wouldn't he? Whether he needed someone. And who to go to.'

She poured steaming pasta into a colander. 'Of course. But I thought we could ask around. Find a name or two.'

'Okay . . .'

Catching the hesitation in his voice, misunderstanding the reason, she said, 'Oh, don't think I'm losing faith in him, Hugh. I'm not. Far from it. No, in fact—' She paused, as if about to say more than she'd meant to. 'I'm actually starting to believe he's going to be all right. I mean, really all right. I've never dared think it before. Not after all the disappointments. But now . . . well, he's been sounding so good on the phone, hasn't he? So together. It's as if he's finally got the message that life's far more wonderful when he's not stoned or high all the time. That he can get through the dark times okay with the help of NA and all the rest of it. Oh, I know it's tempting fate, Hugh. I *know*.' She clutched a hand to her head in a gesture of foolishness. 'But I can't help it.'

Hugh smiled, both to reassure her that the idea wasn't so foolish and to conceal the fact that in recent weeks his thoughts had been running in rather a different direction. It seemed to him that the odds of someone as fragile as Charlie beating his addiction first time round weren't too good, that it would be sensible to prepare for the possibility that he would have to go back into rehab at least once, maybe twice, in the course of his recovery. This thought had seemed rather disloyal at first, but as he took the new rules on board and began to absolve himself of responsibility for Charlie's addictions, to 'release with love' as the rehab centre put it, he began to accept the thought for what it was, not a matter of guilt but of guarding against disappointment.

'Go for it!' he declared.

'You don't think it's unlucky?'

'Totally not.'

'Totally not.' She laughed. 'You sound like Lou.'

'Do I?' The thought didn't displease him. 'Where is she? Still in Madras?'

'Till tomorrow.'

'Then north, is it?'

'Yes. She should reach Calcutta in about a week.'

'By bus?'

'I think so.'

They never worried about Lou, who at eighteen was responsible and level-headed, and far more organised than anyone else in the family. When she had finished trekking through India with her friend Chrissie she was going on to Sri Lanka to do two months' voluntary work in an orphanage before coming home to read medicine at Edinburgh. She e-mailed at least once a week and regularly posted smiling snapshots on a travellers' website.

They carried the supper to the table and Hugh went back for the wine.

'By the way,' he said as they sat down, 'there was a hoodie-style kid hanging around the gate when I got back.'

'Oh?' she said calmly. 'One of Charlie's old crowd?'

'Could have been.'

'You'd think they'd have got the message by now. That he's away at college.'

'Ah, but they don't get the message, do they? That's their trouble – they're too spaced out.'

'You're sure it wasn't Joel? Back from wherever he's been.'

'Canada. No, it definitely wasn't Joel.' Joel was the son of the people who lived two houses away; a gangling monosyllabic youth with bad skin who shared Charlie's passion for IT.

'I can't say I've ever really taken to Joel,' Lizzie said, 'but at least he's not into anything worse than computers.'

'Charlie gets on with him okay.'

'Yes, that's all that matters.'

Now they were back on to Charlie, Hugh was tempted to leave the subject of the youth behind. But he felt bound to add, 'If you see the hoodie hanging around the gate again, you'll call the police straight away, won't you, Lizzie? Or get help from a neighbour.'

'Oh, I'll be all right, darling. Don't forget, I deal with hoodies all day. They don't worry me.'

'Well, perhaps they should.'

She gazed at him for a moment before asking, 'Is that how you got wet?'

'Mmm?'

'Talking to the hoodie?'

'Well . . . *trying* to talk to him.'

'Ah.' She put on a solemn expression, to assure him of her sympathy. 'He ran away?'

'Sprinted, more like.'

'Probably just as well you didn't catch him.'

'Huh. If I'd just had the chance!'

'Well, what would you have done with him if you'd got him?'

'I'd have given him a bloody good hiding.'

Lizzie's eyes gleamed with a suppressed smile.

'And why the hell not?'

'You might have come out of it worse.'

'No way.'

'Anyway, with most of these kids it's all show, isn't it, the hood business. They're just trying to look cool.'

'He was up to no good.'

'Why, because he ran away? He was probably scared out of his wits.'

'It'd be nice to think so. Trouble is, Lizzie, you only get to see the hoodies who make it as far as the Citizens Advice, the ones who're together enough to ask for help.'

'Oh, I get some fairly untogether ones as well.'

'Really? I thought they were too busy robbing off-licences and mugging old ladies.'

She shot him a look of tolerant rebuke, and he withdrew the remark with a wave of his glass. He loved this Merlot, so silky on the throat, so soothing on the brain. Already he felt the day's problems miraculously postponed, his thoughts spiralling happily around Lizzie, the meal, the hours till sleep. He asked, 'What customers did you have today?'

'Well, it was a Monday, so it was non-stop. I had a credit card debt, a couple of eviction notices, a loan-shark victim in hock for ten thousand. Oh and, last thing, Gloria James, the woman from the Carstairs who's so desperate to be rehoused.' Seeing that he was struggling to remember, she prompted, 'The one with the agoraphobic son.'

'Oh yes,' Hugh said, as the story came back to him. The Carstairs was a notorious council estate on the northern borders of the city, a run-down concrete monolith with dark passageways, broken lifts, and litter-strewn landings that had long been a byword for drugs, crime, and anti-social behaviour. The only surprise was that all its residents didn't besiege the offices of the council, the Citizens Advice, and every other agency in the city, demanding to be rehoused.

'Agoraphobia?' he murmured, as something else drifted into his memory. 'I thought the son was living in fear of the gangs, of getting beaten up.'

'That's what Gloria says, yes . . .' Lizzie frowned, as if turning something over in her mind. 'But whatever the cause, the effect is the same. Wesley's terrified of going out, and Gloria's convinced he'll never get better till they move.'

'And he's stayed cooped up *how* long?'

'Two years. Since he was sixteen.'

'He's never been out in all that time?'

'Apparently not.'

'God . . .' Hugh winced at the thought. 'And they can't be rehoused?'

'At the moment they don't score enough points to jump the housing queue. Gloria's got a doctor's certificate to say she's suffering from stress, but then half the estate's got stress-related illnesses so it's not exactly a rarity.'

'So who gets priority? Teenage mothers, I suppose. Lesbian asylum seekers.'

Used to his rumblings against the march of political correctness Lizzie raised her eyebrows briefly. 'The best hope,' she went on, 'is to get Wesley properly diagnosed with agoraphobia and depression and whatever else he's suffering from, then between the two of them they should chalk up enough points. But the psychiatrist's rushed off her feet at the moment. She can't get to see him before the end of the month.'

Hugh said, 'The word agoraphobia comes from the Greek for market-place, you know. It's a fear of going to the market-place.'

Lizzie gave a snuffle of amusement. 'Since when did you know any Greek?'

'Since last week, when agoraphobia came up in a radio quiz.'

'That's cheating.'

'Absolutely.'

'Well, in Wesley's case it's not fear of crowded places. It's fear of going out at all. But at least he's decided to talk to me, to trust me, which is more than he did before.'

A suspicion entered Hugh's mind and settled there. 'What's he been saying?' he asked lightly.

Distracted by some other thought, Lizzie murmured, 'Oh . . . how much he'd like to live somewhere else. That sort of thing.'

He waited for her to say more, but she was concentrating on her food. 'When did you last see him?' he asked, as the suspicion deepened.

'Mmm?'

'Wesley?'

She stabbed at some pasta before glancing up with a quick smile. 'Oh, this evening.'

Hugh absorbed this slowly. 'That was your late meeting?'

'Yes.'

'I thought it was a Citizens Advice meeting.'

'Well, it was.'

As the anxiety bunched in his stomach, Hugh gave up on his food. 'You went to the estate?'

'Yes.'

He gave an unhappy sigh. 'Lizzie . . .'

'It was perfectly safe.'

'I don't think anyone could ever class the Carstairs Estate as *safe*. And certainly not after dark.'

'But I went with Gloria. And John walked me back to the car afterwards.'

'John?' Hugh muttered.

'The community pastor.'

'And he deters the local gangs, does he?'

'No one would try anything with John.'

'You mean the muggers stop long enough to check that he's wearing a dog-collar before they attack? Well, I'm glad they've got so much respect for a man of the cloth.'

'Oh, it's not the dog-collar. It's the fact that he's six foot four and perfectly capable of looking after himself.'

Hugh rapidly amended his picture of John from a saintly grey-haired Bible-pusher to something far more robust, a former army chaplain perhaps, or a Born Again bodybuilder. 'All the same, I can't pretend I'm happy about it, Lizzie. You being there after dark.'

'It's much safer than it used to be even a year ago.'

'But not enough to make Gloria feel secure.'

'That's because she's so worried about Wesley.'

'Well, maybe she's got good reason.' Hearing himself in this mood, topping each point like some smart-arse lawyer, he took a moment to slow down. 'Trouble is, you're always going to be a prime target. White middle-class. A handbag full of credit cards. Everything that's fair game.'

Lizzie shook her head a little, as if the comment was unworthy of an answer. 'I never carry much in my handbag.'

'But they're not going to realise that till they've mugged you, are they?' If he had disliked himself in the role of point-scorer, the part of fretful husband didn't suit him much better. 'Can't you meet people in a café or something?'

'Not if they're old and disabled. Not if they've got children to care for.'

He made an uncertain face.

'I take care. Really I do.'

It was the Denzel Lewis case that had first taken her to the Carstairs Estate, he remembered with an echo of misgiving. Denzel was a twenty-one-year-old serving life for stabbing a youth to death. When Denzel was refused leave to appeal, his sisters had come to Lizzie for advice on raising money for a new legal fight. But then – and Hugh could never work out quite what had triggered it – Lizzie's interest in the case had deepened. Ignoring the training guidelines to keep an emotional distance from her work, she had got involved in the campaign to free Denzel. Perhaps it was Denzel's proud, articulate sisters Jacqui and Sophia who'd convinced her of his innocence, perhaps it was the word on the block, which had it that he'd been framed, but she began to read up on the evidence and talk to Denzel's friends and accompany his sisters to meetings with the new lawyers. Even then Hugh hadn't appreciated how much she'd taken the case to heart until she announced she was going to visit Denzel in prison, and subsequently spoke out for him at a campaign meeting.

If Hugh had been forced to say whether he thought Lizzie's time well spent, he would have been pushed to answer. There was the small matter of the forensic evidence, a jacket splattered with the dead man's blood which had been found in Denzel's bedroom, planted there, according to Denzel, by someone out to frame him. And there was his alibi, which had changed rather too often to inspire confidence. But Hugh tried to keep his doubts to himself. Once, in the early days, he'd uttered a rather sweeping opinion on Denzel's chances of getting off, and been accused by Lizzie of jumping to conclusions without being in full possession of the facts, a charge hard to deny either as a lawyer or a husband. Since then he'd taken a seat very much at the back of the campaign bus, acting as home supporter and sounding board.

'So . . .' he said brightly. 'What's the latest with the Denzel campaign?'

'The solicitor's drafting a new application for leave to appeal but it's not likely to get very far.'

'So, what next?'

'Well, the sisters are planning a new campaign to appeal for witnesses. Sophia's targeting the local radio stations, newspapers and churches, while Jacqui's organising a leafleting operation to cover every household in the neighbourhood – the Carstairs and Summerfields Estates, as well as the shops and offices.'

'Quite an undertaking.'

'Well, there has to be a witness out there somewhere, someone who can support Denzel's alibi.'

'It's been quite a while,' Hugh ventured.

'But that might just work to their advantage. There might be someone who's had the case on his or her conscience all this time and might finally be ready to come forward.' Catching the reservation in Hugh's face, Lizzie added, 'Some people do have consciences, you know. Even on the roughest estates.'

'But their whole culture's about steering clear of trouble, isn't it? And witness statements and court cases are serious trouble.'

'You're not allowing for people's better natures.'

Hugh said, 'That's the difference between you and me, Lizzie. You still believe in people's better natures.'

'So do you,' she said firmly.

Basking briefly in her good opinion, he rather wished he shared it.

Lizzie took some salad. 'Anyway, if anyone's that nervous about coming forward there's always the witness protection scheme.'

It was all Hugh could do to maintain a neutral expression. The idea was so wildly unrealistic he thought she must have abandoned it weeks ago.

She went on, 'I'm seeing Chief Inspector Montgomery tomorrow actually.'

'And what does he say?'

She looked up from her food. 'Well, darling, I don't know till I see him, do I?'

'But . . . he knows you're coming to talk about witness protection?'

'Oh yes. We've talked about it before.'

Hugh stared at her unhappily until she glanced up again, when he busily topped up her drink.

Lizzie put her knife and fork down and, with the air of getting things out into the open, said calmly, 'You're worried about it?'

'Well . . . yes.'

'Why?'

'Because . . .' He hesitated, aware that he was about to overstep his self-imposed boundary and give an opinion. 'Because so far as the police are concerned the case is done and dusted. They've got their man banged to rights. The last thing they want is a new witness crawling out of the woodwork, someone a foxy defence lawyer could use to launch an appeal and get their hard-won conviction overturned.' He stopped abruptly before he could say more and drained the last of the bottle into his glass.

'So why would Montgomery tell me witness protection is definitely a possibility?'

Because he's lazy and incompetent and out to impress you, Hugh felt like saying. Instead, he said with a shrug, 'Who knows?'

'I think I'd realise if he was stringing me along.'

*Ah, but would you?* Hugh thought with a pang. It seemed to him that her innate optimism, her wondrous belief in the possible, could sometimes lead her to take too much on trust.

'And you're assuming the police don't have any interest in justice,' she said, with a hint of challenge.

'Well, yes – I mean, *no*. Their idea of justice is a

conviction, isn't it?' He got up to fetch another bottle from the rack. 'And no matter how well-intentioned a cop might be, he's never going to want to accept that he might have put the wrong man away, not when the evidence is as strong as it was in the Denzel Lewis case.'

Lizzie murmured automatically, 'Or seemed to be.'

'Or *seemed* to be. Though having your victim's blood all over your jacket is a bit hard to argue away, whichever way you look at it.' Hugh drew the cork and came back to the table. 'The thing is, witness protection is incredibly expensive, Lizzie. I mean, megabucks. So the police aren't going to use it unless they're going for a major result, the conviction of a big villain. They're not going to use it to help the defence get someone off, someone who's, well . . .'

'Guilty?'

'In their eyes, absolutely.'

Lizzie had gone quiet, staring down into her wine glass.

'What?' he prompted her.

'Nothing.'

'No, tell me.'

Her eyes glittered with a strange light. 'You think the campaign is hopeless, don't you?'

He was startled as much by the question as by her tone, which was taut, almost accusatory. 'I've never said that.'

'You don't have to,' she said quietly. 'It's obvious.'

Hugh stared at her. 'That's not fair, Lizzie. I don't have any views on the campaign. Apart from anything else I've never met Denzel. I don't know the full story.'

He made a gesture of bewilderment, as much at the fact that they were having a disagreement as anything else. 'Really . . . I wouldn't dream of having an opinion.' What baffled him wasn't that she had guessed at his doubts but that she should accuse him now, and so bluntly, as if he'd been openly disloyal. 'I was only playing devil's advocate, looking at it from the police's point of view, that's all.'

Absorbing this with a small nod, Lizzie picked up her glass and cradled it in both hands.

Hugh felt the tightness above his heart he always felt when their harmony was disrupted. On the few times they argued, it was usually about trivial things, like the route to a friend's house or their memories of some half-forgotten event, and then they tended to argue wildly and inventively, transforming the dispute into an elaborate joke. More serious discussions were conducted according to tacit rules of engagement that required attentiveness and consideration, any emotion directed firmly at the subject, not at each other. Yet here they were, disagreeing for no apparent reason, and worse still, disagreeing unhappily.

Because he couldn't bear to let the situation go on for a moment longer, he came clean. 'Okay,' he said, 'so I've had a few doubts about Denzel's innocence. But only because he seemed to change his story every five minutes. But they were never *firm* doubts. I mean, nothing I'd ever try to defend, and certainly not to you, because you know all about it and I know damn all. And I trust your judgement, Lizzie. If you believe in him then that's all I need to know.'

The sense of injury lingered in her eyes. 'I wouldn't

have minded so much if you hadn't been speaking in your sceptical lawyer tone,' she said. 'No – in your *expert* sceptical lawyer tone.'

He grimaced contritely.

'It was just the last thing I needed.'

'Of course it was.' He reached across and squeezed her hand.

The tension began to slip from her face. 'It's been a long day, that's all.'

'And there I was, talking complete bloody rubbish.'

'I know you didn't mean to . . .'

'And the way I said it . . . sorry.'

'Trouble was, it reminded me of what Denzel's up against.' She gave a painful smile. 'For a while there you almost sounded like the enemy.'

'The *enemy*, Lizzie!' As the word resounded in Hugh's mind, he had a fleeting image of Tom leaving court earlier, talking about orienteering with people as the enemy.

'Listen,' he said, 'why don't you go and ask Denzel's solicitor all about witness protection? He'll know far better than me. Get him to look into it.'

She turned the idea over in her mind, and seemed to warm to it. 'Yes . . . Yes.' Then, with a small shiver, as if to shake herself free of the subject, she began to clear the plates.

When they had loaded the dishwasher, he looped his arm round her shoulders and squeezed her to him. 'I hate it when we have a misunderstanding.'

Her arm came up round his waist. 'Me too.'

'I get this pain in my chest.'

'Ouch,' she murmured sympathetically.

'I feel I can't breathe.'

'Poor you. Is it gone now?'

'Almost totally.' He kissed the top of Lizzie's head. 'How lucky we are.'

'Yes.'

Their good fortune was something they touched on all the time, a thanksgiving in good times, a refuge in bad, and a return to safe ground on the few occasions like this when they managed to upset each other. Sometimes they listed their blessings one by one – the children, their health, the house – sometimes they talked about the outlook over the garden, the view to the hills, the magnificence of the trees, all ways of saying the same thing. Tonight, though, they simply stood side by side, heads touching, for half a minute longer before kissing lightly and separating to do their chores. While Lizzie scooped up the large shoulder bag she used for work and took it to her desk in a corner of the living room, Hugh went upstairs to prepare for the morning. He had to be out of the house by six with his clothes packed for a couple of nights in London. First, Ray, his law partner from pre-merger days, with his unshakeable enthusiasm for networking, had talked him into going to a Law Society dinner. Then, somehow or other, he'd agreed to meet his old friend Mike Gabbay not for the quick drink he'd suggested but for dinner and to stay the night with Mike and his wife Rachel in Belsize Park.

As he was gazing at the open bag wondering what he had missed, Lizzie came in and reeled off, 'Cufflinks? Bow tie? Evening shirt? Shoes?'

'I wish I wasn't going.'

'You'll enjoy yourself once you're there.'

'I'll probably end up drinking too much.'

'Well, try to keep off the port. You know it always gives you a terrible hangover.'

They were in bed by midnight. Before turning off the light they lay face to face, hands linked, legs intertwined, and smiled at each other, taking reassurance that no harm had been done by the unexpected discord at dinner, confirming that their equilibrium was safely restored. After a moment Lizzie's eyelids drooped and, kissing her softly, Hugh reached for the light. She turned away onto her side and drew her knees up. Fitting himself around the familiar shape of her back, Hugh dropped his arm over her waist and, finding her hand, held it close up by her neck. Her breathing steadied quickly, she was asleep within seconds. He would have been close behind, his thoughts were drifting fast, when a worry nudged him back towards wakefulness, something to do with Tom Deacon. At first he assumed it was the hurdle of Price's evidence tomorrow, then the fact that Tom was drinking again, but when he finally fell asleep it was to dream of two small boys leaning into the wind on a rain-swept mountain.

# THREE

Normally Hugh tried to avoid racking up unnecessary expenses on his clients' accounts, but wedged into a standard-class airline-style seat over the wheels of a bumpy carriage, attempting to balance papers and coffee on the minute drop-down table, he wished that for once in his working life he'd splashed out on first class and paid the difference from his own pocket. He had to steady the jolting coffee with one hand, leaf through the bundle of documents with the other until he managed to locate Price's statement. He read it as he had read it many times before in the hope of getting some key to Price and the world of soldiering that had formed such an important part of Tom's life. According to Price, he and Tom had become close mates during the four years they had been in the same unit, drinking and carousing together, standing each other an occasional loan, confiding their hopes and fears. Price described the Tom Deacon he'd first known as outgoing, sociable, a bit of a joker, his personality unaffected by service in the Gulf War. But three years later, after their return from Bosnia, Tom had become moody and short-tempered, the result, Price claimed in the crucial passage, of being unable to cope with the horrors he'd witnessed there. To counter this claim

Hugh had entered in evidence Tom's army record, which also noted a deterioration in Tom's attitude at this time but cited problems at home and his frustration at not being able to obtain a rapid discharge as the underlying reasons. According to Tom, the Army had got it at least half right, he'd certainly been keen to get out, but from disillusionment with soldiering rather than problems at home, while Price's version of events was such a blatant fabrication that he could only be driven by malice. But if Price was lying, the question was why.

In his normal work Hugh had little reason to investigate people's backgrounds and he'd had to go to a family-law partner for the name of a reliable detective agency. The report that came back three weeks later rather shocked him, not for what it revealed about Price, but for the extraordinary detail it provided on what he'd always believed to be confidential matters, such as Price's army and medical records and his two youthful convictions for joyriding. But if Hugh felt uneasy about how such information might have been obtained Desmond seemed unconcerned, or at least discreet enough not to comment, and devoured the report with interest. So far as Hugh could make out, Desmond's plan was to suggest that Price was a loner incapable of making close friendships, a bit of a fantasist who, craving centre stage, had not only exaggerated his friendship with Tom but was using this opportunity to settle an old score, maybe over the girl Tom talked about, maybe over some other grievance that neither would admit to. Why else, Desmond had posed rhetorically, would Price choose to give evidence against his former comrade? Why else would he break the bond of trust wrought in the fires of war?

While Hugh had no doubt this was the right approach, its success would depend on how strongly Price performed in the witness box. If he had learnt anything during this hearing, it was how very differently people reacted under pressure. Perhaps it was the deceptively benign atmosphere of the civil court, with its air of courtesy and consideration, the absence of a jury or any obvious drama, and the leisurely pace dictated by the judge's need to take notes, but for some reason the intricate traps laid in cross-examination seemed to take many witnesses by surprise. Of the ten character witnesses who'd given evidence for Tom four had faltered under pressure, two quite badly. In Price's case, of course, the hope was that he would not simply falter but thoroughly discredit himself.

A refreshment trolley came by but the girl had sold out of bacon, lettuce, and tomato sandwiches, so Hugh settled for a ham baguette which proceeded to shed shards of iceberg lettuce over the next bundle of documents he managed to wrest from his briefcase and balance on the minute table. This bundle contained the large amount of background information that Desmond might want to call on at short notice, though in practice he rarely did so. Facts, figures, statements, correspondence, notes of meetings and conversations: the detritus of four years' preparation, the thousand and one ways of gobbling up huge amounts of time and fees in trying to cover every possible angle: the law in all its obsessive, bloated detail.

It was only as the train neared London that Hugh

remembered the envelope Annaliese had dropped off yesterday which he'd scooped up from the hall table and stuffed into his briefcase as he rushed out of the house early that morning. Opening it, he drew out two letters concerning another case and read them diligently but with fleeting interest. Only as he slid them back into the envelope did he realise there was another, unopened letter at the bottom. The envelope was small and flimsy, the sort sold in corner shops to fit the cheapest writing paper. It was addressed to Hugh in a mixture of scrappy letters and random capitals, his name spelt *Gwinn* without the *y* or *e*. The firm's name was also misspelt and the address lacked a postcode. Above his name was written *Confidential* underlined three times. The thin sheet inside was folded into quarters. It began *Dear Mr Gwinn* . . . His eye flew to the end but there was no signature, just as there was no address at the top. Returning to the body of the letter he skimmed the lines rapidly.

Realisation came fitfully, in small darts of disbelief. His first instinct was to reject the whole poisonous thing, to deny the idea in any shape or form. It was just someone with a grudge, trying to stir things up for Tom. Yet even as he began to read it again, a quiet dread spread through his stomach.

> *To let you know that Tom Deacon went to the family court and got the psyciatrist to say he's OK to get custody of his kids, as per being recovered from the traumatic stress disorder and being sober. Court case was 2 weeks ago – Exeter. Next hearing January. Linda doesn't want to give up the kids but its all going badly*

*for her, she's pregnant and the new man gives her
a hard time. But its not right that she gets to lose
the boys, not when Tom Deacons lying about the
drink and thretening her if she doesn't keep quiet
about it. She thinks she'll get the kids back later,
but she wont. What she needs is some of this
money he's getting from the court. People forget
it was her daughter that got killed too. If he's
going to get rich then its only right that Linda
gets her share. She doesn't know I'm writing
this but somebody had to, it's not right the way
things are.*

As fresh bursts of understanding came over Hugh, his
throat seized, he saw the speeding countryside through
a sudden mist, he whispered savagely, *You stupid
bloody fool! You stupid fucking idiot!* He had an urge
to grab Tom by the collar and shake him furiously,
demanding to know what the hell he thought he was
doing by screwing everything up.

The mist subsided as suddenly as it had come, he
drew a steadying breath and began the reckoning,
trying to calculate what if anything might be salvaged
from the wreckage. He looked at the envelope again,
then the letter, but there were no clues as to who had
written it. The postmark was illegible, the writing semi-
literate. The author hardly mattered though, because
he had little doubt that the contents of this nasty little
note were accurate; they chimed too well with Tom's
view of what was due to him and the sudden confidence he had shown in getting custody of his children.

Hugh wished he could ignore the letter, but it was
too late for that. There was no way to un-read these

words, no way to un-learn their message. To know them was to know them for ever.

In a plunge of despair he saw the case unravelling beyond repair. Desmond would have to be told, and he in turn would be duty-bound to go to the judge and admit that Tom had been playing a double game. The other side wouldn't be able to believe their luck. Tom would be recalled to the witness box for a mauling cross-examination, the judge would decide that the diagnosis of post-traumatic stress was less convincing than he'd been led to believe, and Tom's damages would be slashed.

As the train drew into Paddington and Hugh joined the crowd streaming along the platform he went through the options once again, as if the exercise might conjure up some miracle when he knew there was none. The only hope was that the judge would appreciate that damaged men did stupid self-defeating things, particularly when it came to their children, and that trauma rather than any defect of character had caused Tom to make such a serious mistake.

Hugh reached Court 12 just before ten and waited outside. Isabel was the first to appear, swathed in a long coat, scarf and woollen hat. She said her cold was better, though her blocked nose, watery eyes and rasping voice told a different story.

'Listen,' Hugh said, 'I have to have a long, hard talk with Tom. We may get into court late. If you could hold the fort?'

'Is there a problem?'

'You could say that, yes.' Seeing Desmond and Sanjay coming round the corner, he added, 'But no time to tell you now.'

'Just let me know if there's anything I can do,' she said, and went into court.

Desmond wore an indolent smile. 'Morning, Hugh. Tom here yet?'

'Not yet, no.'

'But we're expecting him?'

*Christ, I hope so*, Hugh thought in momentary panic. 'So far as I know, yes.'

'I've got a query about the leave he spent with Price when they were stationed in Germany. I'd like to know if they *intended* to take their leave together or if it just happened. Did Price tag along or did Tom invite him? You understand what I'm getting at?'

'I'll ask him as soon as he gets here.'

'And Tom'll be around later in the week, won't he?'

'Oh yes.'

'Because I'll probably put him into the witness box first thing on Thursday. But best not to say anything just yet. In case things change.' Then Desmond made one of those gestures that were so characteristic of him, a raising of his eyebrows, an upturning of one hand, as if to suggest that everything of importance was now settled.

'Desmond, something's come up,' Hugh plunged in unhappily. 'I need to talk to Tom first but it's almost certain we'll have to ask for an adjournment.'

Desmond was very still. 'For what reason?'

'To have a conference with Tom.'

'It won't wait till lunch?'

'No.'

'Something serious?'

'Yes.'

'You're making me nervous, Hugh.' But if Desmond

was hoping for reassurance he was disappointed. 'You'll let me know as soon as possible?'

'Of course.'

'Bearing in mind that any significant delays will run us out of time on Friday.'

'I haven't forgotten.'

When Desmond had gone, Hugh paced along the passage to the stairwell, then to the balcony overlooking the Great Hall and back again several times. Finally he saw Tom on the stairs, climbing steadily, head jutting forward, the rucksack high on his back. A few steps from the top Tom twisted round and looked over his shoulder directly at Hugh, almost as if he'd expected to find him there.

'Managed to survive the train,' Tom announced, walking straight past so that Hugh was forced to fall in beside him. 'It was crowded as hell. But I did what my therapist told me. Concentrated on this woman. Oh, not in *that* way.' He gave a derisive snuffle. 'She was fifty if she was a day. But I spent the time trying to imagine what her life was like. You know, the job she did, where she lived, that sort of stuff. And it worked. Took my mind off the fact that we were packed in like bloody sardines.'

'Good. Tom, we need to talk.'

Tom shot him a questioning look which Hugh ignored as he led the way to a window at the end of the passage. The window, tall and arched in the Gothic style, had a seat below, but neither of them sat down.

Hugh began with the simpler of his two tasks. 'Desmond wants to know about the leave you and Price took together in Germany. Did you invite him to join you? Or . . . how did it happen?'

'Didn't have to invite him. He just tagged along like he always did. Most of the unit were away on long leave. The rest of us had twenty-four hours. I was heading for Hamburg with my mate Shortie when Price got wind of it and came and invited himself along. Then Shortie chickened out, so I got landed with Price.'

'Did you ever invite Price to join you on any other leave?'

Tom shook his head. 'Like I said, he tagged along sometimes. But ask him? Nope, I never asked him.' He started to move away.

'There's something else.'

Tom paused, wary now and a little impatient.

'I have to ask you, Tom – have you been to the family court and applied for custody of the boys?'

Tom turned his mouth down in an expression of exaggerated bewilderment. 'Huh?'

'Have you already been to the family court?'

Tom gave him a long stare. 'I don't get it. What's the problem?'

'Yes or no, Tom.'

'But what's it gotta do with anything? I mean what's it matter?'

'It matters.'

The bewilderment again. Then with a light shrug, a gesture of showing willing, Tom said, 'It's like I told you, Emma Deeds put in my application and we're waiting to hear back. But nothing's gonna happen till – I dunno – January, something like that.'

'But has there already been a hearing, Tom? That's what I'm asking. And did you offer new medical evidence?'

Turning slowly away, Tom elbowed one arm free of

his rucksack, then the other, before swinging it onto the window seat. He stared out of the mullioned window, his bony features flattened and calcified by the light, so that for a fleeting moment, set against the Gothic battlements, he might have been a prisoner from long ago, looking out on his lost freedom. 'So what's the big deal?'

'There *was* a hearing?'

'Okay, there was a hearing,' he said on a tense note. 'But it's like I said – nothing's gonna be sorted till January.'

'And did you get a medical report for this hearing, Tom? Something to say you were better?'

A pause, then Tom gave a snort of disbelief. 'How would I do that?'

'I don't know. Go to another psychiatrist?'

'Yeah? And where would I get one? Yellow Pages?'

'I need an answer, Tom.'

Tom's profile took on a haunted expression, and something harsher, like bitterness. Flicking Hugh a dark scowl, he said, 'There's nothing to answer. Okay?'

'Do I have your word on that?'

'You can have whatever you like,' he muttered.

'Just your word, Tom.'

Tom was shaking his head. 'I still don't get what this's got to do with anything, for Christ's sake.'

'Well . . . it's to do with playing it straight, Tom, with not saying one thing to one court and something different to another.'

Tom argued with sudden vehemence, 'Jesus, if you think I'm gonna tell the family court I've still got raging post-traumatic stress, then you must be bloody joking. Christ, they'd turn me down quicker than look at me.

And then the boys would end up in care. *In bloody care*. And then I'd never get another chance. *Never.*'

'Tom, I understand how much you want the children—'

'There's no way I'm gonna risk my boys. *No way!* I love my boys. I *need* my boys. They're all that keep me bloody going. No way I'm gonna give 'em up.' He glared accusingly at Hugh. 'So don't even think about it.'

'But this way you're risking both cases, Tom. You're risking having your damages cut and you're risking' – he almost said 'losing your children' but rapidly amended this to – 'forfeiting the goodwill of the family court.'

'But no one has to know,' Tom argued. 'The family court stuff happens in private. No one's allowed to tell what happens in there. So who's gonna find out? Who's gonna know?'

'*I* found out, Tom. *I* know.'

'It was Emma Deeds, was it? The bitch.'

'No, it wasn't Emma Deeds. I don't know who it was.'

Tom gave an incredulous frown. 'Oh yeah?'

'It was an anonymous letter.'

Tom rolled his eyes. '*Linda.*'

'I don't think so.'

'Come *on.*'

'The person didn't give a name.'

'But it has to be Linda, doesn't it?' Tom scoffed furiously. 'The stupid cow.'

'Well, whoever it was, the fact is that I do know, Tom, and I can't pretend I don't.' But Tom was too busy fuming against Linda to take this in. 'Listen,'

Hugh said when he was a little quieter, 'don't let's get too worried till we see what Desmond says. You never know, there might be a way to limit the damage.'

He had Tom's full attention again now. 'What the hell are you talking about?'

'Well, Desmond's the expert, Tom, not me. He's the one who can advise us on the best way forward.'

'But this stuff – it's just Linda playing stupid bloody games! It's crap. It's nothing.'

'When you say *nothing* . . . ?'

'It's not true. Okay? It didn't happen.'

Voices echoed in the passage, and Hugh glanced round to see two barristers emerging from the next-door court.

Hugh dropped his voice. 'Look, Tom, whatever's done is done. But it's going to be far better to have it come out sooner rather than later. Believe me. Because something like this *will* come out, you know. It always does.'

'I've just told you – it's a non-event! It didn't happen!'

'Are you saying you didn't get another opinion?'

Tom gave a sudden shiver. 'For Christ's sake, just drop it, will you?'

'I can't just drop it, Tom.'

'You're my solicitor, you're meant to be on my side.'

Letting this pass, Hugh said, 'Look, if we go to the judge and tell him the whole story, how you persuaded yourself you were well because you were so desperate to get custody of the kids, then he might take a lenient view.'

'But we're almost *there*, for fuck's sake. We're almost *done*.'

'This is only the hearing, Tom. The case isn't over till the judge hands down his judgement. That could be six weeks away, maybe longer. Till then he can consider any new evidence that comes his way. Recall us for an explanation. Change everything.' Adopting a reasonable tone, he said, 'Okay, he might knock a bit off our damages. But once he understands why you did it – well, he might not clobber us that hard, Tom. With a bit of luck he might give us no more than a small rap over the knuckles, financially speaking. But if we say nothing and the opposition find out – Christ, Tom, they'll tear us apart, they'll take it to appeal, and then we could really lose out. I mean, a serious amount.'

Tom was staring at Hugh in a new way, as if he hated him. 'No way.'

'But it'll be far better in the long run.'

Tom's breath broke into ragged gasps, he lifted a trembling hand. 'This is *my* claim. *My* illness. And I'm saying no deal. You got that? *No deal.*'

'For God's sake, Tom – you could be putting everything at risk.'

Tom's face contorted, his eyes glittered, he seemed on the point of rage or tears or both. He gave another shiver, more violent than the last. '*No deal.*'

'Maybe I've explained it badly . . .' But Hugh trailed off, knowing he had explained it as best he could and that for the moment at least Tom was beyond reasoning.

Voices sounded again, much closer this time. It was the solicitors for the other side, studiously not paying them too much attention, in company with a burly man in a blue suit who, sharing no such qualms, was staring openly at Tom. Realising this must be Price,

Hugh touched Tom's elbow to turn him away from the other man's gaze, but Tom jerked his arm free, and, his mouth drawn down into a grimace, cried again, 'No deal!' Then, the emotion still pulling at his face, the glint of fury in his eyes, he looked round to find Price watching him, and understood that his enemy had witnessed his anguish.

Price strode confidently into the witness box and took the oath as if it was something he did every day. He had the appearance of a travelling salesman too long on the road, with a broad frame run to fat, a belly that stretched the jacket of his suit to its limits, and a plump neck that bulged over the rim of his collar. He was, Hugh supposed, forty-one or -two, but the roundness of his cheeks, the thickness of his hair gave him a deceptively boyish look.

Bavistock began with an unhurried smile, a collusive droop of the eyelids, as if to instil confidence in his witness. 'Mr Price, you have stated that Mr Deacon became a friend of yours when you were both serving together in the Army. How would you describe your friendship? Was he one of a number of mates you had in the Army? Or was he a close friend?'

'A close friend.'

'And you were in the same unit . . .' Bavistock referred to the papers in front of him '. . . for over four years. That's correct, is it?'

'Yes.'

'And at one point you served together in the same armoured vehicle?' Bavistock asked.

'A Warrior, yes.'

'So it would be no exaggeration to say you served side by side?'

'Correct.'

Tom was sitting a yard away from Hugh, far enough to discourage communication but not so far that anyone would think there was a rift between them. Earlier, while waiting for the judge, he had stared darkly ahead, his arms crossed, his mouth tightly pursed, before methodically opening his rucksack and pulling out his notebook and pencil. Now, shaking his head at Price's reply, he began to write.

'You saw Mr Deacon under pressure?' Bavistock asked.

'Correct.'

'In a variety of situations?'

'On exercise and in combat,' said Price, with an edge of pride.

'When you refer to combat, you mean the Gulf War?'

'Correct.'

'And how would you describe Mr Deacon during and immediately after the Gulf War?'

'He was in good shape.'

'How would you describe him in those days?'

'Upbeat. Full of jokes.'

Tom put his pad down and, leaning forward with his elbows on the table, gazed intently at Price as though willing him to look in his direction.

'And off duty?' Bavistock went on. 'You were close friends then as well?'

'Correct.'

'What, you socialised together?'

'Correct.'

'And this was how often?'

'Whenever we had the chance.'

With a slow hiss of disgust Tom resumed his writing.

'Now . . .' Bavistock turned to another page in the statement. 'Moving on to the Bosnian conflict, you served in a different troop from Mr Deacon, but met up again when you returned to the UK?'

'Correct.'

'And it was then that you noticed a change in him?'

'I did.'

'You've stated that he was "down". In what way exactly?'

'Well, he was in a bad mood all the time. Snapping people's heads off. Keeping himself to himself. Not socialising.'

'And he told you what the problem was?'

'He did.'

'And what was that?'

'He said he couldn't get all the stuff he'd seen in Bosnia out of his head.'

'Did he explain what he meant by "stuff"?'

'Yeah. Bad stuff. Mass graves. Men, lads, with their hands tied behind their backs. That kind of thing.'

'He gave no other reasons for being down?'

'No'

Tom flicked to the next page and wrote intently. As Bavistock came to the end of his questions, Tom tore the page out and passed it to Hugh. It read, *LIE 1: GOOD FRIENDS. LIE 2: SERVED SIDE BY SIDE. LIE 3: SAW ME IN COMBAT SITUATION. LIE 4: I NEVER TOLD HIM WHY I WAS DOWN.* Hugh passed it forward to Sanjay, who read it with a brief nod before putting it in front of Desmond.

Desmond began his cross-examination by taking Price through his military service and recent employment, rolling out the questions in a perfunctory way, as if the whole exercise was tedious but necessary, establishing that Price was now a mechanic working on high-performance sports cars. Then, almost as an afterthought, Desmond added, 'As a teenager you lived on an estate in Birmingham, is that right?'

Price clearly hadn't expected the question. 'Yes.'

'How did you get on at school?'

Price shrugged a bit. 'Didn't like it too much.'

'What didn't you like about it?'

'Couldn't see much point.'

Desmond nodded understandingly. 'But you stuck it out until you could leave at sixteen?'

'Yeah.'

'And how did you pass your time when you weren't at school?'

Price hesitated before giving Desmond a sudden, knowing stare. 'If you mean did I get into trouble – yeah, I got into trouble.'

'Oh?'

Desmond instilled the sound with faint surprise, and the first doubts began to play over Price's face. He said woodenly, 'A bit of joyriding.'

'Ah . . .' Desmond made a vague discomfited gesture, as if he had never intended to delve into this area. 'So you enjoyed cars?'

'Yes.'

'I see, I see . . . And, er . . . this joyriding . . . it was a group of you, was it?'

'No.'

'You took the cars on your own?'

Price had the resentful look of someone who has been tricked into overplaying his hand. 'That's right.'

'So you were something of an expert mechanic even then?'

Price wasn't sure how to take this. 'Yeah.'

'And everyone looked up to you for that, did they?'

With an air of having spotted the trap, Price declared, 'Never bothered me what they thought.'

'So you didn't take cars to make an impression – you took them for the pleasure of driving?'

'Well . . . Yeah.'

'And did you take passengers?'

'Never.'

Desmond nodded slowly. 'How else did you pass your time?'

If Price had been wary of Desmond's earlier questions, he looked openly puzzled now. 'I don't follow . . .'

'Well, did you watch TV? Play computer games? That sort of thing.'

'Yeah. Sure.'

'And sports?'

'No chance. Nothing in the way of sports grounds, not for miles.'

'So what did you do by way of recreation?'

Still puzzled, Price gave a shrug. 'I did a few weights at home. Or went down the canal.'

'Ah.' Desmond's tone brightened, as if they had stumbled over a common interest. 'Fishing?'

'Yeah.'

'A bit solitary, though?'

Price frowned. 'Didn't bother me.'

'Difficult to fish in a group of course,' Desmond conceded, with the air of having asked a stupid question.

During the cross-examination Tom had come alive, listening intently, giving occasional snuffles of approval. Now he slid Hugh a quiet look of excitement, as though he knew exactly where Desmond's questions were leading and could hardly wait to see Price's discomfort once the knives were out. Watching him, Hugh realised with a plunge of dismay that Tom had taken none of their conversation on board, that as far as he was concerned it was business as usual.

Desmond leafed through his notes. 'So, Mr Price, you joined the Army at seventeen. And was it all you'd hoped it would be?'

'Oh yes.'

'What was the best thing about it?'

'Doing my job.'

'You qualified as a mechanic?'

'Yes.'

'And what else did you like about the Army?'

Price gave this some thought. 'Serving my country.'

'Anything else?'

Keeping on the same track Price said, 'The challenge.'

'Indeed.' Desmond nodded sagely. 'And your army record . . . how was that?'

'All right.'

'It's army practice to make every soldier aware of his shortcomings, though, isn't it? So that each man can work on them. What were your shortcomings so far as your superiors were concerned?'

Price's gaze flicked down to one side and back again. 'Nothing special.'

'Come now, Mr Price, wasn't the main criticism that you found it hard to work in a team?'

A pause. 'It might have been mentioned once.'

'I put it to you that it was mentioned more than once, Mr Price. I suggest it was seen as a problem throughout your army career.'

Price looked towards Bavistock, as if for rescue. 'No.'

'I put it to you that you were seen as a loner, not just by your superiors, but by your comrades as well. Isn't that right?'

'No,' Price said without conviction.

'You've already told us that you spent your spare time on your own when you were growing up, that you went joyriding alone, weight-lifting and fishing alone. In effect, that you much preferred your own company. It was the same in the Army, wasn't it? That you were far happier taking an engine apart than talking to your comrades?'

'No.'

'Isn't it true that you found it hard to make close friendships, even with the men in your own troop?'

'No. I had some good mates.'

'But close friendships, Mr Price? That's what I'm asking.'

'I had plenty,' Price said defensively.

Desmond left this comment to settle. 'You say you regularly went drinking with Tom Deacon, but you were nearly always in a larger group, weren't you?'

'Sometimes we were, sometimes we weren't.'

'In fact, the only time you and Tom Deacon went

drinking on your own was when everyone else was on long leave, in fact just twice in all the years you served together. Isn't that so?'

'It was more times than that.'

'Three times then?'

Price hesitated. 'I can't remember.'

Desmond waited for the judge to finish taking notes, but also, it seemed to Hugh, to let Price reflect on how badly he was doing.

'You say you became friends with Mr Deacon when you ended up in the same troop, is that right?'

'Yes.'

'Why then, if Tom Deacon was such a good friend, didn't he invite you to his wedding the following year?'

Tom gave a faint chuckle under his breath and, rocking forward, hunched over the table as if to contain his delight. The movement caught Price's eye, he flicked a glance in Tom's direction before looking rapidly away.

'Because I couldn't make it.'

'He invited two of his army friends – Shortie Thomas and John Potter – but not you. Why was that?'

'There was no point in asking me, not when I couldn't make it.'

Desmond tilted his head doubtfully. 'What made you decide to give evidence in this case, Mr Price?'

Price was ready for that one. 'Because I was asked what happened, and I told it like it was.'

'No other motive, Mr Price?'

'No.'

'Nothing to do with getting even?'

Price gave a nervy contemptuous snuffle and glanced at the judge. 'No.'

'Didn't you fall out over a girl quite early on in your acquaintance?'

'No.'

'A girl called Kristina, whom you met in 1990, and who went off with Mr Deacon?'

Price shook his head. 'It was no skin off my nose. She was a—' He paused as if to find a suitable word. 'A slag.'

Desmond glanced at the judge, who murmured, 'I know what the word means, thank you, Mr Riley.'

'My Lord.' Then to Price: 'So what was the bad feeling about?'

'There was no bad feeling.'

'What I'm seeking to establish, Mr Price, is why you should choose to give evidence against a former comrade who was, according to you, a close friend?'

Tom breathed, '*Yes!*' and jammed his fist against his mouth as if to prevent himself from shouting it aloud.

'Because it was the truth,' Price said self-righteously.

'But you could have chosen not to make a statement, couldn't you?'

'When I did the statement I thought I was helping him out.'

'Helping out Mr Deacon?'

'Yes.'

'Come now, Mr Price, you can't have been in any doubt as to which side of this case you were giving evidence for – the side *contesting* Mr Deacon's claim?'

'I wasn't clear. Not then, I mean. Not at the start. I thought I was helping Tom.'

'But the solicitors told you who they were acting for, didn't they?'

'An insurance company, that's all I knew.'

'But the insurance company acting for the driver of the other car?'

'I wasn't clear,' Price repeated sullenly.

'I see. And when you *did* finally become clear as to which side they were acting for, what made you persist with your statement?'

'I thought I had no choice.'

'In what way, Mr Price?'

'Well, being the law, I didn't think I could go back on what I'd said.'

'So you went ahead with your written statement?'

'No, I'd already done the statement,' Price corrected him. 'That's why I thought I couldn't go back on it.'

'I see. But the written statement was something you came to regret?'

'Well . . . Like I said, it was too late by then.'

'But if you could wind the clock back, Mr Price, if you had known at the outset what you know now, that far from helping your friend's case you might actually hinder it, would you still have made the statement?'

Price hesitated. 'Well, I. . . . I suppose not, no.'

'So, if the statement was a mistake, what brought you here today, Mr Price?'

'Like I said, once the truth was out, I thought I should stick to it.'

'Though by appearing here today you would be making matters worse for your old friend?'

'I didn't think there was anything I could do about it.'

'Isn't loyalty almost the first thing instilled into you in the British Army?' Desmond enquired. 'Loyalty to your comrades and your regiment? Isn't that at the very core of what soldiering's about?'

A gleam of sweat had appeared on Price's temple. 'The truth's the truth.'

'But to give evidence that could harm your former comrade's case – why would you want to do such a thing, Mr Price?'

Another pause. 'I didn't think about it that way.'

'Oh, but you must have, Mr Price.' Catching the judge's move to correct him, Desmond turned this rapidly into a question. 'Wouldn't you agree?'

'No.'

'So what were your feelings on coming here today?'

Price's eyes flicked up and down. 'I . . . can't say.'

'Well, satisfaction? Regret? Guilt?'

The whole of Price's face was glistening now, and two trickles of sweat had tracked down the side of his plump cheek. 'Nothing like that . . .'

'What then, Mr Price?'

'Well . . . I felt . . . you know . . . sorry.'

Desmond waited for Price to elaborate before prompting, 'Sorry in what way?'

'Sorry for . . . you know, what happened to Tom. And his daughter . . .'

'But not so sorry that you weren't prepared to come here and give evidence for the side opposing his case?'

Price swallowed, his head settled lower on his thick neck, his skin turned very pink, he said weakly, 'I told you, I didn't realise . . .'


As soon as court rose for lunch Tom hurried forward and spoke to Desmond in a low voice that did little to conceal his elation. By the time Hugh reached them

Desmond was saying firmly, 'Don't forget we've still got the rest of the week to get through, Tom.'

'But you did it,' Tom said with a barely disguised laugh. 'You showed him for what he is – a liar.'

'Well, whatever we've achieved we mustn't make the mistake of counting our chickens. Isn't that right, Hugh?'

'Yes. Absolutely. But, Desmond, we need to have a quick conference before lunch, if that's all right with you.'

Tom took a hasty step backwards. 'Count me out. I've gotta go see someone.'

Hugh said, 'But we need to talk.'

Tom was already turning swiftly away. He was out of the door and halfway down the passage before Hugh managed to grab his arm. 'For Christ's sake, Tom, we can't put this thing off.'

Tom jerked his arm free. 'I told you – it's no deal! Not now, not ever! And don't you go saying anything to Desmond without my say-so. Because you've no right. No right at all!' With a shudder, he strode away.

Joining the rest of the team in the dark wine bar off the Strand, Hugh broke his lunchtime rule and ordered a glass of wine. He needed something to calm him down. Something to nurse him too. He had an ache behind his eyes, a roughness low in his throat, which for him almost always presaged a cold or flu, and alcohol seemed as good a remedy as any. Now and again he tried joining in the conversation, but kept losing track and finally fell silent.

On the way back he warned Isabel he might be late coming into court.

She had been watching him anxiously through lunch. She said immediately, 'This problem again?'

'Yes. Tom and I have a difference of opinion about some information that needs to be disclosed. He thinks we can get away with keeping it secret, I know we can't. But he refuses to discuss it.'

'What sort of information?'

'The fact that he's been making up stories for the family court in Exeter. Like he's perfectly well and fit to have custody of the boys.'

'Oh.'

'And he went and found a shrink to back him up.'

'What! But how could he think . . . ?' She cancelled the question with a sigh. 'Do you want me to try and speak to him? I'd be happy to give it a go.'

'Thanks, but I don't think he'll listen.'

'You're right,' she said. 'I'm a woman after all.'

Hugh shot her a look of surprise. 'What do you mean?'

'He has issues with women. Hadn't you noticed? He switches off the moment a female starts talking.'

'Does he?' Hugh remembered the meetings the three of them had had at the Dimmock Marsh office over the years, the numerous cups of coffee, the lunches at the pub next door, and realised with a slight shock that Isabel was right, he couldn't remember Tom speaking more than a couple of words to her. He thought back to the Sunday Tom had spent at Meadowcroft, the way he had failed to respond to Lizzie's questions or Lou's arrival, a reserve that Hugh had attributed to grief, depression, even a sudden shyness, but that he now viewed in a rather different light. 'I'd never realised. I thought . . . I don't know what I thought. But I'm sorry.'

'Oh, it's not *your* fault,' Isabel said. 'It's just the way he is. But what will you do next, Hugh? What happens if he goes on refusing to listen?'

'It's not an option.' Reaching the pedestrian crossing, they waited for the lights. Then, answering the question properly, he said, 'Theoretically – no, more than theoretically – I'd have to resign from the case.'

'That bad?'

'That bad.'

The lights changed and they started across the street. Hugh said, 'You'd have to resign too, I'm afraid.'

'Of course,' Isabel declared, as if any other idea was unthinkable. 'But what would happen to the case then?'

'Tom would have to find himself some new solicitors.'

'Won't that be difficult so late in the case?'

'Oh, there'd have to be an adjournment. Unless he chose to represent himself.'

'Would the judge allow that?'

'I'm not sure he'd be able to stop him. And with only three days left, he might not even try.'

'And Desmond?' Isabel asked, after they had passed through the security controls. 'What about him?'

Desmond was ahead, progressing smoothly across the Great Hall with Sanjay at his side. Watching him, Hugh felt acutely aware of his own isolation, the fact that he couldn't turn to Desmond for advice. 'No reason why he couldn't stay on.'

'But won't his position be impossible as well?'

'Not if I don't tell him.'

'You can do that – not tell him?'

'Sadly, yes. So long as Tom doesn't want Desmond to know, then my hands are tied. Anyway there's no sense in Tom losing his barristers as well.' At this, the shadow of an idea entered his mind, an idea that was as daunting as it was tantalising.

As they started up the stairs Isabel said with a quiver of indignation, 'Is there no way round it?'

'Not while he refuses to listen.' Aware of Desmond and Sanjay doubling back along the landing above their heads, Hugh lowered his voice. 'And the really stupid thing is, our resignation would achieve precisely nothing. It certainly won't stop the facts coming out, and the longer Tom tries to keep the whole thing quiet, the worse it'll look for him.' The shadowy idea came back to him, stronger than before, and he grasped at it cautiously.

Isabel said something he missed.

'Sorry?'

'Just that I *know* Tom can't help being the way he is, I know he's unwell and irrational and all the rest of it, but sometimes – just *sometimes* – he seems to get paranoid about *us*, as if we're trying to go behind his back or something.'

'I could choose not to tell him of course,' Hugh murmured. 'Not immediately anyway.'

'Not tell him what?'

'That I'd have to resign. I couldn't leave it too long of course – a day at the most – but it might be enough to make him see sense. The worst that can happen is that he fires me anyway.'

'Well, he'd be crazy if he did,' Isabel said loyally. 'You're the best person he's ever going to get.'

The extra day would be useful, but it was the other, more shadowy idea that had taken the greater grip on Hugh's imagination. It would be risky because it would put so much pressure on Tom. And, perhaps more to the point, it would mean deliberately deceiving him. New ethical dilemma for the Law Society *Gazette*: Can it be justified to tell your client an outright lie to save him from his own actions?

Tom was late getting back. As court resumed, Hugh considered waiting inside the first set of doors so that Tom wouldn't spot him till the last minute, but lying in wait felt like a cheap trick, so he stood openly in the passageway, hoping that lunch had put Tom in a more reasonable state of mind.

He heard Tom before he saw him, the tap of his feet on the stairs, the strike of his heels as they hit the level. When he finally appeared, it was at speed. He spotted Hugh straight away but his pace didn't falter.

Hugh stepped forward and said brightly, 'Okay?'

Ignoring him, Tom strode past.

With a leap of frustration Hugh cried, 'Don't be a bloody fool, Tom. I'm going to have to tell them anyway.' It was out, he had said it; the lie had come surprisingly easily.

For an instant it seemed Tom wasn't going to stop, but just short of the court doors he halted abruptly and looked back. 'You can't do that. You can't go against what I want. You're my lawyer.'

'Sorry, but it doesn't quite work like that. My first duty is to the law. I'm not allowed to knowingly mislead the court. I'm not allowed to be party to an untruth.'

'What untruth?'

'You know what I mean, Tom.'

'No, I don't. My life's a load of shit, I can't sleep, I can't work, I can't get through the day without flash-backs and panic attacks. So where's the untruth in that, for Christ's sake?'

'But you've gone and told the family court some-thing else, Tom. And running away from that – and from me – isn't going to help.'

Tom threw his head back and screwed up his eyes in a gesture of patience worn thin.

Walking over to him, Hugh said, 'We're so nearly there, Tom. Please don't throw it away now.'

'I told you – I'm not gonna give up my kids.'

'But hiding the truth isn't going to help get your kids.'

'That's where you're wrong!' he exclaimed avidly. 'It's gonna get me my boys. And by the time anyone gets to hear anything different – *if* they get to hear anything different – I'll have got custody.'

'But this case is going to make the news, Tom. Only a paragraph maybe, but that'll be more than enough. People will talk. What happens then? What happens when the family court gets to hear about it?'

'If they try and get the kids, they'll have to do it over my dead body.' Tom was trembling, the veins standing out on his forehead.

Hugh sighed, 'All right, Tom. All right. But do me one last favour – hear me out one more time. If only for my benefit. Just so I know I've done all I can to explain it to you.' He gestured towards the window.

For a while it seemed Tom wasn't going to move, then with an imperceptible nod he walked stiffly across to the window and, perching on the edge of the seat, hunched forward with his forearms resting on his knees.

Sitting beside him, Hugh went over it again slowly, explaining the advantages of coming clean and the consequences of covering up, counting the important points off on his fingers. He spoke in tones of concern and understanding, sensing that friendship was the only way to reach Tom just then. Only towards the end, as he prepared to repeat the lie, did he strike a note of authority, saying bluntly that he had a duty to put the matter before the court, that if he didn't he risked being struck off.

Tom continued to stare fiercely ahead before cocking his head slightly, as if to determine whether Hugh had finished.

Hugh gave it his last shot. 'What would really crucify me, Tom, is for you to end up with *nothing*. Not the kids, and not the money. We've already turned down three hundred grand. If your award gets knocked right back on appeal, if you end up winning less than the three hundred, then the other side will be able to claim their costs out of your money, and then—'

'I know all that.'

But Hugh said it anyway. 'Then you'll end up with virtually nothing. That's what's at risk here, Tom.'

Tom hunched even lower over his knees and wrung his long fingers. 'So . . . what're you saying?'

'That we go to the judge now. Explain the situation. Get him on our side as far as we can. He should be reasonably understanding.'

'And there's no choice?' He sounded scornful, and for a moment Hugh thought he was about to call his bluff and demand to know why, if there was no choice, they were bothering to argue the point in the first place.

'There's no choice.' And God strike me down for the lie, thought Hugh, but I'm doing it for his own good.

Tom shuddered. 'And then?'

'Then we'll have done all we can.'

'I meant the family court,' Tom growled. 'What happens with them? They get to be told, do they?'

'I'm not sure about that. But I can find out.'

Tom dropped his head still lower and caged his hands around his face. 'Jeese . . .'

Hugh left it a moment before asking, 'So are we on, Tom?'

'I dunno, for Christ's sake. *I dunno.*' He sat up suddenly. 'I've gotta think it through.'

'Okay,' Hugh said soothingly. 'Why don't the two of us meet first thing in the morning? I'll have the information about the family court by then and we can come to a decision and grab a few minutes with Desmond before court begins. How's that?'

Tom gave no sign of having heard. 'All I ever wanted was my life back,' he said with a bitter catch to his voice. 'And now I'm not even gonna get that. Some sort of fucking justice.'


The club lay on the south side of Pall Mall in a row of similar gentlemen's clubs with grandiose facades, wide stone steps, and pillared entrances which occasionally bore a street number but never a nameplate, so that in darkness and rain strangers couldn't be sure of arriving in the right place. In search of the RAC, Hugh found himself in what turned out to be the Reform and was courteously directed two doors further down where he found Ray in the entrance hall, resplendent in a dinner jacket, nose in the *Financial Times*.

'Hugh!' Ray's usual style was a slap on the shoulder and a big grin, but perhaps in deference to his surroundings he greeted Hugh rather more formally, with a handshake. Then, recalling that this was after all his old colleague and friend, he added the usual grin. 'How're you doing, boyo?'

'Okay, thanks.'

Perhaps Hugh's face told a different story because Ray said, 'Look like you need a bloody great drink.'

'I think I'll go and change first, if that's okay.'

'No problem!' Ray declared. 'Your room's on the second floor. But listen . . .' He narrowed his eyes conspiratorially. 'Why don't we slip into the bar for a sharpener first, eh? Come on, just a quick one.'

It was useless to argue with Ray when he was in one of his more expansive moods and, having deposited his coat and bag in the cloakroom, Hugh followed him up the sweeping staircase to the bar. Hugh said he'd have a beer, then, aware of the rawness in his throat, the ache behind his eyes, changed it to a brandy and soda. 'But just a small one, Ray. Really.'

The drink Ray brought to the table was far from small, a double at least, with only the faintest splash of soda, and Hugh made a mental note to hold back on the wine at dinner.

Ray raised his glass. '*Iechyd da!*' he cried. 'To the green valleys of home!'

Hugh was the one born and bred in South Glamorgan, but it was Raymond, brought up in Bristol to a Welsh mother, who in the fifteen years they had worked together had been the keeper of the Welsh flame.

'*Iechyd da!*' Hugh replied dutifully.

Ray took a sip of his drink and gave an enthusiastic sigh. 'Just like the old days, eh, Hugh? Out on the loose.'

A Law Society dinner wasn't Hugh's idea of being on the loose, but then Ray had recently been kicked out by his long-suffering wife of twenty-five years for playing away, and was looking for adventure in even the most unlikely settings. He was sporting a new haircut, Hugh noticed, shorter on top, longer towards the neck so that it looked fashionable in a faintly foreign way. Or maybe it was cool in an English way and Hugh was simply out of touch. He supposed it was another manifestation of Ray's decision to take himself in hand, a rearguard action against the ravages of middle age and the challenges of the singles scene, which had led him to give up alcohol during the week, bread and potatoes at all times, and embark on lunchtime visits to the gym from which he returned looking drained and mottle-cheeked. Ray boasted that he'd never felt better, but beneath his buoyant manner it seemed to Hugh that he was finding his new life a considerable strain. Tonight, though, he was beaming benevolently, perhaps because he was allowing himself alcohol on a Tuesday.

'So . . . how did the big case go today?' Ray asked.

'Oh, all right,' said Hugh, who didn't feel ready to

discuss the Deacon problem with him. 'Desmond Riley did an excellent cross-examination.'

'The press sniffing around yet?'

'Not that I've noticed.'

'But they will, won't they?' said Ray confidently. 'Bound to get huge coverage.'

'I don't see why.'

'Come on, Hugh. There's the size of the damages for a start. It's going to be a record for post-traumatic stress, isn't it?'

'Who said that? Martin?'

Ray turned his mouth down in an expression of intense thought. 'May have been. Can't remember.'

'Well, he's quite wrong,' Hugh said reprovingly. 'We're not there yet, not by a long way. It all depends on the judge, whether he accepts everything the psychiatrists tell him. And there's no way of knowing, not till the actual judgement.'

'Okay, but even if the judge takes a conservative view it's still going to be a stonking great award, isn't it?'

'I'm not banking on it,' Hugh said rather crossly.

Ray waved this aside as natural caution. 'And then there's the story itself. God, every parent's worst nightmare.' He grimaced at the thought. 'No, the press'll go for it all right.' He stabbed an amiable finger at Hugh. 'The important thing is to make sure they spell your name right.'

'The press covered it at the inquest.'

'But how long ago was that? Years. No, they'll cover it again, of course they will. Don't look so glum, Hugh, it'll be a helluva thing for you. And great publicity for Dimmock Marsh. Personal injury hasn't exactly been one of our strengths till now. Though for God's sake don't quote me to our esteemed colleague Martin Sachs,' he said with a roll of his eyes. 'And who knows, maybe you'll end up specialising after all.'

'God, no.'

'Why not?'

'Too late. I prefer muddling along as I am.'

'Ah, but never say never, Hugh. Look at me. If I can do it, anyone can.'

'But you actually like commercial law.'

'Well, yes, I suppose I do,' Ray said, basking briefly in this vision of himself. 'But you don't want to find yourself losing out financially, you know.'

'Oh, I don't care about that.' Then, as the implications of Ray's remark sank in, a tiny warning sounded in Hugh's mind. 'Would I be losing out?'

'Well . . . it could just happen, yes . . .' There was concern in Ray's manner, but also a sudden awkwardness.

'I'm not with you.'

Ray hesitated, as if he regretted having raised the subject. 'Well . . . basically . . . it's this remuneration issue, Hugh. It seems the young lions aren't prepared to let it go.'

Leaving aside who these young lions might be, Hugh asked, 'When you say the remuneration issue . . . ?'

Ray frowned as if it should have been obvious. 'The performance-related pay issue.'

'I didn't know it was an issue.'

'Of course you did . . . you *do*, Hugh. It came up at the partners' meeting.'

'But that was months ago. In June.'

'Yes, well . . . Just because you did your best to kill it dead doesn't mean it went away, you know. It's been rumbling on ever since.'

Absorbing what seemed to be a double criticism, of having taken an unreasonably obstinate line and driven the matter underground, Hugh said, 'I simply reminded everyone that the traditional salary scheme was a condition of the merger.'

Ray fanned out a hand, as though to concede the point and simultaneously brush it away. 'Yes, yes . . . But that was *then*, Hugh. This is *now*. And well, there's a strong mood for change.'

'The issue was meant to be non-negotiable.'

Ray said, 'Nothing's non-negotiable, Hugh. Not in a partnership.'

Suddenly glad of the brandy, Hugh took another gulp. 'So how long's it been brewing, this mood for change?'

'Well, ever since that partners' meeting. I would have kept you in the loop, Hugh, but I sort of hoped the whole thing would blow over.'

At one time they had both scoffed at the new jargon, the blue-sky thinking and joined-up management, the staying outside the box and inside the loop, but now they spoke it with an affected naturalness that was in itself unnatural, old dogs doing their best with new tricks.

Hugh murmured, 'Life seemed a lot simpler before we had loops.'

Ray rolled his eyes. 'God, you can say that again!'

'But if the performance-related lobby felt so strongly why didn't they fight their corner?'

'I think it was more of a kite-flying exercise at the

beginning. Yes . . . definitely,' Ray said, as if this made
the whole thing more acceptable. 'But the young lions
had their finger on the pulse all right, because since
then, well . . . the idea's really gained ground, Hugh. A
lot of people feel, with the best will in the world, that
it's the right way to go.'

Hugh thought back to the old days when he and
Ray and their fellow partners had agreed the firm's
business over a beer and a sandwich at the Old Bell.
Differences of opinion – and they'd had a few, not least
about the wisdom of merging with Marsh & Co – had
been hammered out face to face, sometimes over several sessions, occasionally with some heat, but always
openly and with good grace. Since the formation of
Dimmock Marsh, however, decision making had
become decidedly more opaque, to Hugh at least. A
number of people, and it was usually the same lot,
seemed to turn up at partners' meetings in mysterious
agreement with each other, their arguments ready polished to match. But if Ray was right, and feelings had
been running strong, Hugh couldn't understand how
he had missed the murmurings of discontent. He
hunted back through his memory but he was sure no
one had mentioned the remuneration issue in any of
the time-honoured ways, casually over lunch, or on
leaving a meeting, or drifting into his office on other
business. But perhaps he had been too busy to pick up
on the signs. Out of the loop . . . yes, that seemed to
sum it up.

He said, 'Why didn't you tell me before, Ray?'

Ray made one of those gestures that were so characteristic of him, a sweep of one hand that could have
indicated anything from regret to denial. 'Truth be

told, Hugh, I didn't really appreciate how things were going myself, not until just the other day. And knowing how you felt . . . Well, I didn't want to stir things up unnecessarily.'

Trying not to dwell on the inconsistencies in this statement, Hugh said, 'And they think I won't budge, is that it?'

'Something like that.'

'Well, they've got that right at least.'

'A lot of up-and-coming firms are going for it, you know.'

'Well, that's their choice, isn't it? But in my view they're going in the wrong direction. You know how I feel. The whole point of a partnership is to work as a team. Share the load and share the income. Allow for the fact that everyone has a bad year from time to time.'

'But people's basic salary would be protected, obviously.'

'I don't care. If we went for performance-related bonuses the whole ethos of the firm would change. It would become every man for himself. And then we might as well get shot of the whole partnership and go off and work on our own.'

'I'm not sure it would be as bad as that,' Ray murmured.

Hugh asked, 'So what's your view, Ray? Do you think it's a good idea?'

'Me?' Ray blew out his cheeks. 'God, Hugh – what can I say? I mean, I can see that it has points in its favour. Some of the younger partners are bringing in huge amounts of work – really huge – and you can't entirely blame them for wanting to see more of the proceeds. Age and seniority will always count, of course they will. But it's a sharper, profit-related world out there, isn't it? Everything's getting performance-linked.' He gave a heavy sigh. 'At the same time . . . Well, I hear what you say, Hugh. I really do . . .'

'It'll come up at the next partners' meeting, will it?'

'Yes.'

'And will it get voted in?'

'Christ . . .' Ray gave an elaborate shrug. 'I really couldn't say.'

Yet something in his manner suggested this wasn't quite true. With a descent into disappointment, Hugh asked, 'Which way will you vote?'

'Haven't got that far.'

But I think you've got that far, thought Hugh with another dart of disappointment; maybe even farther. 'Well, keep me in touch.'

'Christ, *everyone's* going to be kept in touch from now on, I can tell you,' Ray protested with a rough emphatic laugh. 'Whether they bloody well like it or not! Full particulars spelt out in bold and underlined. No more of this skulking about in the bloody under-growth.' He drank morosely before looking at his watch and sitting up with a jerk. 'Christ, the time!' He scrabbled in his pocket. 'Could you make it down in record time, Hugh? Sorry to rush you but there're a helluva lot of people I need to talk to before we sit down to dinner.'

The moment Hugh reached the room he checked his phone for messages, but there was nothing from Lizzie. He'd already left one message on her voicemail and, getting no answer again now, debated whether to leave another. She was probably driving or at the supermarket. Or – he couldn't escape the thought – visiting the Carstairs Estate, walking the concrete passageways alone and unprotected. When she'd first started going there in the early days of the Free Denzel Lewis campaign he'd buried his worries, or at least persuaded himself the risk was minimal, but last night his fears had come roaring to the surface, and he wasn't sure why. Because she'd admitted going there after dark? Her alarming belief that it was safe? Or was it linked to his failure to catch the hoodie, who seemed then and now to personify the relentless march of the yob culture? A bit of everything perhaps. Also, if he was entirely honest, he hadn't liked arriving back at an empty house, not knowing how long it would be before she got home. It was entirely selfish, he knew, but when he'd imagined life after the kids had gone to college he'd seen the two of them having more time together, not less.

He had showered and was pulling on his evening shirt when his phone rang and showed 'Lizzie mobile' in the display.

She greeted him over the din of conversation.

'You sound as though you're out on the town.'

She laughed. 'What else?'

'The moment my back's turned. So where are you?'

'Seeing a colleague.'

'Some colleague.'

'She's female and fifty.'

'Well, take it easy on the cocktails.'

'Fat chance. I brought the car.'

'Have you had a good day?'

'Yes, actually. Very good. And you?'

'I've known better.'

'What happened?'

He could only just hear her above the din, and instinctively raised his voice. 'Tom's doing his best to score an own goal.'

'A what?'

'An own goal.'

'Hang on . . .' A pause, then the crowd sound diminished a little and when she spoke again he could hear her better. 'Is there anything you can do?'

'Probably not.'

'Bad luck. Oh, Charlie called.'

'How was he?'

'Fine.'

'He got our text okay?'

'Oh yes . . . yes. A change to his holiday plans, though. He wants to go to Spain immediately after Christmas.'

'*Spain?* But why?'

'Two of his mates are going to Barcelona and he's never been, and well, he thought it would be fun.'

'But he's meant to stay in a safe environment, not go off on trips whenever he feels like it. Spain's full of drugs and God knows what else. It's just asking for trouble.'

'But these friends don't do drugs.'

'I don't care. He'd be away from his counsellor and his NA meetings and all the things that keep him on the straight and narrow. And in a place riddled with temptation. No, I'm sorry, it's not on.'

In the pause that followed, he could picture her standing outside a wine bar, hunched against the cold, wearing the slight frown she always wore when confronting a difficult problem. 'Let's talk about it when you get back,' she said.

'The answer's still going to be no. I'm sorry, the idea's completely crazy.'

Another pause. 'All right. Shall I call Charlie and tell him how you feel? Or do you want to call him yourself?'

Hugh's anger subsided a little. 'No, you call him. I'd only make a mess of it.'

'I'll see if I can get him tonight.'

'I'm sorry, Lizzie, but I really think it's madness.'

'I'm not sure you give him enough credit, darling, really I'm not. He's thought it through, you know. He's worked out how to manage. And it would only be for a week.'

'Thought it through? If he'd thought it through he'd have realised that he's just trying to run away and avoid reality, just like before.' Into the silence that followed, he sighed, 'I'll phone him myself.'

'No, let me do it. But Hugh? When you do eventually speak to him, don't get angry, will you?'

'Of course I won't. Why would I get angry?'

'Well, you're angry now.'

He was about to protest when he played the sound of his own voice back to himself. 'I worry, that's all.'

'I know you do.'

He sighed. 'I wish I wasn't going to this bloody dinner tonight.'

'You'll enjoy it once you're there.'

'And I'm getting a cold,' he said dolefully. 'I have the feeling it's going to be a real stinker.'

But the conversation had risen to a roar again, as if

a door had opened, and she shouted, 'Sorry, darling, what did you say?'

'Nothing.'

'Look, I—' Her voice was lost in the general hubbub or else she had turned to speak to someone. Then she was back, shouting, 'Sorry. Got to go. I'll call you tomorrow.'

'Okay,' he said reluctantly.

She rang off so abruptly, without a goodbye, that he stared at the phone, thinking they must have been cut off.

# FOUR

At first Hugh waited as he had waited the previous day, restlessly, pacing the passage to the balcony overlooking the Great Hall and back to the doors of Court 12. But as ten thirty passed and the court went into session he slowed down, finally stopping altogether at the far end of the passage and gazing out of the window. When he'd arrived that morning it had been drizzling, but now the rain rattled against the glass and guttered down the roofs, while the tips of the ornate spires and pinnacles that rose from every corner and ridge of the rambling building were lost in gloom. He stood there for some time, wondering at the ambition of the Victorian architects, until with sinking heart he accepted that Tom wasn't just late, he wasn't coming at all. It would have been nice to imagine he was taking time to think things through, but more likely he was lying low, nursing a sense of injustice, directing his resentment at Hugh.

Before going into court Hugh left him a message, asking if he was okay, hoping there wasn't a problem, telling him to call, knowing he wouldn't. At lunchtime he called again to relay the news that Desmond definitely wanted him in the witness box the next morning, but if Tom was picking up his messages he wasn't letting on.

'So, can we expect Tom tomorrow?' Desmond asked when court rose for the day.

'I've no idea,' Hugh freely admitted. 'He's not communicating with me at the moment.'

'Would it be wise to make alternative plans then, just in case?'

'Definitely.'

Isabel declared, 'Oh, but Tom'll be here, I know he will.' She faltered momentarily under Desmond's gaze before adding, 'He's been longing to get back into the witness box. He won't miss it for the world, I know he won't.'

Desmond tipped Hugh an enquiring look.

'Nothing's that certain with Tom,' Hugh said.

Desmond nodded philosophically and packed his tote bag. After he'd gone, Isabel eyed Hugh with concern.

'You've caught my cold,' she said apologetically. 'Can I get you anything?'

'I'm all right.' He was croaking badly, his throat was on fire.

'What about some Day Nurse?' She delved into her bag and scrabbled around in the bottom. 'I know I've got some . . . I'm sure I put it . . . Wait – oh, it's Night Nurse. But perhaps you'd like some for later?'

'No, really,' he said more brusquely than he'd meant to.

Isabel paused, the packet in her hand. Then, with the same insistence as before, she said, 'Tom's just in a sulk. It won't last. He'll be here tomorrow, I'm sure of it.'

'I put him under too much pressure,' Hugh said gloomily. 'I don't know what the hell I was thinking of, backing him into a corner like that. I should have played it straight, told him I'd have to resign and left him to make up his own mind. Now he's probably on self-destruct, drinking himself into oblivion.'

'But you've given him every chance, Hugh. You've explained it to him. He might be suffering from trauma, but he can still think for himself.'

'Not when he's stressed out he can't.'

'Well, if you ask me he's a lot tougher than you give him credit for. A lot more—' She broke off abruptly as if to choose a kinder word. 'More *rational*.'

At the doors of the Royal Courts they paused to find their umbrellas. 'That stupid letter,' Hugh sighed. 'I wish I'd never read the bloody thing.'

'But people who write letters like that don't give up, do they? There'll be more letters where that one came from.'

'You think so?'

'Well, they don't write out of the goodness of their hearts, do they? They write to cause trouble, and trouble doesn't go away.'

Hugh shivered suddenly and hunched his shoulders against the cold.

'Here, why don't you take this anyway, just in case?' Isabel pressed the packet of Night Nurse into his hand.

Hugh held it up and pretended to read the label. 'I thought you didn't believe in this sort of stuff.'

'It'll help you sleep.'

'Help me pass out, more like.' He slipped it into his coat pocket, to join the vitamin pastille she'd given him on Monday. Putting up his umbrella, he said, 'The awful thing is, I don't even know where Tom's staying. I can't even go and find out if he's all right.'

'Well, that's Tom all over, isn't it? Not wanting anyone to know where he is.'

'But I should have got his address.'

'I'm not sure he'd have told you. I asked him three times for contact details and he kept saying he didn't have them.'

'Perhaps he didn't, not till the last minute.'

'Oh, I think he had them all right,' said Isabel quietly. 'He just likes to keep things back.'

Two days ago Hugh would have challenged this remark, but now he could only gaze out into the rain and wonder what else Tom might be holding back.


The faded blue front door swung open to reveal the substantial figure of Mike Gabbay. 'For God's sake!' he said. 'How are you doing, you old pagan?' Throwing an arm over Hugh's shoulder he gave him a bear hug. 'God, this rain! Here, give me those!' Hanging up Hugh's coat and umbrella, he urged him deeper into the house. 'How long has it been, for heaven's sake? Two years? Three? Too bloody long anyway. And look at you' – he threw out an accusatory hand – 'you must tell me how you do it. Sneak off to the gym? Practise some kind of Celtic witchcraft? Take a Welsh potion?'

'I don't do anything.'

'What – nothing?'

'Just the garden. And a bit of walking.'

'No justice!' Mike exclaimed contentedly.

Mike's weight battle had been lost in childhood, he had been bald since his early thirties, but his dark eyes, set in the plump smooth-skinned face, glowed with a keen intelligence and love of life. The two of them had been articled to the same firm, but while Hugh had taken the well-travelled route into high street law Mike had set up on his own in what was then the frontier territory of asylum, immigration and human rights, an area which, he liked to complain proudly, was as badly paid then as it was now.

'No justice,' Mike repeated. 'How's Lizzie?'

'Very well, thanks.'

'Glad to hear it! Come and see Rachel. She's in the kitchen.'

The house was Victorian and terraced and had the lived-in look of long occupation, with well-trodden carpets and bulging bookshelves and chipped paint.

'What do you think of this?' asked Mike, indicating the kitchen, which in stark contrast to the rest of the house had undergone a make-over, with modern units, halogen lighting and a tiled floor.

'Looks very nice.'

Rachel broke off from her cooking to greet Hugh. She taught French and greeted him in the French style, with four rapid kisses to the cheeks.

'My wife demanded a new kitchen after twenty-four years of marriage. I ask you!' said Mike in mock dejection. 'Fact is, we needed a project. You know how it is when the kids disappear.'

Rachel shot Hugh a quick smile which suggested that Mike's need for a project had been rather greater than hers.

Mike pressed his hands together and said urgently, 'Now, what'll it be? I've got a nice unassuming little Bordeaux . . .' He was already reaching for the bottle with one hand, a corkscrew with the other. 'Bought it on the off-chance ten years ago and it's done me proud ever since.' Mike had always loved his wine, and when Hugh thought back to their days as articled clerks he always thought of suppers at Mike's flat off the Harrow Road, with spaghetti bolognese washed down by Mike's latest find, and meals at cheap restaurants which suddenly became rather less cheap after the discovery of something worth trying on the wine list. But if Hugh had sometimes had to survive the rest of the month on fish fingers and baked beans, he had always considered it a good bargain.

In another fluid movement Mike placed three wine glasses and a bowl of cashew nuts on the kitchen table. 'First glass for the cook,' he declared, pouring it rapidly.

'Wise plan,' said Rachel.

Mike waved Hugh to a chair at the kitchen table and sat opposite. 'Right, young Hugh Gwynne,' he said, filling their glasses. 'A complete update, if you will. And no time off for good behaviour.'

'Not sure there's much to tell,' Hugh said. But there was plenty to tell, and they had made serious inroads into the Bordeaux by the time Hugh had covered Lou's gap year and her place at Edinburgh to read medicine, and Lizzie's work for her lost and not-so-lost causes, and lastly, because Hugh couldn't bear to let it dominate the family history, the roller-coaster of Charlie's relationship with illegal substances.

'God-awful things, drugs,' said Mike. 'The curse of our age. We've known a few kids who've gone that way, haven't we, Rachel? Such a bloody waste. But Charlie's all right now, is he?'

'So far as I know. As of yesterday. That's all you can ever say.'

'You talk to him regularly?'

'Oh, three times a week.' In fact it was Lizzie who called three times a week, Hugh more like once a week because he worried about having enough to say. He added, 'And we text in between.'

'But it must be tough on you and Lizzie. The worry, I mean.'

'Yes, but we've learnt to get on with our lives. It's a hard lesson, but it's the only way.'

Mike said, 'We worry about Abbie, don't we, Rachel? She doesn't do drugs – at least we don't think she does – but she's been into almost everything else. Body piercing. Purple hair. Raves. Not eating properly. Spectral boyfriends with no visible means of support. Even now we're not sure we're out of the woods – are we, love? All you can do is keep your mouth shut and keep telling them you love them.'

Even as Hugh agreed with this, he wondered if he hadn't failed Charlie on both counts. There had been times when, bewildered by Charlie's capacity for self-sabotage, unable to find anything useful to say, he'd stayed silent, but there had been just as many occasions when he'd said too much, and badly. As for telling Charlie he loved him, he'd tried to say it regularly, but now it struck him with a pang of regret that he hadn't said it nearly often enough.

'We always tell ourselves there's no need to worry while they keep coming home,' Mike said. 'And, thank God, Abbie still turns up every second weekend. Brings her laundry, sleeps all day, raids the fridge, heaves long-suffering sighs if we dare to ask about college.' He raised an open palm. 'Can't ask for more.'

'Charlie can't get home very often.'

'But he comes home – that's the point.'

'And with his laundry,' Hugh smiled, wishing he could take more comfort from this. 'And your boys?'

Both were scholars, one starting his first year at Cambridge, the other a postgraduate at Oxford with all the makings of a history don. Mike spoke of them with a mixture of modesty and awe. 'Don't know where they get the academic bent from. The genes must have skipped a generation somewhere along the line.'

'Speak for yourself,' Rachel murmured in what was clearly an old refrain.

'They're lent to you, these kids,' Mike said reflectively. 'And there's no accounting for how they turn out.' He had been popping cashew nuts into his mouth, but now he pushed the bowl firmly in Hugh's direction as if to distance himself from temptation. 'And what about the big case, Hugh? How's it going?'

At this, several conflicting thoughts went through Hugh's mind. That the rules of confidentiality demanded his silence on the subject of Tom's double game. That he hadn't realised quite how badly he needed to talk to someone. That Mike was the perfect person to confide in, an old friend far removed from the case whose discretion, absolute as it was, would never be put to the test. That secrets, once out, had a habit of spreading.

'It's going okay,' he said.

'Your psychiatrists all singing from the same song sheet?'

For a wild moment Hugh imagined Mike knew all about the two sets of opinions, that in some strange parallel universe he too was acting for Tom. 'Well . . . yeah . . .'

'With our torture clients we find it always comes down to the expert evidence,' Mike said. 'How convincing it is. Because like your Mr Deacon our people don't have much to show for what they've been through, the damage is all up here.' He tapped the side of his head. 'Without the shrinks' evidence they just get categorised as asylum seekers going for the oldest trick in the book. The attitude's, well, they would say that, wouldn't they? Unless they have the scars to prove it, of course. But clever torturers don't leave scars.' Mike added, 'Nothing like an avalanche of pseudo science for bluffing your way through.'

'Pseudo science?'

'Psychiatry. It's all observation, isn't it, not hard science. It's all opinion and fashion. And' – he raised his glass – 'thank God for that. Otherwise half my asylum seekers would get thrown out of the country.'

Hugh said, 'With Tom the issue's not whether he's got PTSD – no one's questioning that – it's whether he's likely to recover, and if so, by how much.'

'And will he?'

'No one thinks so, no.'

'And what do you think?'

'Me?' Hugh echoed, not used to offering a personal opinion. 'No,' he said after a moment, 'I can't see him recovering.'

Rachel said, 'Perhaps Hugh would like a wash and change, Mike.'

Mike's eyebrows shot up, he lumbered to his feet with a scrape of his chair. 'Of course you would!'

'Explain about the water,' Rachel said.

'Yes – hot but deathly slow.'

The room belonged to one of the sons, the walls

decorated with scuffed photographs and old Sello-
tape marks, the available surfaces buried under papers
and music systems. The bathroom was cluttered with
toiletries, many without their caps, and Hugh was
reminded of the kids' bathroom at home. While the
bath filled he went back to the bedroom and phoned
Lizzie's mobile. She answered at the third ring. Her
voice, always a mirror to her mood, was affectionate
but mildly preoccupied, as if she'd been in the middle
of something.

'Where are you?' he asked.

'Home.'

'Not too long a day then?'

'No. You sound awful, love, as if you're getting a
cold.'

'Not getting, *got*,' he said with a nudge of self-pity.
'A real stinker. And I've had a God-awful day. Tom's
gone AWOL, the case looks as though it's going to fall
apart, I'll probably have to resign, and it'll be a miracle
if anyone gets any money, myself included.'

'Is it really that bad?'

'Well, yes, it *is*,' he said, wanting sympathy just
then, not scepticism.

Her small 'I see' drove him to elaborate. He told
the story at speed and without pause, skipping from
point to point without logic or structure, the frustrations of the day pouring out in a fierce, unrelenting
fume of woe and self-reproach. When he wasn't repeating himself he was beating himself up in some new
way, finding fresh sources of gloom. He should have
seen it coming, he should have liaised with the solicitor
in Exeter, he should have warned Tom against having
two different stories, he should have handled the news

differently. Now it was too late, the case would probably implode, Tom would be left with next to nothing.

When he finally came to a halt it was to be met by
silence, as though Lizzie was waiting to be sure the
onslaught was over.

'Why don't you talk to Mike about it?' she said at
last. 'Ask his advice?'

'I can't. Ethically.'

'What about hypothetically then?'

'I can't,' he insisted. Then, hearing himself at his
stubborn worst, he murmured, 'Well, maybe . . .' Then,
aware that he had been talking at her non-stop for the
last five minutes, he asked how her work had gone.

'Oh, I had the most extraordinary day,' she said.
'Something of a breakthrough. Well, I think so anyway.
But I'll tell you about it another time.'

'One of your cases?'

'Yes,' she said shortly, as if she really didn't want to
be drawn.

But Hugh was determined to demonstrate his
interest. 'Which one?'

'Wesley. You remember Wesley?'

'Of course I remember Wesley,' he said, amazed she
should imagine he didn't. 'Have you managed to get
them rehoused?'

'No. It's something else, something . . .' A small rush
of breath while she framed the words. '. . . something
that completely changes their situation.'

'Great. What—'

But she cut across him to say, 'Look, I spoke to
Charlie. He's very upset.'

'Oh?' Hugh said, not wanting the weight of Charlie's problems just then. 'What about?'

'You not wanting him to go to Spain. He feels you don't trust him. That you've got no faith in him.'

'Well, I don't,' he said baldly.

'He feels—'

'Christ! Hang on!' Hugh rushed into the bathroom. The water was an inch below the overflow, and he turned off the taps with a shudder of relief. 'Okay,' he admitted, returning to Lizzie, 'perhaps I don't trust him. No, I'll rephrase that – it's his *addiction* I don't trust, the way it seems to pounce without warning. So what's wrong with that? If he had more sense he wouldn't trust his addiction either.'

'But this is counterproductive, don't you see?'

'I'm sorry, but how exactly?'

'He feels that his achievement over the last few months means nothing to you, that you don't appreciate how well he's done. And it's hurt him. He's really upset.'

'But how did you put it to him? What did you say?'

'I said you were worried about him going to Spain, that you didn't think it was a good idea. That's all.'

'In that case, he's overreacting.'

'Maybe. But that's the way he sees it.'

Hugh felt a sudden weariness. 'I'll call him, okay? I'll call him this evening.'

'If you would, darling. And Hugh?'

'Yes,' he pre-empted her, 'I promise not to get angry.'

'And your cold. Do take an aspirin, won't you? Or a Panadol. Ask Rachel – she's bound to have something.'

Hugh felt better after his bath. Before calling Charlie he sat on the bed, the phone ready in his hand, preparing an argument based on concern rather than distrust, rehearsing a warm loving tone. But when he finally dialled it was to be diverted to Charlie's message service, and then he left a short message, asking Charlie to call. It was only after he'd rung off that he realised how impersonal the message had sounded, and how he'd forgotten to give Charlie his love.

After dinner, Mike and Hugh took some wine to the living room and sat on either side of a flaming mock-coal fire. Over the mantelpiece hung a large abstract painting in wild splashes of scarlet, black and white. 'One of Abbie's,' Mike remarked, following Hugh's gaze. 'We think it's rather good.'

'It's amazing,' Hugh murmured, not being a judge of these things.

'You just have to accept that creative kids aren't going to have easy lives,' Mike said.

And maybe not-so-creative ones too, thought Hugh. It might have been the virus settling low over his brain like a fog, it might have been the comfort of the battered armchair, it might simply have been the wine, but he found himself saying, 'Could I put a hypothetical case to you, Mike?'

'Of course,' Mike said easily. 'But don't rely on me for a textbook answer, Hugh. I'm not exactly a textbook man.'

Hugh went through it all: the personal injury claim of the hypothetical Mr D, the anonymous letter, the custody case two counties away, Mr D's failure to grasp the consequences of his actions, and his temporary disappearance. 'Mr D's solicitor put a lot of pressure on him to come clean, and now he worries that he might have pushed Mr D over the edge.'

Holding up a hand as if to take Hugh back a step or two, Mike said, 'But nothing's come out yet? Hypothetically speaking.'

'Well, no . . . but it will.'

'Why?'

'Because the High Court case will get reported.'

'Not in the law pages. It's hardly ground-breaking stuff.'

'But the popular press.'

'Okay, but they're not going to go into great detail, are they? Could be just a couple of lines.'

'What are you suggesting?' Hugh asked nervously. 'That the solicitor should pretend he doesn't know about the other case and hope it all goes away?'

Mike gave a light shrug. 'You know what they always say – when in doubt do nothing.'

'You know our man can't do that.'

'Why not?'

'The rules of conduct – he'd be in breach. He'd be in danger of being struck off.'

'Maybe. Maybe not.'

'For God's sake,' Hugh breathed.

'Who knows about this anonymous letter? According to our scenario.'

'Oh, several people.'

'Such as?'

'Well, Mr D, obviously. Plus our man's wife. Plus his trainee.'

'No one who's going to talk, then.'

Taken aback by this, Hugh summoned Isabel's argument. 'But the letter writer's bound to try again. People like that always do.'

'So that's a risk our man has to take.'

'A bad risk,' said Hugh, beginning to fight back. 'He can hardly deny he got the letter.'

'Okay, but perhaps the letter never mentioned any new medical evidence,' Mike suggested ingenuously. 'Perhaps our man wrote it off as a poison-pen letter, a fabrication, not to be taken seriously.'

'Christ. You're asking him to cross one massive great line.'

'Am I? It seems to me that the codes of conduct don't always cover every eventuality. That sometimes you have to make a decision that satisfies the needs of natural justice. It happens all the time in my line of work,' he admitted airily. 'And if that means bending the rules a little . . . well . . .'

'A bit more than bending the rules!'

'I deal in human desperation. I tend to avoid sharp distinctions.'

Hugh shook his head, momentarily unable to counter this rush of argument.

Mike swung his wine glass to one side. 'Playing devil's advocate, would it really be such a bad thing to do nothing? Mr D's a genuinely sick man whose condition isn't going to improve. So he's not telling the High Court any lies. He's not trying to obtain money dishonestly. He's just trying to save his kids from going into care, and who can blame him for that? Christ, if it was me, I'd *kill* rather than let my kids be taken away by social services. Okay, so Mr D's been a bit economical with the truth in his dealings with the family court, but that's not going to result in a bad outcome, is it? It's not going to harm any of the people who matter. The ex-wife can't cope and you say Mr D's mad keen to look after the kids. Well, that has to be the best outcome, doesn't it? For the kids. *And* for Mr D. *And* for the ex-wife. Certainly a whole lot better than having the kids shunted round the care system.'

Hugh felt a certain awe at Mike's approach, not simply his readiness to overlook the rules, but his confidence that it was justified. 'You forget what's at stake,' he said. 'If it all goes wrong Mr D could end up with nothing – no money and no children.'

'But our man had spelt out the risks to him?'

'Well, yes . . . But Mr D's deaf to things he doesn't want to hear. He's a man with tunnel vision. Obsessed with the case, obsessed with getting his children back. It's all black and white to him. Either the world's for him or it's against him, and there's not a lot in between.'

Mike gave Hugh a long, thoughtful look. 'Listen,' he said, 'forget the mights and maybes, and all that stuff. There's only one serious piece of advice I'd give our man. And that's not to lose any more sleep over this case. He's done all he can, he can do no more. He should let it go now, leave it at the door.'

'That's what Lizzie says.'

Mike raised his glass a little in tribute. 'Well, she's dead right.'

From the depths of sleep he thought he heard someone calling his name, but the voice was a long way off and faded almost immediately, to be swallowed up by a dream in which people he didn't recognise crowded a strange room and Lizzie was nowhere in sight. Everyone was laughing so loudly they were making Hugh's head ache, he had trouble making himself heard, and without any windows open the heat was stifling. When the voice came again, it was closer, more insistent, a summons. As he began to haul himself into wakefulness, he was aware of clammy heat and a heavy head and a parched mouth. Opening an eye he saw in the dim light a wall with posters and strange curtains, and struggled to remember where he was. Then the voice again, very close now.

'Hugh? Wake up.'

Hugh turned over and saw a large figure silhouetted against an open door. He tried to speak, but his tongue adhered to the roof of his mouth. He swallowed with difficulty and felt fire in his throat. 'What is it?' he managed at last.

'Charlie on the phone for you,' Mike said, holding out a portable.

As he sat up, Hugh's brain felt so heavy he thought he must have been drugged. Swinging his feet to the floor, he said, 'Christ, sorry about this, Mike.'

'Hey.' Mike shrugged it aside and handed him the phone.

As Hugh put the phone to his ear it could have been two years ago, when time had meant nothing to Charlie and he had called in the night, at dawn, whenever he was in trouble or needing money or to be collected from Accident and Emergency, or, once, from the local nick. Are we back into all that again? Hugh wondered wearily. Are we back where we started?

'Charlie?'

'*Dad*,' Charlie said with a ragged gasp. 'I've been trying to find you.' His voice was tense, high-pitched. 'Dad, something's happened.'

'What is it?' Even as he remembered his promise to Lizzie to stay calm, he felt exasperation stirring in his stomach.

'It's Mum. There's been an accident.'

Hugh's heart gave a slow thud of foreboding. 'What the hell's happened?' he demanded. 'What have you done?'

'It's not me,' Charlie protested in a choked voice. 'Dad – it's the house. There was a fire. And Mum – Mum was inside.'

Hugh's heart was so full of dread that everything stalled inside him, he could hardly speak. 'But she's all right?'

Charlie made a stifled sound.

'She's all right?' Hugh demanded again.

A silence, no sound at all, then a deep resonant voice. 'Hugh, it's Ray here. We're at the hospital. Listen, you should come straight away.'

Hugh shut his eyes against the darkness. 'Tell me. Tell me now. Is she all right?'

A soft pause, then: 'It's not too good, I'm afraid.'

'Tell me.'

'I'm so very sorry, Hugh. I'm afraid she didn't make it.'

Afterwards he remembered little of the journey. Just Mike's profile as he drove through the night. The dark motorway stretching westward. A stop at a petrol station, Mike placing a coffee in his hand, though he had the impression he never got round to drinking it. Calls to Ray, Hugh clutching the phone dumbly to his ear for minutes at a time before asking a question Ray couldn't answer or, when he could, that Hugh was too dazed to take in so that he asked the same question time and again. Ray didn't have many details at first, but either during the journey or later at the hospital he told Hugh that the medics had tried very hard to resuscitate her, that she'd been brought into A & E at about half past midnight, that there was nothing the crash team could do to save her. *She. Her.* It seemed neither of them could bring themselves to use her name.

Mike must have spoken several times during the journey but Hugh could remember only one comment he made, that in fires most people died of smoke inhalation, they never knew what had happened to them, they didn't suffer. This had caused a wave of horror to engulf Hugh because he hadn't got that far, not in words or images and, forced to confront the idea, he immediately suspected the opposite, that she *had* suffered, that utterly terrified she had been beaten back by a wall of flames. But there was only so much the mind could take without going mad, and he had the impression it cut out on him after that, plunging him into a sense of unreality.

He had a clearer recollection of the hospital, of going into A & E while Mike parked the car, of announcing himself politely at the desk, of being asked to wait, of taking a seat until a nurse in scrubs took him through a pass-door and led him between rows of curtained cubicles, past a brightly lit area where doctors and nurses sat hunched over computers, to a small room with a few chairs where Charlie and Ray were waiting.

Charlie, white-faced under the lights, came forward
to embrace him, their arms meeting awkwardly so
that they ended up in a half embrace, Hugh's right
arm pinioned, his hand looped up behind Charlie's
shoulder. Charlie held him very tightly and when they
drew apart he was crying. Unable to speak just then,
Hugh squeezed his shoulder. Ray went to find the
doctor, a young girl with dark shadows under her
eyes who expressed her sympathy and explained that
the paramedics had tried to resuscitate Mrs Gwynne
on the way to hospital, but there had been no vital
signs on arrival. The crash team had tried further
resuscitation without success and at a quarter to one
Mrs Gwynne had been pronounced dead. The doctor
looked so young and exhausted, so worn down by the
business of death and bad news, that Hugh offered her
a smile of thanks and commiseration. Maybe it was
this distraction or the numbness clouding his brain, but
when she asked if he had any questions he shook his
head. All he would like, he said, was to see his wife.
The young doctor turned expectantly to Ray who,
taking his cue, said that the police had requested a
formal identification. Assuming Hugh wanted to be the
person to make it, the arrangements could be made
within half an hour.

He did want to be the person, he said. When the
police turned up, Hugh and Ray left Charlie in the
small room and followed the two uniformed men down
long obscure passageways to a door marked Mortuary.
One of the officers rang the bell and after a short wait
a face appeared in the window high in the door and
they were admitted by a youth in overalls. After a
whispered consultation the senior officer explained to

Hugh that at this time of night, without the full complement of staff, it wouldn't be possible to see his wife in the viewing room, would he mind very much seeing her in the mortuary itself? He wouldn't mind at all, he said politely. The youth led them to a room with two raised stainless steel tables in the centre and three large stainless steel doors along the side. As the youth went to one of the doors the senior officer said to Hugh in a tone of mild apology that due to procedural restrictions it wouldn't be possible for him to touch his wife.

The youth swung the heavy door wide open and pulled out a trolley with a white-sheeted figure on it. Hugh stepped forward, bracing himself for the worst, however terrible that might be, only to find himself unprepared. When the youth rolled back the sheet, she was completely unscathed, no burns, no signs of fire, nothing to show for what had happened, her features beautiful but empty, her lovely lips parted to speak words that would never come, her hair wild and windblown.

She was gone, quite gone, but the prohibition against touching her was suddenly a torment, and turning to the senior officer he said briskly, 'Yes, this is my wife.'

# FIVE

Another unfamiliar room, this one clad in busy floral wallpaper with matching curtains and a skirted dressing table. The curtains, operated by some unfathomable cord system, had jammed when Hugh had tried to open them some two hours earlier, so when dawn came the light was grudging, the view narrowed to a single tree. In his confusion he thought the tree was the giant beech on the north-western boundary of his own garden but then it came to him that this was wrong, just like everything else was wrong, there was another garden between this house and Meadowcroft, and Lizzie was dead.

He showered but could not face himself in the mirror to shave. He dressed rapidly and made for the stairs, passing the room where Charlie was sleeping, only to turn back with a pull of concern. He found Charlie sprawled face-down on the bed, deeply asleep, the duvet half off, one leg and arm uncovered. Hugh drew the duvet back over him, tucking it in around his shoulders as he and Lizzie had done when the children were small. In sleep Charlie looked like a kid again, the skin fresh and untouched, the hair thick and golden, the chin dusted with stubble so pale and soft it might have been down. Amid the jumble of images

from the long and terrible night Hugh had a vision of
Charlie in the small room off A & E, barely able to
meet his eye when he came back from the mortuary, of
him trailing behind as they walked to the car park,
shivering slightly when Hugh dropped back to put an
arm round his shoulders, of his shadowy face in the
back of the car staring blankly out of the window,
silent, remote, scarcely responding when Hugh asked if
he was all right. Sleep was the best thing for him.
Awake, Hugh wouldn't have been much help to him
just then.

Closing the door silently, Hugh made for the stairs
again. The muted voices of the Koenig family floated
up from below and he recoiled, as he had recoiled last
night, from the forced intimacy with people he barely
knew and had never terribly liked who had presumed,
decided, arranged to take them in. Before last night his
only connection with the Koenigs had been through
Charlie's friendship with their computer-mad son Joel
and the fact that they lived two doors away. He and
Lizzie had met the parents at the occasional local event,
but it was significant that Hugh couldn't even remember their first names. The father was in public relations,
a smooth hand-presser on the lookout for the next
opportunity, while the mother – Sarah, was it? – was a
fussy, garrulous woman with a relish for gossip. It was
she who had greeted them three hours ago with effusive
sympathy and a relentless determination to tell her part
of the tale, the discovery of the fire and the calling of
the fire brigade. She had tried to gather them into the
kitchen with the lure of food and drink, but only Mike
had obeyed. Charlie mysteriously vanished, while
Hugh stood his ground in the hall, saying she was most

kind but he really would like to go straight to his room
now, a statement he had to repeat twice before she
accepted she would have to tell her story then and
there, standing in the hall, or be forced to bottle it up
till morning. Her husband had gone to bed, she
recounted, and she had let the dog out for his last
widdle when, standing at the back door, she heard a
strange sound. Oh, very faint, she said, so faint she
almost ignored it. But something, *something*, made her
go and look. First she went upstairs to her bedroom
window, then she went to the spare room at the front
which looked out onto the lane. It was only when she
decided to open the window and put her head right
out that she caught sight of something through the
trees, just the tiniest flicker, so tiny she almost missed
it. If it had been summer, of course, she would never
have seen a thing. But with the trees bare, well . . .
Even then, it was a miracle she saw that one small
flicker of light because she didn't see another, not for a
good two or three minutes.

A surge of heat, a sudden panic, brought Hugh out
of his daze. He wasn't ready to hear about wasted
minutes while Lizzie was alone and suffocating from
the smoke. He wasn't ready to face the idea that she
had suffered.

Catching something of this in his expression, Joel's
mother told the rest of her story in a rush, how she
roused John and they drove along the lane and saw
the fire and dialled 999. While she stayed on the phone
to the emergency operator John tried the front door
and the back door but both were locked. They thought
of trying the window but the flames were too bad. They
looked for a ladder but couldn't find one. And then

Hugh understood why she had been in such a hurry to tell him her story; it wasn't just her relish for drama, it was the need to be reassured that she and her husband had done all they could and had nothing to reproach themselves for. Well, reassurance was easy, he offered it willingly, with as much grace as he could muster, longing for the moment when she would be sufficiently consoled to let him be alone. There was more fuss as she showed him the bedroom and bathroom, and, eyes welling, offered a last stream of condolences. When at last the door closed behind her he made his largely abortive attempt to open the curtains before lying down fully clothed on the bed. Then the pain finally overwhelmed him, he sobbed and called Lizzie's name, and then surprisingly he slept. When he woke, it was to the gloomy outline of the giant beech and the aching realisation that it was still true, Lizzie was dead.

The voices were coming from the kitchen away to his right and, reaching the hall, he veered sharp left, treading softly. Passing the open door of a sitting room he saw two black-socked feet sticking over the arm of a sofa and looked in to see Mike lying on his back, his jacket laid haphazardly over the dome of his stomach, a cushion under his head, snoring steadily.

Creeping away, he let himself out as quietly as possible and walked quickly along the lane, propelled by the need to see the damage for himself, to stand alone in the spot where Lizzie had died, even to find in the ruins of the fire some glimmer of an explanation. Last night on the way back from the hospital they had stopped at Meadowcroft only to find everything in darkness, the fire engines gone, just a lone policeman sitting in a patrol car keeping watch till morning. Hugh had wanted to go inside but the policeman had said he was sorry, that wasn't allowed until the investigation was complete. As Mike reversed the car round, the headlights had swept over Lizzie's silver Golf, standing there as if to deliver her back to him, and it was this of all things that had caught Hugh off-guard and brought him into the Koenigs' house with the desperate longing to be alone.

Now, as he came in through the gates he saw parked beside Lizzie's car a white van with its rear doors open and two men lifting out a panel of chipboard, and to the other side of the front door a car and a small van, both in the scarlet livery of the fire brigade. There was no sign of the police car.

What struck Hugh as he drew closer to the house was the relative lack of damage. In newspaper pictures of house fires the outside walls always seemed to be scorched with soot, the roofs holed or collapsed. But the walls of Meadowcroft were untouched, the roof was intact, only the windows looked wrong, all of them wide open, some blackened from smoke or lacking glass.

The two men had a generator going and were about to run the board through an electric saw. One of them looked up as Hugh approached and seemed about to say something, but Hugh ignored him and went straight into the house. And stopped, all sense of normality gone. At first the devastation appeared complete. The walls of the hall were black, the ceiling charred, with gaping holes where the plaster had come down, the floor covered in a layer of sodden debris. But as he made his way slowly forward he looked into the dining room and saw that, though licked with a thick coat of soot, it was largely intact, while the kitchen seemed bizarrely untouched, and it occurred to him in some remote logical corner of his mind that the kitchen door must have been closed. He paused by the living room and knew immediately that the fire had been very bad there. Everything was blackened and contorted, the furniture barely recognisable. The stairs were scorched but solid underfoot. When he reached the turn he looked up and saw that the fire had raged up the stairwell, consuming half the landing rail and banisters, burning into the ceiling above. As he climbed higher, the acrid smell he had dimly registered on entering the house grew much stronger and caught in his throat until he began to cough.

A brisk voice called out, 'Hello?' and a man in a hard hat emerged from the main bedroom. 'You are?' he asked. Then his expression changed and he said in a different tone, 'Family?'

Hugh was overtaken by another fit of coughing, and the man drew him across the landing into Lou's bedroom and an open window. 'Take some long breaths,' he said.

The coughing made Hugh's stomach heave and he struggled not to retch. But at last the worst was over and, panting slightly, eyes watering, he straightened up.

'Mr Gwynne, is it?'

Hugh nodded.

'You'll feel better outside, sir. Why don't you follow me down?'

Hugh shook his head.

'The thing is, you aren't meant to be in here just yet. Not till we've finished our investigation. The police officer should have told you that.'

'Not here,' Hugh managed to say through his raging throat. 'Gone.'

'Has he now? All the same . . . if you wouldn't mind.' The man was short, with a round face and large features.

'Your name is?'

'Ellis. Peter Ellis. Fire investigation department.'

Hugh put out his hand, and Ellis hastily moved his clipboard to his left hand to return the handshake. 'My condolences on your loss, Mr Gwynne.'

'Thank you.'

'I understand you were away on business when the fire broke out.'

'London.'

'And your wife was here alone?'

'Yes.'

'No other family?'

'No. Our children were away.'

'No dogs, cats, other pets?'

'No.'

Ellis nodded, then took a step towards the door, as if to conclude the interview and escort him downstairs.

Hugh said, 'I just want to see the bedroom.'

Ellis hesitated.

'I want to see where my wife died.'

Ellis regarded Hugh thoughtfully before giving in with a quick nod. 'If you could be sure not to touch anything.'

It was becoming a refrain. *Look but don't touch*.

Ellis led the way across the landing. In the bedroom

a second man was standing by the bathroom door, holding a camera to his eye. He acknowledged Hugh's arrival with a sideways glance before lining up another shot. Hugh took a couple of steps into the room and halted, taking in the smoke-daubed walls, a pale grey towards the floor, darker towards the ceiling, the ceiling itself, very black, the trampled carpet, the smashed window with a few jagged shards still adhering to the frame, the harsh acrid smell, and finally the bed itself. The duvet, thrown back on itself, had been dragged half off the bed, the lower sheet was ruckled and pulled free of the mattress, baring some of the mattress cover; all the pillows, grey with smoke, were lying at odd angles and crumpled. By contrast some of Lizzie's clothes were lying neatly folded on the seat of the upholstered chair in the corner, a pair of shoes lined up side by side on the floor beneath.

'She was found in bed?' Hugh asked, selecting a matter-of-fact tone.

Ellis, who had been standing respectfully to one side, eyes averted, looked at him solemnly. 'Yes.'

'Still alive?'

'The men couldn't be sure, so they got her out of the building and undertook resuscitation.'

Hugh tried to imagine the room as it was then, black with smoke and poisonous fumes. 'It must have been . . . difficult. I'd like to thank them sometime if I can.'

'They were only doing their job. But I'm sure they'd appreciate it all the same.'

'It was smoke inhalation that killed her, was it?'

'I couldn't make any comment on that,' Ellis said rapidly, as if to get this absolutely straight from the outset. 'That's for the coroner.'

'Of course. Yes ... With the help of the post-mortem,' Hugh added, to show he understood the system.

'We just report on the fire.'

'Of course you do. Yes ... And what have you discovered so far?'

Ellis shook his head. 'Can't say.'

'Forgive me ... because?'

'My report has to go to the coroner. It's the procedure.'

*Procedure. Look but don't touch.*

'I see ...'

'Sorry about that.'

'No, no. I quite understand.'

The photographer had finished taking his pictures. 'I'll start on the rest of this floor,' he said to Ellis.

'Give me a shout when you're done.'

As soon as they were alone Hugh said quietly, in the manner of someone keen to learn, 'Tell me, Peter, how does this sort of fire behave?' Seeing Ellis's hesitation he added, 'Oh, without going into specifics. Just in general ... I mean what makes smoke travel to one room, fire to another and leave other places untouched?'

'Oh, you can't have fire without smoke. No, no. Fire always produces smoke. But smoke and fumes on their own, they can travel a long way ahead of the fire, and fast too.'

'So ... what makes the smoke travel?' Hugh prompted with the same grave air of enquiry.

'It depends on layout and what you might call opportunity,' Ellis explained, with the air of knowing his subject backwards. 'From the source of the fire it's a matter of what doors and windows are open and where the smoke can get to easiest. Smoke rises, given the chance, so if there's an open door and a stairwell it'll go up to a higher level. If it can't go up, it'll spread sideways across the ceilings and then work its way down.'

'Can you tell how quickly the smoke would have spread?'

'It's only ever a calculated guess.'

Taking it slowly, maintaining a look of almost academic interest, Hugh made a show of absorbing this. 'But you can track the smoke?'

'Oh yes.'

'What, based on the smoke damage?'

Ellis nodded. 'Though certain types of smoke leave more damage than others. It all depends on the type and quantity of the flammable materials.'

Hugh looked around the walls of the bedroom. 'But the fire itself, that behaves differently, you say?'

'Oh yes. Fire needs oxygen and it needs combustible materials, so the speed and intensity of the fire will depend on how much of each it has to feed off. A small fire in an airtight room will burn itself out, while a fire in a room full of combustibles with an open window and a good draught will spread rapidly.'

'And you can always tell how far the fire got?' Hugh looked around the room again and up at the ceiling.

Ellis said hastily, 'Oh, there was never any fire in here.'

'No?'

'No way.' Ellis led the way onto the landing. 'No, this is as far as it got.' He gestured towards the ceiling above the stairwell and the burnt banisters.

It was just as Hugh had thought, but the relief still came at him like a shock. A tightness gripped his chest, his throat swelled, his eyes fired with sudden tears. He would have gone outside then, but Ellis, having taken Hugh into his confidence, was in full swing, pointing out the route of the fire as it came up the stairwell, leading the way down into the hall to indicate the badly burnt ceiling, pausing on the threshold of the living room.

'It started in here,' he said.

Hugh would have held back, the source of the fire seemed so unimportant to him just then, but he knew he would never have such an opportunity again. 'Whereabouts, do you know?'

'Off the record?' Ellis said.

'Off the record.'

The room was in an even worse state than Hugh had realised. Much of the ceiling had gone, some of the joists were scorched and burnt, the walls were black for several feet below the ceiling, and the floor was inches deep in squelching debris.

Ellis went to what had once been a pale sofa, the right side burnt down almost to the frame, the remainder badly charred. 'Just here,' he said, squatting down to inspect the scene again. 'Likely between the arm and the cushion, that's usually the place these things start.'

Hugh said, 'What do you mean?'

'The fire started here in this sofa,' Ellis stated categorically.

Hugh had been expecting an electrical fault, a lamp, a socket, anything but the sofa. 'How could it do that?'

'Cigarette. Match. Candle. But most likely a cigarette.'

'But my wife didn't smoke.'

Ellis indicated the window above the sofa. 'The curtains would have been next. You can see the way the fire fanned out at the top there.' He was pointing towards the devastation that was the ceiling. 'And then this window here was open, just a few inches but enough to provide a draught, the door was open too, so as the fire spread' – he pushed his hands up and sideways – 'it tracked over here towards the door.' He pointed both hands towards the hall.

'My wife didn't smoke,' Hugh repeated.

'No?'

'No.'

'Could have been a candle stood on the surface here,' Ellis suggested, indicating the top of Lizzie's badly scorched desk. 'Which fell over onto the sofa.'

'She'd never use a candle at her desk,' Hugh argued fretfully. 'Why would she use a candle?'

'These scented candles have got very popular—'

'But she'd never use anything like that, not at her desk.'

Uneasy at this sudden change of mood, Ellis regarded him warily.

'She just wouldn't,' Hugh repeated firmly.

Ellis moved towards the door. 'Well, I'd better get on.' Realising that Hugh wasn't going to follow, he said, 'If you could be sure not to touch anything, Mr Gwynne?'

'I won't touch anything.'

Alone, Hugh stared at the charred sofa and blackened desk while he went over what Ellis had told him, but the information clogged in his brain, he could make no sense of it. Why would Lizzie have broken the habit of a lifetime to put a lighted candle on her desk? And so dangerously close to the edge? Even assuming she'd found room next to what were now the gnarled remains of her handbag. Cigarettes and matches were equally implausible. He understood that Ellis was trying to fit the available evidence into the most likely box, but in doing so he was in danger of missing the facts.

Eventually he drifted across the hall into the study, then the dining room, and saw smoke damage. The kitchen seemed untouched. The floor was dry, apples and bananas lay in the bowl, glasses on the draining board, the sun shone through untarnished windows. Only when he touched a surface did he realise everything was covered by a film of grime. A note was wedged under the scales where Lizzie always left money and communications for Mrs Bishop. His heart tightened as he saw her handwriting. *Dear Mrs B, Charlie may be here. If sleeping, best not disturb! I'll be back before three. L.* He could make no sense of this either. Which day was she referring to? Yesterday? Today? And since when had Charlie been coming home?

Outside, the sun was winter bright, the security men were boarding up the living-room windows, and Mike and Ray were there, standing by the fire-brigade car, talking to Ellis.

Mike came over. 'How are you doing, old fella?'

'You should have got some more sleep, Mike.'

'No, I'm fine! No – couldn't sleep anyway!' he lied brazenly, looking crumpled and battered.

'You'll be in no state to drive back.'

'Who said I was driving back? No rush at all.'

'Your work . . .'

'That's what I've got a trainee for. And a mobile phone. And I didn't have much on—'

'Hugh?' Ray's voice interrupted. He was striding towards them, looking spruce and crisp in a suit and tie, only the puffiness round his eyes betraying the lack of sleep. 'Listen, we need to contact your insurance company as soon as possible. You can't remember their name by any chance?'

'Not just at the moment, no.'

'The documents – are they . . . ?'

'In the study.'

'Right.' Ray swung away, only to turn back with an air of having overlooked a vital point. 'Look, you don't have to worry about a thing, Hugh. Okay?' He made an emphatic gesture. 'Not a thing. I'm going to get all this stuff sorted. You just . . . well . . .' He buttoned his mouth down and said in a tone of suppressed emotion, 'You just concentrate on the family.' With a touch to Hugh's sleeve he strode purposefully away.

'Why don't you come and grab some breakfast,' Mike said, 'then we can make a plan.'

But Hugh missed what Mike said after that, as a thought came to him that was so sickening and so horribly obvious he couldn't think why it hadn't struck him before.

'Hugh?'

'Sorry . . . You said . . .'

'Just that we might make a list of people to call.'

'Yes . . . Lou . . . Lizzie's family . . .'

'I was saying, Charlie thinks he knows the name of the people his grandmother's staying with, and he's—'

'I need to talk to the police,' Hugh cut in.

Mike's expression froze. 'Okay . . .'

'Will you drive me there?'

'Well . . . yes, of course. When did you want to go?'

'Now. Right away.'

Mike eyed him anxiously. 'What about some breakfast first? You need to get some food inside you, Hugh. It's going to be a long day.'

But the idea was racketing around Hugh's head, it had to be told as soon as possible. And he wasn't in the least hungry.


In the course of his legal career Hugh had come to this police station in the eastern suburbs of Bristol perhaps half a dozen times, usually to bail out clients for drink-driving, once for an assault. But this was the first time he had been made to sit in the waiting room with the punters, who today consisted of two slumped youths, a heavily made-up girl with glaring eyes, and an older woman whose body spilled out over the sides of the chair. All had the sullen air of regulars. Every so often Mike sauntered up to the desk to make his number with the reception officer, only to get the same message, that nothing could be done until someone became available. What were they doing to make themselves so unavailable? Hugh wondered. Filling out forms in longhand in defiance of the computer age, manipulating the crime figures to meet irksome government targets, hanging on the phone for information that never came; anything, he supposed, to put off an interview with a grief-stricken man wanting to talk about the death of his wife, an event which, though tragic, wasn't going to justify their time or trouble. As the minutes went by, Hugh imagined describing the episode to Lizzie: the absurdity of the wait, the ludicrous inefficiency of the system. But when he tried to conjure up her image he had no hold on her. She was a shadow, an absence, her existence in his memory as a talking, laughing, argumentative being had melted away. He couldn't picture her reaction, couldn't hear her voice, and he missed the idea of her terribly.

When someone finally became available it was a detective constable called Smith, a pallid, paunchy, twenty-something man with bad teeth and a bland expression which sharpened a little when Mike introduced himself as Hugh's legal advisor, an expedient to get Mike into the interview room, which was hot and airless, the surfaces of the chairs and tables tacky from sweat and lies and sweet drinks.

As soon as they sat down Smith went through a standard speech of condolence before expressing concern that family liaison hadn't yet been in touch with Hugh. He could only apologise, he was sure they must be trying to contact him and his family at this very moment. He stressed how experienced they were in these matters, how sensitive to families' needs, how they would be able to deal with all the problems and queries arising from the unfortunate incident.

When Hugh said he hadn't come about that, he'd come about the fire itself, a dullness came over Smith's features, and Hugh knew what he was thinking, that he had more important things to do than be tied down for hours listening to a bereaved man's outpourings of survivor guilt, to be forced to hear the tale of the decorators with blow-torches leaving timbers to smoulder, or the dodgy electrical contractors, or whoever else might be to blame for the accident. Even when Hugh went through the tale of the break-in and the lurking hoodie and the fact that Lizzie didn't smoke, Smith made no attempt to take notes but adopted the pose of the dutiful CID man, sitting back in his chair, head slightly to one side, eyes narrowed, one hand resting against his chin.

When Hugh had finished, Smith was silent for a time. Finally he said, 'So you're saying these events could be connected?'

'That's what I'm saying, yes.'

'In what way?'

Hugh couldn't make out whether he was being slow, or rather clever. 'The hoodie might have forced his way into the house and harassed my wife, even restrained her in some way, and then started the fire.'

'Deliberately, you mean?'

'Well, yes. Oh, not with petrol or anything obvious like that, but with matches, papers stuffed down the side of the sofa, that sort of thing. An act of vandalism, if you like. Or out-and-out arson.'

Now that Smith was having to think up questions his eyes kept tracking diagonally down to the edge of the table, and it occurred to Hugh that he was totally out of his depth.

'The break-in,' Smith said, 'what makes you think it could be linked to this hooded youth?'

'Well, it seems strange to live in a place for fifteen years without any crime, and then to have a break-in and a hooded youth in your garden within the space of a couple of weeks. And then, two nights after the hoodie, to have your house burnt down with—' But he couldn't say it, couldn't say *with my wife inside*. So stark, so matter of fact. 'It's too much of a coincidence by anybody's standards.'

'Do you know of anyone who might have a grudge against you?'

'Nope.'

'What is your line of business exactly?'

'I'm a solicitor.'

Smith's expression didn't change, though like most cops he probably looked on lawyers as the enemy. 'A disgruntled client, perhaps?'

'I do boring stuff, Detective Constable. Conveyancing, wills, probate . . . And none of my clients is remotely young or hooded.' Aware that Smith was only doing his slow, lumbering duty, Hugh added, 'That I remember, anyway.'

Smith seemed to come to a decision. Sitting forward, he said, 'Right, I'll need to get all this down, so while I get set up, how about I organise a cup of tea?'

'Why the hell didn't he take notes first time round?' Hugh murmured after Smith had left the room.

'Modern crime investigation,' said Mike.

The tea was strong but fresh. Smith was left-handed and wrote in the tortured way some left-handers adopt, his arm curved over the top of the paper, his wrist bent inwards, the pen held at a slant. He wrote slowly, frowning over his script.

'The break-in was reported, was it?'

'Yes, but nobody came.'

'And what was stolen?'

'Fifty pounds and some costume jewellery of very little value.'

Smith looked up. 'Nothing else?'

'Nothing else.'

'And a window was used to gain access?'

'It was broken, yes.'

'Any other damage?'

'No.'

Another pause in a long succession of pauses while Smith wrote laboriously.

'And no one – neighbours, passers-by, tradespeople – saw anything suspicious?'

Hugh felt like saying, *Well, if you guys had bothered to turn up you might just have found out.* 'Not that I'm aware of, no.'

After another five minutes they got on to the hoodie, and Hugh went through his account for the second time, how he spotted the youth in the darkness, stopped the car, got out to confront him, set off in pursuit, and was forced to give up the chase.

'How would you describe him in terms of height, weight, age, ethnic group?'

'About five ten or eleven, slim build, young, teens or twenties. White, I think, but I can't be sure.'

'Could you describe his face?'

'I never got a proper look at him, no.'

'So you wouldn't be able to recognise him again?'

'No.'

Another lengthy pause, during which the futility of the exercise was brought home to Hugh. His statement would be logged, there would be the semblance of an investigation, until after a suitable interval the case would be dropped for lack of evidence. The detectives would be polite, regretful, they would offer their condolences once again for his 'loss' – how he was growing to dislike that word – then they would pass him over to a family liaison officer, doubtless female and softly spoken with a diploma in the art of counselling or some other caring and sharing life-skill. Then nothing. With this realisation came a sense of hopelessness and mild panic. By the time Smith reached the events of the previous day Hugh was longing to escape the hot airless room. Yes, he had spoken to his wife in the evening at about seven twenty. What did he mean *in the evening*? he thought despairingly; it was yesterday, just yesterday. Yes, she was alone and not expecting anyone. No, they never knowingly left the front or back door unlocked. No, there wasn't a separate panic button as such, but you could press 999 into the keypad by the front door to set off the alarm. And no, the alarm wasn't connected to a security firm.

Pondering his next question at some length Smith gnawed one side of his lower lip, revealing grey misshapen teeth, and suddenly Hugh felt the blood beat high in his head, he gave an involuntary shiver, and the next instant he was on his feet, sending the chair juddering back over the lino, announcing in a muted voice that he had to go.

Mike craned forward to examine a road sign. 'Is it right here?'

Hugh, who had been gazing unseeing at the road, looked across and confirmed that it was.

'Now, listen,' said Mike as he negotiated the roundabout, 'if you want someone to give the cops a bloody great kick up the arse, then just say the word. I'm your man.'

'I don't know . . .'

'If Smith is half as useless as he looks I suggest

leaving it two or three days then making an official complaint about the way the case is being handled. That'll get the investigation up to detective sergeant level at the very least, maybe even detective inspector. I'll be more than happy to do the stirring if you want me to. Nothing I like better.'

Hugh said, 'You must get back, Mike. You've done more than enough.'

'Happy to stay.'

'Ray can handle any official stuff. And I'll do the rest myself.'

Mike glanced across at him. 'If you're sure.'

'I'm sure.' And it was the only thing Hugh was sure about just then. Well meaning though people were, he didn't want to be taken charge of, presented with decisions, treated as temporarily mentally impaired. He wanted to be with Lou and Charlie, sorting things out in their own way at their own speed. He longed for Lou to get back; he wished she was on her way. He had texted her last night and he remembered Charlie saying he had texted her too, but she hadn't answered and he supposed she was out of range or had turned her phone off to save power. What would he say to her when they finally spoke? How would he find the right words? At some point in the night he'd thought of telling her a white lie, that Mum was ill and she should take a plane home just in case, but he had rejected this straight away. She deserved the truth, though the thought of inflicting such pain at such a distance and with a long flight ahead of her filled him with anguish.

He checked his mobile again but there were no messages. He went to the missed call register but there was nothing there either, only a list of Charlie's numerous attempts to reach him last night. It would have been easy to torture himself for having failed to hear those calls, for having taken some of Isabel's Night Nurse on top of red wine, for having left his phone under a heap of clothes, but of course the delay had changed nothing, it was all over by then, Lizzie was dead. Far worse was the thought that he'd missed a call from Lizzie herself, a last cry for help as the smoke closed in around her, but there was nothing on the register, just as there had been nothing when he'd checked on the long car journey from London. But no amount of logic could entirely banish his fear that a missed call would materialise belatedly out of the ether. So strong was his craving for reassurance that he found himself scrolling through the list again and again.

'Nothing from Lou?' Mike asked.

'Not yet.'

'Charlie may well have tracked her down by now.'

'If she's not in the wilds without a signal. Even then she doesn't always turn her phone on.'

'But the friend she's travelling with – Chrissie, is it? Charlie was going to try and get her number.'

Hugh frowned. 'He didn't tell me that.'

Mike opened his mouth to say something only to think better of it. 'He was going to contact her family. They live somewhere near Bath, he thought.'

'I could have told him exactly where they live. It's outside Frome. But I'm not sure Chrissie's any better at staying in touch.'

'Worth a try, though.'

Of course it was worth a try, but Hugh fretted all

the same in case Charlie should speak to Lou before he
did and get it wrong, though quite what he meant by
wrong he couldn't have said.

Glancing across, Mike said, 'Charlie's pretty amazing at all this technical stuff. What I call technical stuff
anyway. Finding addresses and phone numbers off the
Internet. That sort of thing. '

'Yes. Yes, he is.'

Another pause, then Mike said, 'He did well to track
you down to Belsize Park.'

'Yes.'

'He got hold of Raymond, and Raymond got hold
of your PA.' Another pause as they turned into the lane
to Meadowcroft and the Koenigs' house, then Mike
said delicately, 'He's a good lad, Charlie. But . . . well,
if you don't mind me saying . . . I think he's struggling
a bit. He's doing his best of course, with all this
computer stuff. But I think he needs to talk things
through with you. Hell, I'm saying this all wrong.
What I mean is—'

But an exclamation from Hugh caused Mike to
break off and follow his gaze up the lane. A tangle of
colours had appeared at the entrance to Meadowcroft.
As they drew nearer, Hugh made out flowers, some
propped against the gateposts, others tied to the gate
itself: bouquets in cellophane, bouquets with no wrapping, posies, single stems of red or white roses; perhaps
a dozen offerings in all. They came to a stop and Hugh
got out. He stood in front of the flowers before bending
down to read the messages. People he'd heard of,
others he hadn't. Simple messages, loving messages,
thoughtful messages. The familiar well-used phrases
caught Hugh unawares in a rush of feeling, he read

them through a sudden mist. *A fine lady . . . sadly missed . . . rest in peace.* Standing up he rubbed the wetness from his cheeks with the knuckle of one finger and stared at the flowers until the mist had passed.

His phone bleeped as he got back into the car but it was a moment before he managed to pull it out of his pocket and read the message.

Mike glanced across and said, 'What is it?'

'Charlie's found Lou. He's spoken to her.'

Mike squeezed his arm. 'Thank God. Who knows, she might be able to get a flight out tonight. What a relief.'

But any relief Hugh might have felt was outweighed by the thought of Lou's distress. Desperate to give her what comfort he could, he called her number only to get a long silence followed by a series of beeps. He imagined her weeping and felt a pang of utter helplessness. Following hard on his sense of impotence came a flicker of frustration at not having been able to tell her the full story, to soften the blow by reassuring her that Mum hadn't suffered, that she'd had no idea what was happening.

In the strange new world into which Hugh had passed, the sight of so many cars in the Koenigs' drive seemed unremarkable. There must have been six or seven. None was a police car, unless it was unmarked. But then the CID were hardly likely to allocate scarce resources to a home visit when they had Detective Constable Smith on the case, working out how to sign the matter off as soon as decently possible.

Hugh phoned Charlie and asked him to meet him outside. As Mike went into the house Charlie emerged, squinting into the thin sun, shoulders hunched against the cold. He was in his usual outfit of shapeless T-shirt and baggy low-slung jeans so long in the leg that the bottoms were dirty and frayed where they had caught under the heels of his trainers.

'How was Lou?' Hugh asked. 'How did she take it?'

Charlie thrust his hands into his pockets and shook his head a little as if he found it too difficult to talk about.

'She wasn't alone, was she? She had Chrissie with her?'

'Yeah, Chrissie was there. Yeah . . .'

'Thank God for that. Thank God. But all the same . . . all the same . . . Poor Lou. Poor sweetheart. Where is she? Is she miles from anywhere?'

'She's in Calcutta.'

'That's something at least. She'll be able to get a flight. But I need to tell her to use the emergency credit card,' Hugh added fretfully as he battled another rush of helplessness. 'To get the first flight no matter how much it costs. But how did you break the news, Charlie? What did you tell her?'

Charlie frowned at his feet. 'I just . . . said . . . there'd been a fire.'

'Yes?' Hugh urged him on.

Charlie lifted his shoulders still higher. 'And that Mum was overcome by smoke . . .' His voice was fading. 'And the firemen got her out . . . and tried to – to . . .' He couldn't find the word.

'Revive her?'

Charlie gave a faint nod. 'Yeah.'

'Did you say she was asleep when the fire started? That she knew nothing about it?'

Charlie's downcast gaze shifted a little to one side, his mouth tightened.

'Oh, don't get me wrong, Charlie – you did fine. *Fine.*' Hugh reached out and gripped his arm. 'But I couldn't bear it if Lou thought Mum suffered when she didn't.' He pulled out his phone and chased through the options looking for the redial function. 'Because she didn't, I know she didn't.' In his haste he found himself in a menu he didn't recognise. 'She's left her phone on, has she? She hasn't switched it off? Because I couldn't get through just now. I got some stupid beeps. Poor Lou, she must be—'

'Her phone's not working,' Charlie said. 'You need to call Chrissie.'

'What?'

Charlie drew his phone out of his pocket and handed it across. 'Just press the green button twice.'

'Chrissie?'

'Yeah.'

Hugh pressed the button twice and put the phone to his ear. When the number began to ring he turned to signal his relief to Charlie but he was already walking away.


When he finally went into the house he found Mike waiting in the hall with a sturdy dark-haired woman in a crisp white blouse and black trouser suit. She introduced herself as the family liaison officer. Judging by her manner, her level gaze, the way she offered her condolences simply, without embarrassment or false emotion, he guessed she'd undertaken this task many times before.

Her name was Pat Edgecomb, and she led Hugh
into a room he hadn't seen before, partly a study
equipped with a desk and computer, partly an enter-
tainments room with a wide-screen TV and a baby
snooker table. The Koenigs probably called it the den.

'The Koenigs have given this room over to you for
as long as you need it,' said Pat, 'so you and Charlie
can have some space to yourselves, see people when
you feel like it, get away when you want to be by
yourselves.'

Hugh said, 'We won't be staying that long.'

Pat nodded understandingly. 'Until you move on,
then. Perhaps I should explain my role?' she continued.
'Basically I'm here to do as little or as much as you'd
like me to. If you want information, help of any sort,
if you'd like me to contact any person or organisation
on your behalf, or if you'd just like me to wait while
you decide whether I can be of any use, then that's fine
with me.'

'Thanks, but I haven't begun to work out what
needs to be done yet.'

'Well, if you'd like any suggestions, just say the
word.'

'Food first,' said Mike from the door, clasping his
hands together like an attentive waiter. 'What's it to
be, Hugh? Bacon? Eggs? Toast? Coffee?'

Hugh had lost track of time but breakfast seemed as
good a meal as any. 'Whatever.'

'Whatever, it is!'

Pat sat in an oversized leather chair whose cushion
gave a soft hiss under her weight, while Hugh chose the
matching sofa opposite a window that offered the full
version of the view the jammed curtains in the room

above had denied him that morning: the skeletal branches of the tall beech amid an army of oak and ash, and Meadowcroft two gardens away.

'First of all, what would you like me to call you?' Pat said. 'Mr Gwynne or Hugh?'

'Whatever.' It seemed to be his word of the moment.

'Hugh, then. Shall I just run through who's here?'

'Please.'

'There's a loss assessor from your home insurance company, a Mr Preston. He'd like a quick word with you before he goes, if that's at all possible. Then there's Angela Parfitt, who was, I believe, your wife's supervisor at the Citizens Advice.'

*Was*, past tense. This was to be Lizzie's story from now on.

'And your business partner Mr Wheatcroft.'

Hugh thought Ray had gone to the office hours ago. Perhaps he'd been there and come back.

'Oh, and a young friend of Charlie's who arrived ten minutes ago. I don't know his name.'

'Joel?'

'If you mean the Koenigs' son, he's here, yes. But this is someone else.'

Hugh dragged a hand down his face. His mind was too full of his conversation with Lou to concentrate on all this. Having called to comfort her, he'd found that she was the one comforting him. She realised Mum would have known nothing about the fire, she'd reassured him straight away; she knew smoke killed people in their sleep. What worried her was that he might be blaming himself for not having been there. *You're not, are you, Dad? Because you mustn't blame yourself, you really mustn't. Because if you'd been home you'd have been asleep as well, then Charlie and I would have lost both of you, and then what would we have done?* But if wise, prescient Lou had assuaged one guilt, she had unwittingly unleashed another: that if he'd been home last night then the match-lighting vandal would never have got into the house in the first place, not without the most almighty struggle; that if he'd been home there would never have been a fire at all.

He tried to order his thoughts. 'There's my wife's family to contact,' he told Pat. 'Her mother. Her half-sister. They're both away, I think. Or they were till recently. Her mother was somewhere in Scotland. And Becky – I'm not sure.'

Pat picked up a piece of paper from the low table in front of them and handed it over to him. 'Charlie and I managed to find contact details.'

'Oh.' There was an Edinburgh address and number for Lizzie's mother, and a hotel in Marrakesh for Becky.

'The Koenigs say you're more than welcome to use their phone.'

There was a knock, the door swung open and at first no one came in, then Mike appeared, concentrating hard on carrying a laden tray. 'Scrambled egg, toast, bacon, coffee.' He placed the tray carefully on the low table.

'Thanks.'

Mike waved him towards the food. 'Don't want it to get cold.'

'Thanks, but I should make some calls first.'

'Better on a full stomach,' said Mike, straightening up and revealing his own substantial waistline.

Pat nodded her agreement, and suddenly it was easier to give in, to let himself be led in small matters like food and delayed phone calls, and reserve his energies for the bigger decisions.

He took a token mouthful of egg and toast and was surprised to find he could get it down. 'We've just come back from seeing your colleagues in CID,' he told Pat.

'DC Smith told me.'

'He tell you why we went?'

'Very approximately. I understand you had a break-in two weeks ago, then a prowler.'

'And my wife didn't smoke.'

She gave a slow nod, the sort that acknowledges the information but enquires no further.

'They think that's how the fire started,' Hugh said, 'with a cigarette down the side of the sofa. That or a candle.'

'I see.'

'But your DC Smith didn't seem too interested.'

'You gave him all the details?'

'At some length.'

'I'm sure he'll carry out a proper investigation.'

'Difficult to prove arson.'

Pat gave a concerned smile, like a doctor humouring a valued patient, and Hugh realised it was pointless to say more. Her job, like DC Smith's, was to discharge her duty in accordance with the training manual, then sign him off.

He managed two more mouthfuls of scrambled egg before his stomach began to rebel. The coffee was good though, and he managed a whole cup.

Having fulfilled his duty as breakfast waiter, Mike

stood up and lifted his arms wide before letting them fall to his sides. 'Well . . .'

'God, yes – you must get on your way, Mike.'

'If you're sure?'

'I'm sure.'

'See me out?'

On the doorstep Mike said lightly, 'Why don't you and Charlie take some time out together? I don't know, go for a walk or something. All this' – he flipped a hand in the direction of the kitchen and the murmur of muted conversation – 'the paperwork, the formalities, it can all wait. Charlie needs to know there was nothing he could have done.'

'Of course there was nothing he could have done.'

'But he needs to hear it from you.'

Hugh took a steadying breath. 'You're right . . . I'll talk to him as soon as I've spoken to Lizzie's family.'

'You understand what I'm saying?'

'Yes. Yes . . . he's always been fragile.'

'Well, anyone would be in the circumstances. Seeing his mother . . .'

'Thanks, Mike – for everything.'

'Hell, Hugh . . . I just wish . . .' His face contorted in sympathy.

'I know. Drive safely.'

Mike pulled him into a rough bear hug then stepped outside and paused to delve into his pockets for keys.

'I would never have let him see her,' Hugh commented. 'I would never have put him through that.'

Mike stared at him in puzzlement. 'I didn't mean at the mortuary. I meant at the house, seeing her at the house.'

They exchanged a look of complete misunderstanding, then Mike's round face paled a little. 'He saw them bring her out. He saw them trying to resuscitate her. Christ, Hugh, I thought you knew.'

For a moment no one realised he was there. The kitchen was long with dark wooden fittings and a look of permanent twilight relieved by a sprinkling of down-lighters. Ray was leaning against the central counter frowning at his watch as he listened to a man in a grey suit clutching a sheaf of papers to his chest. Behind them, at the near end of a long rectangular table, Sarah Koenig was sitting with her back to him, next to Angela Parfitt from the Citizens Advice and, opposite her, a weeping grey-haired woman with a handkerchief pressed to her eyes. At the far end was Charlie with the lanky figure of Joel Koenig opposite, and between them a hunched, shaven-headed young man Hugh hadn't seen before.

Ray spotted him and straightened up. 'Hugh! How are you doing? You manage to eat something?'

At this, the other conversations petered out and everyone looked round. Hugh realised with a momentary sense of disorientation that the weeping woman was their cleaning lady Mrs Bishop.

The man in the grey suit was from the loss adjusters. Hugh shook his hand then, with a gesture of apology, moved rapidly on, only to find Sarah Koenig looming up in front of him, wanting to know if he'd like more toast or coffee. He paused long enough to decline with excessive politeness, then Mrs Bishop's tear-streaked face was staring up at him, her dry bird-like hand clutching his, drawing him down onto the chair beside her while she repeated over and over again that she couldn't believe it, she simply couldn't believe it. Finally, counting off the minutes, he accepted Angela Parfitt's condolences on behalf of herself and her colleagues at the Citizens Advice and promised he would contact her if there was anything she or the staff could do.

At long last he reached Charlie's side, to find his gaze drawn to the shaven-headed youth slumped on the other side of the table. It might have been the two scabs high on his scalp where the razor had nicked the skin, it might have been the grubby night-time pallor and unhealthy sprinkling of spots, it was certainly the evasive downcast gaze that refused to acknowledge Hugh's arrival by so much as a glance, but Hugh took a violent objection to his presence. Not only was a casual stranger deeply unwelcome at this most private of times, but in that instant his drooping air of failure and self-absorption seemed to epitomise the whole rotten culture that had led Charlie into drugs. With another lurch of resentment it came to Hugh that he was a fully paid-up addict waiting to lead Charlie back into temptation. Why else would he be here? Why else couldn't he look Hugh in the eye?

Charlie said, 'Oh Dad, this is Elk.'

*Elk?* But it went with the territory: a travesty of a name to go with a travesty of a person.

The creature made a half-hearted attempt to get to his feet. There was a clumsy unravelling of limbs, a forward crouch, a grudging nod, an evasive gaze which flicked up as far as Hugh's shirt front before dropping again as he slouched back in his seat.

Hugh's voice trembled a little as he said, 'Charlie, how about a walk?'

Charlie looked up, his eyes dull and red-rimmed from the long night. He murmured, 'Okay,' before turning to Elk. 'Be right back.'

'No sweat.' Elk's voice was rasping and high-pitched.

There was a delay while Sarah Koenig, swelling importantly to the challenge of finding outdoor clothing for Hugh, searched out her husband's best golfing jacket, only to fret inconsolably when no walking shoes of the right size could be found. Escaping the house in his ordinary shoes, Hugh set a fast pace as they started down the drive, before slowing down abruptly. 'I thought we could do with a bit of time on our own. All those people . . .'

Charlie gave what might have been a nod.

Still in the grip of his incoherent animosity, Hugh demanded, 'Who's Elk? What's he doing here?'

Charlie murmured, 'He's a mate. He just dropped by.'

'I don't understand.'

'He's in NA. He's here to support me.'

'Support you?' Hugh echoed doubtfully.

Charlie made no response as they turned out of the drive into the lane.

'Sorry,' Hugh said in a conciliatory tone. 'Sorry. He just doesn't look very . . .' Abandoning this thought, he explained, 'I'm finding it difficult having strangers around, that's all. I find it . . . intrusive.'

'I was trying to keep him out of your way.'

They were heading away from Meadowcroft, following the route of a favourite Sunday afternoon walk which led up the lane, past the last house to a footpath that trailed across open fields to a copse on the brow of a hill. Charlie's jacket, like all his clothes, was far too thin, and he was walking with his shoulders high, his hands thrust deep into his pockets, his eyes narrowed against the chill wind.

In a rush of remorse and unhappiness, Hugh looped an arm round his shoulders. 'It'll be better when Lou gets here. Then we can get away on our own, we can have time to . . .' But he couldn't imagine what time could do for them, he couldn't imagine an end to this sadness. He said, 'I think the flights from India come overnight, so with luck I can pick her up first thing in the morning.' He squeezed Charlie closer against him, but the two of them weren't in step, they butted awkwardly against each other, and in the end it was easier to let his arm drop.

'Charlie, last night . . . I had no idea you arrived when you did. Why didn't you tell me?'

Charlie's face darkened. Eventually he murmured, 'No chance.'

'What?'

A pause. 'Never had the chance to tell you.'

Confounded by this, Hugh nevertheless let it pass. 'I thought the Koenigs must have called and told you to come. I'd no idea you were already on your way. What time did you get here?'

Charlie might have shrugged, it was hard to tell with his shoulders so high. 'Twelve,' he muttered. 'Just after . . . I dunno exactly.'

'And the fire?' Hugh asked. 'It was still burning? Or had they put it out?'

Charlie's mouth tautened.

Touching his sleeve, Hugh drew him to a halt. 'If you could bear to tell me.'

Charlie whispered, 'Yeah, it was burning.'

'And the fire brigade – they were there?'

'Yeah.'

'You saw them bring Mum out?'

Charlie gave a short nod, his face very pale.

'God . . . I'm so sorry. How awful for you.'

Charlie dropped his head, his thick wavy hair falling forward over his face.

'And then? What happened then?'

'Then . . . then they tried to – to . . .'

'Resuscitate her?'

Charlie nodded.

Hugh's throat constricted, it was an effort to speak. 'Was she still alive when they brought her out?'

'I dunno.' Charlie's voice rose briefly. 'They wouldn't let me near.'

'And nobody told you anything?'

Charlie shook his head.

Eventually they walked on. As they passed the last house and left the shelter of the trees the wind intensified, swooping down off the open fields, and Charlie's face took on a pinched, dogged look, his mouth pulled back against his teeth, his gaze fixed on a point a yard or two in front of his feet.

Hugh asked, 'Was Mum expecting you?' The silence stretched out so long that he thought Charlie hadn't heard. 'You'd called and told Mum you were coming?'

Another pause then a mumbled, 'Yeah.'

They reached the kissing-gate to the footpath. Charlie went first, Hugh followed. 'It was a last-minute thing? You just decided?'

The path ran along the edge of a ploughed field,

they were forced to go single file, and Hugh suddenly wished he'd never suggested the walk, that they were sitting in the warmth of the Koenigs' den where he could see Charlie's face.

'Or had something happened?' he persisted to Charlie's back.

This time the silence drew out for so long that Hugh cried with a flicker of exasperation, '*Charlie!*'

Stopping, Charlie half turned round. 'I wanted to talk to you about Spain.'

'But I wasn't home.'

'You were gonna be back though.'

'But you spoke to Mum,' Hugh asked again, needing to be absolutely sure, 'you told her you were coming?'

'Yeah.'

'What time did you call her?'

Charlie had to think about it. 'Eight?'

'And she was all right when you spoke to her? There was nothing the matter?'

'She seemed fine.'

'Did she say what she was doing?'

'No.'

Hugh looked away towards the brow of the hill where crows were circling over a stand of trees, and was gripped by a sense of loss so profound that for an instant it felt unsurvivable, as if his heart and all his vital organs had seized simultaneously. He sucked in a long breath and felt the wind drag the tears from his eyes. 'If only I'd come home last night,' he cried. 'If *only*—'

'Dad, no—'

'But it's true. If I'd been here none of this would have happened. None of it.'

'Dad . . .'

Charlie took a step towards him but Hugh was beyond consolation. Shaking his head, he turned away and tramped back along the path.

# SIX

He lodged his complaint on the fifth day, acutely aware that he should have taken Mike's advice and done it sooner. He had been too ready to listen to DC Smith's assurances that the matter was being taken seriously, that further investigations were in hand, and – the latest excuse – that they were waiting for the fire investigation report. When it finally dawned on him that nothing was happening, he felt a cold anger, as much at his own credulity as at Smith's inactivity.

He made the call at nine thirty, reckoning it would be the best time to get hold of Smith's superior, a Detective Inspector Steadman, only to be put through to a duty detective who sounded even younger and less experienced than Smith. Selecting his most authoritative tone, Hugh announced that he wanted to make a serious complaint but wasn't prepared to go into detail until and unless he could speak to a senior officer. He was asked to hold. After what seemed a long time but was probably less than a minute he found himself talking to a detective sergeant named Reynolds.

'Nothing personal, Detective Sergeant,' said Hugh, 'but I'm not prepared to discuss my complaint with anyone under the level of detective inspector.'

'Very well, sir. But if I could just log the particulars—'

'Who's your superior?'

'I can assure you that all complaints are taken extremely seriously, Mr Gwynne. But they have to be logged—'

'Who's your superior?' Hugh repeated.

A slight pause, during which Hugh could imagine Reynolds tightening his lips. 'It's Detective Inspector Steadman.'

'Well, it's him I need to see.'

'I'm not sure he's available.'

'In that case I'll come in and wait till he *is* available.'

'I'll just check.' The line seemed to go dead, then Reynolds was back saying, 'Would twelve noon suit you, Mr Gwynne?'

'To see DI Steadman?'

'Yes.'

'Twelve will be fine.'

It was an object lesson, Hugh decided, one he wouldn't need to be taught again. With these guys you had to push, and push hard. What was it the criminal lawyers said? When the cops weren't massaging the crime statistics they were out for an easy life, the path of least resistance towards the pension and the villa on the Costa del Sol. Well, he thought, here's some resistance, and plenty more to come.

'Dad?' It was Lou, standing in the doorway.

'Morning, my love,' he declared, going to embrace her. 'Did you sleep all right?'

'Not too bad.' She pulled away and scanned his face. 'Everything okay?' Something in her expression told him she'd overheard if not the content then the tone of his phone call.

'Just trying to get the police moving, that's all.'

'What is it they're meant to be doing?'

'Oh, just formalities, paperwork.' He hugged her again. 'Nothing important.'

'Anything I can do?'

He shook his head.

'Well . . . don't let them get to you.'

'No.'

She gave the ghost of a smile, and he felt a surge of love and gratitude for this miraculous child. Small, slim and fine-boned, with flawless white skin, broad cheekbones, sweeping eyebrows, and a sweetly curved mouth, she seemed to his partial gaze to be possessed of a commanding beauty. When she had first arrived from the orphanage in China he had secretly wondered if he would ever get accustomed to the alien features, the wide spacing of her eyes, the cruelly winged lids over the inner corners, the jet-black hair which stood up from her head in resolute spikes, but as the years went by he had come to appreciate that her eyes were a perfect almond shape, set just the right distance apart, and that her hair, descending in a heavy curtain, had the lustre of a raven's wings. Serious-minded and hard-working, with a serene intelligence and even temperament, she had never given him and Lizzie a moment's worry.

'Did you manage to find some breakfast?' she asked.

'Plenty, thanks. Oh . . . apart from the butter.'

It was their first morning in their rented house, which was called Oakhill. Lou had helped choose it, advising against a house on the far side of the village, pointing out that it would be more convenient to be in the next lane to Meadowcroft. The interior of Oakhill was painted an unrelenting white and furnished in what the estate agent proudly described as neutrals. The effect was soulless, like a hotel, an impression exaggerated by the absence of family clutter and the host of flowers from well-wishers which Lou had placed in a variety of vases and jugs around the main rooms. The kitchen was polished steel and pale wood, the fridge a giant double-fronted machine which dispensed two kinds of ice and had compartments and drawers for almost everything. Lou delved into one of them now.

'Here's the butter,' she said. 'I'll leave some out, shall I? By the bread.' She put the kettle on and regarded him solemnly. 'How's the cough?'

'Okay.' Immediately after the fire his cold had mysteriously disappeared, only to return a couple of days later in the form of a wheezy chest and persistent cough.

'Did you sleep all right?'

'Sort of.' The doctor had prescribed something to help him sleep but it wore off after a couple of hours and if he took a second dose he woke feeling drowsy and confused. Convinced that at least some of his sleeplessness stemmed from the claustrophobic atmosphere at the Koenigs', he had pressed the estate agent to let them move into Oakhill yesterday, although it was a Sunday and not officially a moving day, but the change had made no difference, he'd still woken at three and spent long restless hours in dull misery punctuated by jolting bouts of intense, almost physical pain.

'Why don't you grab some sleep after lunch?' Lou suggested. 'They say half an hour's all you need.'

He said he'd give it a try, though they both knew he wouldn't get round to it.

'Or a walk? Exercise is meant to be the best.'

'Good idea.' But this too seemed unlikely; the dark-ness came early nowadays and he had no heart for the country walks he'd taken with Lizzie.

Lou made herself some herbal tea and took it to the breakfast table. 'So what's the plan for today, Dad?'

'A whole lot of calls. And people to see in town.'

'Don't forget we've got to go clothes shopping sometime.'

Apart from one suit, he was living in borrowed clothes. He said, 'Tomorrow?'

They had a tacit understanding that it was necessary to keep busy, that this was the best way to get through the day. While Hugh tackled the formalities, Lou had organised the move to Oakhill and the purchase of towels, linen and food. Also, to Hugh's relief, she had taken on the task of returning the calls from relatives and friends, and shepherding the steady trickle of visitors. While Hugh was touched by the people who called briefly with a few faltering words, he became restless and taciturn with those who stayed too long and talked too much, and relied on Lou to step in and rescue him. Charlie, meanwhile, kept busy in his own way, spending long hours on the computer, listening to New Age music, going religiously to his NA meetings.

When Hugh left for the city he told Lou he was going to see the police about security at Meadowcroft while it was empty. While this wasn't the truth, it was close enough for him to persuade himself he wasn't actually lying.

Hugh's grievance with the police had provided a welcome focus for his wider anger. He arrived at the police station in combative mood, ready to do battle at the first obstacle. But there was no delay this time, no request to join the sullen malcontents in the waiting room, no suggestion that DI Steadman wasn't going to be available. Less than a minute after he'd announced himself to the reception officer, a stocky man with a ruined face appeared at the pass-door and introduced himself as DS Reynolds. Hugh followed him down the passage into the same interview room where he had seen Smith.

'DI Steadman's on his way?' Hugh asked immediately.

'He'll be along shortly.'

'I'm not prepared to discuss this without him.'

'I still have to take some details, Mr Gwynne,' Reynolds replied pleasantly. 'DI Steadman will be at least ten minutes. If we could go through a few questions while we're waiting then I won't have to trouble you later.'

In his febrile overwrought state Hugh wondered if he was being fed a line, but something about Reynolds, an air of stolid reliability, made him decide to give him the benefit of the doubt.

Reynolds gestured him to a chair and sat down opposite. Opening his folder, he took out a writing pad and unclipped a pen from his shirt pocket. 'Now, Mr Gwynne, your complaint is that the incident has not been properly investigated. Is that correct?'

'My complaint is that my wife's death has not been properly investigated.'

Reynolds wrote this down, before arranging his features into an expression of sympathy. 'My condolences on your loss.'

'Thank you.'

'And in what way do you consider the investigation to have been inadequate?' Reynolds asked.

'Well, that's what I've come to discuss with DI Steadman.'

'I appreciate that, Mr Gwynne. But this is for the record. If you wouldn't mind.'

Suppressing a sigh of forbearance Hugh said at machine-gun speed, 'Firstly, no proper forensic examination has been made of the source of the fire, no search for matches or accelerants or whatever else was used to start it. Secondly, you have made absolutely no enquiries among the neighbours or the village as to whether they saw anything suspicious on the night of the fire. Thirdly, there was a break-in at my house some time ago, then a prowler two nights before the fire, yet you haven't even begun to look into the possibility that these events might be linked. Fourthly, you've made no attempt to list or profile possible suspects.' He flipped a hand. 'I could go on, but I imagine that's enough for starters.'

Reynolds' notes were suspiciously short.

'How does this work?' Hugh demanded. 'Do you read this stuff back to me?'

'I can do, yes.'

'Well, since this is an official complaint I assume you want to get it right.' If this implied a threat of more action to come, then that was fine with Hugh.

'I'll read it through to you at the end, no problem,' Reynolds said in tone of reassurance. 'If we could just go over a couple of points?' Sliding some papers out of his folder, he began to leaf through them.

Guessing they were Smith's notes, Hugh said pointedly, 'Your man kept telling me investigations were in hand but he could never say exactly what was being done.'

Reynolds read a little further. 'Saturday . . .' He went back a page. 'No, *Friday*, DC Smith asked the fire investigators to review the evidence.'

'Yes? And what did they say?'

'Basically they've confirmed their original findings. As in there being no indication of arson.'

'But they haven't been back to the house. They haven't sifted through the debris.'

'They're satisfied that there was no indication of arson,' Reynolds repeated, studying the report again.

'But if they're not looking for arson, they're not going to find it, are they? An arsonist doesn't need to soak the entire place in petrol to burn it down. All he needs is a match, some newspaper, something to set light to a sofa. If they've got their minds set on it being an accident, then they're going to miss the evidence.' Something about Reynolds' slow nod gave Hugh the feeling he was being humoured. He said sharply, 'But there's no point in this without Steadman.'

Reynolds picked up his pad. 'Shall we go through your complaint for accuracy then?'

Hugh asked him to correct some of the wording. Reynolds had just crossed out *failure to undertake house-to-house enquiries* and begun to write *failure to undertake reasonable local enquiries* when the door opened and Steadman came in. He was a trim sleek man with dark, gelled hair and pale eyes. It might have been the effect of the gel, but the blackness of his hair contrasted so strongly with his skin that it looked dyed. He shook hands briskly and, sitting down, fixed Hugh with an unwavering gaze.

'I regret that you've found it necessary to make a complaint, Mr Gwynne, but I hope we'll be able to answer some if not all of your concerns.' As Steadman was saying this, he swung an open palm towards Reynolds, who placed the details of the complaint in his hand. Steadman glanced down the page then returned his pale gaze to Hugh's face. 'On the matter of the fire investigation, I appreciate that you must have a number of unanswered questions, but the fire investigators can only offer an informed opinion on the source and possible causes of a fire. In this case, all they can say with confidence is that the fire started in—' He turned his head a fraction towards Reynolds.

'In the lounge,' murmured Reynolds. 'In a sofa.'

'In a sofa. And that it appeared to have started accidentally. Beyond that – the exact circumstances of how the item caught light – these are things they can't determine with certainty.'

'I'm well aware of the limits they operate under, Detective Inspector, but they haven't even carried out a proper search,' Hugh argued in a reasonable tone. 'They haven't even combed through the debris for evidence.'

'I'm not sure I follow, Mr Gwynne. What sort of evidence would they be looking for?'

'Well, traces of the materials that were used to start the fire. Evidence that it was started deliberately.'

'The fire investigators are highly skilled, Mr Gwynne. Arson is almost the first thing they look for. And they found no indication of anything untoward.'

'There was no sign of accelerants,' Reynolds confirmed.

'But you don't have to use petrol to start a fire,'

Hugh pointed out. 'It could have been started with anything – matches, newspapers, rags, you name it.'

Steadman's stare narrowed, as if he was gauging the best way to deal with this line of argument. 'I think I'm right in saying that matches and newspapers would burn in their entirety, Mr Gwynne. They would leave no trace.'

'But how can the investigators be sure there's no trace if they don't even look?' Hugh said, letting his exasperation show. 'And they *haven't* looked. They haven't been back since the fire. That's five days ago, and the house clearers are meant to be clearing the house . . .' He drew a steadying breath. 'The point is, Detective Inspector, my wife didn't smoke, she didn't use candles, she didn't light matches at random, and she certainly wasn't in the habit of dropping naked flames down the side of the sofa. It's absolutely inconceivable that the fire could have begun in the sofa while she was in the house. Begun accidentally, I mean.'

'So what else could have happened, Mr Gwynne?' Steadman asked.

'Well, there has to be a strong possibility that someone got into the house and started the fire deliberately. That's obvious.'

Reynolds murmured, 'There was no sign of forced entry.'

'But there are dozens of ways he could have got in. He could have used a ladder and got in through a bedroom window. Or barged his way in when my wife went to answer the door. Or sneaked in and waited till my wife had gone to bed. A hundred different ways. We had a break-in two, three weeks ago. The same guy could have come back again.'

'Access was through a broken window on that occasion,' said Reynolds, getting a prize for doing his homework.

'So he got in a different way this time,' Hugh said, tiring of the argument. 'We reported the burglary but your guys never came, so no chance of fingerprints or DNA.'

Again it was Reynolds who answered. 'When the value of the goods or money is below—'

'Don't tell me, then it's just a crime number. Well, every break-in is a hell of a lot more than a crime number to the victims, I can tell you. My wife was upset. So was I. We no longer felt safe in our own home. And with good reason, as it turned out.'

Steadman looked at the complaint again. 'You say you subsequently had a prowler?'

'Two nights before the fire. A hoodie hanging around in the garden.'

Reynolds said, 'But no sign of a break-in?'

'Well, no. I disturbed him. I chased him off.'

Reynolds went on, 'And you believe the hoodie might have been connected to the fire?'

Maybe Hugh had been slow but it was only then that he realised Reynolds and Steadman were a double act. Not just boss and leg-man, but a well-honed team. He replied, 'Well, it has to be a possibility, doesn't it? Or the break-in was connected to the fire. Or all three were connected.'

Reynolds said, 'Do you have a particular reason to believe they might be connected?'

'Apart from the timing, you mean?'

Neither of them answered that.

'Do you or your family have any enemies?' Reynolds asked eventually.

'No.'

Then, with the air of a busy man keen to move things along, Steadman said, 'What about visitors, Mr Gwynne? Could your wife have had a visitor on the night of the fire?'

'She wasn't expecting anyone.'

Reynolds took over again. 'A friend who just dropped by?'

'They'd have phoned first. She'd have told me.'

Reynolds gave his slow nod. 'You spoke to your wife at what time?'

'About quarter to eight. Roughly.'

'Not very late then?'

'I've told you, she wasn't expecting anyone.'

'Friends of your children perhaps?'

'Both our children were away.'

Reynolds pushed out his bottom lip as if this hardly answered the point. Then, with a glance at Steadman, he reached into the folder and took out a large glossy photograph. Twisting the photograph round he slid it across the table to Hugh. It was a picture of the kitchen. Leaning forward, Reynolds pointed to the draining board where two wine glasses stood in the drying rack. 'Two glasses. And here . . .' He pulled out a second photograph which showed the other side of the kitchen. 'You can just see . . .' His finger pointed to the counter under one of the side units. 'A corkscrew with a cork still in it.'

'So what? That means absolutely nothing.'

They were looking at him as if they pitied him, and

then Hugh understood what they were trying to suggest: that Lizzie'd had a secret lover, that she'd used Hugh's absence to invite him home. He gave a derisive laugh. 'Wrong track. Completely the wrong track.'

They sat and stared at him a bit longer, then Reynolds said, 'You see the point, Mr Gwynne. The visitor could have been a smoker.'

'There was no visitor.'

Reynolds said, 'Then who was the other glass for?'

Not trusting himself to speak just then, Hugh shook his head.

'With respect, Mr Gwynne, it's a reasonable supposition.'

Hugh took a moment to marshal his arguments. 'Okay – the wine. My wife liked a glass of wine at about seven, as indeed did I – *do* I. She liked a second glass at dinner. She preferred white wine before dinner but often switched to red with the meal. She – like me – wouldn't have used the same glass for two different wines. She would have got a new glass from the cupboard. As for the corkscrew, I always forget to take the cork out after I've opened a new bottle. Most people do. So what? But strictly for argument's sake, just supposing someone *had* dropped in, just supposing my wife *had* given them some wine, just supposing they *had* happened to be a smoker – though for the record I can't think of a single friend of my wife's who *does* smoke – then she would also have offered them an ashtray. Which they would have used diligently. They wouldn't have dropped their cigarette down the side of the sofa. They wouldn't have stubbed it out on the cushion. One way or another it comes back to the same thing – the fire couldn't have started by accident.

Quite apart from anything else, my wife would never have left the window open.'

Reynolds raised his eyebrows. 'The window was open?'

'It's in the fire inspector's report.'

After a pause, Steadman pressed his hands together and rested them on the table. The fingers were long and white, the nails manicured, a heavy gold signet ring on the wedding finger. 'The difficulty, Mr Gwynne, is where to go from here. The fire investigators have made their report. There's no indication of a break-in. Your wife was upstairs in bed at the time of the fire, by all accounts asleep.' He spread his hands. 'You appreciate the problem?'

'I appreciate that you're not actively looking for evidence.'

Steadman said with a hint of patience wearing thin, 'But what sort of evidence did you have in mind, Mr Gwynne? Apart from matches and newspaper.'

'Fingerprints. DNA.'

Reynolds said, 'An intruder who uses a ladder is likely to be a professional, Mr Gwynne, and most professionals don't leave fingerprints or DNA. As for the other scenario you mentioned, someone barging his way in, there was nothing to suggest that your wife was attacked or involved in a struggle. She had no injuries. She didn't make any calls to the emergency services.'

'And she was in bed at the time of the fire,' Steadman said again.

Hugh felt he was being argued smoothly into a corner. 'But *something* happened,' he insisted. 'Something that wasn't right.'

Steadman's still eyes became opaque, as if his mind had already moved on to the next problem in his busy afternoon. He laid his palms on the table. 'Mr Gwynne, I appreciate your concerns. They have been logged and will be placed on file. But on the available information there is nothing to suggest that the fire and your wife's death were anything but a tragic accident. As a result I cannot justify the allocation of more police time to the matter. If, however, further information should come to light at some point in the future, information that merits investigation, we will of course give it proper and full consideration. In the meantime' – a half glance at Reynolds – 'family liaison have been on hand?'

'Pat Edgecomb,' Reynolds said.

'Our best liaison officer,' Steadman said, getting to his feet. 'Goodbye, Mr Gwynne. My sincere regrets to you and your family.' Before Hugh could say any more, Steadman gave a quick nod and was gone.

Reynolds made a kindly face as he began to gather up his papers. 'Accidents are often the most difficult things of all to explain. Sometimes you can look for answers and never find them.'

Hugh indicated the photographs. 'Can I see the rest of those?'

'Ah. Regretfully, they're not available.'

'So how do I get to see them?' Hugh asked.

'Best try the coroner's office.'

'And if I wanted to see them unofficially, Detective Sergeant?'

Reynolds inclined his head as if to give Hugh full marks for trying. 'I wouldn't have the authority to show them to you.'

'You've just shown me these.'

'That was by way of illustrating the point. Best stick to the proper channels, Mr Gwynne. Best from everyone's point of view.'

On the way down the corridor, Reynolds said in a tone of wanting to help out, 'My kids' friends, they used to drop by all the time. Never phoned ahead. Smoked like chimneys, girls, boys alike.' He pressed the electronic release for the pass-door. 'Just a thought.'

Reynolds walked him as far as the street door. Rain was drumming against the reinforced glass windows. As Hugh pulled on his coat, the door swung open and a burly man came in, momentarily filling the entrance, bringing with him a blast of cold and damp.

'Afternoon, sir,' Reynolds said in a rousing voice, suddenly all attention and deference.

'Afternoon, John. How's things?'

'Ticking along, thank you, sir. The guv'nor's expecting you.' To Hugh, Reynolds said hastily, 'I'll say goodbye then, Mr Gwynne. Do call if there's anything further we can do.'

The new arrival flicked Hugh a keen look, as if his name had rung a distinct bell, before following Reynolds to the pass-door.

Hugh went out into the rain. It was barely one. His complaint had been logged, heard and discharged in the space of forty minutes. The two detectives probably felt they'd given him more than enough time.

Isabel gave an audible gasp when she heard his voice. 'Oh Hugh, I'm so very sorry about your wife. So very sorry. I would have phoned, I wanted to phone, but I didn't want to intrude, and then Raymond said not to bother you.'

'Don't worry about it.'

'But I'm so very sorry, Hugh. So very sorry.'

He felt the customary dart of anguish. 'Thank you.' He was parked in a service station by the compressed-air machine, the rain sounding a steady tattoo on the car roof. He'd pulled in quite suddenly, without indicating, and got a blast of complaint from the car behind.

'I need a favour, Isabel.'

'Of course. *Anything*.'

'Not for public consumption. Just between you and me.'

'No problem.'

'I need to find an independent fire investigator. And soon, like today. If he wants to charge double for dropping everything to come at short notice, then that's fine. But someone good, Isabel. The best.'

'All right.'

'I think there's a forensic advisory service somewhere, a professional body with a list of experts.'

'I'll find it. And you want this person to . . . ?'

'Carry out a full investigation. The works. Everything he can think of, the latest technology, whatever it takes.'

'I'll do a full Internet search as well. See what names come up.'

'Someone independent.'

'Got it.'

'And Isabel? This is just between you and me?'

'Of course,' she declared, not needing to be told twice.

'I haven't mentioned anything to the children, you see.'

'No.'

'And not to Ray, or anyone else.'

'Of course not,' she agreed, as if any other action would have been unthinkable. 'I'll get on to it straight away and come back to you.'

He almost rang off then, but duty prompted him to ask, 'How did the Deacon case go?'

'Oh, fine.'

'Finish on time?'

'Yes, three o'clock on Friday.'

'And it went well?'

'Desmond thinks so.'

He suspected this left out a great deal but he couldn't begin to face the Tom Deacon problem just then.

He had pulled out into the stream of traffic before he remembered he'd forgotten to phone Lou to say he was on his way home. But it was too late now, the road was busy, the rain was heavy, and he felt an irrational compulsion to keep going, as though time was fast running out and the debris from the fire was even now deteriorating into an indistinguishable soup. Off his guard, he took instinctive refuge in the thought of discussing it with Lizzie when he got home. When realisation came, it was with a beat of despair, and he blinked away sudden tears.

Oakhill was locked, he had to use his key to get in, and when he called the children's names he got no answer. Passing the kitchen door he saw a note propped up on the counter. He recognised Lou's neat handwriting even before he got close enough to read it.

The anxiety bumped against his chest. He pulled out his phone hastily.

'Hi, Dad,' she answered.

'You're at Meadowcroft?'

'Yes.'

'Well, could you stop whatever you're doing, please? Stop straight away.'

'What's the matter?'

'Just stop now. Just go downstairs and don't touch anything on the way.'

'Dad, what is it?' She was sounding upset.

'Nothing must be touched, Lou. I can't explain. Just leave everything as it is and come back. No,' he corrected himself, 'I'll come and fetch you. Just leave everything as it is and wait in the hall. Don't touch anything. Okay?'

'Okay,' she said in a small whisper.

As he drove round he berated himself for having snapped at her. It was hardly her fault, after all. Slow down, he said to himself, just slow down.

There were two cars parked outside Meadowcroft, one he thought he recognised as Pat Edgecomb's, the other was certainly Sarah Koenig's.

Lou was waiting under the porch, a bundle in her arms. 'I came to pick up some clothes,' she said. 'Do you want me to put them back?'

'*Your* clothes?' he asked, as if she would be picking up any others.

'Mine, yes.'

He embraced her, bundle and all, and said into her

hair, 'Darling heart, of course you can take them. Of course. I'm sorry.' Pulling back, he saw Pat Edgecomb standing in the open door with Sarah Koenig just behind.

'It's the insurance people,' he announced. 'They don't want anything touched.'

Pat Edgecomb looked puzzled. 'I thought they were all finished.'

'Has anything been touched?'

'Well, in Lou's room – yes.'

'What about the other rooms?'

Pat Edgecomb shook her head.

'Sarah?' Hugh demanded.

Her eyes shifted guiltily. 'I had a quick look at a couple of rooms,' she said in a small voice. 'Just put my head round the door.'

'What about the living room?'

Her eyes hunted from side to side, as if seeking help. 'I had a small look, yes.'

'Did you go inside?'

'I . . . well . . . just a step.'

'No more than a step?'

Her face had turned a mottled crimson. 'Maybe two.'

'Well, was it two or was it more than two?' Perhaps the words came out rather more sharply than he'd intended because there was a startled pause.

Lou was the first to speak. 'Dad—'

'I'm sorry,' Hugh argued, looking at Sarah, 'but I have to know if the room's been disturbed.'

'It was just a couple of steps.'

'Did you touch anything?'

Sarah shook her head rapidly.

'What about the door?'

'The door?'

'Did you touch it?'

'No.'

'Has anyone else been into the living room?' Hugh said to Pat.

'Dad,' Lou said insistently, trying to draw him away.

'I'm sorry but I have to know. It's important.'

Pat hesitated and looked at Lou. 'I didn't go into the living room, no.'

'Dad, would you lock up, please?' Shifting the bundle under one arm Lou pressed the keys into his hand. 'Sarah, Pat, thanks for all your help.' She stood back to let the two women pass before following them out into the rain.

When he joined her in the car she was staring impassively ahead.

'Sorry,' he said. 'Was I very rude? I didn't mean to be. But it was important.'

She gave a tight little nod. 'Let's get back.'

As they set off he asked where Charlie was.

'He's at the Koenigs', with Joel.'

'Well, I suppose that's marginally better than being with Elk or whatever his name is. Though I'm not convinced Joel isn't into pot, you know. I'm sure I smelt it on his clothes the other day.'

Lou said nothing but her forehead was clouded by a slight frown.

'You don't think so?'

'Charlie wouldn't hang out with him if he was into drugs, Dad.'

'No?'

'No.'

When they reached Oakhill he went ahead to open the front door while she followed with her bundle, walking unhurriedly through the rain.

'I'll make some lunch,' she said, dusting the rain from her hair with a light brush of her fingers.

While she put cold meat and salad on the kitchen table he elaborated on his story about the insurance people, how on Friday it looked as though they wouldn't be sending their own investigator, how they'd changed their minds, how he'd got in a sudden panic about anything being touched.

Again the slight furrow sprang up between her eyebrows, again she said nothing, and this time her silence was like a rebuke.

He said, 'No excuse for overreacting though. Sorry.'

Lou accepted this with a slow nod. 'What are they hoping to find?'

'How the fire started. The fire brigade people did their best of course, but they don't have the time or resources to make a proper job of it.' Hugh held up a hand. 'Oh, I know it's not going to change anything, Lou. I know it's not going to bring Mum back. But I need to know how the fire started. I need to know if there was anything that could've been done.'

Lou went back to the fridge and took out a bottle of mineral water. 'I thought the fire started in the sofa.'

'Yes, but what set the sofa alight? How did it happen?'

Lou poured the water and sat down, gazing at him anxiously.

'Oh, I realise they might not find anything,' he said, as if to answer some unspoken challenge. 'But at least we'll know there was nothing to find.'

Lou gave another slow nod and, sliding the food towards him, urged him to eat. It wasn't till they had finished lunch that she said, 'Dad, about going to the house . . .'

'Yes?'

'When you asked if anyone had been in the living room, the answer was yes. Charlie went and got Mum's computer to see if he could salvage anything from the hard disk.'

'*What?*'

'It was because of what you said last night, about the friends we hadn't managed to contact, the phone numbers we were missing. Well, Charlie thought he'd get Mum's computer and see if he could retrieve her Christmas card list and e-mail addresses.'

'He went to her *desk*?'

'Just to get her computer.'

Hugh groaned.

'Dad, you said you'd been to Mum's desk yourself.'

'But I was careful not to touch anything!'

'I'm sure Charlie was careful too. He was only there for a minute—'

'But he didn't know what to be careful about!' Hugh retorted, hearing himself at his fretful worst. 'He could have trampled on something important, picked up stuff on his feet.'

'Dad . . . please . . .'

Hugh took a deep breath. 'It's just . . . I wish he could have asked me first!'

'But this thing about not touching anything, it's just come up today, right? So we couldn't have known, either of us.'

'But we were always going to have to wait for the

okay from the insurers—' Angry with himself for arguing the matter, angrier still for having believed his own
fiction, he waved the rest of the excuse aside. 'You're
right.'

'He was only trying to help, Dad.'

'I know.'

She said in a small voice, 'You won't get stressed
with him?'

'Of course not. When do I ever get stressed with
him?'

'Well . . .' She struck a diplomatic note of doubt.
'Just now and then?'

Hugh opened his mouth to protest before accepting
the accusation mutely, with a grimace. 'I haven't since
Mum died.'

'I know you haven't.' Again the two small furrows
creased the perfect smoothness of Lou's forehead.
'Another thing . . . Charlie's still blaming himself about
not getting home sooner on the night of the fire.'

'But that's crazy. He got there when he got there.
He's got nothing to blame himself for. Nothing at all.'

'If you could just tell him that, Dad.'

'But I *have* told him! I have!'

'I mean, if you could just tell him again. You know
how he is . . . he never believes anything first time
round. He always thinks everything's his fault.'

Hugh gave a baffled nod. 'Sure.'

'He's finding it really tough going at the moment.
We all are, of course,' she added rapidly. 'But with him
. . . well, he needs to feel you're right behind him,
Dad.'

'Of course I'm right behind him.'

'On the drug thing, I mean.'

'Ah well, I do worry about that. I can't pretend I don't.'

'Trouble is, he's sort of picking up on that. Thinking you don't trust him.'

'But I haven't said a thing about not trusting him, Lou. Not a thing.'

'I know, Dad. I know. But if you could . . . perhaps, well, show your support when he goes to NA meetings. Tell him he's doing well. That sort of thing.'

'It's that Elk creature I can't take. Why does he have to spend so much time with him?'

'Elk's his mentor.'

'Some mentor. Looks like he's still using.'

Lou said in fond exasperation, 'Dad . . . Dad . . .'

'Okay. Okay. I'll try harder. I promise.'

'Just tell him you're proud of him. That's all he needs. Just say you believe in him.'

It was exactly the sort of thing Lizzie would have said. It might have been this thought or his sense of failure over Charlie but Hugh suddenly felt immensely tired, as if he'd run into a wall and lost the energy to pick himself up again. 'You're right . . .' He rubbed his eyes vigorously. 'I'll talk to him. I'll find a time . . .'

'That'd be great.' She reached out and gripped his hand. 'Really great.'

The child becomes parent to the man, Hugh thought, controlling his emotions with difficulty. And so much sooner than you expect.

'And, Dad? If there were some more jobs you could find for him to do? Computery things. And helping to choose hymns and readings for the service.'

'I thought I heard you talking about hymns last night.'

'We were. But it'd be better if it came from you.'

'Okay.'

Reading his expression, she came round the table and planted a kiss on his cheek. 'Oh, Dad, don't take it wrong.'

'No, I'm glad you told me.'

She bobbed down at his elbow, and for an instant she was a child again, wanting his attention. 'For sure?'

'For sure.'

'Love you.'

'Love you too.'

She squeezed his arm. 'I'll make some coffee.'


He drank two cups, but it was the gnawing sense of lost time that did most to recharge his flagging energy. Going into the dining room where he had set up a temporary office, he found a phone number for the fire brigade headquarters and called to find out if Ellis was based there, little imagining the switchboard would put him straight through. At the sound of Ellis's voice he rang off abruptly, fearing a rebuff if he made his request over the phone.

Before leaving the house he laboured over a text message to Charlie. *Great idea to search computer. Back about 7. Much love, Dad.* This, like so many of his communications with Charlie, seemed inadequate, but it was the best he could do, though that didn't prevent him from fretting over how it could have been improved.

When he called upstairs to tell Lou he was going out, she leant over the banisters and listened to his story about needing to go into the office with the same faintly troubled expression as before, so that for the second time that day he felt he had managed to disappoint her in some crucial way.

The rain had eased off and he drove towards the city through a light drizzle that seemed to infiltrate the car, misting the screen. He fiddled with the ventilation controls, but either there was too little air or it was too cold, because suddenly the screen fogged completely. Almost blind, he slowed down and rubbed at the glass with the palm of his hand. Pushing at the ventilation controls again, he was finally rewarded with a blast of air and looked up to see a red light with a mother and child walking across. He stopped in time, there was never any danger, but his nerves were so taut, his dread so acute, that he felt cold suddenly; he gave an involuntary shiver.

He parked in his allocated place beneath the Dimmock Marsh office and walked the four blocks to fire brigade headquarters.

'Mr Ellis is away from his desk at the moment,' the receptionist announced after speaking into the phone. 'He's expecting you, is he?'

'I was hoping so,' Hugh said.

She wrote his name down and gave him a professional smile, bright but detached. 'If you'd care to wait?'

The fire brigade obviously had a better class of visitor than the police: the waiting area was open plan, the seats comfortable, the windows large and unbarred. There were stands containing leaflets with such titles as *Fire Safety in the Outdoors*, *Caring for your Smoke Alarms* and *Candle Safety*. He picked up *Candle Safety* and read it through twice. His eye kept returning to a caution halfway down the list: 'Keep candles out of draughts and away from furnishings and clothing.' Had it really been that simple after all? Had she put a lighted candle on her desk then gone to the kitchen to make some supper and forgotten about it? That much was just about possible. But she'd still have gone back to turn off her computer. When it came to saving energy she was a proselytising green; she liked to quote the fact that machines left on standby overnight burn enough energy to light two large cities. Unless there had been something to distract her. Ranging through the possibilities, he gave her a bad headache and saw her taking an aspirin and lying down, intending to close her eyes for just a minute or two, only to fall into a deep sleep. He gave her food poisoning, so virulent that she could get no further than the bathroom before collapsing into bed. He saw her getting uncharacteristically frustrated with her work and finding comfort in another few glasses of wine. But no matter which scenario he chose he couldn't see her abandoning their deeply ingrained night-time ritual of turning off all the lights and checking the doors and windows. Even with the lights on she could hardly have failed to notice a candle burning: candles were brighter than you thought; the Victorians had read by them after all.

He had just started on a leaflet entitled *Close that Door!* when the receptionist called him over. 'Mr Ellis says he wasn't expecting you.'

'Oh?' Hugh made a show of mild surprise. 'Could he spare me a few minutes anyway?'

She went back to the phone and relayed the message. 'He'll be right down.'

In a short while Ellis appeared through a swing

door, looking wary. 'Mr Gwynne,' he said with a taut nod, 'what can I do for you?'

'I was wondering if we could have a quick word.'

'Concerning what exactly?' He was more than wary, he was defensive.

'A couple of things I wasn't clear about.' Sensing that Ellis was about to turn him down, Hugh added quickly, 'Just small details.'

'Mr Gwynne, I'm sorry but I'm unable to enlarge on my report or discuss any issues relating to my report. If you want further information then you'll have to apply to the coroner's office.'

Aware of the receptionist a few feet away, Hugh dropped his voice a little. 'Off the record?'

Ellis said under his breath, 'Your idea of being off the record doesn't appear to be the same as mine, Mr Gwynne.' The note of injury was unmistakable.

'Oh.'

'I understand you've made a complaint as to the quality of the investigation.'

Hugh thought: I'm getting slow, I should have realised the police were bound to tell him. 'My complaint was with the police.'

'That's not what they told me.'

'Well, they told you wrong. I never complained about the quality of your investigation, only its scope, and I laid the blame for that firmly at their door, not yours.'

'Scope?' he queried touchily.

'The fact that they didn't treat the house as a crime scene. Didn't bring in a whole team of experts to go through everything with a fine-tooth comb.'

Ellis's expression relented a little, but he wasn't quite

ready to abandon his sense of injury. 'They'd need good reasons to do that.'

'That was my point – there *were* good reasons.'

Ellis exhaled slowly. 'Look, Mr Gwynne, while I have every sympathy for you at this difficult time, I regret that it's impossible for me to be of any further assistance. I've made my report, and that's as far as I can go.'

'I loved my wife, Peter.'

The declaration and the use of his first name caught Ellis off-balance. He shot Hugh an awkward glance.

'I feel I owe her this one last thing – to try and find out what happened. I realise there may be nothing to find. But I have to try.'

Ellis began to shake his head.

'Just a couple of questions.'

'Listen, Mr Gwynne, when we make a report we offer an *opinion* as to the cause of a fire, that's all. We offer it in good faith, to the best of our knowledge. But the way the world is now, people try to sue us. It's got so bad that the lawyers have told us not to discuss our findings with anyone, and that includes people like yourself . . . relatives, loved ones. So you see—'

'I won't sue. I give you my solemn promise.'

Ellis's round face betrayed his indecision. 'But telling the police you knew about my report – it landed me right in it.'

'I apologise if I betrayed a confidence,' Hugh said humbly. 'It was unintentional. It won't happen again, I promise.'

When Ellis gave in, it was with a small sigh, as though he was still going against his better judgement. With half a glance towards the receptionist, he led Hugh closer to the window. He said, 'Nothing gets quoted, officially or unofficially, to anyone under any circumstances?'

'Absolutely.'

Another sigh. 'Go ahead.'

'The window,' Hugh began. 'You said a window had been left open?'

Ellis frowned with concentration. 'One downstairs. A second upstairs.'

'The one downstairs was where?'

'In the lounge, about a metre from the sofa where the fire started.'

'Opposite the door then.'

Ellis thought about that. 'On the other side of the room, certainly.'

'And which upstairs window was open?'

'In the en suite bathroom.'

'The one in the bedroom was closed?'

'Yes.'

Hugh nodded, as if this tallied with his existing knowledge. 'The window in the living room, was it open very far?'

'Depends what you mean by far. It was on the stay.'

'The stay . . . ?'

Ellis mimed a push–pull action. 'The long handle at the bottom of the window that fits over the pin and stops it banging about.'

'Of course, yes. Yes . . . So what are we talking about? A few inches?'

'The fire officer observed that the window was open. It's beyond his remit to take measurements.'

'I just wanted to be clear that the window wasn't on the vent setting. There was a second groove – *slot*, do

I mean? – on the main latch so you could open the window just a crack but still leave it secure.'

'According to the lads it was on the stay.'

The stay. A new word for his window vocabulary. 'And the living-room door had been left open?'

'Yes.'

'And the bedroom door?'

Ellis hesitated, as if he could see where these questions were leading and didn't want to be implicated in the conclusions. 'Yes.'

'And the window in the bathroom, how far open was that?'

'A couple of inches, no more.'

Hugh suppressed the picture of choking darkness that threatened to engulf his imagination. 'What about the smoke alarms?' he asked. 'Were they working?'

'Couldn't be sure about the one in the entrance hall, it was too badly damaged. But the one on the first-floor landing was operating.'

'It had gone off?'

'It was sounding all right when the firemen got into the house. But the battery was almost flat.'

'Why didn't she hear it?' Hugh murmured as much to himself as Ellis.

Ellis shrugged. 'Often these battery-powered alarms aren't so loud as mains-powered.'

'But it would have been loud enough to be heard before the battery went flat?' Hugh made a baffled gesture, inviting ideas, but if Ellis had any more thoughts on the subject he wasn't forthcoming.

Struck by new uncertainties, it was a moment before Hugh managed to get his thoughts back into some sort of order. 'The smoke,' he said at last. 'How is it that people don't wake up? Why don't they cough or choke?'

'Carbon monoxide makes people sleepy, so if they're deeply asleep already . . .' He turned his mouth down.

'That's what's meant by toxicity, is it? Carbon monoxide?'

'And a whole range of other gases. Each fire's different, depending on the amount and type of toxic materials.'

'Is a house very toxic?'

'Can be. Old foam cushions are the worst offenders.'

*Old foam cushions* hung in the air like an accusation: the crime of having failed to succumb to the craze for refurbishment.

Once again Hugh struggled to find his thread. 'So it's not unusual for people to sleep through smoke?'

'It's all too common, unfortunately.'

'Hence the campaign to install smoke alarms. Battery operated or otherwise.'

Not sure how to take this remark, Ellis let it pass.

'The front door,' Hugh went on. 'It was locked? They had to break it down?' He knew the answer already but he wanted to hear it from Ellis.

'Yes.'

'Any record of whether the mortice lock was engaged?'

'No.'

Such information had been too much to hope for. Hugh gazed out of the window at a rain-streaked concrete wall across the street. 'Last question,' he said pensively. 'What was my wife wearing when they rescued her from the building?'

Ellis was uneasy again. 'Not something we put in our reports.'

'No . . . But you could find out?'

Ellis hesitated unhappily.

'I'd be very grateful.'

A last hesitation, then Ellis gave a reluctant nod. 'But no promises.'

At a quarter to five Bristow's was almost deserted, a few shoppers dawdling over their coffee, a lone drinker hunched over a newspaper, the staff polishing tables and stocking the bar in preparation for the onslaught of thirsty office workers, usually well represented by the staff of Dimmock Marsh, located twenty yards down the street.

Isabel was waiting for Hugh at a corner table. She stood up, her eyes very grave, and said rather formally, 'I'm so very sorry, Hugh.'

'Thanks.'

She sat down rapidly, as if to get on to business, and passed him a batch of envelopes. 'Cards from the staff. They don't expect a reply. And these' – she reached for a folder – 'are letters from clients and associates. There's a lovely letter from Desmond. And another from Sanjay. I don't know what you want to do about them . . . if you'd like to draft a standard reply which I could send out for you? I've kept a note of all the names and addresses.'

He had no idea what he wanted to do. The protocol of bereavement, the need to make decisions of this sort, was beyond him. 'Thanks. I'll probably draft something in the next day or so.'

'People have been asking if there's a date for the funeral.'

'It's not decided yet. But . . . well, we're thinking of a small affair. Just family and close friends. Perhaps you could explain?'

'Would flowers be all right? A joint wreath from everyone?'

'I . . . Yes, of course.' He could see his hope of a simple, austere funeral with a single wreath of white flowers slipping away.

Guessing something of this, Isabel said, 'But let me know nearer the time.'

'Yes.' Then, unable to hold back any longer, he asked, 'It's all set for tomorrow then?'

'Yes. David Slater will be at the house by ten to ten thirty, depending on the traffic. I've got his mobile number' – she handed him a slip of paper – 'and I've given him yours in case he's delayed.'

'And he's the best?'

'Well, he's registered with two of the top forensic advisory services, and when I double-checked with their senior staff they all said he was highly respected. And when I Googled him, he came up straight away. He's written several papers on fire investigation and appeared as an expert witness in some high-profile legal cases. I found the names of some other consultants on the Web, but Slater seemed to be the most experienced. And of course he was available.'

'You told him a bit about the job?'

'As much as I could.'

'He sounded confident?'

'He was a bit concerned about how long it'd been

since the fire. And he wanted to know if the roof had been damaged and whether any rain had got in.'

'He thought the delay might be a problem?'

'He didn't actually say so. He just asked how long it had been.'

'Anything else that worried him?'

'Whether the site had been kept secure. I said I thought it had. And whether there were limits on the budget. I said there weren't. I hope that was okay.'

'Absolutely.'

'He's bringing a team, he said. And they might need to be there for several hours.'

'Good.' Hugh added impulsively, 'How about a glass of something?'

'No, thanks. A bit early for me.'

'For me too, but what the hell.' He had been advised by the doctor that after a bereavement it was best not to drink for at least two weeks. Five days struck him as a fair compromise. He decided on a Scotch for rapid effect and wasn't disappointed. As the warmth curled around his stomach he felt his anxiety, if not fading exactly, then pleasantly blunted.

'You must put your time down to me, Isabel,' he said. 'Don't want Ray on your back for failing to keep an accurate time sheet.'

She waved this aside. 'Before I forget – Raymond's been trying to get hold of you. Something about the house insurance.'

Hugh couldn't think what it could be. 'I thought I was dealing with that. Did he say if it was urgent?'

'You know how it is with Raymond.'

He knew. When Ray wanted an answer to something

it was always urgent, no matter how trivial the question.

'I'll call him later. But tell me about the Deacon case, Isabel, and what happened with Tom.'

Isabel blinked rapidly, as if she had been preparing for what was always going to be a difficult moment. 'I had to make a couple of decisions that I need to square with you.'

'Go ahead.'

'The first was about our little difficulty with Tom, about him coming clean or us having to resign. Well, I wasn't sure what to do. In the end I decided I wasn't in a position to take action without proper authority. Authority from you, I mean. So I did nothing. I didn't say anything to Tom. I didn't tell him I knew about the problem, I didn't ask him for a decision or anything like that. I just ignored it. It was only afterwards that I wondered if I should have referred it to one of the other partners.'

'Christ, no. That would really have blown it. No, you did the right thing, Isabel. And Tom didn't mention anything, I suppose?'

'No.'

'He was probably relieved that I wasn't there to put him on the spot.'

'That's the other thing,' Isabel said. 'On Thursday morning when Raymond called and told me about the fire, I wasn't sure what to do. Whether to tell everyone. Everyone in the team, I mean. But then – well, I realised . . .'

Hugh breathed, 'Tom.'

She nodded vehemently. 'He was already in a state when he arrived at court. Nervous. Shaking and sweating. I thought if I went and told him he'd just freak out, which wasn't going to help anyone. And then I thought it wouldn't help to tell Desmond either, not just then, not when he was about to start Tom's re-examination. So I just told everyone you had a family emergency. Then when court rose for the day, Tom rushed away before I had the chance to tell him. And he didn't turn up at all on Friday. I tried his mobile all through Friday and the weekend, and today as well, messages and texts, but he hasn't answered, so I still don't know if he's heard.'

How strange, Hugh thought, that he should have missed the obvious, that in his shock and confusion, in the closing of his mind to everything but the impossible task of coming to terms with Lizzie's death, it hadn't struck him until this moment that he and Tom now shared an extraordinary and terrible bond, that their greatest common experience was not after all to be the law case but the loss of a loved one to fire. The thought gave him no comfort; rather, it touched him with a nameless anxiety.

Into the long silence Isabel dropped a soft, 'Hugh?'

Hugh emerged from his thoughts with an effort. 'Yes, it was the right thing, Isabel. Yes . . . So, tell me about Tom's evidence. Tell me what happened.'

'Well, he was amazing.' Isabel shook her head in wonder. 'After all that sweating and shaking I thought he'd fall to pieces, but once he got into the witness box he was calm as could be. No, not calm – *focused*. He kept his answers short and simple, like Desmond had told him. But he was really moving as well. So sad and sort of *dignified*. You felt he was telling it from the heart. It really got to you. And it wasn't just me that thought so,' she added, as if her own judgement had been a bit suspect. 'Desmond did too. And Sanjay. Anyway, Desmond took him through everything, all of Price's evidence, how he'd never known Price that well, how Price used to tag along, how Tom never had mental problems as a result of his army service, only worries about his marriage and the strain of being away so much. And how he felt he was doing health-wise, whether his hopes for the future had changed at all. When it came to the cross-examination I thought he might lose it – Bavistock launched in with some fairly aggressive questions – but he stayed totally cool. If anything he just got more and more – well, *dignified*. The judge seemed impressed. He made a big thing of thanking Tom anyway. Said he hoped it hadn't been too much of a strain, that kind of thing. So . . .' She tipped her head to one side. 'It looks like he went and pulled it off.'

Hugh breathed, 'Good old Tom.'

'But he'll still have to face the music, won't he? I mean, the whole thing's still going to come out?'

Hugh drained the last of his whisky. 'Who knows? The way his luck's going at the moment he'll probably get away with it.'

Driving out of the city, Hugh left the line of slow-moving traffic to stop at a supermarket and buy some wine for dinner. The choice of reds was limited; there were only two that looked vaguely promising. He was reading the label of a Chilean Shiraz, looking for he knew not what information, when Ray called.

'Hugh? Where are you?'

'Shopping.'

'You're still in town?'

'On my way home.'

'Oh. But I saw your car here. I thought you'd drop in.'

'I had to get back,' said Hugh, who couldn't think of anything worse than dropping into the office.

'But everything's okay, is it? I was a bit worried at not having heard from you.'

'I've been tied up. Is there a problem?'

'Oh no – no problem at all. No, it's just the house insurance people. They want a bit more information. And then I thought we might try the coroner's office first thing in the morning to see if there was any progress on the death certificate.'

For a moment Hugh thought his memory must be playing tricks. Though much of the first two days had passed in a blur, he had a distinct recollection of a conversation with Ray on what must have been Friday morning. They were sitting in the Koenigs' den, drinking coffee, Ray defaulting on a year's hard-won abstinence to chain smoke, while they went through a list of calls and paperwork. There had been no sudden decision on Hugh's part to reclaim the arrangements, just a gradual realisation that he didn't want his life to be taken over by other people, however well meaning. He had interrupted Ray politely, thanked him for everything he was doing, and said he thought he would take on the arrangements himself. He remembered the phrases he'd used, even the tone, grateful but resolute. But perhaps Ray, still exhausted from the previous day, hadn't taken it in. Or, in a fit of paternalism, had decided to ignore it.

'Very good of you,' Hugh said now, 'but I'm already in contact with the coroner's office. And the insurance people – I'm fine to deal with all that now, Ray. So—'

'But I'm more than happy to do it, Hugh. God, it's the least I can do! You don't want all the hassle and red tape. Like the stupid house clearance people. I've just discovered they've gone and mixed up the dates. They seem to think they're not coming till next month. Well, you don't want to be—'

'I cancelled them, Ray. I cancelled them this morning.'

A pause. 'Oh.'

'Postponed them, rather. It would've been too soon. We need more time to sort out our personal stuff.'

'I see. But—'

'Look, I appreciate everything you've done, Ray. I can't tell you how much I appreciate it. But I need to do this stuff myself, if only to keep my mind off things.'

'Oh . . . well, if you're sure.'

'I'm sure.'

There was a taut silence. 'Okay. No problem. I'll get the papers round to you first thing in the morning.'

Ringing off, Hugh felt a passing guilt at denying Ray his chance to contribute, perhaps even to grieve. Ray had always adored Lizzie in a boyish, hopeless way, an admiration that relied on mystery and unavailability.

Lou was chopping vegetables when he got back to Oakhill. She came forward to give him a kiss. 'Hi, Dad. How was your meeting?'

'Oh, all right.' He lifted the carrier bag onto the side and began to unload the shopping. 'I'm sorry I was so long. Everything okay?'

'Yeah.'

'Charlie around?'

'He's just got back from Joel's.'

'You've been on your own?'

She shrugged. 'It was okay.'

But he sensed she had been lonely and therefore more unhappy than she need have been, and looping an arm round her he kissed her hair. He watched as she started on the vegetables again. She chopped like a practised chef, keeping the tip of the knife on the board, working the blade so fast over the carrot that the slices fell in a gentle cascade.

After a while she looked up questioningly. 'Hey,' she said.

'Mmm?'

She put down her knife and waited for him to speak.

'Oh, I don't know, Lou. I don't know . . .'

Still she waited.

'I keep thinking it's all a bad dream,' he said. 'Keep thinking I'll wake up and Mum'll still be here.'

She gave a minute nod.

'And when I'm not thinking that, I—' But he broke off, not wanting to burden her.

'Yes?' she prompted softly.

He shook his head. What could he tell her? That he still blamed himself for having stayed in London, that he felt sure none of this would have happened if he hadn't left her mother alone, that he felt driven to find out what happened, that he feared he never would. 'I just miss her so much, that's all.'

Lou's eyes welled. 'Yeah.'

They stood in silence for a moment, then Hugh went in search of a corkscrew, finally locating one in the dining room.

'You won't forget about Charlie?' Lou said when he came back.

'What?'

'The hymns and readings?' she reminded him.

'Oh . . . Yeah. Sure.'

'And any computer jobs you need him to do?'

Hugh tried the Shiraz. It tasted a bit sharp, even metallic, but like so many of these cheaper wines it would probably improve on further acquaintance. He took another gulp or two to find out. 'I'll go and talk to him now.'

'Supper's in half an hour.'

'Right.' As Hugh drained the glass and topped it up he caught Lou's glance. 'The doc told me not to drink for a while,' he said. 'But I can't take the tablets, Lou. I can't take the chemical fog.'

'You do it your way,' she said. 'Don't listen to anyone else.'

'Even when it's a doctor?'

'Especially when it's a doctor.'

It had been a joke of theirs ever since she'd decided to apply for medical school, but the smile he won from her now was fleeting, troubled, and he couldn't rid himself of the suspicion that something he had said or done was adding to her unhappiness.

The throb of amplified music guided him unerringly to Charlie's new domain. Arriving at the open door he saw that Charlie had wasted no time in imposing his style on the room. The bed was unmade, clothes lay strewn over the floor, the booming music emanated from a hi-fi system wired to four speakers ranged around the room, while at a rectangular table under the window Charlie was sitting in front of two computers, tapping frenetically on a keyboard.

'Charlie?'

Charlie jerked round and reaching for the volume control turned the music off. 'Hi.'

Hugh tried not to notice the cigarette burning in a saucer beside the keyboard. Lizzie, who'd tolerated Charlie's smoking because it was the lesser of the available temptations, had drawn a firm line at smoking indoors. But, much as Hugh supported the idea of a ban, this wasn't the time to take Charlie to task. It was only tobacco, and Charlie was someone who needed a prop.

'How are you doing?' he said.

His eyes back on the computer screen Charlie gave a grunt. 'I dunno . . . I thought I'd got it. I thought the disk was okay, I mean it *is* okay, like it's not badly corrupted, you know? Just a small section, not much at all. But the data's got shifted somehow. And I can't work out how . . . *where* . . . it's gone . . .'

Hugh sat on the bed and watched Charlie as his fingers sped over the keys, the absorption in his face, and the concentration.

'See, even when something gets corrupted there's like a record left behind,' Charlie muttered. 'It's gonna be here, I'll find it okay. Just takes longer when you dunno the path names.'

'Which is Mum's computer?' Hugh asked, recognising neither.

'Wasn't safe to use. I took out the hard disk, cleaned it up and installed it in this old machine of Joel's.' He indicated the computer on the right. 'And then I'm running everything through this one as well' – he pointed to the other machine – 'to make sure I'm backing it up okay.'

Hugh had only a vague idea of what he was talking about, but nodded anyway, glad to see Charlie in his element. Obtaining the list of friends and their addresses wasn't that vital, they could probably get by without it, but he wasn't going to interfere with anything that kept Charlie fully occupied.

Charlie drummed his fingers rapidly on the table top and glared at the screen, as though willing it to give up its secrets. 'Can we get fixed up with broadband, Dad? It's just I don't wanna have to go to Joel's the whole time when I need to download stuff. And it wouldn't mean getting tied in for ever. There's like two, three providers you can sign up to by the month.'

Did this mean he was aiming to stay out of college till Christmas? Hugh wondered in passing. 'Sure. Go ahead and fix it up.'

Charlie attacked the keys again, his mouth clamped tight shut, his eyes staring with concentration, and Hugh hoped he wasn't getting too hyper. In his early teens he'd developed bursts of almost manic energy. It was one reason he'd taken to cannabis, he'd told them on one of the few occasions he'd talked rationally about his addictions: to calm his head down.

When he paused again, Hugh said, 'After supper, how about we all sit down and choose some hymns for the service, eh? And any poems or readings you like?'

Charlie dragged his attention away from the screen and fixed his gaze on the table top. 'Can't tonight.' His eyes flicked up and veered down again. 'Elk and I are going to a meeting.'

'Oh. An NA meeting?'

'Sort of.'

'Sort of . . . ?' Hugh added a smile to soften the question.

'It's like a Buddhist group.'

Hugh maintained his smile. 'For recovering addicts or . . . ?'

'It's just a regular meeting, I think.'

The silence threatened to stretch out. 'Well, so long as it does the trick,' Hugh said. 'So long as you feel it helps. I mean, if you want to go to a Buddhist meeting or any other sort of meeting, then, hey . . . that's fine with me. Whatever. And don't think I'm worried or anything like that. About the drugs, I mean. Because . . . well, I'm really not. And you know I'm here for you, if you ever . . .' He had drunk the wine too fast, it had gone straight to his head, he felt a little dizzy. '. . . if you ever want to talk.'

Charlie gave him an uncertain glance. 'Sure, Dad.'

Another silence then Hugh stood up and gripped Charlie's shoulder. 'Take care, eh?'

Hugh was halfway down the stairs when the music boomed out again, so loud that he almost missed the buzz of the doorbell. 'Cut it down, will you, Charlie?' he yelled.

Lou came out of the kitchen and looked at him questioningly.

'Are we expecting anyone?' he asked.

She shook her head.

'It's probably Elk,' he said in a stage whisper. 'Let's just hope he's not expecting supper.'

But it wasn't Elk. In the pouring rain and darkness beyond the porch light, as though uncertain of having found the right address, was a cyclist with a helmet shading his face, waterproofs, and a reflective yellow jacket. The cyclist pulled his bike back onto its stand. Only as he advanced into the light, the rain trickling down his face in glittery runnels, did Hugh recognise Tom Deacon.

Tom stepped into the hall and pulled his helmet off. 'Couldn't get here sooner,' he gasped breathlessly. 'Had the boys for the weekend.'

'Tom, I . . .' Hugh was still struggling to overcome his surprise. 'Listen, it's good of you to come at all. I . . .'

Tom was staring at him with such a fiercely pained expression that the rain on his cheeks might have been tears. 'Christ! Of *all things*. Of all *the sodding things* . . . Wish I could save you this, Hugh. Wish I could save you the grief.'

'Thanks. I . . .'

'If there's a god in heaven, you bloody wonder where the hell he's gone, don't you?'

'Yeah . . .'

'You got my message okay?'

Hugh racked his brains. 'Um . . . When did you . . . ?'

'It was tied to the gate. With the flowers.' There was an awkward silence punctuated by Tom's gasps. 'To the gate,' he repeated.

'In that case we'll have got it. And the flowers too.' Saying this, Hugh wondered if he'd got it right about Tom bringing flowers. It didn't seem likely somehow.

Tom said tautly, 'You didn't see it? The message?'

'I'm sure we did . . .'

'I left it on Friday. I came over specially. It was with the flowers, tied to the gate. I didn't know where you were. I thought the gate was the best place. I wrapped it in plastic in case it rained.'

'We must have got it then. We took everything off the gate. We collected all the messages.'

Tom was in a strange panic. 'You didn't see it?'

'I probably did, Tom. But to be honest the whole of Friday's a bit of a blank.'

Tom glared at him uncomprehendingly before clamping his eyes shut in a gesture of light dawning. ''Course it was bloody blank. 'Course. Memory's the first thing to go. Christ, I should bloody remember that, shouldn't I?'

'What did it say, the message?'

'That I'd be here for you,' Tom declared, as if this should have been obvious. Shrugging his rucksack to the floor, he peeled off his dripping top by grabbing the back and pulling it over his head.

'You've cycled all this way,' Hugh said.

'I would have cycled all night if I had to. You know that.'

Hugh took the waterproof from him. 'But in this rain . . .'

Tom balanced on one leg then the other to peel off his waterproof trousers. 'I wasn't going to let you down, was I? No way.'

'I don't know what to say.'

'Nothing *to* say.'

Hugh took Tom's gear and hung it on a coat hook. Returning, he summoned a tone of welcome. 'What can I get you, Tom? Coffee? Beer?'

He trailed off as Tom came towards him, raising both arms. For a crazy instant Hugh thought he was going to close his eyes and say a prayer, then he thought he was going to make a speech. Only as Tom got closer did Hugh realise it was to be an embrace. It was a stiff, self-conscious affair, Tom keeping most of his body well clear, only their shoulders touching, and Hugh guessed such gestures didn't come naturally to him.

Stepping back, Tom said formally, 'Please accept my deepest sympathy.'

'Thank you.' Seeing Lou at the kitchen door, Hugh said, 'You remember my daughter, Lou?'

Tom nodded and said a brief, 'Hi.'

'Can I get you anything?' Lou asked.

Tom addressed his answer to Hugh. 'Wouldn't say no to a glass of red.'

Collecting wine and glasses, Hugh led the way into the living room. 'How were the boys?' he asked.

'Good,' Tom grunted.

'You took them walking?' Hugh asked as he worked out how to ignite the mock-coal gas fire.

'The sports field. Nowhere else to go.' The lack of a car, the reliance on public transport for activities with the boys was a recurrent complaint with Tom.

'So . . .' Hugh said when they were sitting down. 'Isabel tells me it went well on Thursday, that you did a great job in the witness box.'

'Haven't come to talk about that,' Tom said firmly, from behind a cloud of cigarette smoke. 'I've come to listen. To talk. To be here for you.' By way of emphasis, he sat forward, resisting the comfort of the armchair, his gaze fixed on Hugh.

'Well . . . that's very good of you, Tom. I appreciate

you coming, I really do. But, well . . . we're coping reasonably well at the moment. You know . . . so far as we can.'

'But you need to talk, Hugh. You have to talk. It's the best therapy. Believe me – I've tried them all.'

'Of course you have! Yes . . . I'm sure you're right. But I'm lucky, you know – I have Lou and Charlie, and they have me. We've done quite a bit of talking, one way and another, and I'm sure we'll do a lot more in the days and weeks to come. And sometimes . . . well, you run out of talk.'

'It's never good to stop talking, Hugh. It means you're avoiding the painful stuff.'

'Very probably.'

Tom said in an intense way, 'You're feeling guilty.'

Hugh took a slow sip of his drink while he rehearsed a response.

'You feel you should have saved her.'

'Well, yes. That goes without saying. I wouldn't be human if I didn't think that.'

'It's called survivor guilt.'

'I know what it's called,' Hugh said, not caring to go in that direction.

Tom drew on his cigarette, exhaling smoke as he said, 'You feel you should have been there to get her out. You feel you should never have left her alone.'

'Sure,' Hugh said.

'You're trying to punish yourself for the fact that it happened, that's all. It's a form of denial.'

'I'll take your word for it, Tom.'

'But you'll get through it. That's what you've got to keep sight of. You'll get to accept it wasn't your fault. You'll get to accept there was nothing you could've done. It's one hell of a journey, to get that straight in your head. It takes one hell of a lot of therapy. But you *will* get there, Hugh. You *will* get through the guilt.'

The insistent tone, the relentless stream of advice, were getting on Hugh's nerves. Hearing the clatter of plates through the open door, he longed for Lou to come to the rescue and announce supper.

'But you can't do it alone,' Tom said, flicking his ash into the flames. 'You know that, don't you?'

'A therapist, you mean? Maybe,' Hugh said, knowing he'd only try it as a last resort.

'Everyone needs help, no matter how strong they think they are.'

'I get all the help I need from the kids.'

'You can't offload guilt onto other people, Hugh.'

'I wasn't suggesting you could. What I meant was, they get me through the day. They give me a reason – *the* reason – to keep going.' The argument, even the phrase, were oddly familiar, and Hugh realised with a sense of unreality that he was echoing Tom's words.

Tom said, 'So, who gets to hear about your guilt?'

Feeling oppressed, Hugh took refuge in a flippant tone. 'Well, I certainly do.'

'You've got to understand the process, Hugh.'

And why do I think you're about to explain it to me? Hugh thought, bracing himself with another gulp of wine.

Tom put his wine down. 'Okay . . .' He began to count off the points on his fingers. 'First comes the numbness, the shock, and the *denial*. The refusal to believe it's true. Yeah?' He narrowed his eyes and cocked his head a little, the instructor waiting for a glimmer of understanding from his student, and it struck Hugh that he was relishing his rare moment of authority.

'Yeah,' Hugh murmured.

'You might not realise it, but you're still in the denial stage. Okay? You're still trying to believe it's not true.'

Next, thought Hugh with growing tension, you'll be telling me it gets worse.

'Second' – Tom bent another finger – 'comes the anger.' He regarded Hugh impassively. 'And I think you're already into the anger, right?'

Hugh made a non-committal gesture.

'Well, it's okay to be angry. Angry with yourself for not being there. Angry that you didn't realise she needed help even though you were miles away at the time. Angry with the whole bloody world for letting it happen. Yeah?'

Tom was sounding like a walking textbook. But then after five years' therapy he probably was.

'Am I angry?' Hugh posed rhetorically as the wine took charge. 'Well, why not? Might as well go the full gamut.'

'And when you've stopped being angry with yourself, you'll start looking for someone else to get angry with. Someone else to blame.'

Already there, thought Hugh. Just five days and I'm onto stage three. Or were they still on stage two? He'd lost track.

'You know how it was with me,' said Tom. 'It wasn't just that stupid old man' – he never mentioned the other driver by name – 'it was his fucking doctor for letting him stay on the road when he was a heart attack waiting to happen, it was the car makers for their crap safety features.'

'You had good reason to be angry,' said Hugh.

Tom stated with unwavering certainty, 'You'll find targets for your anger too.'

'Not sure who or what I'd be angry with. Apart from myself. And that's keeping me pretty busy.'

'You'll look for conspiracy theories.'

Not trusting himself to answer that, Hugh gave a snorty little laugh.

Tom's eyes darkened. 'I don't mean like international plots,' he said touchily. 'I mean like whatever might've started the fire. The last electrician in the house. The last plumber. Whatever.'

'Hadn't thought of that. Why not?' Hugh reached for the bottle to top up their glasses.

'Do they know what caused the fire?'

'An accident, they think. But the jury's still out.'

'They're not sure?'

'Who knows?' said Hugh, setting the bottle back on the table and taking a gulp of his wine. 'They don't say much.'

'How're you dealing with that?'

Hugh thought, Christ, he's been among the shrinks so long he's come to rate his talent as a therapist. 'Doesn't bother me.'

''Course it bothers you. It bothers you to hell.'

Close to outright rebellion, Hugh waved this aside with a swing of his glass.

Tom insisted, 'It bothers you to hell because you want someone to blame. But that's okay. It's part of the process.'

'Nothing's going to bring my wife back,' Hugh said, taking refuge in platitude. 'So the cause of the fire doesn't make any difference.'

Ignoring this entirely, Tom said, 'You might never know what caused it. That could be the toughest thing of all, tougher than having someone to blame.'

'Wouldn't be surprised!' Hugh declared with a sudden smile. 'So . . .' He made a thrusting movement of one hand as if to move them rapidly forward. 'What comes after guilt and anger, Tom? What's the next stage?'

Tom's frown made his bony face seem more emaciated than ever, the eyes burning fiercely above the skeletal cheeks. 'I know this is hard for you, Hugh.'

'Yeah, well, now you come to mention it I don't know if I don't prefer denial and make-believe and muddling through with the help of some red wine.' He raised his glass in tribute. 'You do at least have the benefit of feeling numb.'

Tom nodded understandingly, as if this were another predictable phase in the official process of grieving. He stubbed out his cigarette on the hearth and reached for the packet to pull out another. 'Self-medication isn't always the best way.'

Hugh's eyebrows lifted. 'Sorry?'

'Alcohol.'

'Isn't that just a touch of the pot and the kettle?' Hugh added a smile to lighten the criticism.

'If I had my time again I wouldn't have used drink.'

'You use it now, Tom!'

'That's what I mean. It got a grip on me.'

'Well, hey – each to his own. I'm sure as hell using it tonight and I have to say it feels wonderful.' Hugh was well on the way to getting drunk and hadn't the slightest intention of slowing down. 'So, you haven't told me what next. The guilt and anger gets to go, does it?'

'Yeah.'

'When does that happen?'

'When you get to accept deep down that there was nothing you could have done.'

'Aha! Deep down? Not sure where that's located just at the moment.' Hugh took another swig of wine. 'And then?'

Tom's gaze took on a distant look, as if his thoughts had turned inwards. 'You keep looking for the person you've lost. You keep searching for them.'

'And after that? Just wondering if it gets better.'

'Then you begin to get over it. You begin to accept it.'

'Glad to hear it,' Hugh said airily. 'Very glad. Is that what the textbooks say?'

Tom nodded.

'Must be true then.'

Tom's expression became opaque, his jaw muscles clenched rapidly, the sinews quivering visibly beneath the tight flesh.

Playing his words back in his head, hearing the flippancy in his voice, Hugh said in a spirit of remorse, 'Glad for the information, Tom. Don't get me wrong.'

'It helps to know.'

'Sure. And your case taught me about post-traumatic stress.'

'You've got grief reaction.'

'Yes . . .' Wishing more than ever that he could escape, Hugh said lightly, 'Good old Ainsley. He spelt it out to the court, didn't he? The difference between grief reaction and PTSD. I should have remembered. A good find, Ainsley. Came up trumps. Wowed the judge. Wouldn't be surprised if his evidence does the trick, eh, Tom? Wins you the jackpot.'

Tom held his gaze unblinkingly.

Hugh signalled another retreat with a twist of one hand. 'So,' he said. 'Grief reaction. . . . no flashbacks, eh?'

'No.'

'Except in the imagination.'

'You don't get flashbacks unless you've seen something for real.'

'Depends on the imagination, surely.' When Tom didn't reply, Hugh argued strongly, 'Come on, if you have a clear picture of what happened, of what you *think* happened, then it's going to come back to you, isn't it? It's a flashback by any other name.'

'You recover from grief,' Tom said doggedly.

'But not, I think, from flashbacks,' said Hugh, unable to imagine a time when he wouldn't be able to picture Lizzie in the smoke-filled bedroom. 'These distinctions sound great in the textbooks, but it's just an attempt to tidy people into compartments, isn't it? To superimpose a neat model. That's psychiatry for you. I'd be no bloody good to Ainsley, would I? As a patient, I mean. Refusing to fit into my slot.'

'You fit,' said Tom. 'You don't realise it, that's all.'

That just about summed up the therapy industry, Hugh decided. Allow yourself to be led by us and we will show you the true light! Hallelujah!

The second wine bottle was empty and it wasn't going to replace itself without positive action. Hugh hauled himself out of his chair. 'Just going to see . . .' He indicated the kitchen.

Lou was at the sink, draining a pan in a cloud of steam. 'Dad, is Mr Deacon staying for supper?'

Hugh couldn't work out why there was no more wine. He opened a couple of cupboards to look.

'Dad . . .' Lou came up beside him. 'You don't need any more to drink.'

'No?'

'You've got through two bottles.'

'Have I? Oh . . .'

'The food's almost ready. Come and sit down.'

He whispered, 'I don't want him to stay, Lou.'

She gave a small nod. 'I'll find a way . . .'

Hugh sat down, his elbows on the table, his head resting in his hands. He heard the murmur of Lou's voice in the next room then footsteps in the hall. The footsteps paused then grew louder as Tom came in and stood beside him.

'Take it easy, eh?' His hand dropped onto Hugh's shoulder.

Hugh lifted his head. 'Yeah, yeah. Just tired . . .'

'Remember, I'm here for you, eh? And I ain't gonna go away.'

Hugh made no answer.

'I'll come back tomorrow. Yeah?'

'Look, I'm going to be busy tomorrow.'

'That's okay.'

Overcome by a sense of oppression, Hugh said, 'Let's meet on Friday. I can't think about anything else before then. We'll meet on Friday and talk about the case then.'

'No need to talk about the case.'

'Oh, but there is, Tom. There is.'

Tom removed his hand. 'If it's about what you told me on Tuesday, forgive and forget, eh? Water under the bridge.'

Hugh twisted round to look up at him. 'What?'

'The lie you told me about needing to see the judge. I was a bit pissed off when I got to find out. But, hey' – he gave a bleak smile – 'you did what you had to do, just like I did.' At the door he paused to say, 'Go slow on the vino, eh?'

# SEVEN

Slater dropped down onto one knee in front of the sofa. 'This hasn't been moved or touched at all?'

They had been inside the burnt-out room for several minutes but this was the first question Slater had asked. He was younger than Hugh had expected, no more than forty, a lean tidy man with quick eyes and a precise, energetic manner. He was wearing disposable overalls and carrying a clipboard on which he made frequent notes. On entering the room he had stood still and looked about him quickly, then slowly, and a third time for good measure before walking into the centre of the room and repeating his visual examination in the same methodical way.

'It hasn't been moved, no,' Hugh replied. 'And so far as I know it hasn't been touched. Though I can't answer for Ellis, the fire brigade investigator.'

Slater studied the charred remains of the sofa, then the wall behind it, shining a torch beam on the electrical socket, before standing up and looking at the window and the ceiling immediately above it. 'There were curtains here?'

'Yes.'

'Similar to the ones over there, were they?' He indicated the smoke-blackened curtains at the other window.

'Yes.'

'And how long were they, the curtains? To the floor, or did they stop under the window?'

Not entirely trusting the first impulse of his overtired brain, Hugh double-checked his memory. 'To the floor.'

'Anything else in the room that has been moved or altered in any way?'

'We've taken some papers – and a computer – from my wife's desk.'

'The computer – it was definitely on the desk?'

'I'm pretty sure. But I'll check with my son. He was the one who took it.'

Slater threw Hugh a swift mechanical smile, as if to reassure him, before moving closer to the desk and bending over to inspect the fire damage. His eyes went back to the window then up to the ceiling and back to the desk again.

'Did the fire report mention whether any windows were open?'

Hugh gestured towards the window over the sofa. 'This one was, yes.'

Slater gave a sharp sigh of satisfaction as if this confirmed the evidence of his visual inspection.

'I thought it might have been on the vent setting,' Hugh explained, 'but they said no, it was definitely on the stay.'

Slater nodded avidly as he made his notes.

'Just one problem – my wife would never have left it open.'

Slater's eyes fixed on him with keen interest. 'No?'

'We always check' – Hugh corrected himself with barely a pause – '*checked* every window and door last thing at night. Without fail. My wife wouldn't have forgotten, particularly when she was on her own, particularly when we'd had a break-in two, three weeks ago. It wasn't anything serious, the break-in, just a broken window and a bit of cash, but it made us extra cautious.'

Slater absorbed this with the same show of interest. 'I see.'

'The door was open as well,' Hugh volunteered.

Slater nodded rapidly as if he had been well aware of this. 'But the window – that was unheard of?'

'Completely.'

With a last thoughtful stare at the window Slater said briskly, 'Right, I'll get the men started.' There were two of them, both ex-firemen, who had arrived in a large white van. They appeared wearing overalls, one bearing a camera, the other an instrument Hugh didn't recognise, possibly an electronic tape measure, or maybe it was laser. While they began work in the living room Slater continued his tour of the ground floor, circling each room, paying particular attention to the floors and carpets. For a wild moment Hugh thought he must be looking for broken glass from a window, for a wilder moment still for footprints, until it dawned on him that he was looking for the remains of further, less successful attempts to start fires.

Back in the hall Slater gazed long and hard at the scorched ceiling, before following the track of the flames up the stairwell. On the top landing he turned in a slow circle, scouring the walls and ceiling for information, before inspecting each room. He left the main bedroom till last. As he went in, Hugh started to speak, but Slater silenced him with a brief, apologetic gesture while he began his visual sweep.

Hugh hung back in the doorway. When he had last seen this room he had been numb, almost devoid of feeling, but now the sight of it made him breathless with misery. Here were the ghosts of lost happiness. Here he and Lizzie had loved and laughed and slept and made their plans; here they had also worried and disagreed, but the years seemed flawless to him now. Her absence was like a chasm, endless and unbridgeable; yet even as it yawned before him he felt fresh anger on her behalf, and it was the anger that finally carried him forward into the room.

Completing his final scan, Slater threw Hugh an expectant look. 'You were going to say?'

'According to the fire report the door was open.'

Slater nodded to show he'd already worked that out. 'And the windows?'

'They were closed apparently. Apart from the small one in the bathroom.'

Catching the note of misgiving in Hugh's voice, Slater raised his eyebrows. 'And would that be normal?'

'The windows maybe. But the door, no. We never left it open at night. Never. Not since the children were small anyway. The only time recently was the summer before last, in that bad heatwave, to get a through draught. But that was the last time, the only time. Normally we always closed it. I can't think of any reason my wife would have done any differently.'

'I see.'

'Our son was expected home, but not till late,

midnight or so. She would have been expecting him to come and knock on the door to tell her he'd arrived. That was the rule if the children got in late – they had to let us know they'd got back safely. So, you see, she wouldn't have had the door open, she would have had it closed, waiting for Charlie's knock.' Even as Hugh said this it occurred to him with faint alarm that he might be quite wrong, that far from it being impossible, this was the one occasion when Lizzie might have gone against all habit and left the door open. With Hugh away and Charlie in an agitated state, she might have decided to wait for Charlie's arrival and call him into the bedroom to talk things through. He could see it now, the door open, the light spilling in from the landing, Lizzie in a light doze waiting for the sound of the front door and Charlie's steps on the stairs. But if she'd been keeping one ear open for Charlie, how come she hadn't heard the smoke alarm? How come she hadn't smelt the fumes?

It was a while before he realised Slater had asked a question. 'Sorry?'

'It was normal for you to keep the windows closed, was it?'

'At night we always opened at least one' – Hugh indicated the smashed and boarded window – 'but in winter we had it on the vent setting, open just a crack. The fire fighters probably didn't notice when they broke in.'

Slater awarded the information a solemn nod before going across to the bathroom.

Alone, Hugh looked down at the bed, the rumpled lower sheet, the slewed duvet and jumbled, indented pillows, and felt a lurch of doubt and inadequacy. Why doesn't any of it make sense, Lizzie? Why do I feel such foreboding? Would you approve of what I'm doing? Or would you suggest that I was off on one of my wilder tangents?

The disrupted bed worried him. He saw again the smoke-filled room of his imagination and the fireman arriving to find Lizzie still breathing. He saw the fireman throwing the duvet back and shoving his arms under Lizzie to lift her clear of the bed. He imagined the confusion, the need for haste, and how the sheet and all four pillows might have got rucked up in the process. And then it came to him – stupid not to have thought of it before – that the fireman wouldn't have been working alone; there would have been another fireman close behind, maybe even a third, who in the thick murk would have yanked the duvet back and pushed the pillows aside to check for a second victim.

No sooner was this question settled than his gaze turned to the button-back chair and his unease returned.

Slater was a fire investigator not a detective, this wasn't strictly his province, but Hugh had reached the point where he had to tell someone. When Slater came out of the bathroom he said quietly, 'My wife never left her clothes like this.'

Slater looked at the neat pile of clothes with the perfectly aligned shoes on the carpet beneath. 'Go on.'

'Dirty clothes went in the basket. Anything she was going to wear the next day she hung over the back of the chair. Well, she folded them a bit first, I suppose, but then she sort of draped them. She never folded things like this, not on the seat of the chair.' They contemplated the stack of smoke-blackened clothing.

'And shoes . . . she never left her shoes out. I don't know why, but she always put them away.'

'Let's get this photographed before we touch anything.'

Once the pictures had been taken Hugh picked up the first article. It was a cardigan folded in half, arm against arm, and then again the other way. The quarters not exposed to smoke damage proved to be a pale greeny-blue. Next was a shirt, once white. 'My wife would never have worn a shirt twice,' Hugh commented in a low voice. 'She'd have put it in the laundry basket.' Underneath the shirt were some jeans. Last of all, tights, bra, panties. He held them in a small bundle. 'The bra, the tights maybe,' he said. 'But never the panties.'

'She'd have put them in the wash?'

'Always.'

After a while Hugh turned away and went into the bathroom. He raised the lid of the laundry basket and dropped the underwear inside. The flimsy shapes fell lightly onto a bed of shirts and boxer shorts. He closed the lid abruptly.

'Anything else that doesn't seem right?' Slater asked when he got back.

Hugh stared at him. The folded clothes, the shoes, the open door seemed more than enough. 'What did you have in mind?'

Slater shrugged. 'Anything that strikes you.'

'Nothing that I can see, no. '

Slater's team had brought piles of equipment into the hall and were laying plastic sheeting over the living-room floor.

'What happens now?' Hugh asked.

'What happens now, Mr Gwynne, is that we make a hundred per cent certain we don't miss anything.'

'What are you looking for?'

Slater said cheerfully, 'Good question.' He went to the living-room door to give the men some instructions before going out to his car and returning with a Thermos flask and an extra cup. Pouring Hugh a coffee, he apologised for the fact it was sugared. 'My only vice,' he said, and Hugh believed him.

They drank their coffee standing in the hall where Slater could keep an eye on the work in the living room.

'What are we looking for?' Slater echoed. 'Everything and anything is the short answer. No stone unturned. If there's something to find, we'll find it. Needles in haystacks a speciality. But there's always going to be a risk that we'll find nothing, you do realise that, don't you, Mr Gwynne?'

'It's Hugh. Call me Hugh. Yes . . . Yes, I understand.'

'Or that we might find it was an accident after all.'

'I can't see how.'

'I appreciate that, Hugh, but at the end of the day we have to keep an open mind. We can't rule it out altogether. And it's David.' He gave his quick smile.

'She didn't smoke, David.'

'Smoking's not the only cause of accidents.'

'What else could it have been, then?'

Slater paused thoughtfully, gazing at his men as they folded the surviving curtains and placed them in a transparent plastic bag. 'Well, we can safely rule out lightning, gas leaks, sunbeam magnification. Which leaves appliances, faulty or misused, electrical faults, or careless use of other combustibles. Out of those . . . well, the fire started on the sofa, no question of that, on the right-hand side, so that rules out the wiring and the sockets. Appliances . . .' He shook his head. 'There was no sign of an appliance near the sofa, no lamp, hair drier, computer, or similar. You say the computer was definitely on the desk there?'

'Yes.'

'And not damaged, apart from smoke?'

'I don't think so. Though I'll have to ask my son.'

'So in the accidental category we're left with human error involving cigarettes, cigars, candles, lighters. If it was a lighter, we'll find it, plastic or metal. A candle . . . we might find some wax if we're lucky. Cigarettes, cigars . . . they don't leave any trace. But we'll take the sofa away and try burning a cigarette on it, test it for combustibility, see what happens. Ditto with a candle.'

'Ellis kept going on about candles, no matter how many times I told him my wife wouldn't have lit one.'

'Eighty per cent of house fires are accidental, Hugh. In the absence of other evidence he was always going to go for an accident.'

'Well, he didn't look too hard. He was only here a couple of hours.'

'They're never going to dig deep unless there're obvious indications of arson.' Slater finished his coffee and, crunching across the debris to the front door, shook out the last drops from his cup.

Hugh said, 'If it was a lighted cigarette or a candle, it could still have been deliberate, couldn't it? It could still have been arson.'

Slater came back with his cup. 'Too right.'

'So how can you tell? Whether it's deliberate?'

'Ha! The million-dollar question,' said Slater, screwing the plastic cup back on his Thermos flask. 'Like I said before – there may be nothing to find. I could put five men on the job, sift through every shred of debris in the room two, three times over, run every kind of chemical analysis in the book, and we'd be none the wiser. That's the first thing.'

'I understand.'

'Next, if this *is* arson, then it could be clever stuff. Someone who did his homework. Not impossible to get the technical knowledge nowadays, unfortunately, not with all these websites and real-crime books and stuff. You have to hunt around a bit, but it's there, most of it. He left no obvious traces, you see. If he used petrol or paraffin, then he was careful to use very little. No irregular burn patterns, no obvious smell. And he didn't try to light more than one fire – always a bit of a giveaway – instead he made sure that the one fire ignited properly. And he didn't do anything stupid like breaking and entering to make it into a crime scene. No, he planned it well.'

'Go on,' Hugh urged, wanting an end to the bad news.

'So he's a clever boy, but with luck he's not going to be *that* clever. With luck he'll have left a trace. If he used one of the common accelerants, then we should find some residue. If he used something like acetone, then . . . well, that's more difficult. Leaves no residue, acetone. But he'll have used *something*, that's for sure. A cigarette on its own isn't enough, you see, not for a serious arsonist. A cigarette might just smoulder, burn a hole, but fail to ignite the cushion.'

'Why not just put a light to the sofa?'

'What, and wait till it takes hold, you mean? Because he'd want to be well away before the fire started,' Slater declared. 'First rule of the clever arsonist. Get your alibi fixed up. Make sure you're having a drink with your mates when the fire breaks out.'

'Supposing he didn't care about that,' said Hugh after a pause. 'Supposing he cared more about the fire.'

Slater pulled his mouth down. 'A simple torching job? Possible. Yes . . . I certainly wouldn't rule it out. But nine times out of ten that's your habitual arsonist. Someone who's been fire-raising since he was a kid. Gets his kicks out of watching the fire go up. They usually get caught from the breaking and entering. Fingerprints, basic stuff like that. And you said there was no breaking and entering?'

'No. Nothing obvious anyway.'

'And not a lot of disaffected youth in this neighbourhood, I assume.'

Another pause while the image of the hoodie ran through Hugh's mind. 'More than you'd think.'

Slater's eyebrows went up. 'Proximity to Bristol, I suppose.'

'Yes.'

'And your wife wasn't in social work or anything like that?'

Hugh shot him a startled look. 'Well, yes. Yes, she was. She worked for the Citizens Advice. But she kept her work quite separate.'

'Yes?'

'She would never have let clients know where she lived,' Hugh insisted, as if Slater were arguing the point. 'She would have been well aware of the risks.'

'Just asking, that's all. One house fire I investigated,

the couple had retired after thirty years as foster parents. While they were away in Spain one of their previous foster kids came out of prison and came looking for them. Knew where the key was kept. Got upset that they weren't there, or started a fire to keep himself warm, depending on his story. The house was gutted.'

Hugh's phone rang. Digging into his pocket he hauled it out and silenced it. 'Well, we've never done any fostering. And my wife didn't have any clients who were into arson. She would have told me, you see. She always told me about her clients. Not the names necessarily, but the sort of problems they had.'

'There we are then.'

While Charlie's druggie friends were a different matter, Hugh thought suddenly. What did we ever know about them, Lizzie? Apart from the fact that most of them were capable of stealing and cheating to feed their habit? In the dark world Hugh now inhabited, where suspicions were two a penny, arson didn't seem such a big leap from drug addiction, not when he remembered some of the types Charlie had hung about with in the bad days, types, he couldn't help thinking, who looked and behaved like Elk.

Hugh said, 'So . . . if it was a kid with a lighter, we'll never know?'

Slater sucked in air through his teeth. 'Unlikely to find evidence from the fire itself, no.'

'And if it was this clever guy?'

'Ah,' said Slater, brightening up again, 'he'll have wanted to get well clear before the fire started. He'll have set up a delaying mechanism, something nice and dependable. With a bit of luck that's what we'll find –

some trace of the device he used.' With this thought Slater pulled on some blue latex gloves and, excusing himself, went to work.

Hugh watched as the three men shifted the sofa onto a large plastic sheet and began to seal it up. Remembering the missed call, he checked his phone. The number wasn't one he recognised.

It was Ellis who answered. 'Ah, Mr Gwynne,' he said tersely. 'Thanks for returning my call.'

'Not at all. Have you—'

'Just wanted to check something,' Ellis cut in.

'Sure.'

'Just wanted to check that we'd got a deal.'

'You mean . . . on the confidentiality issue?'

'That's exactly what I mean,' he shot back.

'Yes, we have a deal. Absolutely. Why?'

'Because I've had the police here, and I'll be in deep trouble if they know I've been talking to you.'

'They're going to investigate after all?'

'I don't know about that. All I know is that it was a chief inspector, and he was here for a good hour, wanting chapter and verse. If it gets out that I've been talking to you I could be in deep trouble, Mr Gwynne. I just wanted you to be aware of that. All right?'

'All right,' Hugh said in a calming voice.

'He said not to discuss it with anyone. He made a point of it. Not to discuss it with anyone at all.'

'Did he say why?'

'He didn't have to. He's a chief inspector.'

'What was his name?'

A sharp pause, then Ellis said reluctantly, 'Montgomery. Chief Inspector Montgomery.'

The name was familiar, though Hugh couldn't immediately place it. Work perhaps. Or the local news. 'He's Inspector Steadman's boss, is he?'

'Don't know. One last thing, Mr Gwynne,' he said in a different tone. 'About my report, I just wanted to say that the opinion I arrived at was the best I could do with the time and facilities at my disposal. If I was wrong – if I missed anything – I want you to know it wasn't for lack of looking.'

'I realise that.'

'We don't have the power to call in the forensic specialists. That's for the police.'

'What did Montgomery tell you about the investigation?' Slater and his men were starting to manoeuvre the packaged sofa out of the living room. Moving further away, Hugh lowered his voice. 'Did he say they were thinking in terms of arson?'

A short defensive silence. 'Nothing. He didn't say anything.'

'But he went through it with you?'

'I told you, I can't discuss it. He came on really strong about that. Not to be discussed with anyone.'

'But—'

'No buts, Mr Gwynne. Sorry.'

'Okay,' Hugh said. 'Before you go – did you manage to get an answer to my question? Did you find out what my wife was wearing?'

'Look, Mr Gwynne, it's like I said – I really can't discuss it.'

'This one last thing.'

A silence.

'I'll keep it confidential, I promise.'

'That's not the point any more, Mr Gwynne. The point is . . .' But he was weakening, Hugh could hear it in his voice.

'It's just to put my mind at rest,' Hugh said, even as the mixture of dread and anticipation gripped his stomach. 'That's all. For peace of mind.'

This time the silence seemed unbearable. Finally Ellis exhaled softly into the mouthpiece. 'She wasn't wearing anything, Mr Gwynne.'

'Thanks,' Hugh said levelly. 'Thank you for telling me.'

Ringing off, he pushed his way into the kitchen and stood blindly in the middle of the room while a succession of scenes racketed through his mind, forming and re-forming, appearing possible and impossible, often at the same time. She had been so ill she hadn't had the time or energy to put on her nightie. She had decided to sleep naked on a sudden whim. She had been overcome by smoke before she was properly in bed. She had been drugged and dumped naked on the bed by an intruder. Or maybe it was a friend: nothing seemed impossible just then. She had been raped; though signs of a struggle would surely have shown up in the post-mortem. And then the policemen's favourite scenario: she had been entertaining a lover. And why not? If she was going to break the habit of a lifetime by sleeping naked, why not break every habit in the book? Take a lover, leave two glasses on the draining board, light a candle on the desk, leave it on the very edge ready to fall onto the sofa, open a window to fan the flames; choose this one night of the entire year to go completely against character, conviction, temperament, everything she'd ever believed in.

How long he stood there he wasn't sure. Eventually his phone rang. When he answered, his voice sounded strange to his own ears.

'Hi, Dad,' came Lou's voice. 'How are you doing?'

'All right, love. How about you?'

'Okay. You still at the house?'

'Yeah. The insurance people are taking their time. You know how it is.'

'I'm calling because Angela Parfitt from the Citizens Advice just dropped by and left a message about a Reverend John Emmanuel wanting to have a meeting with you.'

Hugh had a moment of confusion. 'What about? The funeral?'

'No. Her message says' – a pause while Lou browsed the note – 'he worked with Mum and has something important to discuss with you and can you phone him, please. There's a mobile number.'

'Okay,' Hugh said, and took the number down.

'You be home for lunch, Dad?'

'Not sure yet.'

'Shall I bring a sandwich over?'

'No.' He didn't want her seeing what was happening, he didn't want her getting worried. 'No, I'll just come and grab something when I get the chance.'

It was after two by the time Slater and his men had finished parcelling and labelling debris and sections of carpet, and begun to load their equipment into the van. While he waited to lock up, Hugh went through the drawers of Lizzie's desk. Though everything on the flap had been reduced to congealed ash or charred, water-welded globs of paper, the contents of all but two of the drawers and compartments had survived, albeit with varying degrees of water damage. The day after her death he had found her passport and birth certificate, miraculously intact, in the drawer furthest from the flames. Now in a lower drawer he found some of her old diaries and notebooks, though nothing dated later than April. He was flicking through them for a second time when Lou's voice startled him.

'Dad?'

'Lou!'

She was standing inside the door with some cling-filmed sandwiches in her hand. 'I thought you might be hungry.'

'Sweetheart . . . Thank you. Yes, I'm hungry.'

As she came forward she stared at the space where the sofa had been and the rectangle of bare floor where the carpet had been removed and the reference labels on the walls.

'They're very thorough,' Hugh explained.

She nodded, her mouth flexing slightly. 'Are you coming home soon?'

Where was home? *Where the heart is.* And my heart's still here, he thought. 'No,' he said, 'I'm going to meet this vicar or pastor or whatever he calls himself.'

'You'll be back for supper, though?'

'Yes.'

'Because Charlie and I need to have a talk with you.' Before he could ask more she turned and walked out of the room. He called after her, but with a brief backward wave she was gone.

\*

Lowering clouds had brought an early dusk to the city; a few lingering bands of brightness lay in thick yellow streaks across the western sky. From a distance, silhouetted against the last of the light, the cluster of tower blocks had a deceptively elegant look, a suggestion of Manhattan, until Hugh had climbed the hill to the edge of the estate, when the towers loomed up directly in front of him, grey and forbidding, the corrugated concrete streaked with grime, and the strings of lights that had looked so enticing from the bottom of the hill revealed themselves to be the regimented illuminations of the stairwells. School was over for the day but few windows were lit and there were no kids playing on the concrete aprons beneath. The place had a deserted air. There were conflicting rumours about the Carstairs Estate: one that it was due for demolition any day, the other, surreal in its predictability, that the conservationists were applying for it to be preserved as a paradigm of late sixties estate architecture, but perhaps this proposal had died a death or local reaction had driven it underground because he didn't remember reading anything about it recently.

The church was on the far side of the estate, between a parade of shops and an electricity substation. Most of the shops looked closed for good, their shutters daubed with graffiti; only one blazed with light, a corner shop with a large handwritten sign in the window which, like some reactionary diatribe against single mothers, read 'Only 2 children at same time'. The church was constructed in the ubiquitous corrugated concrete, as low-built as the towers were high, a wide, spindly, sixties take on flying buttresses giving it the appearance of a crouching spider. For a spire it had a metal spike with a light on top. Above the door was a brightly painted sign saying 'All Welcome'.

The interior was plain, the adornment minimal. There were four or five people scattered around the pews, sitting in silent contemplation. Hugh could see only one door that might belong to the vestry. He knocked and heard the sound of a chair scraping back, then the door was flung open by a tall man, broad and powerful as a boxer, with a large face, polished-ebony skin, and metal-rimmed spectacles that had the effect of magnifying his eyes. He was wearing a bright blue tracksuit and white trainers. He reached out a broad hand and shook Hugh's solemnly.

'Mr Gwynne. Very good of you to come. Please . . .' With a sweep of one arm the Reverend Emmanuel gestured Hugh inside.

'I'm sorry I'm late, Reverend. I hope I'm not delaying you.'

'By no means. And it's John.'

'John,' Hugh echoed obediently.

Hugh was surprised to find someone else in the room, a strikingly beautiful woman with deep-coffee skin, wide features, and extravagantly braided hair. She was smartly dressed in a black suit and white shirt, and was standing very straight. The reverend introduced her as Jacqui Lewis.

'I'm Denzel Lewis's sister,' she explained, shaking Hugh's hand.

'Of course. My wife often talked about you.'

'My sister's sorry she couldn't make it. She's still at work.'

Hugh nodded, not quite sure why the sister should have been expected.

'But our whole family offer their sincere condolences, Mr Gwynne,' Jacqui said. 'Denzel phoned specially just to say how sorry he was. He appreciates everything Lizzie did for him and the campaign. We all do. She never lost faith, she kept with us all the way. That meant a lot. And now—' She broke off with a glance at the reverend.

'Thank you,' Hugh said.

John said in his deep melodious voice, 'Mr Gwynne, may I also extend my deepest condolences to you and your family. Such a sudden and pointless loss is always the worst to bear. I hope you will find some comfort in the knowledge that your wife was held in high esteem by those she helped in this neighbourhood. People have been coming to pray for her and to leave messages of condolence for you and your family.'

'How very kind. If you'd thank them . . .'

The reverend tipped his head in acknowledgement. 'For myself I will miss her more than I can say, both as a sister and a friend.'

'I know she valued your friendship.'

'Ah yes . . . we fought many a good fight together,' John said in a reminiscent tone. 'She would find the person we needed to see at the council, the social services, the police, wherever it was. *The man*. That's what she used to say: "We have to find *the man*, John." And when we got to see them she'd wear them down with sweetness and reason. That was her great gift – to wear them down so sweetly that they never minded one bit. Yes,' he said with a show of feeling, 'I will miss her greatly.'

'Thank you.'

John drew a chair forward. 'Please . . .'

They sat in a semicircle, Hugh facing a wall of blue surplices hanging in two neat rows with names tacked up above the pegs. There must have been at least thirty in the choir, and Hugh wondered what sort of music they sang, gospel or spiritual, or something more Caribbean. Whichever it was, he bet they made a fantastic sound. Without warning, his mind projected into the future he had taken for granted while Lizzie was alive, and he had a vision of the two of them sitting side by side in the church, listening to the choir in full swing, as they had sat in churches discovered at random on foreign holidays. Remembering all the things they had planned to do and now never would, he felt a foreshadowing chill of the lonely years ahead.

John said, 'If there is any way I can be of help to you and your family, I hope you will ask, Mr Gwynne. I will be glad to do what I can.'

'Thank you. And please call me Hugh.' Bereavement seemed to encourage formality, and this plea, like the statement 'how kind', was one he seemed destined to repeat many times.

'Hugh.' John placed his elbows on the chair arms and made a cage of his fingers. 'Thank you for agreeing to meet me today at a time when I'm sure you have many things to attend to. The reason I asked you to come was to hear what Jacqui has to say. Jacqui came to see me on Sunday and told me something which I thought you would want to know about. Jacqui?'

Jacqui was ready to say her piece; she had been ready ever since Hugh arrived. 'Mr Gwynne,' she began in a low, tight voice, 'you know that my brother's in prison for a murder he didn't commit. He's got fifteen years minimum, and a bad chance of parole so long as he refuses to admit his guilt, which he's never going to do when he's innocent. Lizzie went and found us some new lawyers – and they're good, we're happy with them – but lawyers can't do anything without new evidence. And that's the one thing we haven't got, Mr Gwynne. New evidence.'

Hugh gave a nod as he tried to imagine where this was leading.

'Lizzie called me a while back to give me the name of a journalist who might be interested in doing an article on Denzel, and we chatted a bit. She asked how the plans for the public appeal were going, and I said okay. But I guess I sounded a bit down because she asked me what the matter was, and I said I wasn't holding out much hope after all this time, and she told me I mustn't lose heart because you never know what's round the corner.'

'The public appeal . . . ?'

'To ask people to come forward with information. Sophia and I are doing leaflets, TV interviews, stuff like that.'

'Oh yes,' Hugh murmured as it came back to him.

'But, like I said, I was really down,' Jacqui continued, 'so I went on about why the public appeal was going to be a waste of time, how no one was ever going to come forward, not unless they were crazy or wanted to get themselves targeted. And Lizzie said, "But there has to be information out there." And I said, yeah, but we know where *that* is and we're never going to get anything from *them*, meaning the police. And she said, "I mean in the community." So I said,

"So what's going to make someone come forward now?" and that sort of stuff. And then she said' – Jacqui paused while she got it right – 'then she said, "Listen, there's just a chance I might have found some information. And when I say just a chance, that's what I mean, Jacqui. Just a chance." Well, of course I asked her what she meant, I asked her what it was, this information, a witness or some other kind of evidence, but she wouldn't tell me. She kept saying, "It's only a small chance," and she'd let me know one way or the other when she had news. I thought maybe she'd just said it to keep me going. You know? But then I realised she'd never have done anything like that – said something for the sake of it. No, she must have found something, and it *had* to be a witness, there was nothing else it could be. It had to be someone who'd seen Denzel exactly where he said he was that evening, out Clifton way, trying to find that girl's address.'

With the air of having reached the end of her story, she gazed intently at Hugh. Not sure what was expected of him, Hugh glanced across at John.

John said, 'I think Jacqui wants to know if Lizzie said anything to you about this information, Hugh. What it might be.'

'No, she said nothing to me. No . . .'

'She didn't talk about the campaign?' Jacqui asked.

'Yes. Often. But she only gave me the bare outlines.'

'She didn't say anything about . . . I don't know . . . new developments? Anything like that?'

'No.'

'Nothing about what she was doing? Who she was going to visit?'

Hugh thought of Lizzie's phone call from the noisy bar. 'No.'

Jacqui cast around desperately. 'There was no one else she could have told?'

'Outside work? No.'

Jacqui gave a sharp sigh of disappointment and looked helplessly towards John.

In the short pause that followed, snatches of his last evening with Lizzie came back to Hugh, her talk of the Free Denzel Lewis campaign, of going to see the police about the witness protection scheme, but he saw no point in mentioning that now, when it would only raise artificial hopes.

Jacqui turned back to him. 'Can I ask you a favour, Mr Gwynne?' she said gravely. 'I know it's a lot to ask at a time like this. I know you and your family have enough on your plate at the moment. I wouldn't trouble you, I really wouldn't, if it wasn't so important. But if there was any chance you could take a look through Lizzie's work stuff, her Filofax, her mobile phone, see if there's anything there, anything at *all*, that might give us some lead as to what she was talking about . . . well, we'd be so very *very* grateful.'

Hugh said, 'That's not going to be possible, I'm afraid.'

'Just some idea of who she went to see, who she phoned. This could be our only chance to find out, Mr Gwynne. Our one and only chance.'

'No, you see, my wife's handbag was burnt in the fire.'

'Oh,' Jacqui said, taken aback. 'And there was nothing left?'

'Nothing like that, no.'

Jacqui sighed again. 'I see.'

'What about her mobile?' John suggested mildly. 'Was it pre-pay or billed?'

'Yes,' Jacqui declared, flinging him a look of gratitude. 'Did she get bills with the numbers itemised?'

'Yes, her bill was itemised,' he admitted reluctantly. 'When it comes in I could have a look at it, see if there are any numbers that might be relevant.'

'And what about the bill for last month?' Jacqui ventured.

'I've no idea if it got burnt. Everything's in a terrible mess.'

'Of course,' Jacqui said, deflated again.

There was a dejected pause which prompted Hugh to say, 'Look, if it's any consolation I'm sure my wife would have told me if she'd come across anything as important as a witness. We talked about the campaign on our last evening together. I'm sure she would have said something.'

Jacqui's gaze told him it was no consolation at all.

After another pause John said, 'Perhaps at some future date, Hugh, if anything should come to light you will let us know?'

'Yes, of course.' Hugh stood up, and the others followed.

Jacqui gave him a card with a phone number. 'Thank you in advance for any help you can give.'

'Not at all.'

He was almost at the door when she called after him.

'One last thing.' She came up and fixed him with her fierce gaze. 'There are some people who find it easier to believe Denzel's guilty, that he's just making it up about being framed to get out of prison. But they're the people who come with preconceived ideas, a head full of stereotypes, a fixed mindset. Lizzie wasn't like that. She came with an open mind, no preconceived ideas. She just listened. And when she got to know the facts she realised everything we were telling her was true, that the case against Denzel never added up. She recognised the truth when she saw it, and then she did everything she could to see justice done.' Jacqui paused, as if to add weight to these last words, before ending quietly, 'Just thought you'd like to know.'

As John walked Hugh to the church door he bent his head and murmured urgently, 'You come by car, Hugh?'

'Yes.'

'Could I ask you to wait there a while, till Jacqui's gone? I would very much value a word in private.'

'Yes . . . of course,' Hugh said, because it seemed unreasonable to refuse.

Hugh had been sitting in the car for less than a minute when he saw Jacqui and the reverend appear at the church door, exchange a few words, and Jacqui walk quickly away into the estate.

'Thank you for this,' the reverend said as Hugh came back into the church. Evidently it wasn't to be a quick word because instead of saying what he wanted to say there and then John led the way back to the vestry. When the door was closed and they had sat down again, he said, 'The reason I asked you to return is because I am facing a dilemma and I believe you are the one person who can help me towards an answer.'

For a wild moment Hugh wondered if they were

going to talk about God or the law, or some juxtaposition of both.

'My dilemma,' John continued in a voice so deep and soft that it seemed to come out of the ground, 'is that Lizzie chose to impart some information to me on the understanding that it should remain strictly confidential between us. In normal circumstances it would of course remain so. But with her passing . . . well, am I to keep my vow or consider myself released from it? I have thought long and hard about this, Hugh, and on reflection I have decided that I must be guided by what Lizzie would have wanted. And I believe she would have wanted me to use the information in the best way possible.'

'I'm sure that's right,' Hugh said. 'I think you should go right ahead and do whatever you feel is best.'

'I'm relieved to hear you say that, Hugh. Most relieved.'

Hugh waited, wondering if this was the end of it.

'But maybe you're ahead of me, Hugh?' John asked hopefully, his eyes amplified by the lenses of his spectacles. 'Maybe you can guess what I'm talking about here?'

'No. Go on.'

'What she told me was—' John lifted his head to the sudden babble and whoop of high-pitched young voices outside the heavily barred window. As they began to fade, he resumed in the same low voice. 'What she told me was that she had found a witness who could prove Denzel's innocence. She'd gone and met up with him, talked to him personally, but he wasn't prepared to speak out until he got protection, and she was having a hard time knowing where to go for protection.' Something in Hugh's face made John stop and ask, 'She said nothing to you?'

'No,' said Hugh, trying to contain his hurt. 'No . . . only in general terms.'

'She said she'd been to the police to ask what would happen if a witness was to come forward. She was careful not to say anything too definite, she said, not till the witness could be guaranteed protection. Same reason she didn't want me saying anything to anyone, not even the Lewis family. She didn't want their hopes getting raised. Most of all she didn't want talk on the estate – talk that would get the witness running scared.'

'She actually met this witness, you say?' Hugh asked quietly, needing to hear it again.

'That's right.'

The hurt was like a small torment, eating away at him. 'I see. I didn't—' But he gestured the thought away. 'Go on.'

'The reason she told me all this was by way of asking if I would take this witness into my home if anything should happen, if word got out and he began to run scared. I agreed. My wife and I, we often lay an extra place at our table. But I said to Lizzie I wasn't sure our home was the best place.' He gestured over his shoulder. 'We live just down the road here. People come knocking on our door all times of the day and night. It wasn't going to be a safe place. You understand me? It wasn't as if people weren't going to find out someone was there. But Lizzie, she said it would only be in an emergency, if there was no other place for him to go.'

Hugh gazed blindly at the wall of blue surplices. Why didn't you tell me? he demanded of Lizzie. How could you sit across the table and talk about the campaign and say nothing? How could you look me in the eye?

'So,' said John with the air of reaching the end of his story, 'as soon as Jacqui came and said she was going to ask for your help, I thought of what Lizzie would want me to do . . .' He spread a massive hand.

'You did the right thing.'

'I didn't feel it was right to tell Jacqui. You understand me?'

Hugh nodded, his mind still racing through fragments of conversations with Lizzie. After a while he became aware of John gazing at him expectantly. 'Yes . . . I understand.'

'I appreciate that you already have a heavy burden to carry, Hugh. One of the heaviest burdens a man can bear. I know this will do nothing to alleviate it. But if there's anything you can do to help. Anything at all.'

Driving back, overcome by sudden exhaustion, Hugh played loud music and opened the windows to stave off the threat of sleep. I'll do what I can for them, Lizzie, he decided emotionally, because it's what you would want me to do. But not straight away. I have you to worry about first. I have to find out how you died, to bury you, to put you to rest, body and soul. To work out how to live life without you.

He made the turn for Oakhill with minimal hesitation. How quickly one adjusts, he thought; soon the turn would become automatic. There were two extra cars outside the house. One was Pat Edgecomb's, the other he wasn't sure about.

Lou met him in the hall. He put on a pantomime of weariness, a slumping of his shoulders, a blowing out of his lips, as he went to hug her. 'Oh, Lou, I'm so glad to be back. What a day. How've you been? And Charlie?'

'All right, Dad.' Her tone told him nothing. 'Pat Edgecomb's here. And the vicar.'

'The vicar? Oh . . .'

'About the service.'

The new vicar was female with a masculine haircut, a stern manner and no discernible sense of humour. 'You'll help me talk to her, won't you?' he said, in momentary panic. 'And Charlie too, of course.'

'We'll need to be finished by seven thirty. I've ordered an Indian and Mr Ravikumar's delivering it specially.'

And after the takeaway, Hugh thought, will come the conversation Lou had made such a point of arranging when she brought his sandwich to Meadowcroft.

Pat Edgecomb and the vicar were in the living room. As he came in, he heard the vicar say, 'Of course when the parents are working all hours, the children never sit down to a decent meal . . .'

'Hello, Hugh.' Pat smiled, getting to her feet.

'Mr Gwynne,' the vicar said in a voice so grave she might already be conducting the funeral.

Pat only wanted two minutes, so they went into the hall.

'I just dropped by to make sure there was nothing more I could do,' she said in her calm, businesslike way. 'I understand from the coroner's office that they're ready to issue the interim death certificate.'

'They left a message, yes.'

'And the other arrangements – they're all in hand? You don't need any help there?'

'I don't think so, no.'

'So there's nothing else I can do at the moment?'

'You know I went to see Steadman yesterday?'

'Yes, he told me.'

'And why?'

'Yes. I only wish we could have found more answers for you, Hugh. I only wish we could have put your mind at rest as to the cause of the fire. But perhaps the insurance investigators will be able to shed more light. Was it today they came?'

'Yes.'

'How did they get on?'

'Oh . . . All right, I think.'

'Did they say anything about possible causes?'

'Nothing in particular, no.'

'But they've taken samples away for analysis, that sort of thing, have they?'

Hugh gave a vague shrug. 'I don't know about that.'

'If it's a detailed investigation I expect that's what they've done. Were they on site long?'

Hugh made a show of searching his memory. 'An hour or so.'

Pat's unassuming gaze held his. 'They sent a team, did they?'

'Not a team exactly, no.'

She waited expectantly for him to elaborate. When he didn't, she said, 'But they'll be letting you know their findings in due course?'

'Hopefully.'

'Well, whatever the outcome I hope it gives you the answers you want.'

They moved towards the door.

'Shall I wait to hear from you then?' Pat asked as she lifted her jacket off the hook. 'I'll be glad to come any time, any time at all. And of course I'm always on the end of the phone.'

'Thanks.'

'Well . . .' Pat held out her hand. 'Good luck. And don't forget – if there's anything I can do . . .'

On the doorstep Hugh said, 'Oh, yes – I was trying to remember the name of your chief inspector. What is it . . . ?' He circled a hand, as if to fire his memory.

'You mean, in CID?'

'I think so, yes.'

'It's DCI Mitchell.'

Hugh shook his head in puzzlement. 'No, that's not it. Perhaps I meant detective superintendent?'

She mentioned another name he didn't recognise.

Hugh said mildly, 'Why did I think it was Montgomery?'

'Oh, there's a DCI Montgomery all right. But he's based at Trinity Road.'

'Nothing to do with you then?'

'No.'

'Ah, I remember now . . .' Hugh said. 'Yes, of course . . . it related to something else altogether.'


The three of them sat down to lamb rogan josh and chicken jalfrezi, with pilau rice, and onion bhajis, which Mr Ravikumar had brought up from the village in his ageing Cortina and delivered with a speech of condolence and a hand pressed against his heart. Indian food had always been a favourite of Hugh's, preferably

washed down with a cold beer, but after his perform-
ance with the wine last night he was glad there was no
alcohol in the house.

'Well,' he said, 'what did you think of the vicar?'

Lou glanced at Charlie before answering, 'A bit
uninspiring.'

'Charlie?'

Charlie made a face. 'I dunno. I mean, a vicar's a
vicar . . .'

'Well, forgetting the vicar bit, what did you think of
her as a person?'

Charlie took his time loading his fork. 'Sort of
creepy.'

'That's what I thought too,' said Hugh.

'Mum wasn't keen on her,' said Lou.

'No, Mum didn't take to her at all. So here's an idea
– how about us having the pastor from the Carstairs
Estate to do the service instead? The Reverend John
Emmanuel? He worked with Mum quite a bit. They
were friends.'

'They did the Denzel Lewis campaign together,' Lou
said.

'He's a great communicator, and because he knew
Mum he'd be able to give a proper eulogy.'

'Sounds good,' Lou said. 'Charlie?'

'Mmm.'

She nudged him into a fuller response.

Looking up from his food Charlie said more posi-
tively, 'Yeah. Has to be an improvement.'

'Shall I go ahead and ask him then?' Hugh said.

Lou nodded.

'I'm sure he'll agree. He was very fond of Mum. He
said some really nice things about her.'

'What was the important thing he wanted to discuss?' Lou asked.

'Oh . . . nothing,' Hugh said, with an obscure sense of having been found out.

They talked about the service, the atmosphere it should have, not too dismal, with a strong element of celebration, and all the time he was aware of Lou waiting for them to finish eating so she could launch the conversation she had been so anxious to set up.

Finally Lou took a sip of water and, setting her glass down, said with an air of rehearsal, 'Dad, Charlie and I want to ask you something.'

'Of course, sweetheart.'

Charlie, who was cleaning the last food off his plate, paused and, with a sideways glance at Lou, took his cue and put his fork down, as if to provide a united front.

'We know you've been doing what you think is best, trying to protect us and all that. But we need to know what's going on. And, well . . . we'd like to hear it from you, not from other people.'

Hugh said, 'Why? What've people been saying?'

'Oh . . . just things.'

'Like what?'

Lou seemed thrown, as if she hadn't foreseen the conversation taking off at quite such a tangent. 'Like . . . well . . .'

'Pat,' Charlie murmured.

'Yes – Pat. Saying she was sorry you weren't happy with the police investigation. And us not knowing what she was talking about.' She shot Charlie a glance as if for corroboration. 'And then . . . well, Ray—'

'*Ray?*'

'Yes, he kept calling us because he couldn't find you. He asked if you were at the police station, like he thought that's where you must be, and of course we didn't know where you were, or why you'd be at the police station.'

'Forget Ray.'

'But not telling us where you're going, Dad. And going mad when we touched things at the house. And all the people this morning – why were they there, Dad? You said you wanted to find out what caused the fire, but . . .' Faltering, Lou turned to Charlie for help.

Charlie looked up and Hugh noticed how tired he looked, how marked were the shadows under his eyes. 'Yeah, what's it matter what caused the fire? I mean . . . nothing's going to bring Mum back.'

Hugh's throat tightened. 'I know it's not going to bring her back. I know . . .'

Lou said, 'But is there something you're not telling us, Dad? Something we should know.'

Hugh sighed, 'I didn't want to worry you unnecessarily. I didn't want to leave you with questions that may never be answered.'

'But, Dad, we're old enough to know,' said Lou, looking immensely young and grown up all at the same time. 'And we'd rather know than not know.'

Charlie's eyes had been back on the table again, but now he was gazing obliquely at Hugh, waiting for an answer.

'You're right,' Hugh said. He took a sip of water to ease the thickness in his throat. 'At the beginning, it wasn't just that I didn't want to worry you – I thought perhaps I was imagining things, looking for something or someone to blame for Mum's death. But then . . . well, I realised I wasn't. Imagining things, I mean.'

In the heightened silence the telephone began to ring but no one thought of answering it.

'There were just too many things that weren't right,' Hugh said with new certainty. 'Things I noticed that first morning when I went round the house with the fire brigade investigator. He said the fire started in the sofa, with a match or a cigarette or a candle. Well, that's just not possible. Mum would never have lit a match or a candle, not when she was working at her desk. And cigarettes . . . She wasn't expecting anyone that evening. She would have told me. And who leaves cigarettes smouldering on a sofa anyway?'

Lou was gazing at him steadily, while Charlie was frowning at the table.

'And then there was an open window,' Hugh went on. 'Mum would never have left a window open, not after she'd gone to bed. One of us always checked the doors and windows last thing. And it wasn't just on the latch, the window, it was properly open. And you know, it takes air – oxygen – to feed a fire. To make it spread.'

Lou was so still she seemed to be holding her breath.

'Then the door to the hall was open. Okay, sometimes we did leave it open. Well, perhaps more often than not. But our bedroom door, that was open too, and we *never* left it open at night. Unless Mum was hoping to catch you when you got home, Charlie.'

Charlie looked alarmed, as if he was being accused of something.

'She didn't say anything about wanting to speak to you when you got in, did she?'

Charlie shook his head.

'Well, that's right. She'd have left a note on the stairs if she'd wanted to talk to you, wouldn't she? She wouldn't have left the door open on the off-chance of hearing you come in. No. So the door was open. And her—' But he broke off, loath to tell them about the clothes and the way they were folded, and how their mother had been naked when she was pulled from the house.

Both children were motionless, waiting for some sort of conclusion.

'There was no sign of a break-in of course,' he said. 'But . . . I think there must have been someone there.'

Lou whispered tentatively, 'Someone who started the fire on purpose?'

'I think so.' Then, more definitely, 'Yes, that's what I think.'

After a short silence Charlie got up to refill the water jug.

Lou was biting hard on her lip, close to tears. 'But Mum wouldn't have known anything, would she?'

'No,' Hugh said. 'Absolutely not.'

'And the men at the house this morning?'

'Independent fire investigators. I hired them to see what they could find.'

'Oh, Dad . . .' Lou reached for some kitchen paper to dry a sudden tear.

'That's what I mean, sweetheart. There may never be any real answers.'

Charlie put the water jug on the table and sat down.

'But who could've done such a thing?' Lou cried.

Hugh gestured mystification. 'There was the break-in of course. And—'

'Break-in?' Lou interrupted, looking startled.

'It was nothing much. Just a broken window and a bit of cash.'

'But when was this? Why didn't you tell me?' She threw a glare at Charlie as if to accuse him of being in on the plot.

'It was about three weeks ago. We didn't want to worry you, not when you were so far away.'

She shook her head despairingly.

'Then, a couple of days before the fire, I got home and saw a hoodie lurking in the garden – '

Lou clapped her hands over her face as if she could hardly bear to hear any more.

' – but he ran off when he saw me. Probably just a local kid fooling about.' The statement sounded unconvincing even to his own ears.

Lou lowered her hands. 'The police are looking for him?'

'No. That's one of the things I complained about.'

'But why on earth not?'

'They've accepted the fire brigade report, that the fire was accidental.'

'But what about everything you told them? The doors, the windows . . . someone being there?'

'Well, that's the thing, you see. They think Mum had a visitor, someone she knew, someone who smoked.'

Lou said plaintively, 'I don't get it.'

'There were two wine glasses on the draining board. To their minds that's as conclusive as it gets.'

Charlie reached for the water jug and pulled it closer to his glass. 'What about fingerprints, stuff like that?' he said.

'Exactly. But they don't want to be bothered with any of that till they have evidence of foul play.'

Lou said, 'What's going to happen, Dad?' She was a child again, seeking reassurance.

'We see what the independent fire investigators come up with.' What would happen if they found nothing hung uncertainly in the air between them. 'And we keep up the pressure on the police.'

There was a silence which Charlie broke hesitantly. 'The, um . . . addresses on Mum's computer? Found them okay.'

'Well done,' Hugh murmured.

'I could look for more stuff . . . if, you know . . . it was any use . . .'

'Sure.' Fearing this had sounded half-hearted, Hugh added an encouraging smile. 'Anything to do with Denzel Lewis and the campaign would be really good. His family want to know.'

'Denzel Lewis. Yeah, sure.'

No one could think of anything more to say. They cleared the plates in silence, then Lou came to Hugh for a hug. Laying her head against his chest she said in a voice still muffled by tears, 'Thanks for telling us, Dad. It's better to know.'

He leant his cheek against her raven hair. 'I'm sorry, my darling. I'm so sorry.'

For an hour they watched a TV game show together, then Charlie disappeared to work on his computer, Lou to have a bath, while Hugh fell asleep in front of a police drama, to be woken by his mobile phone. Digging it out of his pocket, he stared at the name on the display for a long time before deciding to answer.

'Hi, Tom.'

'How're you doing?'

'Okay.'

'Yeah?'

'Yeah.'

'Tough day?'

'Yeah.'

'What did you do?'

Hugh thought, Oh, just told my children their mother was probably the victim of arson. Just ensured they'd never get to have another moment's peace. 'It was just stuff, you know. Formalities.'

'Feeling stressed?'

There was no answer to that. 'You know . . .'

'You have to work on your breathing. Take it real slow. Count the breath in and out.'

'Sure.'

'I mean it. When you get your breathing right, then you can get through the shit better.'

'I'll work on it.'

'Had a drink?'

'What? No.'

'That's good. Very good,' came the relentless voice. 'Support system up and running?'

'I've got the kids. That's all I need.'

'One lucky guy.'

'And you, Tom? How're you doing?'

'Hey. Forget about me. This is about getting you through the night.'

'Thanks,' Hugh said with a sinking heart.

'Don't forget, Hugh – she felt no pain.'

Hugh wasn't sure why it seemed so important to do

it just then, but immediately he had rung off he went into his makeshift office in the dining room and, taking Lizzie's charred handbag out of its cardboard box, opening it very carefully, looked through the contents.

# EIGHT

Hugh sat in a corner of the open-sided lounge where he could watch the flow of people strolling through from the foyer. Most were making for the lifts at the back of the hotel but now and again someone came into the lounge itself: a willowy woman with a briefcase, two men talking with forced jollity, a Japanese tourist drifting aimlessly. Hugh had two opposing visions of what Montgomery would look like, one a grey-haired version of DI Steadman, lean and incisive, the other a fleshy pasty-faced figure gone to seed after too much desk-work. Both guesses were wide of the mark. The man who headed unerringly across the room to meet Hugh was well-built rather than overweight, with keen eyes, coarse pink skin, a broad nose, and ginger-grey hair combed over a bald crown from a low side-parting. The guesswork had anyway been unnecessary as Hugh realised he had seen him before.

Montgomery shook his hand. 'Extremely sorry to hear about Mrs Gwynne. My condolences to you and your family.'

'Thanks.'

Unbuttoning his jacket Montgomery sank into the adjacent chair and crossed his legs as if to set a relaxed tone. 'Campaigning groups aren't always the easiest of people. Tend to get a touch confrontational. But Mrs Gwynne was always most pleasant and professional to deal with. We didn't see eye to eye on the merits of the Free Denzel Lewis campaign of course but it was never personal. She was a most delightful lady.'

'You met regularly?'

'Oh no,' Montgomery said, as if such a thing had never been on the cards. 'No, it must've been three times in the last two years. Ah . . .' Spotting a waiter he lifted a hand and kept it up until the waiter took notice. 'Would you like a coffee, Mr Gwynne?'

When they had ordered, Montgomery remarked, 'Don't often get decent coffee in my line of work.'

Was this why the chief inspector had suggested meeting in a four-star hotel, Hugh wondered: for the quality of the coffee? Or was it out of sensitivity to Hugh's widowed status, a place away from the clamour and interruptions of the police station? Or was it a desire to keep their meeting away from curious eyes, an extension of the secrecy he'd tried to impose on Ellis?

Montgomery said, 'DI Steadman and his team completed their investigations, have they?'

Hugh took a moment to frame his answer. 'They think they have.'

If this reply raised any questions in Montgomery's mind he made no comment. 'And the fire brigade have made their report as to the cause?'

Hugh was tired, he had slept even worse than usual, it was all he could do not to snap, *You bloody know they have, you talked to Ellis.* Instead he selected a level tone to say, 'I believe so, yes.'

'And it was a tragic accident?' The conjunction of

'tragic' and 'accident' was delivered matter-of-factly, like 'serious incident' or 'immediate response'.

'That's what they're saying.'

Montgomery creased up his eyes in a show of sympathy.

Hugh wasn't sure what he took most exception to, the facile compassion, the ridiculous strands of hair pasted over Montgomery's shiny pate, or the way he pretended ignorance of the fire report.

With the air of having completed the preliminaries, Montgomery ventured, 'So . . . what can I do for you, Mr Gwynne? I wasn't quite clear when you called.'

Nor was I, thought Hugh, but I'm much, much clearer now. Proceed with caution.

'I've come on behalf of the Lewis family,' he said.

'Oh? In a legal capacity?'

'No. Just helping out.'

'Ah.'

'It was about the meeting you had with my wife last . . . Tuesday, was it?'

'Yes. Tuesday morning.'

'The Lewises wanted to know what the outcome was.'

Montgomery's eyebrows rose slightly. 'They know why she came to see me?'

'Something to do with witness protection, I believe.'

'Yes . . . Yes, that's right. Mrs Gwynne wanted to know how the scheme worked, whether it would be available in the event of a new witness coming forward. I wasn't able to offer much hope.' A semblance of regret passed over Montgomery's pink face. 'Once there's been a successful conviction, well . . . it takes a lot to reopen a closed case.'

'She must have realised that, surely?'

'She did, yes. But she wanted to know if there was any way round it.'

'And was there? Is there?'

'I told her it would take strong evidence.'

'How strong?'

Montgomery had a think about that. 'A sworn statement, a reliable witness prepared to stand up in court and swear to dates and times. Something along those lines.'

Feeling a duty to argue Lizzie's corner, Hugh said, 'That's Catch-22, surely? You're not prepared to offer protection until you get the statement, but no witness in their right mind is going to be daft enough to make a statement without a guarantee of protection.'

Montgomery conceded with a dip of his head. 'Put like that . . .'

'Very good of you though.'

'How's that?'

'To give time to people who're out to prove you got it wrong.'

'If I've learnt anything in my thirty years in the force, Mr Gwynne, it's never to close the door on people.'

'Even when they're trying to undo all your good work.'

Montgomery gave a humourless smile. 'Even then.' The coffee arrived and he sat forward to select a sachet of sweetener.

'My wife certainly believed in the campaign.'

'Yes.'

'But you don't think there's anything in it?'

'My team put Denzel Lewis away on solid evidence, Mr Gwynne.'

It would have been surprising if he'd said anything else, yet there was no hint of conceit or triumph in his manner. The glib sympathy had given way to an open accommodating manner. He seemed without malice or vanity. Yet he couldn't have reached the rank of chief inspector without a sliver of steel in his spine, the same steel that was making him conceal his knowledge of the fire report.

'Solid evidence isn't necessarily infallible evidence,' Hugh pointed out.

'I would never suggest that it was. But it's sufficient for the justice system. And as you're aware, Mr Gwynne, that's all we do at the end of the day, feed the facts into the justice system.'

'Remind me, what *was* the evidence exactly?' Hugh asked, not because he wanted to hear it again but because he wanted time to think.

Montgomery gave him an appraising look, as if unsure of the spirit in which this request had been made.

'I've always heard it from the other side,' Hugh explained.

'Of course.' Montgomery made a business of stirring his coffee while he assembled his facts. 'Well, for some months before the killing Lewis and his gang had been intimidating Jason Jackson for no other reason than Jason was a good, hard-working, clean-living kid who was an easy target. On the night of the murder Jason was walking home from basketball practice at the local sports centre. At approximately nine thirty he was stabbed three times and dragged into a dark alley. None of the wounds was immediately fatal, but left without medical attention he bled to death, probably within the space of an hour. When apprehended Lewis was unable to provide an alibi and his Nike jacket was found to have bloodstains on the right cuff which DNA tests showed to be a one-in-fifty-million match for that of Jason Jackson. Then of course Lewis had two previous convictions for violence, one of them for ABH with a knife.'

'The family say the jacket was planted.'

'That's what they maintained, yes.'

'But it wasn't likely?'

'My team didn't think so. Nor did the jury.'

'And wasn't Denzel Lewis meant to have been getting his act together? To have got a job and be going straight?'

'That's what his defence said, yes.'

'But there was no doubt as to his guilt?'

'The verdict was unanimous.'

'So you got it right, Chief Inspector?'

'We sincerely believed so.' Montgomery sipped his espresso and replaced the cup carefully on the saucer. 'But if any evidence were to come to light that was to suggest otherwise then we'd be anxious to hear about it, Mr Gwynne. Most anxious.'

'But not so anxious that you're prepared to offer witness protection?'

'Not in the first instance, no. But we'd be prepared to provide a halfway house, something reasonably secure.'

This was beginning to sound like a negotiation, though quite what Montgomery was hoping to achieve

Hugh wasn't sure. 'Well . . . I'll let the Lewises know. In case anyone comes forward.'

Montgomery gave him an odd, indecisive look. 'Your wife didn't mention anything about having found a witness already?'

'No. Why?'

'Just an impression I got, that's all.'

'She said nothing about it to me.'

Montgomery eyed him thoughtfully. 'Well, if you come across anything perhaps you'd let me know?'

I think not, Hugh decided with a bump of antagonism. If Lizzie wasn't prepared to trust you, then I'm certainly not going to take the risk. 'We've seen each other before,' he said abruptly. 'In the entrance to Staple Hill police station on Monday.'

Montgomery said, 'That's right.'

'I'd been to see Steadman.'

'Yes.' His tone was neutral.

'Did he tell you why I'd come?'

'He made a brief mention, yes.'

'He told you I wasn't happy with the investigation into my wife's death? That I'd made an official complaint?'

Montgomery gave a short nod.

'Did he tell you why I wasn't satisfied?'

A hesitation, which was more noticeable for being Montgomery's first. 'Not in any detail, no.'

'No?' Hugh echoed in open surprise. 'Though presumably you told him you knew my wife?'

'It wasn't my patch, Mr Gwynne. It wasn't my case. And DI Steadman was having a busy day.'

'He told you the fire investigators were sticking to their original findings?'

'He mentioned something like that, yes.'

'Did he tell you he was intending to close the case?'

'Not in so many words, no.'

'Well, he has. But for what it's worth I believe my wife was killed unlawfully and I intend to get the case reopened.'

Montgomery absorbed this solemnly. 'May I ask on what basis?'

'There was an intruder.'

'I see.'

'An arsonist. Not necessarily someone who did it often, but someone who'd done his homework very carefully.'

'You have evidence for this, Mr Gwynne?'

'I do indeed.'

'Is DI Steadman aware of it?'

'Some of it.'

'Well, if you have any more evidence, Mr Gwynne, then I urge you to take it to DI Steadman without delay. Arson is an extremely serious offence.'

Rankled by Montgomery's lack of curiosity, Hugh felt driven to say, 'And the timing wasn't random either, the arsonist was intent on harming my wife.'

Montgomery pulled his head back in surprise. 'You've got evidence for this?'

'Yes.'

'What kind of evidence?'

'I'm building up a dossier.'

Montgomery gazed at him uncertainly. 'In that case I can only repeat, you must take it to DI Steadman so he can start making the appropriate enquiries.'

Hugh said pointedly, 'Not something that would be of interest to you then, Chief Inspector?'

'I wish I could be of help, Mr Gwynne, but as I explained—'

'Not your patch.'

'That's right.'

Hugh's coffee wasn't that good. He didn't wait to finish it.


He got back to an empty house. Lou and Charlie were in town shopping. The answering machine was blinking frenetically as if to admonish him for the numerous calls he'd failed to return the previous day. There had been a message from Lizzie's mother, anxious to know the date of the funeral but also longing to be asked to come and stay, and another from Lizzie's twice-divorced sister Becky, whose boyfriends got more foreign and youthful by the year, and whose bossy managerial nature had extended to making lengthy suggestions for the funeral service. A cousin and several friends had offered to help in any way they could. They all deserved a proper response, but he didn't feel capable of speaking to them now. Later perhaps, with a warming drink inside him.

He picked up the mail, diverted from Meadowcroft, and shuffled through it as he made his way to the dining room. The ringing of his mobile had him reaching into his pocket with such haste that he dropped half the letters over the floor. But it wasn't Slater, it was Tom Deacon again: the fourth time that morning. Tom had left no message the first three times so, deciding it couldn't be urgent, Hugh let the phone ring till the voicemail kicked in.

Collecting the mail from the floor he spotted an

envelope marked HM Coroner and ripped it open, hoping for the full post-mortem report, getting instead a notification that the inquest would be formally opened on Monday and immediately adjourned until further notice.

He had arranged his papers over the far end of the polished oak table, but now he slid the stacks of funeral plans, letters of condolence, insurance and legal documents to one side and, sitting down, took a pad and pen and started to make a list. He headed it *Facts*, though a more accurate title might have been *Evidence of Crime*. He wrote down everything he had gone through with Slater, from the impossibility of a naked flame finding its way onto the sofa to the pair of shoes sitting under the button-back chair. Leaving enough space at the bottom for the scientific findings, he briefly considered calling Slater to ask how they were coming along. But Slater had said he would phone the moment he had anything to report and he wasn't the sort of man to delay.

On the next sheet of paper he started a second list which he headed *Facts Open to Interpretation*. By its very nature this list took more thought. He began with *No signs of breaking and entering – L let him into house?* Realising he needed to break this down further he started again, making *No signs of breaking and entering* a subheading and listing the possible explanations below. At first he managed only two. *L invited him in* and *He tricked/barged his way in*. After a while he added a third: *He sneaked in through an open window/door*. Once again he realised he was setting it out all wrong and began a third draft with more space between the propositions to allow for elaboration. Under *L invited him in*, he listed: *Friend of L's, Friend of family, Neighbour, Trusted acquaintance*. He had an image of Lizzie opening the door to the visitor and welcoming him inside. After that, his imagination stalled. He could think of no reason why anyone they knew should want to harm her. Nevertheless he added a column down the right-hand side headed *Motive?* and, leaving it blank, moved on.

Trying to think of people who might have tricked or barged their way into the house was even less satisfactory because the possibilities were almost limitless. In the end he split the options into two: a nutter who'd chosen the house at random, and someone who'd targeted it specifically; a distinction which, though marginally tidier, was hardly more productive.

Coming to the last proposition, an intruder who might have sneaked his way into the house, he deleted 'door' as a possible means of entry on the grounds that Lizzie wouldn't have left either front or back door unlocked on a dark autumn evening. The kitchen window was a brief candidate – Lizzie sometimes opened it for a few minutes when she was cooking something hot and steamy – but alone for the evening she wouldn't have cooked anything elaborate, an omelette or stir-fry at the most, neither of them high on the hot-and-steamy scale. Which left an upstairs window. This, however, would have required a ladder or the talents of a cat burglar who, having gained access, decided not to steal anything and to commit arson instead. Both these alternatives seemed so unpromising that he left the space blank and moved on.

*Facts Open to Interpretation.* Subheading the second . . .
There was one obvious candidate, but something

made him hesitate to put it down quite yet, as if there was another point that should come first. To jog his mind he traced Lizzie and the visitor from the door to the living room but, when the idea still refused to form, he went for the obvious contender after all.

Subheading the second: *The two wine glasses.*

Proposition the first: *L drank a glass of white wine then a glass of red.* He had argued this idea fiercely in reaction to Steadman's pathetically predictable assumption that two glasses was evidence of a secret lover. Yet in the cold light of reason, free of the need to defend Lizzie, he considered the chances of her drinking two different wines when on her own for the evening were fairly unlikely.

Proposition the second, therefore, that Lizzie, of her own free will, in the name of hospitality, poured a glass of wine for her visitor.

He saw her in the kitchen, uncorking the wine, taking the glasses from the cupboard, carrying them through to the living room.

To whom? Friend or foe? Both, obviously. Didn't you realise, Lizzie? With your intuitive nature, didn't you see?

*Ah, easy to say that now*, she told him crossly. *You have the benefit of hindsight. But I sensed nothing in the way of danger. Why should I?*

You're right, he thought, why should you?

*Conclusion: The visitor was a friend.* Immediately spotting his error he crossed out 'Conclusion' and made it into a proposition. Underneath, he added a second: *Acquaintance on business.* This was quickly followed by a third: *Friend/acquaintance of another member of the family.* By which he supposed he meant a friend of

Charlie's, since Lou had been abroad and he himself in London. He pictured a mentally unbalanced young man, high on drugs, shaven-headed and saturnine in the Elk mould, who had come to beg money off Charlie. With Charlie absent, he had demanded money from Lizzie instead, and gone mad when she refused, attacking her—

Except that, according to the post-mortem findings relayed to him over the phone by the coroner's office, she had died of smoke inhalation, no more no less. No marks, no bruises, no signs of a struggle. And Lizzie would hardly have offered a glass of wine to a kid high on drugs, someone she barely knew if she knew him at all. Whenever Charlie brought a friend round, the most they ever got offered was beer.

Nevertheless he wrote *Friend of Charlie's?* before moving on.

Subheading the third: *Wine glasses placed on draining board, not in dishwasher.*

There was only one possible answer to this, and he wrote fiercely, digging the point of the pen into the paper: *Glasses placed on draining board by intruder.* Having been washed to eradicate DNA and fingerprints, naturally. Organised intruder, then? Or panic-struck intruder trying to cover his tracks? Clever anyway. Or did he mean cunning? Or maybe neither, maybe he was just an assiduous student of crime dramas.

Stupid or clever, I'll get you yet, he thought with a shudder of savage excitement. I'll get you if it's the last thing I do.

Subheading the fourth: *L naked, clothes folded strangely.*

His mind jumped to the rumpled bed. Not ready to go there, he tried to reject the vision, but his imagination had other ideas, and, giving in, he crossed out what he'd just written and substituted under subheading the fourth: *Bed rumpled*. The options were simple. The firemen had simply rumpled the bed while searching for a second victim. Lizzie had been raped. Raped while unconscious. Raped while conscious. Or entertaining a lover.

He considered the last possibility with as much detachment as he could muster. Spur-of-the-moment lover. Hardly. Not Lizzie's style. Long-term lover. Well, if so, the arrangements had been unbelievably discreet. He remembered Lizzie remarking about an adulterous couple, 'How did they ever find the *time*? That's what I can never work out.' Excellent point, Lizzie. When would you ever have found the time? Quite apart from the inclination, of course, which unless their life together had been a complete fantasy would have been unthinkable. They had trusted each other. They had never had secrets.

He corrected himself with a pang of bewilderment: until now. He clambered to his feet and went to the window to stare out at the leaf-strewn grass. Why didn't you tell me about the witness, Lizzie? Surely you trusted me to keep a secret like that? Or had you given your word to tell absolutely no one, not even me? Or – he had the sense of grasping at straws – was there some conflict of interest involved, something that touched on my work?

Finally he took refuge in what he had chosen to believe last night – that she hadn't wanted to burden him, that she'd known he would worry and, once worried, would try to talk her out of getting more deeply involved. She had been determined to pursue this first chance of fresh evidence, and determination was no sin, even if it resulted in a little subterfuge. The more he thought about it, the more certain he became that this must be the answer, and he returned to the table with a sense that his past had been restored.

Conclusion: no lover.

Sorry for even considering it, he told her, but you know I must unturn every stone. It was one of those phrases that had become part of the family's vocabulary. Whatever was mislaid – passport, book, iPod, keys – the owner was required to unturn every stone in search of it. Gone now, he thought, the sharing of private language, cryptic jokes, our shorthand, our past.

With new anger he scrawled *Rape*.

The word stared up at him, charged with a thousand brutal images. He added in his neatest handwriting: *Conscious? Drugged? Restrained by . . . ?*

He gazed at this for several moments before taking a fresh sheet of paper and starting another list headed *Action Points*, under which he wrote:

*1) DNA*

*2) Post-mortem*

The house phone began to ring. He waited for the answering machine to pick up before returning to the subject of the rumpled bed and finding he had nothing more to add.

*L naked, clothes folded strangely* was now subheading the fifth.

Here at least was one firm conclusion: that at some point the intruder had been in the bedroom. But if not to rape, then why? And what possible motive could he have had for folding her clothes? From the knot of competing ideas that had been clogging his mind for days a half-glimpsed truth finally emerged into the light; he realised it was the clothes, not the rumpled bed or Lizzie's nakedness, that was the key. Cautiously at first, then with more confidence, he wrote: *He wanted to make it look as though she'd gone to bed of her own accord.* He examined the statement for flaws. It had to be right; the only other possibility was sheer insanity, a nutter with a fetish for tidiness. But there was too much organisation, too much guile in the intruder's actions for that. Failing to put Lizzie in her customary nightdress had merely been a bad guess on his part.

Conclusion: Lizzie did not go to bed of her own accord. Ergo, either she was forced to get into bed or she was placed in bed while unconscious or otherwise immobilised. But if you forced someone to get into bed, how did you make them stay there while you went downstairs, started a fire and left the house? You didn't, was the answer. You couldn't. What victim, realising the house was on fire, wouldn't try to get out even at the risk of being attacked? He moved on to the last alternative with a mixture of relief and dread, relief that she might already have been unconscious, dread that she might have been 'otherwise immobilised', by which he supposed he meant tied up. But the tied-up scenario fell at the same hurdle as the force argument. If she had been tied up only to be released before the fire started, what would have prevented her from trying to escape? Particularly when the smoke alarm was screaming its head off.

She must have been unconscious. But not, according to the post-mortem, drugged with anything obvious.

A date-rape drug then. What was it called? Rohyp-something. Or was it GHB?

Something that left no trace, anyway. Something that could be slipped into a glass of wine.

Sorry it took me so long, he told her. Sorry. But I'm there now.

The urge to reach for the phone and start making calls was very strong, but he resisted it and went back to the window to gaze out at the spiralling leaves while he waited for his thoughts to settle. Even when he was certain what he needed to do, he delayed a little longer, making some coffee, reading his notes again, going over everything a second time, making a list.

Finally he began. His first call was to Isabel to ask if she could find the name and availability of a good forensic pathologist, his next to the coroner's office to notify them that he wanted to apply for an independent post-mortem and to fix a time to go in and sign the necessary paperwork. Then he called Slater to ask if there was a way of salvaging damaged papers and documents, but Slater wasn't answering and he had to settle for leaving a message. Lastly he called Ray and asked him to stand by on the legal side.

'Glad to help,' Ray cried immediately. 'God, *any* time. You don't even have to ask! But can you give me an idea of what you might want me to do?'

'Probably to lodge information with the police and the coroner.'

'I see,' he said in a puzzled tone. 'Can I ask what sort of information?'

'I'll let you know.'

'Right. Right.' A pause, while Ray struggled to

contain his curiosity. 'My imagination's going crazy, Hugh. Can you give me some idea . . . ?'

'Proof that Lizzie was killed unlawfully.'

There was a taut silence, then he exhaled sharply. 'God, Hugh, I don't know what to say. God, that's *terrible.*'

'But not for public consumption. Okay? Not till I say so.'

'No, no. But are you absolutely *sure* about this, Hugh?'

'Absolutely sure.'

'You mean it was *arson?*'

'At the least, yes.'

'*Christ,* Hugh, what are you saying? I don't even want to think what you're saying.'

'The arsonist meant to get Lizzie.'

'*What?* But why would anyone want to get *Lizzie,* for Christ's sake? Lovely, *lovely* Lizzie. *Why?*'

Hugh was reminded of a line his old law tutor Dewey had liked to quote: *To ask the hard question is simple – to ask the right question is far more difficult.*

'Lovely, *lovely* Lizzie. *Why?*' Ray repeated emotionally.

'I don't know.'

'What about the police, Hugh? I hope they're bloody moving on this.'

'Not yet.'

'Why the hell not?'

'They didn't see the point.'

'You mean they're *ignoring* the fact that it's arson?'

'They've refused to mount a proper forensic investigation into the fire, so I've had to hire my own people.'

'Your own fire experts?'

'Yeah.'

'And it's them who've found evidence of arson?'

'I'm waiting for confirmation.'

A pause. 'Right.'

'And I'm applying for an independent post-mortem as well.'

'I see.' Ray's tone had become thoughtful. 'When's that going to happen?'

'Don't know yet.'

Another pause. 'Well . . . Call me as soon as you need anything done, won't you? I'll get straight onto it.'

'And Ray? Not a word to anyone.'

Ringing off, Hugh looked at what he had written on his pad: *The hardest question.*


It took the best part of an hour to search Meadowcroft, find what he could, and transport it back to the rented house. Sliding the funeral plans, letters of condolence, insurance and legal documents even further down the dining table, he arranged his haul in a semicircle. Phone bills and correspondence straight ahead, Lizzie's note-books in date order to the right, household papers to the left. Many of the papers were water- or smoke-damaged. Some were scorched, while others from the desktop and pigeonholes were plain burnt. He also fetched Lizzie's handbag. He had looked inside it before, but now he gingerly removed the contents. Mobile phone. Black leather purse, one side burnt and brittle, the rest damp. Yield: thirty-odd pounds and a full complement of credit cards. Lipstick, compact, hairbrush, comb. Headache tablets. Indigestion tablets.

Pens, lots of them. Sunglasses. Reading glasses. Receipts which fell apart in his hands. Scraps of what might have been shopping lists. No Filofax. And no sign of it at Meadowcroft either.

He tried the mobile phone but it was dead. He connected it to a charger and waited a few minutes before trying it again, but there was still nothing. He was starting on the notebooks when the front door sounded and Lou's voice called hello. He called back and heard her and Charlie talking as they went into the kitchen. There was the slam of cupboards and the duller thud of the fridge door while they unloaded the shopping, then Lou came through.

'Hi, Dad.'

'Hi, darling,' he said, glancing up briefly. 'You have enough money for the shopping?'

When she didn't answer, he looked round to find her gazing at the table.

'What's happening, Dad?'

'I'm going through as much stuff as I can. See what's here.'

'What are you looking for?'

'Not too sure at the moment. Anything. Everything.'

She peered at a sodden notebook. 'Can I help?'

'No.' Realising how dismissive this had sounded, he threw her a pale smile. 'What I meant was it's a bit of a one-man job at this stage. Later, when it comes to prising pages apart, then I'll be glad of some of your patience. Where's Charlie?'

'Making a sandwich.'

'Well, when he's finished – no, no,' he fretted, getting up and heading for the door. 'No, let's talk now.'

Charlie was hunched over the kitchen table, biting

into a thick sandwich, the contents bulging out from the sides. His eyes flicked up to Hugh then his sister, then down to the table again. Lou stood behind Charlie, leaning back against the central island, while Hugh stationed himself in the middle of the room. 'Listen, guys,' he began, 'I'm sorry but we're going to have to delay the funeral. We probably won't be able to have it till the end of next week, maybe the beginning of the week after. I know it's not ideal. I know it means everything's in limbo. But there's no way round it.'

'But why, Dad?' Lou asked unhappily.

'Some things are taking longer than we thought.'

Charlie abandoned his sandwich to his plate and sat back, shoulders hunched, arms folded.

'But you said—' Lou paused in confusion. 'Yesterday you said there was nothing to stop the funeral going ahead.'

'There wasn't *then*. But we've had to put everything on hold, you see.' Knowing he couldn't put it off any longer, Hugh braced himself to say, 'What's happened is that we're having to organise a second post-mortem. Using an independent pathologist. And that'll take time, I'm afraid.'

'Why?' Lou breathed.

'To make sure they got it right.'

'I don't understand.'

'To make sure they didn't miss anything. On the cause of death.'

Lou flung a look at Charlie, as if for support, but he was staring intently at the table. 'Who's decided all this? Who's this *we*?'

'Well . . . when I said *we* I really meant *me* on behalf of *us*.'

Lou stared at him reproachfully, her eyes filling. 'Why didn't you ask us, Dad?'

'It's only just happened, Lou. This morning. And I *am* asking you. I'm asking you now.'

'What's only just happened?'

What a mess he was making of this. Taking a steadying breath, he said, 'What's happened is I've reviewed everything we know, all the facts, everything from the fire investigators, and as a result . . . well, I've worked out that Mum must have been unconscious before the fire started. It's the only explanation for all the things that weren't right in the house. For how she was found. For – well, everything. So the point is, if she was unconscious, there must have been a reason, something they may have missed. A bruise, something in her blood – whatever.'

'But, Dad, if there'd been anything to find, they'd have found it already,' Lou argued.

'You say that, but pathologists vary a hell of a lot, just like doctors. There was a report only the other day saying that post-mortems are often seriously sub-standard.'

'What report?'

'Can't remember. It was in the paper somewhere.'

Lou closed her eyes despairingly. 'Oh, Dad . . .'

'There's no such thing as infallibility, Lou. You should know that better than anyone. Apparently a lot of these pathologists work on their own, completely unsupervised. They get sloppy over the years.'

Lou dropped her head.

'It's the only way to find out what happened, Lou. Don't you want us to find out what happened?'

Lou said in a muffled voice, 'Of course I do.'

'So . . .' Hugh made a gesture of appeal towards Charlie, who gave him a depressed glance. 'And if it tells us nothing new, then at least we'll know there was nothing new to find. We won't spend the next twenty years wondering.'

Lou pressed a hand to her eyes and gave a ragged gasp. Hugh reached out to comfort her but she gave a sharp shake of her head and made for the door. 'I can't bear it, that's all,' she choked. 'I can't bear it!'

'Lou—'

But she was gone. They heard her run upstairs and into her room.

Hugh stood irresolutely, then sank into the chair beside Charlie. 'God.'

Charlie murmured, 'She'll be okay, Dad. She's just . . .' He gave a slow shrug, a forward movement of the shoulders, a downward bow of the mouth. 'You know . . . stressed out about the funeral . . . moving all the stuff she's fixed up.'

'I just wish . . .' But Hugh wasn't sure what he wished just then, except for an end to shocks and surprises, both received and inflicted.

Charlie said, 'It's got to happen, this thing?'

'Yes, it does, Charlie.'

A sharp shrug this time. 'Well, then . . . Don't beat yourself up about it.'

'Perhaps I should go up and talk to her.'

'Leave it a while, Dad. She'll be okay.'

'Yeah?' Bowing his head, Hugh gave his eyes a harsh rub and emerged blinking.

'I got some stuff off Mum's computer last night,' Charlie offered tentatively, as if to test the temperature of the conversational water.

'Any good?'

'Um . . . Maybe. I dunno. She worked on three files that night. Modified them anyway. It was all Citizens Advice stuff.'

'You've got the names of the files?'

'Sure. You want them now?'

Hugh gestured him to stay where he was. 'No, no. Eat your sandwich. You need to eat. Can you get into the files?'

'Sure.'

'There wasn't a password?'

'I've always had Mum's password. I installed half her software.'

'Of course.'

'Um . . . And I should be able to see what she added to the files, if that's any use.'

Hugh thought about that. 'I don't know. It might be.'

'Well, it's no big deal to print them both off. Like, the modified file and the original.'

'Thanks.'

'Um . . . And it looks like she did her last work about nine forty. That's when she saved the last file anyway. Nine forty-one, I think it was.'

'You can tell all that?'

Charlie gave his slow shrug. 'Sure. It's basic stuff.'

'Not to me it isn't.'

Nine forty-one. Hugh imagined her shutting down the computer. Then what? A cup of tea? Some reading until the doorbell interrupted her? He had imagined the scene so many times that it ran like a film in his mind's eye, the way she lifted her head in surprise, marked her page and put her book down before walking across the hall to open the door. Only the person or persons at the door remained unclear. Sometimes Hugh saw the hoodie, sometimes two yobs out to thieve and rob, sometimes a figure hiding behind a smile.

Charlie frowned at his sandwich. 'Um . . . and then the clock stopped at twenty-three forty-seven.'

'The clock?'

'In the computer.'

Hugh sat up a little. 'Because of the fire, you mean?'

'Had to be. There was a system failure logged at the same time.'

'Twenty-three forty-seven?'

'Yeah.'

How long before this had the fire started? Hugh wondered. Five, ten, fifteen minutes?

'For a system failure to register it means the computer must've been on standby,' Charlie added, watching Hugh's face to make sure he'd got the point.

But Hugh was already there. 'And she hated things to be left on standby.'

'She was always on at me about it.'

The film sequence which had started with Lizzie sitting on the sofa reading a book faded in Hugh's mind. He repositioned her at her desk, working on her computer, conscientiously saving the open file when the doorbell rang, intending to return to work when she'd answered it.

'Well done, Charlie,' Hugh said.

Charlie had propped his head on one hand, a wave of golden hair obscuring his eyes. Now he glanced up, embarrassed but not displeased, and gave a jerky, diffident smile. He had never seemed so youthful, so flawless, with his hazel eyes, clear skin, sweeping eye-brows, the extraordinarily thick hair. Only his colour was unnaturally pale, almost anaemic.

'Go on – eat your lunch.'

Needing no further encouragement, Charlie bit deep into his sandwich, while Hugh attempted to put some order in this new sequence of saved files and doorbells and wine glasses. Nine forty until roughly eleven forty. Two hours.

'Could she have been working on a file later than nine forty? One she never got round to saving?'

Charlie struggled to swallow his mouthful. 'Could've.'

'It wouldn't have shown in the system failure record or whatever it was?'

Charlie shook his head.

Hugh got up and stood in front of the kettle, not sure what he wanted, coffee, food or nothing at all. In the end he cut a slab of bread, mashed a banana over the top, added a skim of jam, and folded it over into a makeshift baguette.

Back at the table, he wondered if he should take the opportunity offered by this computer-forged harmony to ask Charlie how he was doing on the drug recovery front. The timing was never easy. Charlie was so sure, so focused when he talked about computers, and so unknowable, so touchy when it came to the rest of his life. The recovery programme was meant to be about honesty and communication, yet he seemed to entrust his thoughts to no one but a few fellow travellers in drug recovery and, occasionally, Lou.

'Going to another meeting tonight?' he asked lightly.

Charlie's mouth was full. He nodded, but his eyes held a wary light.

'With Elk?'

Another nod.

'And your therapist? You're seeing him soon?'

'Yeah.'

'And you're doing all right, Charlie? You're okay?'

It was like pressing a button, all the old defensiveness came shooting back. Charlie's gaze hardened. His expression seemed to shout *Don't start!*

'Listen, when I ask about the meetings, it's not because I'm checking up on you or anything like that,' Hugh argued levelly. 'It's because I'm right behind you, and I want you to know it. Okay? Nothing else.'

Charlie nodded.

'It's the same when I ask how you're doing. It's not a roundabout way of asking how the recovery programme's going. Well, it's *partly* that, I suppose – it's bound to be. But mainly it's to know you're all right, Charlie. That's all. Just like I need to know Lou's all right.' When Charlie didn't immediately respond, he prompted, 'You understand?'

Charlie breathed, 'Yeah.'

'I know you'd rather talk to your mates. I know you think no one else understands. But Mum and I, we always tried our best to understand, Charlie, we really did. And—'

'I know that, Dad!' Charlie protested on a rising note. 'I *know*.'

'And I'm going to go on doing my best. But it's hard when you don't give me any sort of clue. When I don't know what's going on under the surface.'

'Dad, it's just . . . like, I don't wanna offload any of my stuff onto you. Not when you're stressed out already.'

'I'd be less stressed if I knew you were okay.'

'I'm okay,' Charlie declared unconvincingly.

'There's nothing you want to talk about?'

Charlie looked uncertain and tormented by turns. 'Not right now, Dad.'

'No time like the present.'

'It's just . . . I'm sort of, you know, busy with computer stuff . . .'

'I want us to be able to talk, Charlie.'

Charlie hesitated, as if he might yet be persuaded, when the ringing of Hugh's phone sounded through the open door from the dining room. Thinking it might be Slater, it was all Hugh could do not to rush out and answer it. With an effort he brought his attention back to Charlie, but it was too late, the moment had passed, Hugh could read it in his face.

'When you get back from your meeting then?' he suggested.

'I was going to hang out with Elk. Go to a movie or something.'

'Tomorrow then?'

Charlie had a trapped look. 'Okay.'

'Maybe we'll go for a walk.' But remembering the failure of their last open-air conversation Hugh cancelled the suggestion with a gesture. 'No, we'll grab a coffee and escape the phone, shall we?'

'Okay.'

Hugh gripped his arm encouragingly before getting up. At the door he paused long enough to ask, 'Oh, and would you look at Mum's mobile phone? I think it's a goner, but could you check it out?'

'Sure.'

'It's in here,' he called as he hurried into the dining room.

He reached eagerly for his phone but there was no message from Slater, no message from anyone, just another missed call from Tom Deacon. He couldn't face calling back. He wasn't ready for more amateur therapy, or any other sort of therapy, come to that. He didn't want to be told what he was supposed to be thinking or feeling, or what stage of the grieving process he'd reached. Anger suited him fine; it gave him a sense of direction. He certainly didn't want Tom telling him that he needed to work through it. It seemed to Hugh that there was an essential fraud in the idea that grief was treatable, that by disgorging your most precious and painful thoughts your so-called condition would somehow improve. The idea stemmed from the modern conviction that everything should be fixable; and if it wasn't, you found someone to sue. Well, there was never going to be a remedy for death and grief, that was for sure. But if you were lucky there was justice and, if you were luckier still, retribution, and the prospect of attaining them was therapy enough for him.

It was different for Charlie. He relied on therapy to stay clean, though Hugh sometimes wondered, probably unfairly, if for an addictive personality like Charlie therapy wasn't just another form of addiction. Certainly no therapist was going to encourage Charlie to break free, not while Daddy was paying the bills. The one thing Hugh didn't understand was how the constant revisiting of weaknesses and insecurities was meant to do anything for Charlie's self-esteem. Wallowing in it, he'd once said to Lizzie: to be told he hadn't grasped the basis of therapy, how the process helped people to identify and address issues in their lives. Hugh had enquired mildly if the issues really needed to be identified and addressed weekly at seventy quid a throw, to which Lizzie had argued with unassailable logic that the financial pain was surely preferable to the risk of Charlie going back on drugs.

Charlie wandered in and picked up Lizzie's phone. He tried switching it on and, having no more success than Hugh, took it off to his room.

Hugh was looking through one of Lizzie's drier notebooks when Lou came in swiftly and, looping an arm round his shoulder, pressed her cheek against his head. 'Sorry, Dad.'

He kissed her pale, slender, child's hand. 'No, it was my fault,' he said. 'Did it all wrong.'

'There was no right way to tell us, Dad.'

'I'm not sure about that.'

Straightening up, she said in a no-nonsense voice, 'Well, *I* am. Now, what can I do? I need something to do.'

'Well, there's a load of messages on the answering machine. And the family to call. Could you bear it?'

'What shall I tell them about the delay?'

He hadn't thought that far. 'I don't know. The truth?'

She shot him a look of dismay. 'They'd ask all kinds of questions.'

'Say it's the coroner then. Say there's a delay with the inquest.'

'And Granny? She wants to know when she can come and stay.'

'Say we'd love to see her at the weekend.'

'And Aunt Becky? She was talking about coming as well.'

'No. Tell her . . . tell her there'd be nothing for her to do.'

'And if she says she's coming whatever?'

'Put her on to me,' Hugh said ominously.

Lou took a long breath as if to prepare herself for the fray, before going into the hall and rewinding the messages. Disembodied voices were still issuing from the answering machine when Charlie came in with some printouts.

'Here's the three documents Mum saved that evening,' he said. 'And the earlier version of two of them.'

'Thanks . . .' Hugh was already skimming the first page. 'And Charlie? Can you find out what documents Mum had worked on in the previous week or two?'

'Sure,' Charlie said, rising to the challenge. 'So long as none of it's in the corrupted sector of the hard disk.'

'Oh. Could it be?'

'It looks like it's mainly a couple of programs that got fouled up. So . . . should be okay.'

'Well, whatever you can find, Charlie.'

'Sure.'

The first file was labelled 'CA/Kizito Paul/housing app3.doc' and was an application letter to a housing association on behalf of a Ugandan asylum seeker and his family, presently in temporary accommodation. The letter was a page and a half long and appeared to be finished. The earlier version showed that Lizzie had made substantial changes. Was she satisfied with the final draft? he wondered. Well, she should have been. It was a well-crafted letter. Charlie's pencilled note gave the time it was saved as 19.20.

The next document was a report on Lizzie's campaign to get Gloria James and her son moved away from the Carstairs Estate. The report, which ran to ten pages, was cumulative, starting with Lizzie's first meeting with Gloria, covering eighteen months of referrals, psychiatric reports, phone calls, communications with local authorities, consultations with Angela Parfitt, and visits to Gloria's flat. Hugh skimmed quickly through to the last page. The penultimate entry, dated the day of the fire, noted a conversation with a council official which confirmed an offer of a two-bedroomed council flat in the north of the city. The final entry, dated later that day, recorded Lizzie's phone call to Gloria to give her the good news. What a rewarding moment it must have been for Lizzie after such a long, uphill struggle. He was glad she'd known about it before she died. This thought and the ones that came rushing after it brought a lump to his throat, a tightness in his chest, a sudden heat behind his eyelids.

I want you back, he told her. I want you back now and for ever.

*Well, that's not possible, is it? You'll have to manage as best you can. And concentrate, please. Keep going. Don't miss anything.*

But I'm so exhausted, Lizzie. Half the time I'm not sure I'm thinking straight.

*In that case you must get more sleep, mustn't you?*

*Remember what I used to say – it's no good tossing and turning. You must learn to switch off at night. You must learn to let go.*

But night's the hardest time of all.

*All the more reason to let go. I give you permission.*

'Easier said than done,' he whispered aloud.

He took a quick look at the time. Allowing for traffic he had ten minutes before he had to leave for the coroner's office. As he started on the printout that Charlie had marked 'Saved 21.41' his mobile rang. Picking it up, he saw 'Tom D' on the display. He wavered for several seconds before putting the phone back on the table and letting it ring. 'Sorry, old chum,' he muttered under his breath, 'you'll just have to wait.' After the allotted five rings the voicemail kicked in and the phone fell silent.

The last file was labelled 'CA/Jacobs John/request to be sectioned.doc', and contained exactly what it said on the label, a letter on behalf of a mentally ill man who was asking to be sectioned under the Mental Health Act. The letter ran to four paragraphs. Halfway down the second paragraph there was a break in the text preceded by an unfinished sentence: *At this point Mr Jacobs' case notes were mislaid and*

And the doorbell had rung.

Feeling a sudden drag of exhaustion, Hugh went through to the kitchen and made a strong coffee cooled down with a splash of cold water. Having downed it in three gulps, he put his head into the sitting room where Lou was on the phone. He made a questioning face to ask how things were going and she held out a piece of paper to him. It read *Tom Deacon (2 calls)*. He mimed going out and she nodded.

Pocketing his mobile, he pulled on the new padded jacket Lou had bought for him, grabbed his wallet and car keys and went out into a blustery wind. As he opened the car door his mobile rang. It was Tom. He got into the car and started the engine before answering.

'Hi, Tom.'

A pause. 'You're there, then.'

'I'm in the car.' Hugh unreeled his seatbelt, stretching it out to gain length before curving the tongue towards the buckle.

'I've been trying to get you.'

'I've been rather tied up, I'm afraid.' The metal tongue wouldn't quite reach the buckle and Hugh yanked at the reel to gain more length.

'Not trying to avoid me?'

Hugh hesitated, before gently clicking the buckle into place. 'No, Tom. Just busy.'

'How're you doing?'

'Well, I'm still here. All I can say really. You know how it is.'

'Got the kids with you?'

'Not right now, no. They're at home.'

'That's what I mean. You've got 'em with you.'

Recognising one of Tom's more abrasive moods, Hugh made no reply.

'Keeping you going, are they?' Tom asked.

'Yeah.'

'That's what kids do. Keep you going.'

'Sure do.' Aware of the time, Hugh began to search for his hands-free kit.

A silence followed, which Tom didn't seem inclined to break.

'Hello?' Hugh said after a while.

There was a rushing sound as Tom breathed hard against the mouthpiece. Finally he said in a taut monotone, 'Crazy how things get to you, how you look back and what seemed like the worst thing that could ever happen wasn't so bad after all.'

The hands-free wasn't in its usual place, and it didn't seem to be in the foot well either. Giving up, Hugh jammed the phone against his shoulder while he put the car into gear and drove off.

'I used to think Bosnia was the worst thing that was ever gonna happen. Wasn't too bad at the start. I thought, it's war, this is what happens, this is what I'm trained to do, go up this hill, follow the stink that's like no other stink on earth, start sorting through the bodies . . .'

'Tom, listen—'

But Tom was talking over him. 'I thought, it's not like it's any of my mates who've bought it, not like Northern Ireland where some of the guys got to see bits of their mates plastered all over the road.'

'Look, Tom, can we leave this till another time?'

'But then it started to get to me,' Tom went on doggedly. 'We had to put yellow crosses on their foreheads. Or their feet if the head wasn't in good shape. In among the women there were small babes. But it was the two-, three-year-olds that really got to me. Some, you could see the bullet wounds. Others, you couldn't see how they died and you began to think they'd been buried alive.'

Belatedly, it dawned on Hugh that Tom was drunk or high, or both. 'Just stop it there, Tom. Okay? I really can't talk now.'

'Must've been the fourth grave,' Tom continued as if Hugh hadn't spoken. 'Sipovo it was. Outside Sipovo. It was full of OAPs and kids. Crazy thing was, it was the OAPs that did my head in as much as the kids. Never worked that one out. Still can't. OAPs!'

Hugh had reached the T junction at the end of the lane. With fast-moving traffic ahead and a car coming up behind, he dropped the phone into his lap while he concentrated on finding a safe gap. Once onto the main road, he picked up the phone again and, hearing silence, prompted reluctantly, 'Hi?'

'What happened?'

'Traffic.'

'So . . . the fourth grave was at Sipovo. Just outside Sipovo. It was full of OAPs and kids—'

'I got that bit!' Hugh interrupted, dangerously close to exasperation. 'Look, Tom, can I call you back?'

'No, you can't!' Tom answered furiously. 'No! I'm telling you, and you're gonna listen. You're gonna fucking listen!'

Hugh would have rung off there and then but for the certainty that Tom would call back and keep calling back until he'd got this off his chest. 'Okay, Tom, but I'm driving and I don't have a hands-free and I may have to put the phone down sometimes.'

'So,' Tom said, moving on tenaciously, 'when I got back to the UK, that's when the nightmares started. Did my head in. Saw the dead climbing out of the graves, yellow crosses on their foreheads. Coming after me, trying to grab me, pull me down. Saw the babes under the earth, half dead. It seemed like the worst thing that could ever happen.' He gave a bitter snort. 'Bit of a joke now.'

Coming into the village, Hugh veered left into the only parking place available, a disabled bay outside the Star of India. Halting, he saw Mr Ravikumar in a window of the restaurant, fixing a menu to the glass. The top and sides of the glass had been overpainted to form an Eastern arch ornamented with elephants and stars, so that Mr Ravikumar appeared to be framed by a stage set of India.

Tom was pressing on in a fierce monotone. 'That's when I got into dope. Not like before, at weekends and shindies, but all the time. Only way I could get through the days, let alone the bloody nights. And then Holly arrived. Changed my life, she did. Loved her to bits right from the start. With Matt, I hadn't taken to him, not as a babe. Hardly seen him, for one thing. Screamed the whole bloody time. But once my little girl came along, it was like she stole my heart. I got my act together, cut out the dope and the worst of the booze, went to the doc for stuff to calm me down, got regular work . . .'

Mr Ravikumar had spotted Hugh and was waving from the arched window. Hugh waved back and reached forward to turn off the engine.

Another blast against the mouthpiece as Tom snorted again. 'It was like I was being set up, of course, taken sky high just so I could be dropped as low as I could go. Like I was being taught that Bosnia didn't come close to being the worst thing that could ever happen. But then you know what it's like, don't you, Hugh? To be sky high one minute, then low as you can go.' There was an edge to Tom's voice, a challenge or a warning.

In the window Mr Ravikumar was smiling enquiringly at Hugh as if to ask after his health.

'Sure,' Hugh murmured as he mustered a brief smile for Mr Ravikumar.

'Then so-called God in his so-called fucking wisdom decided he'd make me watch Holly die. At least you didn't have to go through that, did you, eh, Hugh?'

'No, I didn't.'

'That's right,' said Tom, pushing his point. 'Only thing that stopped me from topping myself was the thought of getting some justice. What a joke. The only real justice would've been if that old man hadn't died in the crash, if he could've been made to suffer like I'd suffered. But the case, the money – it was the next-best thing. That's what I told myself. But then I got to realise the money didn't count for anything without my boys. Got to love 'em like I loved Holly. Never thought I would, not like I loved Holly, but I did. Got to love 'em to bits. Broke me up whenever I had to take 'em back to Linda and that scumbag she took up with.' His voice was rising and cracking slightly. 'And then for once in my life I get a break. Linda wants to give 'em up, to let 'em come and live with me! My boys! All I've ever wanted – to have my boys at home with me! And I'm sky high. Sky high!'

Hugh pressed his head back against the rest and exhaled sharply.

'Oh, excuse me.' Tom's voice plunged sarcastically. 'Not boring you, am I?'

'Don't be stupid, Tom. Go on.'

'*Not fucking boring you?*'

'No – you're worrying me. Come on, what's happened?'

'You know what's fucking happened – you went and fucked it up for me.'

'Tom, whatever's happened, it wasn't me that told them.'

'You *shit*.'

'It wasn't me.'

'Why didn't you listen? Why didn't you fucking *listen* when I told you?'

'Is it the family court? If so, there may be something we can do. It may not be as bad as you think.'

'Not as bad?' He gave a great gasp. 'They're taking my boys into *care*! My boys . . . into *care* . . .'

Hugh sighed, 'Oh, Tom . . .'

'My boys . . . *My boys* . . .'

'Look, I'll get on to your lawyer in Exeter. See what we can sort out. I'll do it now. Okay?'

'Why the hell didn't you fucking *listen*?'

'Tom . . .'

But he had rung off.

# NINE

Hugh operated the coded padlock fitted by the home security people and let himself in. As he peered into the gloom, the keen wind sent a dry leaf scurrying past him to settle on the fire debris which had been compressed into a hard patchy layer, like worn lino. The house was fusty with mould and damp and stagnant air, and he opened windows in the kitchen and dining room to create a through draught. Then, because he was early, he began a search of the kitchen drawers and cupboards.

The previous evening he had eaten little, drunk more than he'd meant to, and slept fitfully if at all, disturbed by vivid nightmares which drove him out of bed before six to reread some of Lizzie's notebooks and make toast and coffee and wait for the first glimmer of dawn. When at last the trees had begun to separate themselves from the sky, he had bathed and shaved and put on warm clothes. Downstairs again, he had drunk more coffee while he packed his briefcase with a notebook, Lou's digital camera, his memo recorder and two of Lizzie's water-damaged notebooks whose pages were melded together. Restless, with two more hours to kill, he had driven down to the village and bought a newspaper, more coffee and a bar of chocolate, and sat in the car skimming the news and working his way through the chocolate while he waited for his drink to cool. He had read three pages before he realised he had taken nothing in.

And so he had come to Meadowcroft early and begun to search drawers and shelves he'd searched before, knowing there was nothing to find, but driven to look all the same. The drawer beneath the kitchen phone yielded a clutter of bills, receipts, promotional leaflets, and numerous slips of paper torn from the jotter pad, with suppliers' names and phone numbers in Lizzie's slanted handwriting. One marked 'Labrador breeder' must have dated from the time four or five years ago when they'd thought of getting a replacement for their much-loved Buster, parentage unknown but probably a mixture of Labrador and Doberman, who had died at thirteen. In the end they'd decided against another dog because the children were older and they themselves were getting too busy. Remembering Buster's last summer, his determination to keep up on walks as the arthritis locked his joints, Hugh saw that it was the end of the untroubled years, the time before Charlie took to drugs, before Hugh's parents died, before the intense pace set by Dimmock's merger with Marsh & Co, before Lizzie got embroiled in campaigns against injustice. If they'd had worries Hugh couldn't remember what they were. His father's heart condition, certainly. Money, possibly, though not in any serious way. Most likely their greatest preoccupation had been whether to go skiing or save up for a more ambitious summer holiday.

Coming across a petrol receipt, he wondered if Lizzie had ever bothered to claim a mileage allowance from the Citizens Advice, and if so whether she had specified the clients she was visiting. He slid the receipt into his notebook and scribbled a reminder to check with Angela Parfitt.

He went into his study and sat at his desk, alert but directionless, and leafed perfunctorily through some old letters and bank statements. Once, when Lizzie was beginning to take on more work, he'd suggested they swap study areas, but she'd insisted there was no need, she had room enough. By the time her little desk in the living room was overflowing with papers and the floor lined with printers and scanners, she was too deeply ensconced there, in no mood for upheaval.

The restlessness took him into the dining room to open a drawer at random, knowing perfectly well it contained cutlery. Wandering out again, he finally surrendered to the pull of the living room, though he managed to stay away from Lizzie's desk for a good ten minutes while he went through a chest of drawers containing family memorabilia. The numerous photo albums, neatly arranged by date, seemed to have escaped the worst of the smoke damage, though they gave off an ominous hint of mould. The children's school reports were more obviously damp, the covers stained and curling, while their kindergarten paintings were soggy along the edges. Finally, he went and stood in front of Lizzie's desk. He'd searched it thoroughly and removed everything of interest, but this didn't prevent him from taking a last look. All that was left was stationery and a collection of brochures, theatre programmes, postcards, business cards and old year-books. He went through them, flicking through the pages that weren't stuck together. In a pigeonhole, wedged between some envelopes, he found a leaflet he'd missed before. It was damp and when he tried to prise the leaves apart they threatened to disintegrate in his hands. By starting from the marginally drier top corner and taking it slowly, however, he managed to unglue the leaves by a couple of inches to reveal a schematic map of the Carstairs Estate with a jotting in Lizzie's handwriting giving the name 'James' and a block and flat number. He wrote down the address on the basis that he wrote down all information concerning the parts of Lizzie's life he hadn't shared, that, useful or not, it added to his bank of knowledge. The lower half of the leaflet was noticeably damper, the leaves stuck more resolutely together, and when he tried to separate them they began to fall apart. He was contemplating another attempt when he heard the sound of a car and abandoned the leaflet to the desk flap.

He arrived at the front door to see DS Reynolds climbing out of a grey car, a cigarette clamped between his lips. Spotting Hugh, he dropped the cigarette onto the ground and stepped on it. DI Steadman emerged from the passenger side and, with a glance over the house and garden, went to the rear door to extract his raincoat, which he pulled on before coming across the gravel.

Steadman gave a solemn nod of greeting. 'Mr Gwynne.' Then, as if to get on with the business in hand, he strode past Hugh into the house with Reynolds in his wake.

'Slater's coming from London,' Hugh told them. 'He might be held up.'

Steadman was staring at the remains of the hall ceiling. 'But he's in no doubt, you say?'

'None. He says it's definitely arson.' Recalling Slater's words on the phone, the barely suppressed excitement in his voice, Hugh relived his own shock at having been proved right, the vindication and the anguish.

'Did he indicate what sort of evidence he'd found?'

'He said it was best explained in person. But I imagine the evidence is strong. For him to be so sure.'

Steadman gave a slight nod. Noticing his hair again, how immaculately combed and blow-dried it was, how unnaturally dark it was against his face, Hugh tried not to hold his vanity against him.

Steadman indicated the living room. 'This is where the fire started, is it?'

'That's right.'

He swung his gaze towards the kitchen and dining room. 'And no signs of a break-in?'

'No.'

'And your wife wasn't expecting anyone that evening?'

Hugh said tightly, 'We've been through this before.'

Steadman shaped his mouth into an understanding smile. 'I appreciate that, Mr Gwynne, but in view of developments I'm afraid it's going to be necessary to go through certain aspects again.'

'The facts haven't changed since Monday.'

'It's a question of establishing the details.'

It might have been the amount of coffee he'd drunk or a sugar-rush from the chocolate or the suspicion that Steadman hadn't bothered to read Reynolds' notes, but Hugh was shaken by a small rage. Only with an effort did he keep his voice steady. 'Well, I'm not prepared to go through the whole thing again unless it's to make a proper statement.'

Steadman's steady gaze betrayed nothing. 'As you wish, Mr Gwynne. Perhaps you could take us through the house then?'

Destined, it seemed, to reopen his wounds on a daily basis, Hugh started on the familiar tour. Like a well-trained guide he set the scene with care, describing the location and appearance of the absent sofa, the state of the windows and door, the work Lizzie had been doing on her computer, the time she had closed the last file, before leading his visitors along the track of the fire, directing them to points of interest, pausing now and again to let Reynolds catch up with his note taking. Unlike a well-trained guide, however, he deserted his visitors at the final attraction. With no stomach to watch the two men casting their cold inquisitive gaze over the unmade bed, he hung back on the landing. Once, Reynolds came out and asked a question about the window. Otherwise Hugh paced slowly back and forth, listening to the men murmuring to each other as they moved about the room. Despite the cold, he had sweated through his shirt; his stomach felt nauseous.

Steadman reappeared, wiping his hands on a large cotton handkerchief. 'Nothing been moved or altered since the fire?'

'No. Why?'

'Just a routine question.' Steadman went on wiping his hands, as if he'd come into contact with something nasty he couldn't shift.

Hugh said, 'The bed's in such a mess because the firemen were searching for other victims.' *Other victims?* He had caught the plague of official-speak. He corrected himself. 'Searching for *me*.'

'I see,' Steadman said impassively. 'You mentioned the clothes on the chair, the way they were folded.'

'Yes – my wife would never have left her clothes like that.'

'Could you be more specific?'

'Well, she never folded them. Ever. Any clothes she was going to wear the next day she draped over the back of the chair. And she always, *always*, put her underwear straight into the laundry basket, never left it out. And she wore a nightdress except in hot weather, and when she was found she was naked.'

Steadman waited for Reynolds to finish writing this up.

'And the clothes haven't been touched since the night of the fire?'

Hugh hesitated. 'I looked at them once, just to see what was there. But I replaced them exactly as they were. And we were careful to take photographs beforehand. Slater was, rather. He took pictures of everything.'

'So . . . that would have been two days ago?'

The implication was clear: it was too long after the event to count. 'But absolutely nothing was touched before then,' Hugh said firmly. 'No one's been allowed into this room, not even the family. I knew there'd have to be a proper investigation. I knew nothing must be touched.' Sensing that Steadman remained unpersuaded, Hugh added, 'And Ellis's photographs must show the clothes.'

'Ellis?'

'The fire brigade investigator.'

Absorbing this with a slow nod, Steadman cast an eye around the landing and up at the ceiling. 'I'm not

clear about one thing, Mr Gwynne. You say your wife
was alone in the house and no one was expected.'

'That's right.'

'But your son arrived sometime that evening.'

'He arrived late. After the fire started.'

Reynolds looked up from his notepad. 'Your son's
name, Mr Gwynne?'

'Charlie.'

'Is that Charles?'

'No. Charlie.'

Steadman said, 'And you weren't aware he was
coming?'

'His mother knew. He phoned her earlier that
evening.'

'Ah. And how would he have got here?'

'Sorry?'

'What transport would he have used?'

'Well . . . coach from Birmingham. Then a bus.
Except it might've been a taxi because it was so late.
But what's that got to do with anything?' Realising this
had sounded rather abrupt, Hugh added a conciliatory
shrug.

Steadman paused, as if deciding whether to break
with his normal practice and reveal his thinking. 'If
your wife was expecting him, she might have answered
the door rather more readily than otherwise.'

'But she knew he was going to get here late – at
eleven or twelve. And he would have let himself in.'

Steadman's gaze turned inward, as if Hugh's reply
had confirmed the foolishness of entering into discussions with civilians. With a glance towards Reynolds,
he said, 'Thank you, Mr Gwynne, I think that's everything up here.'

When they reached the hall Reynolds said, 'The wine glasses, they're still in situ, are they, Mr Gwynne?'

They trooped into the kitchen and stared at the glasses standing upside down on the draining board, their surfaces tarnished with a faint film of soot. Hugh explained how Lizzie always used the dishwasher for glasses because she believed it cleaned them better.

Reynolds referred to his notebook. 'Previously you said she might have used two glasses in one evening.'

Hugh could see where this was leading. He said, 'It's possible, yes.'

'But you're suggesting someone else washed them up?'

'All I know is Lizzie wouldn't have washed them up by hand.'

It was Steadman who voiced the obvious. 'The second glass could have been for an unexpected guest.'

*But not a lover*, Hugh thought with a warning glare. But if Steadman's mind was journeying down that route, he didn't say anything.

'Have the glasses been touched?' Steadman asked.

'No.'

Steadman's gaze settled thoughtfully on the bay window before coming back to Hugh. 'Anyone have a grudge against your wife, Mr Gwynne?'

'Not to my knowledge, no.'

'She worked at the Citizens Advice, I believe?'

'Yes.'

'She mention any troublesome customers there? People who might have threatened her?'

'No. Some of her clients got upset now and then, when they got turned down for housing or whatever it was. But they didn't take it personally. They knew it was the system that was against them, not Lizzie. But you should ask Angela Parfitt, her team leader. She'll be able to tell you more than me.'

'And outside her work? Your wife was involved in some high-profile campaigns, I believe.'

'No. I mean, there was only one you could call high profile – the Denzel Lewis case.'

'And what was her involvement there?'

'She helped him find a new lawyer. And she did what she could on the campaigning side.'

'What, leaflets, that sort of thing?'

'More, contacting useful people, getting their help.'

'What kind of useful people?'

'Forensic experts, criminal barristers . . . And Chief Inspector Montgomery. She saw him a few times.'

Steadman's impassive features showed something like mystification. 'Oh?'

'She saw him only last week, in fact. The day before she died.'

Steadman gazed at him while he considered this information. 'You know why?'

Maybe it was his lawyer's training which had taught him to divulge the minimum information, maybe it was his natural caution when dealing with something he didn't fully understand, but Hugh said, 'Best ask him yourself.'

'Indeed.' Steadman glanced around the other half of the kitchen before asking, 'Your wife have any contact with Lewis's associates? His fellow gang members?'

'Not as far as I know.'

'Or with rival gangs?'

'No,' Hugh said emphatically.

In a tone of enlightening him, Steadman said, 'The

Carstairs Estate is rife with gangs, Mr Gwynne. The Yardies are in charge at present. They make it their business to know who's who. If she was going there on a regular basis, her presence would have been noted.'

'Well, she never mentioned any trouble to me.'

Steadman wandered towards the side counter and peered at the half-drunk bottle of red wine, and beside it the corkscrew with a cork still in it. 'You stated you'd seen a hoodie in the garden two days before the fire. Could you give us a description?'

It seemed so long ago that Hugh struggled to summon up an image. 'I don't know . . . He was about five nine or ten, I suppose. Skinny. Young. Fit. That's about it. It was very dark.'

'Ethnicity?'

'White. I think so, anyway.'

'You saw his face, then?'

'For a second. But it was raining hard, I didn't get a good look at him.'

'And he was acting suspiciously?'

But Hugh had picked up the sound of an approaching car and was already moving towards the hall.

'Traffic,' Slater said, as he came energetically into the house. He was wearing a dark suit and crisp white shirt, and carrying a cabin bag which he set down on the floor. He looked around expectantly. 'CID here?'

'In the kitchen.'

Slater's quick eyes brightened. 'Excellent.'

Hugh took him in and made the introductions. Slater handed Steadman his card. 'Done quite a bit for the Met, Thames Valley, Hampshire Force,' he announced. 'Always glad to help in any way.'

Steadman put the card in his pocket without reading it.

Slater pressed his hands neatly together, like a lecturer summoning his students. 'Well, shall we get started then?'

Hugh collected his memo recorder and followed the others into the living room, where they formed a loose semicircle around the absent sofa. Slater crouched down and, unzipping the case, extracted first a laptop which he opened and set up on the seat of an armchair, then some enlarged photographs of the sofa, which he offered to Steadman.

'Right.' Slater looked from face to face, as if to gauge the attentiveness of his audience, perhaps even to heighten the dramatic effect, and it occurred to Hugh that this was a high point of his career, a tale he would recount many times in the future. 'Right . . .'

Hugh held his recorder out to catch Slater's voice.

'The fire brigade and ourselves agree on the source of the fire – that it started on the sofa which stood here, under the window. The right-hand side of the sofa, to be precise. On the seat, close to the arm.' He directed Steadman to the photographs. 'You can see the frame at this point was burnt right through to the wood.' He waited for Steadman to look up again. 'And the fire damage clearly emanates from this area, spreading sideways, but mainly up and over. The window behind the sofa was slightly open, the door fully open. So, once the fire had got a grip it travelled towards the door and out into the hall, getting as far as the upper landing before it was extinguished.' He paused enquiringly to make sure everyone was with him so far.

'Now, in cases of suspected arson I'm looking for one or both of two things – first, how the fire was started, and second, the way or ways it might have been encouraged to spread. As you'll be aware, most arsonists are what you might call amateurs, they use accelerants like petrol which leave detectable residues and telltale burn patterns, and they often start more than one fire at the same time. But our arsonist was in a different class. He had two clear aims: a) to leave as little evidence as possible, and b) to be well away from the scene by the time the fire started. So he didn't use an obvious accelerant, and he started only one fire.' A glimmer of satisfaction crossed Slater's face. 'But that doesn't mean he left no evidence.'

DI Steadman inclined his head a little, as if to urge Slater to get on with it.

'So . . .' Slater said, gaining pace. 'Because the sofa was the sole source of the fire we were able to concentrate our examination there. And we found evidence of a simple but effective method by which he could be away from the scene by the time the fire started. If I could demonstrate . . .' Like a conjuror producing a rabbit, he reached down and took a packet of cigarettes out of his case and extracted one. 'He lights a cigarette . . . he places it on the sofa . . .' In the absence of the sofa, Slater perched the cigarette on the edge of Lizzie's desk. 'Then . . .' Reaching down into the case again, he brought out a book of matches, the sort restaurants and hotels used to give away before smoking was banned. 'He flips the matches open, he bends the cover right back so the matches are standing up . . . and he places the matches over the near end of the cigarette . . .' Slater took a moment to balance the book of matches in the right position. 'Now, a cigarette takes between seven and eleven minutes to burn to the end, then the cover of the matches will catch light, then the matches themselves. From that point on, the fire will take anything between ten and twenty-five minutes to take hold, depending on the proximity of flammable materials and the use of accelerants. So, adding it all together, our man had at least a quarter of an hour to get away. How do we know he used this method?' He went back to his case and extracted a sealed, transparent plastic bag. 'We know because all book matches, no matter where you obtain them, are fastened with the same unique staple.' He held up the plastic envelope in front of him, the staple just visible in one corner. 'And it was just such a staple we found at the epicentre of the fire. A staple, in other words, that could only have come from a book of matches. As the fire got going, the staple worked its way down through the foam and ended up on the sofa frame, which is where we found it.'

Hugh tried not to imagine the number of ways a clever lawyer would find to challenge this sort of evidence. Where was the proof that the book of matches hadn't been lying down the side of the sofa for years? Or hadn't fallen onto the sofa with an unattended candle?

'But it's not enough for this arsonist to start his fire,' Slater said. 'He has to make sure it's going to get a good hold. The way our man achieved this was very simple. He took the floor-length curtains that were hanging at the window here and brought them forward over the front of the sofa onto the seat cushions, in close proximity to the cigarette and matches. How do

we know he did this? Because we found residues of the
curtains on the sofa. If I could just demonstrate . . .'
He went to the laptop and brought up a diagram
showing a line-drawing of a sofa, sideways on, with
the curtains brought forward onto the seat cushions.
He pressed a key and the diagram came to life. A small
red flame appeared on the cushion and began to spread
up the curtains towards the ceiling. As the curtains
burnt, the residue, shown as a series of bright green
specks, formed on the cushions of the sofa. When the
lower halves of the curtains had burnt through, the top
halves swung back towards the window and the residues began to fall onto the floor. 'This is the only
scenario consistent with the evidence,' Slater said. 'The
curtains were used to get the fire going.'

Here was proof, but Hugh felt no elation, no triumph, only a dull, persistent anxiety.

Slater was facing them with an eager enquiring look,
as if to invite questions, but it was a full half minute
before Reynolds asked, 'There was no accelerant used?'

'We've found no evidence so far, certainly nothing
obvious like petrol, but absence of evidence isn't evidence of absence when it comes to accelerants. In my
opinion it's highly likely one *was* used, but since this
guy knew what he was doing, he'd have chosen acetone
or something similar, which leaves no trace.'

Hugh's recorder clicked as the tape ran out. He
extracted the cassette and turned it over.

'Your reasons for thinking an accelerant was used?'
Steadman asked.

Slater acknowledged the validity of the question
with a quick nod. 'Partly a gut feeling – this guy was
leaving nothing to chance. Partly the intensity of the

fire, the pattern of the damage. But that's just my opinion,' he added, with an eye to his expert status. 'Nothing I could swear to in court.'

Hugh pushed at the cassette but couldn't get it to click into the slot. Giving up, he asked Slater, 'How would someone acquire this sort of know-how? Is it freely available?'

'They say you can get it off the Internet if you know where to look. Anarchists, terrorists . . . they'll post up anything.' He looked to Steadman for confirmation and got none. 'But if it's there it's in a deep, dark place, because I've never managed to find it.'

'But the method's well known in your profession?'

'Oh yes. We share this sort of info, pass it around. Particularly when it's something sophisticated, designed to pull the wool over our eyes.'

Another pause. 'Thank you,' Hugh murmured. Then again with genuine gratitude: 'Thank you. Your people must have worked flat out.'

'They did,' Slater declared with a puff of pride. 'They stayed late on Tuesday evening. And the lab people dropped everything to help out. But they were glad to, in view of the urgency and importance of the investigation. Oh!' He made a gesture of memory and plunged his hand back into his case to bring out a charred, vaguely rectangular object in a plastic bag. 'We found this on the sofa frame as well. Bound in leather, ring-binder. A diary or Filofax. Must have been lying open because all the leaves were destroyed.' He offered it to Steadman. 'Need this for evidence, Detective Inspector?'

'Everything you've got. When will your report be available, Mr Slater?'

'Interim report Monday. Final report two weeks max. Unless you need it sooner?'

It wasn't needed sooner, and almost as one they began to move, Slater to pack up his laptop, Reynolds to go back through his notes, Hugh and Steadman to stroll to the front door and stand in the porch, gazing out at the wind-blown garden.

Steadman said tautly, 'I owe you an apology, Mr Gwynne.'

Hugh shook his head. 'So long as you can get things moving. Find this man.'

'Most arsonists are rank amateurs. They usually make it blindingly obvious. Never seen anything like this before.'

'That's what worries me. What kind of person would plan something like this? Go to so much trouble to kill my wife.'

'Like I said, if you could think about any enemies your wife might have made, Mr Gwynne. Someone who had an obsession about her. Or a grudge. A local troublemaker . . . A neighbour . . . Someone she'd been kind to who'd got the wrong idea. A road rage incident she'd been involved in, maybe recently, maybe some time ago. A client from the Citizens Advice who started playing the blame game. Any yobs, crackpots, gang members who'd come her way.'

'Well, it's not likely to be a yob, is it? They wouldn't have the brains.'

'Ah, but you get bright yobs just like you get stupid ones,' Steadman said in the tone of having seen it all. 'And drug users are often the brightest of the lot . . .'

Hugh shot him a defensive glance, wondering if he knew about Charlie.

'. . . Mrs Gwynne must have met a few in the course of her work. Maybe she encouraged one of them to shop a dealer? Maybe she aggravated a gang member without realising it? That's what I'm getting at, Mr Gwynne. We can't rule out anything at this stage.'

Dazed by this new range of possibilities, Hugh said, 'What next?'

'The house will have to be sealed off until the SOCOs have had a chance to go over the place. Meantime, we'll set up an incident room, start gathering statements. We will of course keep you fully informed of any developments.' Behind the rigid composure Hugh thought he detected a note of pessimism in Steadman's voice, a sense that the case had got off to a bad start and would continue as it had begun. Or maybe Steadman was simply careworn from a heavy caseload and too few resources. Either way, Hugh made a mental note to keep the pressure up.

Steadman took out a card and wrote on it. 'My mobile number. Call me or DS Reynolds if you have any thoughts. Anything at all.'

A gust of wind hit them. Reaching a pale hand up to smooth his hair, Steadman turned to go back into the house.

'You talked about Lizzie getting noticed for going to the Carstairs,' said Hugh, following him. 'But apart from the Lewis family the only people she visited were families wanting to be rehoused or people with mental health issues or old age pensioners too frightened to leave their flats. Why would that have attracted attention?'

'Visiting the Lewis family would have been enough.'

'Even with Denzel in prison?'

'Once a gang member always a gang member. Being inside doesn't stop them dealing drugs, waging turf wars.'

'And you really think they could be capable of something like this?'

'They're capable of most things when they set their minds to it.'

'But why Lizzie? What could she have done to upset them?'

'If we knew that, Mr Gwynne, we'd be a long way to finding the person or persons responsible.'

Hugh hesitated, caught between his instinct for caution, his urge to help, and his reluctance to point Steadman in what might be the wrong direction. 'There was talk of a witness,' he said abruptly. 'Someone who could give Denzel Lewis an alibi.'

'Oh yes?'

'I thought it was just a rumour, but . . . well, it seems Lizzie might have been in touch with this person.'

Steadman gave his unblinking stare. 'Chief Inspector Montgomery know about this?'

'In theory anyway. Lizzie asked him about witness protection.'

This time there was a marked tension in Steadman's silence. 'When was this?'

'At their meeting last week.'

Steadman turned his face towards the light while he digested the information. 'And this witness, did she tell you his name?'

'No.'

'What about other people? Like the Lewis family? Did she tell them who this person was?'

'I don't think so, no.'

'But they knew there was a witness?'

'Yes.'

'Anyone else know?'

'I couldn't say.'

'But your wife definitely talked to Montgomery about it?'

'Yes.'

With a pensive nod, Steadman straightened his back. 'Right, well, thanks for that, Mr Gwynne. I'll look into it further.'

'There's another thing.'

Steadman lifted his head to the question.

'My wife must have been unconscious.'

'Why do you say that, Mr Gwynne?'

'Because there was no other way this guy could have undressed her and folded her clothes and put her into bed. No other way he could have persuaded her to stay there once the fire started and the smoke alarm went off.'

Steadman took his time to consider this idea. 'There's nothing in the post-mortem to suggest she was unconscious.'

'Yes, but what about date-rape drugs? They don't show up, do they?'

Steadman took even longer over this thought. Finally he offered Hugh a mechanical smile. 'I hear what you say, Mr Gwynne. I hear it loud and clear.'

Back in the house, Hugh gave Lizzie's water-damaged notebooks to Slater for delivery to a specialist document restorer, then left for Oakhill to face the task of telling the children.

*

*Gone out*, Lou's note said. *Back later*. The message was so abrupt, so devoid of information that Hugh felt a beat of alarm.

She answered her mobile instantly. 'Dad.'

'Sweetheart. You okay?'

'Can't talk now. Waiting for a call.'

'Anything the matter?'

'It's Charlie,' she said in a tight voice. 'He didn't come home last night and he's not answering his phone.'

It had only been a matter of time, Hugh thought wearily, though that didn't prevent him from feeling a plunge of disappointment.

'Where are you?' he demanded. She seemed to be in a car, but it couldn't be Lizzie's because that was sitting outside in the drive.

'We've just tried the place where Elk was meant to live, but he's not here any more.'

'Who're you with?'

'Sarah.'

His mind was a blank. 'Sarah?'

'Koenig. But Dad, I can't talk now. I'm waiting for a call from Joel. He thinks he might be able to find out where Elk's gone to.'

'Lou – don't expect too much.'

'What do you mean?'

'I mean . . . if Charlie's decided to start using again, then there's nothing we can do about it. Believe me, darling – nothing.'

'Well, if he *has* started again that's all the more reason *not* to give up on him – not when he needs us,' she declared emotionally. 'And he needs us, I know he does! I'm going to be there for him – even if you're not!'

'Lou, I didn't—' But she'd rung off, and he didn't call back. He'd wept for Charlie once on discovering he was into heavy drugs, and again the first time Charlie had relapsed after swearing faithfully, absolutely, cross-his-heart-hope-to-die that he'd given up, but at some point in the succeeding months his tears had dried up. The disappointment, which had seemed so acute a moment ago, had already faded, another fact to be absorbed and somehow lived with, like the fire and Lizzie's death.

Heading upstairs, he pushed open Charlie's door and surveyed the jumble of strewn clothes, cigarette stubs and half-drunk cans of Coke that littered the place. Only the computer table was relatively uncluttered. Wandering over, he saw Lizzie's mobile phone lying face down with its back removed, and on a stack of papers next to it a handwritten list of names and phone numbers. From entries such as 'Plumber Dave' and 'Electric Paul' he realised it was a summary of Lizzie's SIM card. This was what baffled him, how Charlie could make such a neat, methodical list when for so much of the time his mind, like this bedroom, seemed to be in a state of confusion. On the next sheet was a printed list of computer file names, perhaps fourteen or fifteen in number, which, according to Charlie's handwritten note, had been modified in the last two weeks. In the pile beneath were printouts of the fifteen files. 'Charlie . . .' he murmured with a mixture of admiration and despair.

Collecting up the printouts, he took them to his

bedroom and put them on the side table while he went into the bathroom and splashed his face repeatedly in cold water. Then, lying on the bed, propped up on the pillows, he began to go through them, skimming over Lizzie's Citizens Advice cases, reading the remaining files in more detail. Coming to the file marked 'Denzel Lewis Campaign' he skipped to the end to see if she'd had time to write up her meeting with Montgomery, but there was nothing. It was only when he leafed backwards that he found a paragraph headed 'Meeting with DCI Montgomery', with notes on the witness protection scheme. The date was some weeks back, which surprised him. Or had he simply got the time-scale wrong?

Reaching the second-to-last document, there it was suddenly. A file entitled 'Statement' kept in a folder labelled 'W'. The heading read: *Summary of conversations with W.*

August 1, 6: W first tells me he's frightened of the gangs because of something he's seen. Clams up when I ask him for details.

August 13, 20, 27, Sept 1: Steady progress in winning W's trust. He seems genuinely terrified of consequences of having seen 'bad' thing. Says 'they' would get him if they knew. Tells me 'they' are local gang, but won't say which. I passed all this on to Dr S for information. She said it could be an attempt to rationalise his fear of the outside world, i.e. a fabrication.

Sept. 18: On my return from holiday W is wary and withdrawn, as if to punish me for my absence, but then begins to respond. I feel I'm regaining his trust. I think he's missed my visits.

**Sept. 23:** W told me it was a knifing he saw. I didn't press him. I feel he'll tell me more as and when he's ready.

**Sept. 28:** Most positive talk yet re practical issues in his life: occupational training, getting fit, etc. W excited at my idea of theme park outing for his birthday. Something to aim at, if nothing else.

**Oct. 1:** Another positive visit, though W still needs a lot of reassurance, encouragement etc. Towards the end, JE dropped by. As he, G and I talked, W became agitated, then aggressive & withdrawn. Reaction made no sense till I worked out only thing that could have upset him was talk of Denzel Lewis campaign.

**Oct. 2:** Reassure W. Swear formally on the family Bible that I would never break his trust, that whatever he tells me will always remain confidential. I then ask him straight out if it was the killing of Jason Jackson he saw. His reaction says yes. After a lot more reassurance it all comes out. To the best of my recollection, this is what he told me:

Three years ago, on the night in question, W had been to the sports centre to watch basketball practice with a view to taking up the sport. He was walking home sometime after nine o'clock. There was a kid ahead of him, also walking home from basketball practice. He knew this kid by sight only; not well enough to walk with him. A distinctive red Ford XR3 with spoilers and white metal wheels went by, then reappeared and stopped alongside the other kid. At first there was some sort of talk between the kid and the people in the car. Then

two white guys got out of the car and surrounded the kid.
There was a shout, then the guys stabbed the kid. At this
point one of the white guys saw W and shouted something,
and W ran away in the opposite direction. Hearing the car
coming up behind, he dived down an alleyway and made his
escape through some back gardens.

When I questioned W further, he said

1) He was in no doubt the two guys stabbed the kid. (He
   mimed the stabbing movements for me.)
2) The two guys were definitely white. He saw them
   clearly.
3) He was certain about his description of the car because
   he loves cars and always notices them. He said the car
   belonged to a white gang from the adjoining estate.
4) W couldn't name the exact date of the attack, only that
   he'd just turned fifteen, which tallies with the murder
   of Jason Jackson.

Oct. 3, 5: W is relieved to have told me, but also very
defensive re Denzel being in prison for something he didn't
do.

Oct. 8: W tells me he recognised one of Jason's attackers as
one of the Forbes brothers, well-known racists and gang
members. I talk about witness protection, a new home in
another city, but he's scared stiff.

Oct. 10: No progress on idea of witness protection.

Oct. 12: Same.

Oct. 15: Same.

Oct. 17: We talk about God and faith and bravery. Could be the way forward.

Woken by the buzz of the doorbell, Hugh opened his eyes to the featureless neutrals of the Oakhill decor and saw it was one o'clock; he had slept for almost forty minutes, and now Isabel had arrived, precisely on time. He got to his feet, scattering papers over the floor, and hurried downstairs. Swinging the front door open, the smile he'd mustered for Isabel died on his lips as he saw Ray standing at her side. From Isabel's expression it was obvious that Ray's presence wasn't her idea.

'What brings you here?' Hugh said, suppressing his irritation.

Leading the way in, Ray hauled off his coat. 'Just a couple of things to clear with you, old fellow. Thought it would be easier to make it into a visit. And then Isabel told me she was coming, so . . . well, here we are.'

Isabel threw Hugh a helpless look.

Hugh said, 'Well, there are things I need to discuss with Isabel.'

'Fine. No problem. But how's it going, old fellow?' Ray asked, with a doleful expression. 'You've seen the police—'

'You came in the same car?' Hugh cut in.

'What? Well, yes. Didn't seem much point in bringing two.'

'Then you'll have to amuse yourself while Isabel and I have our meeting.'

'Yes, but . . . well, it's the Deacon case you're discussing, isn't it?' Ray asked, looking from Hugh to

Isabel and back again. 'I'd be glad to sit in. You know, throw in some ideas.'

'Thanks, but it's not practical.'

Ray lowered his voice confidentially. 'Look, I do actually know the shit's hit the fan, if that's what you're worried about.'

Isabel widened her eyes to confirm it.

'Oh?' said Hugh.

'Desmond Riley told me about the, er . . . awkward discrepancy in Deacon's story. '

'How did that come about?' Hugh said with deliberate calm.

'Sorry?'

'That you spoke to Desmond?'

'Ah . . . well, you see, he wanted to talk to whoever was standing in for you and so the switchboard put him through to me.'

Hugh exchanged another glance with Isabel. 'I tell you, it's not practical. We haven't got time to go through the back story.'

'Well, I could—'

'It wouldn't work,' Hugh insisted.

'Well . . . fine,' Ray said, baffled and a little hurt. 'I'll take a turn round the garden . . . or whatever.'

Isabel held up a carrier bag. 'I've brought some lunch.'

Hugh delved into his pocket for money. 'Here . . . let me . . .'

'Raymond paid for it,' she said.

For some reason this rekindled Hugh's irritation. 'Bung it on my expenses, will you, Ray?'

'Don't be idiotic, man,' Ray said, following Hugh into the kitchen. 'But how did it go this morning?' he asked urgently. 'The police getting moving at last?'

Scooping up some water glasses, Hugh almost bumped into Ray, hovering at his elbow. 'Looks like it, yes.'

'They're setting up a proper criminal investigation?'

'Yes.'

Ray raised his eyes heavenward and gave an exaggerated sigh of relief. 'Thank God for that! About time too! Your expert came up with the evidence, did he?'

'Yup.' Hugh grabbed some mineral water and took it to the table where Isabel was distributing sandwiches. He sat down briskly. 'So what's up, Ray?'

Sitting down next to him, Ray gave another sigh. 'I still can't believe it, you know. I can't—' He gulped, as if to suppress a sudden upwelling of emotion. 'I can't believe anyone could start a fire *deliberately*, knowing what—'

'Water?' Hugh interrupted, holding up the bottle to Isabel.

'Please,' she said.

'So what is it, Ray?' Hugh demanded as he filled the glasses.

Reading his mood at last, Ray said in a steadier tone, 'Um . . . well, with everything that's happening I wasn't sure if you'd had time to think about the press. Because the moment they get to hear about the police investigation they'll be down here in droves. I wondered if you wanted me to fend them off – so far as possible anyway.'

'The police have sealed the house off.'

'That won't stop them coming here, though, will it?'

'They're not going to bother with us.'

Ray's expression suggested he wasn't so sure. 'What about keeping the gate shut?'

'Then we'd have to get out of the car to open it. I tell you, it won't be a big media thing. Why on earth should it be?' Hugh was beginning to regret his impulsive decision to ask Ray to stand by on the legal side; it was a request Ray was always going to interpret liberally.

'Well, let me know if you're getting any hassle, won't you?' said Ray.

Hugh tore the wrapping off his sandwich. 'Anything else?'

'Um . . . yeah. One thing . . .' Ray was nervous, he was having trouble looking Hugh in the eye. 'It was just that – in view of what you told me – I thought I'd better check the position vis-à-vis the police and the second post-mortem—'

'The second post-mortem's got nothing to do with the police.'

'Well . . . yes and no,' Ray offered gingerly, as if negotiating a minefield. 'You see, it occurred to me that . . . well, in view of the fact the police are mounting a criminal investigation . . . they might order their own second post-mortem. In which case we could be in danger of, well . . . getting our wires crossed. So . . .' Ray gave a terrible smile. 'I spoke to the coroner's office and they confirmed what I thought, that now it's a criminal investigation the police could well order a second post-mortem . . . using a forensic pathologist of their own. In which case their request would . . . well, take precedence . . .'

Hugh argued, 'But it's all arranged with – what's his name, Isabel?'

'Professor Alan Ritchie.'

'Professor Ritchie.' To Isabel again: 'And he's doing it when?'

Isabel hesitated because he'd specifically asked her not to tell him when it was going to take place. 'Um . . . tomorrow.'

'Tomorrow when?'

'Morning.'

'Tomorrow morning,' Hugh declared. 'So what are you saying, for Christ's sake? That they're going to withdraw permission at the last minute?'

Ray raised a calming hand. 'No. I mean . . . Apparently the normal practice in such circumstances is for the family's pathologist to attend as an observer. You know – sort of sit in. So—'

'You're saying they're going to stop it going ahead?'

'Well, um . . . like I said . . . the coroner's office are going to find out from the police if they might want a second PM, and they'll let us know either way by the end of the day. It would only be a question of postponing for a day or so at the most . . .'

The anger came over Hugh in a red-hot wave. He shot to his feet, sending his chair juddering back over the floor. 'For Christ's sake!' he said. 'Why couldn't you just for once in your life have left well alone? Why did you have to interfere? If you hadn't bloody well interfered—' He flung out a hand in exasperation and, frightened of what he might say next, marched out into the dining room where he stood blindly at the window until the worst of his anger had passed. Then, reaching for a chair, he sat at the table and dropped his head into his hands, assailed by the terrifying thought that he was going the way of Tom Deacon, into the realms of victimhood, ungovernable anger and violent mood swings.

Lizzie, what's happening to me? Tell me how to get through this.

But his vision of her was fragmented, reduced to a series of snapshots which drifted through his mind at random. He tried to recall what she used to say to him when he was stressed. But that was it of course – she'd said almost nothing, just the occasional 'Did he?' or 'Really?', listening solicitously, patiently, until his anger burnt itself out. That had been her skill, to know how to handle him in such a mood, just as she'd known how to handle so many other people. Except perhaps Charlie. They had both failed with Charlie, and there was a dubious sort of consolation in that.

There was a sound at the door and Ray appeared. He stood abjectly, arms hanging loosely at his sides. 'I'm sorry, old friend . . . Didn't intend to . . . The last thing I meant . . . Thought I was being useful . . .'

Hugh made an indeterminate gesture, a spreading of one hand.

'I just admired Lizzie so much . . . Everything a woman should be,' Ray said mawkishly, adding hastily, 'Oh, don't get me wrong. Never had designs . . . As if she'd have looked at me . . .' He gave a self-deprecating grimace. 'No, just admired her from afar . . .'

Not sure he was ready for an outpouring of this sort, Hugh started to get up, but it was too late, Ray was already dropping heavily into a chair.

'Always so bloody kind to me . . .' Ray went on. 'Wonderful when Milly and I were breaking up . . . Used to prop me up, you know . . . Well, maybe you didn't. But I used to phone her sometimes . . . when

I was desperate. Didn't think you'd mind. Needed a sympathetic ear, and she always found time to listen, you see. Didn't take sides. Made me think I wasn't quite such a bastard as Milly made out. Gave me hope for the future. Began to think there might be more women like Lizzie out there somewhere. Haven't found one yet . . . but I live in hope . . .' He made a contrite face. 'God, this is sounding awful. All I meant to say was that I thought she was simply bloody wonderful and I'd like to kill the bastard that did it.' His eyes filled suddenly. 'Sorry . . .' He pushed a knuckle against an eye. 'Didn't mean to blub.'

'Glad you told me,' Hugh murmured, terribly embarrassed.

Ray shook his head. 'It's my own bloody stupid fault, overstepping the mark.' And for a moment Hugh thought he was talking about his feelings for Lizzie. 'Shouldn't have rushed into action like the bloody cavalry,' he went on. 'Should have kept to your brief and stayed on standby. Won't happen again, I swear.'

Desperate to get away, Hugh made for the door. 'The coroner would probably have delayed the post-mortem anyway.'

'You really think so?' Ray said inconsolably.

Hugh left him staring morosely at the table and went back to the kitchen, where for a brief moment the tangled affairs of Tom Deacon seemed to offer a welcome respite.


Isabel was searching a cupboard. 'I was trying to find ground coffee,' she explained.

Hugh dug it out of the fridge. 'What about you?'

'Coffee will be fine.'

'Thought you didn't drink it.'

Her eyes rounded. 'Oh, sometimes I do. Oh yes . . . definitely.'

'There's herb tea somewhere. Lou buys it. Rosehip, peppermint . . .'

'No, coffee will be fine, really. But I don't know how strong to make it.'

Hugh upended the half-used packet into the cafetière and thought of Lou, wondering if she'd managed to find Charlie, and what sort of state he'd be in, glassy-eyed with dope, bright-eyed with something harder, comatose with drink, or a combination of all three. He held up the cafetière to find he'd overfilled it. Shaking a random quantity of grounds into the sink, he poured in the boiling water. He was staring blankly at the wall tiles when Isabel said, 'Do you want me to do anything about Professor Ritchie, Hugh? Warn him the post-mortem might have to be postponed?'

'What? Um, yes . . . No. No . . . The coroner's going to let us know by the end of the day . . . isn't that what Ray said? They're going to let us know the . . . the . . .' He struggled for the thought, but his mind had stalled, he was beset by darkness and a constricting panic halfway between dream and memory.

'The police's decision?'

'Yes . . . So, wait until . . . until . . .' His chest was so tight he could hardly breathe, the room was swimming, he felt in danger of passing out.

'Hugh? Are you all right?' Isabel's words seemed to come to him slowly, from a long way away.

'Uhh?'

'Come and sit down.'

She was tugging at his sleeve. He let her lead him to the table, where she brought him a glass of water, followed by a cup of coffee.

'Have something to eat,' she urged him. 'You haven't touched your sandwich.'

'I'm not hungry.'

'You've got to eat,' Isabel insisted, pushing the sandwich closer.

Dutifully he took a mouthful and chewed on it half-heartedly.

'Shall we leave this till another time?' Isabel asked, gazing at him anxiously.

'No . . . No, let's get on . . .' He took a gulp of coffee to wash the food down and scalded his tongue. 'No . . . tell me about Tom. Tell me how it all came out, the business with . . . with the . . .' His brain was still thick, he felt as if he were drugged. 'The alternative psychiatric report . . .'

'Sure you're all right?'

'I'm fine.'

'Well, the first I heard was from Emma Deeds in Exeter, to say the family court had been in touch with her, wanting to know what if any High Court proceedings had taken place.'

'Another letter . . .'

'What?'

'Must have been another anonymous letter. It was bound to happen sooner or later.'

'Emma Deeds didn't know what it was. Or she didn't say. Anyway, I put her off till I could speak to you. Meantime *our* judge's clerk called, saying something had come to the judge's attention regarding certain family proceedings involving Tom, and could we come and see him in chambers as soon as possible.'

'No surprise there, either. The family judge would have phoned him direct. Almost the first thing she'd have done.' The coffee was beginning to kick in, and Hugh downed the rest in one. There was something else that would help clear his head, he realised, and that was a quick drink. He got up to pour himself a Scotch and heard the murmur of Raymond's voice next door.

'That's when I thought I'd better speak to Desmond Riley,' Isabel was saying.

'Absolutely right.'

'I filled him in as best I could, but he only had a minute before going into court. And when he called back, that's when he got put through to Raymond. I don't know why.'

Hugh took a sip of his drink and brought it to the table.'Because Ray told the switchboard, that's why,' he said, his exasperation coming to the surface again.

'Oh,' said Isabel, not quite sure what to make of this. 'Anyway, when I managed to get back to Desmond and we had more of a chance to talk, he seemed to think the judge would be understanding. Up to a point anyway – that's how he put it: "up to a point". But he thought the judge would want to see the psychiatric report from the family proceedings, perhaps ask for the psychiatrist to give evidence in person.'

'I'm sure that's the very least he'll want,' said Hugh, feeling the Scotch work its magic. 'Can you manage all that?'

She nodded keenly. 'I've already asked Emma Deeds to send a copy of the psychiatric report.'

'You should have backup for a meeting in chambers, Isabel. It's not fair to send you on your own.'

'But Desmond'll be there.'

'You should still have backup in case the judge has some questions.' Thinking aloud, he murmured, 'Perhaps I should ask Martin Sachs . . .'

Isabel looked alarmed. 'Not so sure that'd be a good idea.'

Picturing Martin Sachs at his most insufferable and patronising, Hugh gave a sigh of agreement. 'Raymond then?'

'It would still mean a briefing,' Isabel said unhappily.

Finally Hugh understood what she was trying to tell him, that a briefing could put her on the spot, force her to admit that she'd known all about Tom's stunt while the hearing was still in progress. 'Christ, what a bloody mess.'

'No . . . *No* . . . You did the right thing, giving Tom a chance.'

'I let him think he could get away with it.'

Isabel shook her head. 'He'd already made up his mind to get away with it, which is something totally different.'

'He screamed down the phone at me last night.'

'That's the other thing,' Isabel said. 'I got a call from Dr Ainsley on the way here. He said he was worried about Tom's mental state. Wanted to know if we knew where he was. If there was anything we could do.'

'Like what?'

'Get him some help, I suppose.'

'When did Ainsley speak to Tom?'

'A couple of hours ago, I think. Said he'd never known him in such a bad way. Talking about grabbing the boys and going into hiding—'

'Just the sort of stupid thing he *would* do.'

'But what worried him most was what Tom might do if he lost the boys altogether.'

Hugh tried to shut out the images that raced through his mind. 'Can't Ainsley do something about it himself?'

'He's in Canada.'

'Christ.'

'I could go to his place, see if he's there,' Isabel volunteered without enthusiasm.

'Wouldn't do any good.' Knocking back the last of his drink, Hugh pulled up Tom's number on his phone and tried to think of what message to leave. It would be a mistake to offer false hopes and wild promises. The only chance was an assurance that everything possible was being done. 'What's the precise situation on the care proceedings?'

'Care proceedings?' Isabel said, puzzled. 'Emma Deeds didn't say anything about care proceedings.'

'That's what Tom told me last night, that they were threatening to take the children into care.'

'God, no wonder he's lost it.'

'Check it out with Emma Deeds, will you?'

While Isabel made the call, Hugh poured a cup of coffee and took it into the dining room, where Ray was slumped in his chair, staring into space, though Hugh had the feeling he'd only just come off the phone.

Ray jerked round and, seeing the proffered coffee, declared profusely, 'Hey, just what I needed! Thanks!' Then, apropos of nothing, added warmly, 'My old friend . . . I've been sitting here going down memory lane, thinking about the old days. Don't really appreciate them at the time, do you? Not till after the event.' Again, Hugh thought he must be talking about Lizzie. 'Wasn't such a bad set-up, was it, the old firm? Never would've made us a fortune, but we did all right, didn't we?' Ray gave a nostalgic sniff. 'Those partners' meetings in the pub. Home by six. Taking the odd Friday off. Not sure how long we'd have survived, of course. But they were good times while they lasted, eh?'

'I'm going to resign,' Hugh said.

Ray made a face of almost clownish incredulity. 'What? Don't be crazy, Hugh. What the hell are you talking about?'

'I'm not made for a big firm. Never was.'

'Listen, *listen*, my old friend – this isn't the time to be thinking about things like that! Not while you've got this terrible, *terrible* business hanging over you.'

'I'm sure.'

'But why? *Why?* It's not the Deacon case, is it?'

'If you like.'

'Come on.'

'No, I'm serious.'

'I don't get it,' said Ray helplessly.

Hugh shrugged, incapable of explanations.

'Are you worried about the case making a loss? Is that it?'

'Should I be?'

'For Christ's sake, Hugh – no one's going to judge you on one case, not when you've been such a – such a

– *player*! And not when you've just lost your beloved
Lizzie. Jesus, the partners aren't made of stone. They're
right behind you. Believe me – one hundred per cent.
Anyway, it's not as if the Deacon claim's about to be
thrown out altogether, is it? Just knocked back a bit.
Who knows, it may not show a loss after all!' He
gripped Hugh's upper arm encouragingly. 'That's why
I wanted to sit in – see if I could take at least one
worry off your shoulders.'

Hearing a phone ringing in the kitchen, Hugh made
an abrupt gesture and swung rapidly away.

Ray called after him, but Hugh was already in the
hall where he almost collided with Isabel emerging
from the kitchen. She was holding up his mobile phone.
'It's Charlie,' she breathed.


The road was short, with just six terraced houses
crammed along each side and a tall weed-clad chain-
link fence blocking off the end. The houses were two-
storey red brick, each with a small front area filled
with dustbins and assorted rubbish behind a dilapi-
dated wall. Hugh knew the district only from the
arterial roads that encircled it and its reputation for
ethnic restaurants and evangelical churches. It was here
the respectable West Indian community had moved
when they were pushed out of St Paul's by the motorway and the drug dealers, though from the look of the
place now the drug dealers couldn't have been very far
behind.

Number six was the last house on the left and, either
for lack of an outside neighbour or from subsidence,
was noticeably crooked, not a windowsill straight and

the front door remade to fit. Hugh parked almost opposite, between a white van and a Ford Escort painted scarlet with a broad white stripe down the bonnet. As he got out, the hum of vibrating metal and the approaching howl of a diesel engine announced a railway line behind the chain-link fence.

There was a mouldering mattress wedged behind the dustbins of number six and a pile of dead leaves blown up against the door. There were two doorbells, neither labelled, so he pressed both. Hearing no ring, he pressed again, then rapped a knuckle on the door. After a while a door sounded deep in the house, then creaking boards, then the latch clicked and the door swung open to reveal Charlie.

'Dad!' He was wearing ragged jeans and a thin T-shirt and no shoes, and seemed overcome, almost as if he hadn't expected Hugh to turn up.

'You okay, Charlie?'

'Yeah.'

But he looked pale and tired and edgy, and Hugh found himself looking for other signs of drugs.

'Thanks for coming,' Charlie said in a constricted voice and, eyes averted, stood back to let Hugh in. The hall was cold and gloomy, with scuffed paint over Anaglypta wallpaper and a smell of dirt and stale cigarettes and old food.

'Why didn't you call, Charlie? We've been frantic with worry. Lou's been out looking for you everywhere.'

'Sorry . . . *Sorry* . . . My phone ran out . . .'

'We thought something terrible must have happened. Not to phone!'

'I couldn't leave Elk.'

'Why?'

'He's sick.'

'*Sick?* Christ, Charlie, Lou thought you must have been mugged or worse. And I thought—' Hugh lifted both arms and dropped them again. 'Well, I thought you must have got into trouble again.'

For once Charlie didn't bristle at the suggestion. 'Lou knows I'm okay?'

'I called her straight away. Wasn't there another phone you could have used?'

Charlie shook his head.

'And I suppose Elk—' Hugh pulled himself up short and said in a calmer tone, 'Look, why don't you tell me all about it on the way home, eh? Let's get going.'

'Can't leave yet. Not till Elk's in better shape.'

'Well, if you can't leave, why did you—' Breaking off again, Hugh said mournfully, 'I don't understand.'

With a glance up the stairs, Charlie moved away down the passage, looking back to make sure Hugh was following. They entered a dank kitchen with a filthy stove, cluttered surfaces, a sink full of dishes, and a floor that was dark and tacky underfoot.

Charlie extracted a mug from the sink and, filling it with water, gulped greedily, as if he hadn't drunk anything for a long time. 'Elk's been sick,' he said.

'What's the matter with him?'

'He OD'ed accidentally.'

'Did he now?' Hugh said tightly. 'I thought he was meant to be in recovery.'

'He was. For more than three hundred days. But he had a row with his dad . . . Basically told him he was rubbish . . . never wanted to see him again.' Charlie's shrug suggested this was quite enough to send anyone back to drugs. 'And when he shot up he didn't allow for losing his tolerance.'

'Heroin?'

'Yeah.'

'Shouldn't he be in hospital then?'

'The worst's over.'

'But you're really okay, Charlie?'

'Sure,' he breathed, though the tension in him suggested a different story.

'Isn't there anyone else who can look after Elk?'

'No.'

'But this place, Charlie . . . It's God-awful.'

'I've promised to stay. For another day. Two at the most.'

'So what are you telling me? That Elk comes first?' Hugh said, hating himself in the role of martyr.

'No, Dad, *no* – but it's part of the deal.'

'Some deal,' Hugh growled.

Suddenly the tension in Charlie was unbearable. 'Listen, Dad . . . Elk's got something to tell you.'

'*Me?* What can he have to tell *me*?'

'Dad, whatever happens you've got to promise you won't get mad at him. He can't take it right now. He'll only clam up.'

'Why should I get mad at him?' Hugh asked with a pull of dread.

'Just say you won't.'

'I can't promise something like that when I don't know what the hell he's going to tell me.'

'You've got to promise, otherwise it won't be any good,' Charlie pleaded.

They glared at each other for an instant. Then Hugh nodded rapidly. 'Okay . . .'

Charlie hesitated, looking doubtful.

'I promise,' Hugh said as the dread circled his stomach.

Charlie led the way into the narrow hall and up the stairs to the back of the house where he opened a door just enough to step into the opening. 'Hiya,' he called into the room. 'My dad's here.' There must have been some kind of response because Charlie said, 'Now?' Another pause, then Charlie said, 'Yeah,' and moved forward to let Hugh in.

The room was small and painted a violent shade of blue. There was just enough space for two single beds pressed against opposite walls, a chair in between, a chest of drawers hidden under a jumble of clothes, and an ancient electric heater which at any other time Hugh would have marked down as a serious fire risk. Elk was in the bed nearest the window, lying on his side in a grey T-shirt, one tattooed arm bent over the grubby duvet. His eyes followed Hugh into the room. The rest of his body was so still that Hugh had the impression his eyes were all he could move. His stubbled head was matched by a stubbled chin, while the pallor of his skin was accentuated by two livid, pustular spots that blazed from his cheek. Charlie sat down on the unmade bed opposite and Hugh sat next to him.

'I told Dad how I'm gonna stay till you're okay.' Charlie glanced at Hugh for confirmation. 'I told him how you'd had a row with your dad and accidentally OD'ed, and that you just need time to get straight again. So we all know where you're coming from. Yeah?'

Elk's gaze lost focus and turned inward.

'Hey, it's gonna be okay . . .' Charlie waited for a moment, then leant forward and tapped Elk's arm. 'I'm telling you – it's gonna be okay.'

Elk's stare suggested he wasn't convinced.

'Wanna sit up?' Grabbing a pillow from the spare bed Charlie folded it over to form a head cushion and, standing over Elk, waited attentively as he hoisted himself higher in the bed. The cushion in place, Charlie sat down again and said, 'So . . . just tell us. Yeah? What you saw.' When Elk didn't speak, Charlie repeated firmly, 'I'm telling you – it's gonna be okay. Nothing's gonna happen.'

Just when it seemed Elk was never going to speak he said, 'Yeah . . .'

'So . . .'

'So . . .' Elk inhaled wearily. 'I came by your place, I saw this guy—'

'But the reason you were there?' Charlie interrupted. Elk frowned.

'Elk's phone had got nicked,' Charlie explained. 'He knew I was coming down from college, but he didn't know when, so he came looking for me. That's why he was at the house – to find me.' Charlie gestured for Elk to go on. 'Tell us what happened when you got there.'

'Yeah . . . there's these lights on . . . so I go round the back—'

'He didn't want to ring the bell, he wanted to see if I was there first,' Charlie chipped in.

'Yeah . . .'

'And then?' Charlie prompted.

'This is the night of the fire?' Hugh asked quietly.

Charlie nodded.

'What time? Roughly?' He aimed the question at Elk.

Elk gave a shrug. 'Must've been ten . . . something like that.'

'That's another reason he didn't want to ring the bell,' Charlie said. 'Because it was late. So . . . you looked round the back.'

'Yeah. No one there. So I go round the front again and . . . see what I can see . . .'

'He tried looking in the living-room windows, but the curtains were drawn.'

Elk lowered his eyelids in agreement, and the livid spots flared like beacons on his face.

'Then you went to the dining-room window.'

'Yeah . . .'

'And the hall door was open so he could see through to the stairs,' Charlie said to Hugh.

'Yeah . . .'

'Go on,' Charlie urged.

'Yeah, well . . . when I get there, it's like I just miss this person. All I see is this . . . this . . .'

'Glimpse.'

'It's like the moment I look, they're gone.'

'Man? Woman?' Hugh asked, his mouth dry.

'Dunno. Couldn't see that much.'

This time it was Hugh who urged him forward. 'And then?'

'Didn't know what to do . . . without a mobile to call Charlie. So I wait a while . . . Then, just when I'm thinkin' there's no point in hangin' about . . .' In the pause that followed, Elk tightened his mouth and Charlie flung a tense glance in Hugh's direction. '. . . I see this bloke . . . He's, like, headin' upstairs . . . carryin' someone. . . . A woman.'

Blinking a sudden heat from his eyes, Hugh said, 'What could you see of her?'

'Huh?'

'You could see it was a woman?'

Elk had another think. 'Yeah . . . saw her feet . . . Knees. Yeah . . . her knees.'

'So he was carrying her in his arms?' Seeing that Elk didn't get the point of the question, Hugh added, 'Not over his shoulder?'

'In his arms, yeah.'

'And this man – what did he look like?'

'Never got a look.'

'But was he dark haired? Fair? Young? Old?'

Elk's eyes swivelled in Charlie's direction, as if for rescue.

'Short? Tall? Fat? Thin?' Hugh persevered. 'Anything you can remember, Elk. *Anything* at all.'

'I wasn't gonna hang around, was I? The moment I saw the way things were, I was out of there.'

The way things were: a man carrying a woman up to bed. Hugh bowed his head.

Charlie said, 'But you thought he was wearing jeans?'

'Dunno.'

'But you said—'

'I dunno. Okay?' Elk said irritably.

'And you can't remember anything else?' Hugh asked.

Elk lowered his eyes: a no.

Charlie said, 'The motorbike, Elk – tell him about the motorbike.'

Elk said reluctantly, 'Yeah . . . there was this motorbike . . .'

'Where?'

'Side of the house.'

A lot of things raced through Hugh's mind as he absorbed this. That it was the perfect means of transport for an arsonist. That it seemed to rule out your average drug addict, drifter, schizophrenic, general all-round maniac. That various people he knew owned motorbikes, a couple of the partners in Dimmock Marsh, a few neighbours. That the information both worried and excited him.

'What kind of motorbike?'

'I dunno.'

'Well, was it large?'

Elk was getting drowsy. 'I dunno . . .'

'What about the colour?'

Elk was already indicating a don't know.

Hugh searched desperately for more questions. 'Did it look shiny?'

Elk paused to consider. 'Yeah . . . Yeah, shiny.'

'With lots of metal over the front?' Hugh sketched a shape in the air.

'Might've.'

'And . . . it was parked down the left-hand side of the house?'

Elk's eyelids were drooping heavily now, he was battling to stay awake and Hugh had to ask him again.

'Yeah . . .'

'And was it facing outwards? Ready to go?'

'Yeah . . .' Elk turned his head away and closed his eyes.

'Thanks,' Hugh said. 'And if you remember anything else . . .'

But if Elk heard him, he gave no sign.

'You'll keep asking him?' he said to Charlie.

'Sure.'

As Hugh led the way down the stairs he said, 'I don't know why you thought I'd be angry, Charlie. God – anything *but*.' Then, with the sense of having known it all along, a realisation came to him. Reaching the narrow hallway, he said flatly, 'Elk came looking for you two days before that, didn't he? He was the hoodie I chased down the lane.'

Charlie nodded.

'Why did he run away?'

'Thought you wouldn't be too welcoming, I guess.'

Hugh didn't bother to deny it. 'But these things he saw, Charlie – we need him to make a statement to the police. Will he agree, do you think?'

'Yeah.'

'You're sure?'

'It's part of our deal.'

Once again Charlie had managed to take Hugh by surprise. 'So, if I can arrange it for tomorrow . . .'

'I'll make sure he gets there.'

'I'll come and collect you.'

At the door he said, 'First I'll get your phone topped up at a cash dispenser. That's how you do it, isn't it, at a cash dispenser? And food. I'll get some food and drop it back for you. And then you'll come back, won't you, Charlie? As soon as you can. You'll come home?'

# TEN

The morning was still and bitterly cold, with ice warnings for country roads. Hugh had set off in good time, hoping to have a quick word with the Rev Emmanuel before collecting Elk and Charlie for their appointment with the police, but as he drove up the long hill towards the Carstairs Estate he realised the reverend was otherwise engaged: a hearse and three black limousines stood outside the church.

He slowed indecisively. With forty minutes to spare, he didn't want to hang about in the dismal house by the railway line, nor get the boys to the police station too early and run the risk of Elk taking fright. Seeing an entrance to the Carstairs coming up ahead, he made up his mind and turned in. He paused by a large map of the estate. The print was faded, the colours bleached, some block names had been almost entirely scratched out, but after checking his notebook he identified the block he was looking for. The road, marked by low kerbs and concrete bollards and punctuated by speed bumps, circled the five giant high-rises, passing between concrete aprons on one side and patches of worn grass on the other. The block he wanted was on the far side. Like the rest of the estate it looked cleaner and brighter close up, though that was probably the effect of the sunlight. He parked in an area marked 'Residents Only' because all the other places seemed to have hatched yellow lines and warning notices. Nearby, some kids were kicking a ball around, while outside the entrance two large ladies were talking intently. It all looked very normal, but then what had he expected?

Beyond a pair of battered swing doors was a cramped lobby with a concrete floor that sported a scattering of cigarette ends, a chocolate wrapper and a large ink-like stain. There were two lifts, one of which arrived within a minute or so, which he guessed was fast for a block this size. The lift interior was small but well lit, with an emergency intercom that appeared intact. The cage rattled and rumbled, but delivered him safely to the twelfth floor. He stepped out into an altogether darker world. Two gloomy corridors stretched away in opposite directions, illuminated only by small end-windows and the occasional low-powered ceiling light. There was a strong smell of disinfectant and the loud beat of bass music. Opposite the lift a patch on the wall with torn fixings suggested there had once been a sign to say which flats lay in which direction. He tried right and when the first flat number looked promising kept going. He passed the blaring music and was nearing the end of the corridor when he saw the door of the last flat. The jamb had been compressed and splintered, the door gouged around the battered lock, while two shiny new locks had been fitted top and bottom. Caught up by a dull, incoherent anxiety, he rang the bell once, and again, followed by a series of firm knocks.

After a time he retreated to the flat with the bass music and rang the bell. There was a long pause, then a male voice called though the closed door, 'Who's that?'

'I wanted to ask about the Jameses.'

'Say a-gain,' came the voice.

Hugh put his mouth closer to the edge of the door and repeated the request at a shout.

After a moment the latch sounded, the door opened a little, and the music boomed out. A face filled the opening, young and black, with shrewd eyes that appraised Hugh coolly.

'Who wants to know?'

'My wife was with the Citizens Advice,' Hugh said, raising his voice over the music. 'She used to help Mrs James. We wanted to know if Mrs James and Wesley were all right.'

The young man gazed impassively at Hugh while the music thumped out behind him.

'I saw the door . . .' Hugh gestured towards the end of the corridor. 'It looks as if it's been forced.'

The young man canted his lower jaw to one side.

'What happened?'

A minute shrug.

'We're worried. That's the only reason we're asking.'

'They came. . . . They took him away.'

'Who took him away?'

The young man looked mildly entertained that Hugh should ask.

'Was it the police?'

Another shrug.

'We're really worried, otherwise we wouldn't ask.'

'Police, social services . . .' His expression suggested they were all the same to him.

'You didn't see them, then?'

He gave a minute shake of his head.

'You just heard about it?'

A nod.

'And when was this?'

'Two . . . three days . . .'

Hugh thanked him and swung away. Waiting for the lift, his anxiety hardened, he pressed impatiently on the button. When the lift finally arrived, the downward journey seemed endless; he had a sudden fear of being trapped. Emerging fast before the doors were fully opened, he bumped into a youth who cursed him loudly. Driving away, he hit the first speed bump too fast and the car rabbit-hopped. He made himself slow down, but the anxiety was still there, bunched high in his stomach.

Pulling out into the main road, he saw a trickle of black-clad figures coming out of the church and pall-bearers sliding a flower-decked coffin into the hearse. He drew up behind the last limousine. John Emmanuel was standing in the porch, resplendent in white and blue vestments, shaking hands with the mourners, listening and talking, his breath vaporising in the freezing air. Hugh hung back until the last mourner drifted away, and approached John as he was locking the church door.

'Hugh! Hey, how you doing?'

'John, you know a boy called Wesley James, don't you?' Hugh asked.

'Yes.'

'Can you tell me what's happened to him?'

'Why, yes . . . he's gone to the hospital. He's not been well, not well at all.' Casting a glance towards the waiting cortège, John gestured for them to walk.

'So it was an ambulance crew that took him away?'

'No . . . No, I believe it was social services.'

'To hospital? You're sure about that?'

'That's what his mother said. It was for his own safety. He'd threatened to throw himself out of a window. He couldn't be left alone.'

'He's committed himself voluntarily, then? Under the Mental Health Act?'

But John didn't know about that. 'Why you asking, Hugh? What's happened?'

'Social services can't take people away for treatment, John. Not without a court order. You're sure it wasn't the police?'

'His mother never mentioned the police. What's the problem?'

They had paused by one of the black cars. The occupants, dressed in deepest mourning, gazed out at them with melancholy interest.

'Wesley was Lizzie's witness. Wesley saw two white boys kill Jason Jackson.'

John Emmanuel stared at him in astonishment. '*Wesley?*' He shook his mighty head. 'Now you're making me worried, Hugh. You're saying that's the reason he's got ill?'

Worse than ill, Hugh thought, though he didn't say so. 'Did you know the door of the flat had been forced?'

John was momentarily dumbstruck. 'But Gloria never said nothing about that. You sure?'

'Well, it looked forced to me.'

One of the mourners leant his face close to the car window and fixed the reverend with a pointed stare.

'I have to go, Hugh.'

'Have you heard of someone called Forbes? Part of a white gang?' Hugh asked.

'Sure. There's not many haven't heard of the Forbes boys. Why? Are you saying—' But, unable to postpone his duties any longer, he abandoned the question and reached for the car door handle. 'How can we check Wesley's all right? What can we do?'

'I'll start with social services and the hospitals.'

'And I'll speak to Gloria. I don't understand about the door. She never said anything about the door.'

It was fifteen minutes since Elk had emerged from the interview room and Charlie, armed with money and the number of a taxi firm, had taken him off for a meal, an NA meeting and a final night of moral support in the squalid house by the railway line. Hugh and Steadman were sitting alone in the interview room, which was hot and airless and imbued with the scent of industrial air freshener. DS Reynolds had brought water for Hugh and coffee for DI Steadman before vanishing, apparently never to return. Steadman had taken off his jacket and hung it over the back of his chair to reveal a deep-collared cream shirt with wide cuffs and gold cufflinks. He slid his elbows onto the Formica table and clasped his white hands together.

'If I could just get this straight, Mr Gwynne – you're saying that the person or persons who set fire to your home are also behind the disappearance of this witness?'

'Yes.'

'I'm not clear what makes you so sure the two events are linked.'

'The fact that my wife was the only person who knew the identity of the witness, and now the witness has disappeared.'

Steadman gave a slow nod to show he was getting the picture. 'So it's the timing that's significant, is that what you're saying?'

'Yes.'

'And you're suggesting that the arsonist went to the house with the purpose of silencing your wife?'

'Yes. And—' As the thought clarified and found expression in his mind Hugh was ambushed by a fresh throb of anxiety; he had to catch his breath. 'And to get the name.'

'The name of the witness?'

'Yes.' *Please don't let me imagine how he did it. Please* . . .

'I see. And the witness – you're certain he's disappeared?'

'Yes . . .' *Perhaps he didn't hurt her, perhaps he just threatened her. Perhaps* . . . Hugh took a sip of his water, which tasted warm and metallic. 'The neighbours said he'd been taken away. But I've had my assistant check the hospitals and social service departments, and he's not there.'

'I see. So you know his identity?'

'Yes.'

'I'm not clear – when we talked yesterday you said you didn't know his identity.'

'I didn't then. I do now.'

'And how did that come about?'

Hugh thought of the printouts lying openly beside

his bed at Oakhill and the computer sitting in Charlie's room, and felt a twinge of unease. 'I can't say.'

Steadman tilted his head as if to get the measure of this remark. 'Can I ask why?'

'I need to protect my source.'

Steadman gave a sage nod, though behind the show of equanimity it seemed to Hugh that he didn't have much time for the niceties of source protection. Coming fast on this thought, it occurred to Hugh that having made such basic errors at the start of the case the inspector must be under a lot of pressure to make up for lost time. 'I see,' Steadman murmured as he picked up his pen and started to write.

'We've checked the hospitals and social services,' Hugh said. 'But the one place we haven't checked is the police stations.'

Steadman went on writing for a moment before looking up. 'In case the witness is in custody for an unrelated matter, you mean?'

'Well, yes, that's one possibility, I suppose. But I was thinking more of him being held somewhere for his own protection.'

'I don't follow.'

'I thought maybe your colleague Chief Inspector Montgomery might have got him in a safe place.'

Steadman went through the motions of considering the idea. 'Why would you think that?'

They exchanged a look of mutual incomprehension.

'Well, Montgomery investigated the Jackson murder. He's the only other person with an interest in spiriting him away.'

'If there was a witness in police protection I assure you I'd have heard about it, Mr Gwynne.' Steadman returned to his writing. 'His name?' he murmured, eyes on his note pad.

'Sorry?'

'The witness's name?' Steadman glanced up.

Hugh hesitated as the incoherent anxiety pulled at him again.

'Mr Gwynne, I can hardly search for him if I don't have his name.'

'No ... I realise that. No ... But it'll be kept confidential?'

'I'll have to inform my team.'

'But so far as possible? The witness confided in my wife because he trusted her. I'd hate to feel that I was betraying that trust without ... well, some sort of guarantee.' Sensing that Steadman was unmoved by this argument, Hugh said, 'Perhaps I should explain – this young man didn't just witness the killing of Jason Jackson, he actually recognised one of the gang who did it. So if they got to hear ... if they got hold of him ...'

'But you're suggesting they already have, Mr Gwynne.'

Hugh paused uncertainly. 'Yes ...' he conceded at last. 'Yes, I suppose I am.'

'And the assailant he was able to identify? Do you have a name?'

'Yes. It was Forbes.'

Steadman was writing again. 'First name?'

'Don't know. But I gather he's one of two brothers – or more than two brothers – who're part of a well-known gang. You've heard of them?'

The pale eyes lifted briefly. 'They're not on my manor but yes ... yes, I know the name.' He prepared to write again.

'And if one of them had a motorbike . . .'

'Yes . . .'

'It might be on CCTV somewhere. There's a camera in our village, by the parade.'

Steadman acknowledged the information with a brisk nod. 'And the name and address of the witness, Mr Gwynne?'

A last hesitation, a last unaccountable twinge of doubt, and Hugh told him.


In the car he tried calling Lou but she wasn't answering her mobile and there was no reply from the house line, so he left messages on both. He drove in silence, with no radio and no music and, after cancelling an incoming call from Ray, no phone either. He needed to slow his head down, to get a grip on his anxieties, to prepare himself for the inevitable delays and frustrations of the police investigation. What did they have to go on, after all? No hard evidence, no fingerprints or DNA, just one motorbike with a shiny cowling, make and colour unknown. The CCTV in the village was primitive: one camera aimed along the shopfronts with an oblique view of the road; knowing the local council, the thing probably wasn't even loaded. And how many motorbikes passed through in any one evening? Ten? Thirty? A hundred for all he knew. As if to emphasise their ubiquity, one passed him now, with another coming up behind, weaving fearlessly in and out of the car slipstreams, its rider bent low in helmet and blacked-out visor.

He tried to imagine a future in which the arsonist wasn't caught, and saw his life going on as it was now, in a succession of journeys and restless nights, reading, questioning, searching for the evidence the police had missed, and if that should fail resorting to campaigning, like Denzel Lewis's family, becoming a master of soundbites and articulate outrage and appeals to the public. Perhaps Lizzie would be proved right, perhaps he too would invest his hopes in the public's better nature.

Coming to a supermarket, he decided to pick up some food. It would be a diversion; also a much-needed grounding. He looked for meals the kids might enjoy. Lou was easy; she liked anything to do with pasta and vegetables, but he couldn't remember if Charlie's latest passion was for spare ribs or spicy chicken. He was keen to get it right, not just because Charlie had done so well to persuade Elk to make a witness statement, but because Oakhill didn't feel complete without him. Deciding to cover all possible shifts in Charlie's tastes, Hugh loaded the trolley with spare ribs, spicy chicken, chips and potato skins, adding a pizza for good measure. Then, persuading himself he had arrived in the wine section by chance, he went along the row of New World reds till he found a nice Merlot. Wine as medication. The question was, as a sleeping potion, half a bottle to be consumed over dinner, the remainder before bed? Or to be administered in heavier doses as a general anaesthetic? There was a long week ahead, with the opening of the inquest, the arrival of Lizzie's relatives, the funeral itself. He felt he must decide there and then to keep things under control or deny himself even the evening glass he loved so much. In the end he took just three bottles, to see if he could make them last for three days.

Driving out of the car park he registered the presence of a petrol station and the fact that he needed fuel at virtually the same instant, which was an instant too late to make the turning safely. He went for it anyway, stamping on the brakes, swerving sharply without indicating, grinding a wheel into the kerb, but if the driver behind took exception to this violent manoeuvre he didn't show it. At the pumps Hugh had another unsettling moment when for a split second he thought he was filling the car with petrol instead of diesel. I'm finally beginning to lose it, he thought.

Back on the road, he tried to drive with attention, keeping to the speed limit, watching out for ice, using his indicators in good time. But his concentration must have drifted because the next thing he knew he was in the wrong lane for his turn, and was forced to indicate and slow down until someone let him in. A horn sounded angrily, he thought he must have misread the other driver's willingness to give way, only to realise the horn was aimed at a car further back which was trying the same last-minute lane switch.

On a smaller road now, with no lanes to worry about, Hugh nevertheless didn't entirely trust himself not to miss the next turning or, God forbid, the next car, and he made a fresh effort to stay alert. At a village with a renowned farmers' shop he made another stop to buy local beef and cheese. The strange thing about paying attention and looking in the mirror more often than usual was that you noticed the cars behind. Setting off again, he realised the car pulling out from a parking place some way beyond the farmers' shop was the same dark-blue Honda that had made the sudden lane switch at the last turn-off. Another strange thing

when you were thoroughly tired and overwrought was
how easy it was to imagine that this same car had been
with you all the way from the supermarket car park,
maybe even earlier. His readiness to believe he was
being followed unnerved him. Paranoia was setting in.
At this rate he'd be as bad as Tom, seeing conspiracies
everywhere.

Approaching a junction he saw a road sign to a
place that lay in the direction of the village where Tom
was living. Even as he argued with himself that it was
miles out of his way and Tom probably wouldn't be
there and it was crazy to imagine for a single second
that the dark-blue Honda would take the same turning,
he indicated and, his pulse quickening, moved towards
the crown of the road to make the turn. Behind him,
the dark-blue Honda also began to indicate and move
over. Poised on the crown of the road, waiting for a
gap in the oncoming traffic, Hugh watched the Honda
coming up behind him and stopping some three or four
yards behind. He tried to get a look at the driver's face,
but the visor was down, the sun low, and only the
man's chin was visible over a dark polo shirt.

Hugh made the turn and set off along a meandering
road through a string of suburban villages. At one
point he took the wrong fork and had to follow two
sides of a triangle to get back on track. The Honda
stayed with him, cruising some fifteen yards behind.
Yet even as Hugh's nerves tautened and the sweat
began to prick against his skin, a part of him still clung
to denial. Who on earth would want to follow him?
The press? The police? For what possible reason? They
knew where he lived. They only had to lift the phone.
Who else, then? The driver might be many things, but

from the look of the well-maintained car, the neat polo shirt, he was no hardened gang member from a rough estate. Hugh began to concoct wild plans for ambush and confrontation, only to realise he'd almost missed the obvious. He went fast round a bend then slowed, so that when the Honda appeared it was close enough for him to see the registration number clearly. The figure 5 in mirror image gave him a moment's hesitation, but then he had it. Not trusting his memory, he kept repeating it aloud until, with one eye on the road, he managed to operate the memo function on his phone. Even then he checked the number a second time when the Honda drew up behind him at a T junction.

He couldn't have said why he went on after that; from a need for company perhaps, or reassurance. Approaching Tom's place he decided to maintain his speed till the last moment then swing in across the entrance so he could get a look at the Honda driver as he went past. But he had been to Tom's cottage only once before and the sprawling suburban village with its string of garden centres and electrical-goods warehouses confused him; he didn't see the narrow side lane until he was almost on top of it. Braking hard for the second time that afternoon, he pulled in, only to hit ice and feel the back of the car skidding sideways. Wrenching the wheel over had no effect, he watched the corner of a brick wall advancing inexorably towards the passenger side until it met the rear door with a firm crunch. He jerked round to look at the road but he was too late; the Honda was already passing by, the driver's face obscured.

He pressed his head back against the seat-rest and swore once, loudly, with feeling. Climbing out of the

car, he saw a familiar long-legged figure hurrying up
the lane towards him.

'What the hell?' Tom called.

'I was being followed. I was trying to get rid of him.'
It sounded even more fantastic spoken aloud, but Tom
merely raised his eyebrows and went round the car to
inspect the damage.

'It's just the panel,' he announced. Then: 'Maybe
the whole door. Let's get you clear. Start by moving
forward a touch, full right-lock . . .'

Hugh got back in and followed Tom's instructions,
inching back and forth on one full lock or the other
until the car was free of the wall.

'Are they still around?' Tom said, tipping his head
towards the road.

'Don't think so.'

'What are we looking for?'

'A dark-blue Honda.'

Tom went and looked up and down the road, then
turned back with a shake of his head. 'You look like
you need a drink, hot and sweet variety,' he said.

Tom walked ahead of the car and waited for Hugh
to park alongside a high wall opposite the terrace of
tiny artisans' cottages where he lived.

'Who was following you, then?' Tom asked as Hugh
climbed out.

'Don't know.'

'Who'd have *reason* to follow you?'

'Don't know.'

'Well, either they're for you or against you. Has to
be one or the other. Work it out.'

'It's not that easy, for Christ's sake.'

Tom led the way towards his front door. 'What do they *want*, then? What're they *after*?'

But Hugh wasn't listening. He was too busy staring at the shiny motorbike parked in front of Tom's cottage. 'Where did that come from?' he asked, maintaining a level tone.

'Huh?'

'The motorbike.'

'My landlord's.' Tom indicated the cottage next door. Then, with a dismissive grunt: 'Well, it's never gonna be *mine*, is it?'

Seeing that the motorbike was in fact parked half in front of the next-door cottage, knowing full well that Tom had no money, Hugh felt a dart of shame at the thoughts that had raced so readily into his mind. 'No,' he murmured. 'No . . .'

Dusk had come early to the narrow lane; the tiny cottage was shrouded in a premature gloom. With its slimy bricks, sagging gutters and dark peeling paint it had an air of irretrievable damp and decay. The front room was cosy enough, with a fire burning in the grate, posters on the walls, and photographs of Holly and the two boys on the mantelpiece, but the kitchen was freezing and through the door to the bathroom extension Hugh could see mould blooming along one wall.

'Was he tailgating you?' Tom asked, cigarette jammed between his lips as he filled the kettle. 'Trying to push you around?'

'No. Just following. Unless I'm going completely mad . . .' The more he replayed the journey from the supermarket in his mind, the more he began to wonder if it hadn't all been a wild coincidence.

'You'll go to the cops?' Under the overhead light Tom's features were jagged, his eyes two deep shadows.

'They'll probably think I'm being paranoid.'

'Yeah, well, that goes with the territory, doesn't it? People thinking you've gone off the rails. The shock, you know,' Tom added in a high-pitched parody of concern. 'Never the same since.'

'Listen, Tom, I came to check – you're not thinking of doing anything crazy, are you? You're not thinking of going into hiding with the boys or anything stupid like that? Because it's not going to help, you know.'

'I'm sure as hell not gonna let them be dumped in care.'

'Emma Deeds says there's been a case conference, that's all. No application to the court.'

Tom shot him a look of exaggerated incredulity. 'You think social services are gonna give *warning*? You think they're gonna *tell* anyone? No way! They'll just grab the kids and argue later.'

'They'd still have to make an application—'

'Yeah, at dead of night! On the sly! I know how they work. They're like the fucking Gestapo.'

'There'd still have to be a hearing, Tom. And if you try to do a runner you can kiss goodbye to any hope of getting the kids.'

'Already done that,' he spat.

'But you haven't, Tom! That's the whole point. Your chances of getting custody are still *good*. Despite everything you've still got a great chance!' It was a rash statement, but Hugh was prepared to say anything just then. 'If we can persuade the family court that the two sets of psychiatrists were looking at your illness from two entirely different angles – your capacity to work versus your capacity to look after the kids – well, they'd buy that, I'm sure they would.'

'Like hell,' Tom muttered, though part of him was listening hard.

'We'll get Ainsley to tell them what a great father you are.'

'Oh yeah?'

'Just promise me you won't even think about running for it, Tom. Just promise me that.'

Tom gave a bitter down-turned smile. 'What, make for Spain, you mean? A nice little villa with a pool. Though the weather's not so good at this time of year, so they tell me.'

'You've got to keep faith, Tom.'

Tom screwed his eyes up, as if to reject more useless talk and, grabbing two mugs from the draining board, shoved them down on the counter with a clunk. Then, his cigarette between two nicotine-stained fingers, he spread his hands out in front of him as if to check for tremors. 'I was out of order the other night,' he grunted. 'Got the wrong side of a bottle of whisky.'

'That's okay.'

'Sorry for sounding off at you.'

'Sure.'

'I try not to keep booze in the house, but come evening . . .'

'It seems to help at the time.'

Tom gave an unhappy laugh on a breaking note. 'It's fucking great at the time! That's the trouble – it's fucking great!'

'How are you doing for counselling, Tom? Are you seeing someone while Ainsley's away?'

'Been checking up on me, has he?'

'He's worried about you.'

'What, thinking I'm gonna top myself? Can't say it doesn't have its attractions.'

'Don't you bloody dare,' Hugh growled.

Abandoning the flippancy, Tom said in despair, 'It's the hanging on . . . the sheer fucking effort of hanging on . . .'

Hugh said quite roughly, 'But look what you're hanging on for. The boys. The settlement.'

Shaking his head, Tom made the tea. 'But listen to me, for Christ's sake,' he murmured after a moment. 'Going on about my own sodding troubles when you're the one who's had the stomachful. Lousy bloody friend.'

'You've been a good friend, Tom.'

'No,' he stated with unexpected vehemence. 'No – I've been a crap friend.'

Without feeling the need to explain this, he picked up the mugs and, cigarette jammed in his mouth, led the way into the front room. Jabbing at the fire with a makeshift poker, he threw another piece of wood onto the flames. 'Come on then,' he demanded fiercely. 'This car – who'd wanna follow you? Who'd wanna know where you are?'

'Haven't a clue. I thought it might be the police. But that's crazy. Why would they want to follow me?'

'How many in the car?'

'Just one.'

Tom shook his head authoritatively. 'The cops always hunt in pairs.'

'Do they? Yes, I suppose they do. Then I thought it might be the press. But that doesn't make any sense either. If they wanted to talk to me they'd come and ring on the doorbell. Or phone.'

'But why'd they wanna hassle you, for God's sake? No reason.'

'Oh, they'll have heard it's arson by now. They'll probably come sniffing around.'

Tom stalled with his tea mug halfway to his mouth and stared at Hugh in a strange way. 'Arson?'

'The police took their time, but finally they've accepted it's arson, yes.'

Tom's mouth jerked, as if in spasm.

'Oh, I always knew,' Hugh said, as if to soften the news. 'Right from the beginning. Never had any doubt.'

'For Christ's sake . . . But *who*? *Why*?'

'To silence Lizzie. That's what we think anyway.'

'Silence her for *what*?'

'She knew about this witness. It's all rather complicated . . . But we think they were after the name of the witness. And . . . to stop her telling anyone.'

Tom's face contorted. 'They set the fire knowing she was upstairs?'

'Yes.'

'Christ . . . *Christ* . . .' Jamming his tea mug down on the hearth, Tom rocked forward in his chair, clamped his hands over his face and gave a howl of fury and pain.

For Hugh there was something disturbing in witnessing such emotion on his behalf. He wished Tom would stop. He found himself staring at the cigarette in Tom's fingers as it burnt perilously close to his hair.

'*Christ* . . .' Tom raged into his hands.

'Don't . . .'

Eventually Tom lowered his hands a little and fixed Hugh with blazing eyes. 'What kind of *animal*?' he hissed emotionally. 'What kind of *vermin*?'

'Hopefully the police are going to find out.'

'*Scum!*' Tom clenched his fists. '*Scum!*'

Hugh put his tea down.

'If it was me I'd put the bastard up against a wall' – Tom mimed grabbing someone and thrusting a pistol against his head – 'and *phut*!' He bared his teeth as he pulled the imaginary trigger. 'Except shooting's too bloody good for them.'

Hugh looked at his watch. 'Listen, Tom, I really have to—'

'But the cops – they're gonna get these bastards?' he went on furiously. 'They're gonna nail 'em?'

'They've got a full team on it.'

'Forensics? DNA?'

'Yeah.'

'And what ideas they got?'

'Well, it's early days.'

'They must have some ideas, for Christ's sake!'

Hugh stood up abruptly. 'Look, Tom, I've got to get going. Sorry, but I've got a helluva lot to do.'

Tom froze slightly, before getting slowly to his feet. 'Yeah, sure . . .'

Hugh gestured towards his untouched tea. 'Sorry, it was a bit hot . . .'

Tom said, 'You need to talk this through.'

'Thanks. But we're fine.'

'I could come over tonight. I've got nothing on till the boys come for the weekend. I could come over and we could—'

'No.' Hugh interrupted more bluntly than he'd

intended to. 'No . . . I'm having supper with my daughter, you see. It's all arranged.'

Tom's gaze dropped, his mouth made a fierce line, and he gave a quick nod before chucking his cigarette into the grate and going to open the door. They went out into a twilight that was clear and still, the air already sharp with frost.

'That guy following you – watch your back, eh?' Tom grunted as Hugh prepared to drive off.

'Sure.'

Tom levelled a finger at him, as if sighting along the barrel of a gun. 'Remember – he's after something.'

Even as Hugh began to shrug, a realisation came to him. It was so shocking and so horribly obvious that he couldn't believe he hadn't thought of it before. He was overcome by a sense of danger so acute that when Tom asked what the matter was his throat seized, he couldn't speak, and he drove away without answering.


He slowed as he approached Oakhill and turned in through the gate at a trickle, making almost no sound. He was tensed for battle, his heart pressing against his ribcage, his pulse beating high in his head, but there were no strange cars, no signs of anything out of the ordinary. He drifted to a halt and cut the engine and listened hard. Getting out, he listened again before unloading the shopping. Approaching the front door he had the key ready in his hand, only to jam it into the lock upside down. As he fumbled to get it the right way up, the latch sounded and Lou swung the door open.

'You're all right?' he asked, in a flood of relief.

'I'm *fine*. But what's all this about, Dad? You scared me half to death on the phone.'

Dumping the shopping on the floor, Hugh closed the door behind him and flicked the deadlock. 'No one's come to the door?'

'No.'

'You drew all the curtains?'

'*Dad!* Will you *please* explain?' She was angry because she was frightened, and he couldn't blame her.

'Well, there's some evidence here in the house, you see. And they know it. I thought . . . Well, I'm not sure what I thought. But as long as you're all right, that's all that matters.' He tried to put an arm round her but she pulled away.

'You're not making any sense, Dad.'

He tried to slow down. 'It's Mum's computer,' he said, 'there's something on it they want. I've got to get it out of here.'

'But who wants it? The police?'

'Not the police, no.'

'Dad.' She made a gesture of exasperation.

He had hoped to avoid telling her, but she deserved to know. 'The witness Mum found in the Jason Jackson murder? Well, he's been abducted. Maybe even killed. Which means the only evidence left is sitting in Mum's computer. And I think they know that, Lou. I think they're going to come and get it.'

'But who's "they"?'

'I don't know. Jason's murderers . . . their friends . . . All I know is I've got to get the computer out of here.'

Lou was looking at him in a different way, with

concern. 'Okay . . .' she said carefully, as if treading on eggshells. 'If it'll make you feel safer, Dad.'

'And I want you to go and stay with friends.'

'*What?*'

'You could go to the Koenigs. They'll understand.'

'I'm not going to stay with the Koenigs!'

'Sorry, but I want you out of the house, Lou.'

'Dad, this is *crazy*. You're completely overreacting!'

'Maybe. But do it for me anyway. Please, Lou.'

'Why can't we just call the police?'

'I will. But they may not come. Not in time anyway.'

Holding back tears, Lou bit hard on her lip and shook her head sadly. 'Dad . . . Dad . . .'

'Do it for me, Lou. So I know you're safe.'

A tear squeezed from her eye and she brushed it impatiently away.

'I'm sorry you had to know about all this.'

'It's not that. It's—' But she gave up further explanation with a hopeless gesture. 'Okay . . . there's a bunch of friends going to a film tonight. I'll go with them. But I'm absolutely *not* going to stay somewhere. I'm coming back here.'

He would have argued but he could see that her mind was made up. 'All right,' he said reluctantly. 'But phone me before you start back. Promise?'

'Promise.'

Hugh picked up a holdall from his bedroom and took it into Charlie's room. Faced by the assortment of laptops, printers and hard drives, not knowing where Lizzie's data was stored, he disconnected the cables and loaded everything but the printers into the holdall. Jamming the pile of printouts into a side pocket, he took the holdall down to the dining room and left it behind the door. It looked so obvious there that he thought better of the idea and took it out to his car and put it in the boot. Then, in another change of plan, he removed the printouts from the side pocket and, wedging them under his arm, prepared to take them back into the house. The faint murmur of traffic from the main road only served to emphasise the silence of the garden and the crunch of his footsteps as he walked back towards the house. Pausing on the threshold to listen again, he wondered if Lou wasn't right after all and he was overreacting.

*You react in any way you like,* Lizzie whispered to him. *You're accountable to no one but yourself.*

And to you, Lizzie.

*Fine: to me as well. And I give you permission to see as many conspiracies as you choose. Dozens, hundreds. So long as you get there in the end. So long as you see my story through.*

Trouble is, Lizzie, I'm not sure I trust my judgement any more.

*Of course you do. Didn't we always say that gut instinct was the most reliable guide of all? That however much you rationalise and chop and change your ideas later, you nearly always come back to your first reaction?*

It's so hard not being able to talk things through with you, Lizzie.

*You're not listening to what I'm saying. Go with your instincts. Stick to your guns.*

Lou was in the hall putting on her coat.

'It's going to be icy tonight,' he said. 'You'll drive carefully, won't you?'

She nodded mutely and indicated a list by the phone. 'Thousands of people have called. I've told them the funeral's likely to be on Wednesday. Pat Edgecomb wanted to come round but I told her it wasn't convenient at the moment.'

She seemed worn down by it all, and he said with a surge of remorse, 'Sorry you've had to bear the brunt.'

With a small shrug she moved towards the door. He opened it for her and walked her to the Golf.

'What film are you going to see?'

'The latest Bond,' she said before pausing to stare at something behind him. 'What happened to your car, Dad?'

In the porch light the dent looked worse than before. 'I hit some ice.'

She gave a sigh, as if this was another symptom of his frightening slide into emotional instability. 'Oh Dad, I think I'd better stay. I really do—'

'No! *No!* I'm fine!' He smiled to persuade her it was true.

'But you'll be on your own.'

'Ray's on his way over.'

'Promise?'

'He'll be here any minute.'

After a last hesitation she got into the car.

As soon as her tail-lights had disappeared, Hugh hurried back into the house and sitting at the dining room table started on his calls. When he tried DI Steadman he was told he was unavailable and was put through to DS Reynolds.

'Followed?' Reynolds echoed. 'You sure about that, Mr Gwynne?'

'Absolutely.'

'When did this happen?'

'After I left you this afternoon. I'd gone a mile or two when I realised he was behind me. I took a long detour to try and shake him off, but he stayed with me all the way. There's no doubt about it.'

'So he followed you home?'

'Not actually home, no. I stopped to see someone on the way.'

'So he followed you till you made this stop, but not after that?'

'Well, he might have, but it was getting dark, I could well have missed him. Look, I can give you the registration number. You can check it out.'

In the pause that followed, Hugh heard muted voices in the background and wondered how many people were working on Lizzie's case. 'Right, Mr Gwynne,' Reynolds said, 'fire away.'

Hugh gave him the registration number, using an approximation of the phonetic alphabet, and asked Reynolds to repeat it back to him to make doubly sure. 'It was a dark-blue Honda,' he added.

'Dark . . . blue . . . Honda,' Reynolds confirmed at writing speed.

'Shall I hang on?'

'Sorry.'

'While you look it up.'

'Ah, well, we'll need to investigate the matter first, Mr Gwynne. We'll get back to you in due course.'

'But the owner's name – that's simple enough, surely.'

'Sorry, Mr Gwynne. You have to leave this to us.'

'And how long will that take?'

'Can't say. But we'll get straight onto it. And if there

are any developments you can be sure we'll let you know.'

'And what happens if these guys turn up here? What am I meant to do then?'

A slight pause. 'If anyone should harass you in any way, then you should contact us straight away, Mr Gwynne.'

His pronunciation of harass in the American style, with the emphasis on the second syllable, only served to increase Hugh's frustration. Ringing off, he took a couple of turns around the room before calling Isabel and asking if she could find the car owner's details. But quickly; a formal application involving paperwork would take too long. If all else failed she might try the private detective they had used in the Deacon case, the one who'd got all the dirt on Price.

Hugh began to rearrange the papers on the dining-room table, spreading the computer printouts out in front of him, mentally reviewing everything from Lizzie's desk, deciding what might be worth looking at again. To focus his search he pulled a pad towards him and constructed a timeline, starting with *Wesley tells Lizzie he saw JJ killing*, followed rapidly by *Lizzie discusses witness protection with Montgomery* and *Break-in at Meadowcroft*, then a gap of some weeks before *Fire*, and finally, *Disappearance of Wesley*. What he was missing, he quickly realised, were the dates when Lizzie had told John Emmanuel and Jacqui Lewis about the existence of a witness. In his mind he replayed the conversation in the vestry, but if there had been any mention of timings he couldn't remember what was said. Yet, even if the dates coincided, was it likely that John or Jacqui would have let the information slip?

Not John, he decided immediately. A man used to bearing secrets bears them easily. But Jacqui was a different matter. In her excitement at the news she might well have told family and friends, and inadvertently set off the rumour mill.

Glancing at the time, he called Ray to ask where he'd got to.

'Pulling up outside,' he answered.

Turning an ear towards the window Hugh could hear the car. 'Well, stay there,' he ordered. Bundling up the printouts, collecting his keys from the hall table, he hurried outside to find Ray walking towards the door.

'How's it going, old friend?'

Hugh went to his car and opened the boot. 'I need you to keep this in a safe place.' He stuffed the printouts into a side pocket of the holdall, zipped it up and hauled the bag onto the ground. 'Take it home with you tonight. Don't leave it in the car, whatever you do. Then take it to the office and see if they've got room for it in the safe.'

Ray looked at the holdall doubtfully. 'Bit large for the safe.'

'Your office then, but keep the door locked whenever you're away from your desk.'

Ray exhaled in an awkward half laugh, his breath briefly fogging the air. 'But Hugh, you know how it is at the office – no one ever locks their doors.'

'Maybe. But I don't want anyone walking off with it, accidentally or otherwise.'

Ray made a show of considering the problem. 'Well . . . I'm sure we can find some space in a cabinet somewhere.'

'Even better if it's got a key.'

'What's so precious?'

'Evidence.'

'Right.' Ray nodded rapidly, as if to humour him. 'About the fire, you mean?'

'About the person who killed Lizzie.'

'Christ,' Ray said in a shocked voice.

Hugh took the holdall to Ray's car and waited for him to unlock it.

'You know who it is?'

'More or less.'

'Well, *who*, for Christ's sake?'

'Long story.' Hugh jerked at the handles of the holdall to prompt Ray to open the boot.

'What, a nutter? A madman?'

'It was to do with her work.' Hugh swung the holdall into the boot.

'*Christ*. I always knew she met some fairly rough characters at the Citizens Advice, but I never realised . . . *Jesus.* Are the police on to this guy?'

'More or less.'

'But if this is evidence, don't they need it?' Ray asked, gazing into the open boot. 'Shouldn't they be examining it?'

'Not at the moment, no.'

Ray stood there uncertainly, his face very white in the thin light. 'I could take it over in the morning. First thing.'

'No,' Hugh said firmly, in no mood for discussion.

'But Detective Inspector Steadman's meant to be as sharp as they come, Hugh. I checked up on him. They say he gets results.'

Hugh moved forward and slammed the boot shut. 'Just keep this stuff safe, okay? Don't give it to anyone.'

Ray finally gave up with a baffled, compliant shrug. 'Sure.' Reverting to a tone of disbelief he murmured, 'Through her work . . . *God* . . . It's an obvious place, I suppose. But all the same . . .' Then, as if voicing a shared relief, he added, 'At least it's not . . .'

'What?'

Ray made a nervous sound, an awkward chuckle that emerged as a cough. 'Well, at one stage you were worried about the people Charlie was hanging around with, weren't you? All those addicts.'

Hugh moved towards the house. 'I'll call you tomorrow, Ray.'

Following him, Ray said in the tone of someone trying to make amends for an inadvertent slight, 'Charlie's in recovery, of course. I do realise . . . I didn't mean to—'

'Bye, Ray.'

'You're all right, old friend?'

'I'm just fine, thanks.'

'How about a quick cup of tea?'

'Too much on.'

'You sure you're okay? Why don't I come in for a while?'

'I'm all right, for God's sake!'

Closing the door on him, Hugh felt a brief remorse. He could hardly blame Ray for sharing what until recently had been such a burning suspicion in his own mind about Charlie's friends. But that didn't stop him resenting Ray for voicing it. He considered going out and catching him before he left, but he had no time for explanations, let alone apologies. Pausing only to make a hasty sandwich and unplug the house phone which was ringing again, he went back to the dining room and ate while he studied the timeline and added events from his own memory, including his sighting of Montgomery at Steadman's headquarters and his meeting with Montgomery in the hotel. His mobile rang but seeing it was Tom he didn't answer. When it rang again a minute later, he left it for a while, thinking it would be the voicemail, only to see Isabel's name and snatch it up.

'No joy with the DVLA,' she reported. 'Not if we want the information quickly. They only supply information on receipt of a written application citing reasonable cause. And I didn't have any luck with the private detective either. He said he couldn't do it because of the data protection laws. It would leave him open to prosecution.'

'Well, the data protection laws didn't seem to bother him too much when he was getting Price's medical records, did they? He must have a mate in the force. Someone who owes him a favour. Every private detective on the planet has contacts in the police, surely.'

'I did ask, Hugh, but he wasn't going to budge. He said everything's logged on the central computer now. He couldn't ask his contacts to put themselves on the line in that way.'

Hugh sighed hard into the mouthpiece.

'Sorry.'

'No . . .'

'But, Hugh?'

'Yes.'

'Can't you ask the police?'

'No, actually. I can't.'

A puzzled silence. 'Oh.'

'I can't,' he repeated, as if she'd argued the point.

Another silence. 'Are you all right? I mean . . . is there anything you need? Any valerian or . . . ?'

'*Valerian?*'

'It's a natural sedative.'

Even Isabel seemed to think he was cracking up. 'Thanks, but I prefer something stronger.'

Sitting in the quiet house, pausing to take stock, Hugh persuaded himself it would be no great loss to wait for Reynolds to report on the Honda driver. After all, what would he have done with a name and address? Gone round and asked the guy why he'd been following him? Knocked on the neighbours' doors asking for information? Fouled up the police investigation?

Returning to his timeline and the missing entries, he found Jacqui Lewis's card and keyed her number into his phone, ready to press the dial button. Then, following his usual work practice, he took a fresh sheet of paper, wrote her name at the top, and prepared to take notes. As a preliminary, he noted the date of their meeting in the vestry and what he could remember of their conversation. He'd written a couple of lines when a memory came back to him. But had he got it right? In his exhausted state had he confused this fragment of conversation with another? But no: the more he replayed the scene in his mind the more certain he became. Jacqui had been convinced that Lizzie had found an alibi witness for Denzel, not a witness to the crime itself. And – he tested his memory again – he was pretty certain John had thought the same thing. This changed the timeline in some profound way, yet for a while he couldn't decide why or how. To help clear his mind, he wrote the statement down: *Jacqui believed Lizzie had found an alibi witness.* Even then, the significance came to him slowly, clogged by tangential ideas and irrelevancies. But finally it was there: no one would bother to abduct an alibi witness. He examined this idea from every angle, he turned it over again and again in his mind until he was satisfied it was right. Yes: even if Jacqui had shouted the news of an alibi witness from the rooftops of the Carstairs Estate it wouldn't have induced the real killers to lose a moment's sleep, let alone come looking for Lizzie. What did they care if Denzel was in or out of jail?

He fretted over his next thought as well, not because it was coming too slowly but because it had come too damn fast. While he turned it over in his mind, he padded around the silent house, pulling back a curtain to stare into the darkness, putting an eye to the peephole in the front door, finding himself in the kitchen unable to remember why he'd gone there. Pouring himself a glass of water, he took it back to the dining table and stared at the timeline for another five minutes before picking up his mobile and calling Mike Gabbay.

When he told Mike what he wanted, he heard a rush of breath. 'Hell, Hugh, that's not so easy.'

'But you've got friends in the immigration service with access to the database.'

'*Friends* would be a strong word, Hugh. We're usually in opposite camps, remember.'

'But someone who'd do it as a favour.'

'I guess so,' he said doubtfully. 'But surely you can apply to the DVLA yourself? I'm sure you can.'

'Haven't got the time.'

'Ah. And when you say it's important, Hugh – we're not talking a case of road rage, a shunt on the motorway?'

'No. It's to do with Lizzie.'

'Lizzie? Hell, why didn't you say so? In that case I'll try an old client of mine. Ex-illegal immigrant. Poacher turned gamekeeper. Been working in the immigration service for the last five years. I can't promise of course. He might turn all ethical on me. He might feel he's run out of favours. But I'll do my damnedest.'

'One more problem – I need the information quickly, like now.'

'Hell, Hugh. It's ten to five.'

'I know.'

Ringing off, Hugh sat immobile in his chair for a while. Then, restless, seeking distraction, he wandered into the hall and peered at Lou's list of the day's phone calls. The vicar. Lizzie's mother. Lizzie's sister. Various cousins. Old friends. The church organist. Work colleagues. Neighbours. Reading the notes Lou had made against each name – 'funeral time confirm', 'offered help with funeral food', 'wants name of good local hotel' – he felt he was occupying a parallel universe in which these issues were diminished and distorted, as if he were viewing them through the wrong end of a telescope.

He lifted his head to the sound of a motorbike in the lane, a faint hum that grew steadily and faded abruptly, as if the engine had been cut. I'll be hearing footsteps next, he thought. Seeing shadows in the garden. But the dark figures wouldn't be hoodies this time; they would be altogether more conventionally dressed.

The idea that had come to him so rapidly had

refused to die, and with a small thrill of fear he returned to the timeline to relive the last few months of Lizzie's working life from her point of view.

As early as April she sees the fight to rehouse Gloria and Wesley as a mission. The bureaucratic difficulties, far from wearing her down, have made her increasingly determined to win through. And not just because of the Jameses' vulnerability and need, though these are reason enough; she has also, against the Citizens Advice guidelines, let herself become emotionally involved. She sees Wesley as another Charlie, a sensitive, over-imaginative boy ill-equipped to withstand the rough and tumble of street life. In drawing him out and trying to build his confidence she is subconsciously re-enacting her early attempts to support Charlie, but without the misjudgements and emotional barriers. She grows very fond of Wesley, and thus, intentionally or otherwise, finds herself taking on the second, arguably more difficult challenge of overseeing his rehabilitation. She arranges for the psychiatrist to come to Wesley, but the sessions are too irregular to do much good. Her own visits, however, produce a steady improvement in Wesley's confidence. He talks more freely, he agrees to think about undertaking some sort of vocational training, he looks forward to going to the theme park. Then comes the crucial day when John Emmanuel drops in and Wesley overhears Lizzie and Gloria talking to him about the Denzel Lewis campaign. Wesley's reaction is so immediate, his fear so obvious that Lizzie, always attuned to people's deeper motives, realises instinctively what it's about. To coax the full story out of Wesley, she swears on the Bible never to tell anyone.

But the secret brings her an acute dilemma. She finds herself torn between her duty to protect Wesley and her wish to see Denzel Lewis cleared of a crime he didn't commit. She can see only one way out. If she can obtain witness protection for Wesley, then she might be able to persuade him to give evidence. She knows only one senior police officer personally, the very person who put Denzel behind bars. This must concern her, she must realise she's asking Montgomery to help demolish his own case, but perhaps she believes in his basic decency, perhaps she trusts to his better nature, perhaps she thinks a simple enquiry isn't going to alarm him. She doesn't give him too much information of course; quite apart from anything else she mustn't break her oath to Wesley. She speaks hypothetically, asking what protection would be available for any future witness. But Montgomery is wary. This is before the Lewis family decide to launch their new public appeal; why would she come to him now unless she actually knows of a witness? Still more worrying from his point of view, she makes it clear that this hypothetical witness would be able to identify the real killers.

Perhaps there was more. Perhaps in her eagerness to win protection for Wesley Lizzie hints at a racial motive to the crime, she mentions a white gang. Whatever, Montgomery is now seriously rattled. He sees Denzel Lewis's conviction being quashed and an investigation being launched into his conduct of the case. He sees his reputation being damaged. He hears mutterings about corruption, and fears that however hard he tries to distance himself from them some of the mud will stick.

So . . . what does he do? The great unanswerable

question. Does Montgomery pretend to be sympathetic to Lizzie in the hope that the problem will simply fade away? Or – a darker thought – does he take measures to protect himself? A quiet word in someone's ear, a whisper that will get back to the Forbes family? Yes, perhaps Montgomery has more reason than most to fear the finger of suspicion. Perhaps he himself is corrupt. Perhaps he's been corrupt all along. It would explain why the Jason Jackson case went wrong from the very beginning. It would explain Montgomery's strange obsession with secrecy. Why not? Almost anything seemed possible just then.

The ring of his phone made him start slightly. He snatched it up, hoping to see Mike's name in the display, seeing instead a number the phone memory hadn't recognised. Leaving the call to the voicemail, he picked up the message a minute later without enthusiasm, expecting a request for funeral details or a neighbour offering food. But it was John Emmanuel, who announced himself in a low sonorous murmur, asking him to call back urgently. He answered Hugh's call in the same deep whisper, as if in danger of being overheard. Despite his low tone, he was perfectly audible, there was no mistaking his words, yet Hugh was so startled he asked him to repeat them.

'Wesley's here,' John whispered. 'In my home. He arrived half an hour ago.'

'Is he all right?'

'Scared. Jumpy as a cat. But otherwise he seems okay, yes.'

'Where's he been?'

'He's not saying. And I don't like to push him.'

'God. And I thought . . .' Hugh's relief that Wesley

was alive and safe was overtaken by a new concern. 'Does anyone know he's there?'

'Not unless he's told people.'

'What about his mother?'

'He's not saying, so I guess not.'

'If you could keep him there till I work something out, John. Do you think you'll be able to keep him there till morning?'

'I'd say so. My wife's cooking a meal for him now. And there's the big match at quarter to eight.'

'Tell him he's in the safest possible place. Tell him everything's going to be okay. Tell him anything he needs to hear.'

Ringing off, Hugh pushed the timeline slowly aside. Lou had been right, he had got things ludicrously out of proportion. He imagined how he must have looked to her when he got home, obsessive and wild-eyed, barely in control. No wonder she'd treated him as if he were off the rails. He rested his head on his fingertips, eyes closed, and finally admitted to the depth of his exhaustion. Yet he couldn't begin to think about sleep. He had to go on to the end now.

His phone buzzed the arrival of a text message. It was from Mike Gabbay, giving the name and address of the registered car owner. *Paul Louis Pertusio.* The address was in the east of Bristol. Directory Enquiries said the number was unavailable, which he took to mean ex-directory. He hunted round the house for the Bristol phone directory and found it in the kitchen. There was only one Pertusio listed, initial M. With such an unusual name it had to be a relation.

The number rang for a long time before the reedy voice of an elderly woman answered.

'Oh, Paul doesn't live here,' she told him.

'I see. Could you possibly . . .' Distracted by the sound of a car Hugh moved into the hall. 'Er . . . give me his number, Mrs Pertusio?'

'Oh no,' came the soft inflexible voice. 'No, I couldn't do that.'

A car door slammed. 'Could I get him at work?'

'Yes, that would be the best thing.'

Hugh went towards the front door. 'Would you have the number?'

'It's in the phone book.'

'What should I look under?' Hugh put his eye to the peephole and saw two men walking towards the door.

'Well . . . "police".'

The bell rang.

'Police?'

'That's right.'

The images were distorted by the lens of the peephole, but one of them was definitely Montgomery.

'Thank you very much, Mrs Pertusio. Sorry to have bothered you.'

Hugh swung the door open.

'Evening, Mr Gwynne,' said Montgomery, holding up his warrant card, 'Detective Chief Inspector Montgomery. We met the other day. And this is Detective Constable Pertusio. Could we come in for a moment?'

Staring at DC Pertusio, Hugh guessed he was about twenty-five. A grandson, then.

'What's it about?' he asked Montgomery.

'A number of matters, including the whereabouts of a young man called Wesley James.'

# ELEVEN

Montgomery was sitting on a pale sofa, heavy forearms resting on his knees, hands clasped in front of him. DC Pertusio had taken a chair on the far side of the room by the window. When he wasn't looking at the back of Montgomery's head or flicking the occasional glance in Hugh's direction, he was gazing at the floor and chewing his lip.

The conversation had begun badly. Asked by Montgomery if he had any idea where Wesley might be, Hugh had said, 'Why would you want to know that, Chief Inspector?'

'Because we believe he's in need of protection.'

'Isn't it a bit late to be offering him protection?'

Montgomery said gravely, 'We hope not.'

'But if he's disappeared you must know where to start looking, surely?'

Letting that pass with a set of his mouth, Montgomery said, 'So . . . you don't know where Wesley might be?'

'Even if I did, I'm not sure it'd be in his best interests to tell anyone.'

Montgomery held his gaze. 'No,' he agreed unexpectedly. 'No . . .' He looked older than before, the strands of combed-over hair strewn haphazardly over the bald crown in wispy ginger-grey feathers, the pink face turned tired and sallow. 'Perhaps I can explain?'

'You can try.'

Montgomery made a cage of his hands and took a slow breath. 'I've been in the force thirty-five years, Mr Gwynne, all but three of them in CID,' he said in the manner of someone beginning a long story. 'After a time you like to think you get a feel for cases. Whether they hang together properly. Whether they've got holes. The Jason Jackson murder seemed to hang together all right. Couldn't see any holes. The forensic evidence was strong. Denzel Lewis had form for violence. The gangs were getting their kicks from hitting easy targets like Jason – kids who had no gang protection. It was the local sport, you might say. No reason to look elsewhere. And then, after Lewis was put away . . . well, I'd seen justice campaigns come and go. Thought this one would fade away like the rest. When it kept going, well . . . you start thinking. You go back over the evidence. You wonder what you could've missed. But if we'd got it wrong, if that jacket was planted on Lewis like he claimed, then I couldn't see how it was done. Not when we'd picked him up so quickly.' His voice stiffened. 'You can't see how it was done unless the whole case was rotten from the start. And you don't want to have thoughts like that, not without good evidence. So you file your worries away at the back of your mind and you—' He broke off momentarily as Pertusio's phone rang and was answered. 'And you hope like hell you're wrong.'

'But you weren't wrong,' Hugh said.

Montgomery lifted a hand, as if to ask for more time to tell the story. 'When your wife first came and asked me about witness protection, well, I can't say I took it too seriously, not to start with. When she said it was hypothetical, I took her at her word. But when she started talking about her hypothetical witness being able to identify a white boy as one of Jason Jackson's killers . . . well, I sat up and took notice. I asked her straight out if the witness was for real, and she didn't deny it. I don't like to get things wrong, Mr Gwynne. Never have. And a racial killing – that was even worse. Problem was, like I told you, my hands were tied. I had no chance of getting my boss to agree to protection without a statement from the witness, and Mrs Gwynne – correctly in my opinion – wanted guarantees first. We tried to find a way round it, but . . .' He shook his head.

His call over, Pertusio came and murmured something in Montgomery's ear, which he acknowledged with a faint grimace. Turning back to Hugh with an air of hesitation, as if coming to the most difficult part, Montgomery continued, 'When your wife died in the fire, well . . . we had to address the possibility of a connection. The possibility that your wife had been targeted in some way. So while the fire investigation was in progress I set up a team—'

'But the fire investigation wasn't in progress,' Hugh protested, needing to make the point. 'Nothing was happening.'

Again Montgomery accepted the criticism without objection. 'Yes . . . If I could come back to that, Mr Gwynne?' Taking Hugh's silence as agreement, he went on, 'We knew we had to get to the witness fast, so we worked round the clock and finally got to Wesley yesterday and took him to a place of safety—'

'You had him?' Hugh exclaimed, thoroughly startled.

'Until this morning. We took him to a police officer's flat and put a watch on him. But unfortunately he made a run for it while one officer was in the shower and the other was making breakfast.'

'You had him?' Hugh repeated in disbelief.

'We could hardly keep him under lock and key, not without his permission. It was hard enough persuading him we were there to protect him.'

'Breaking down his door can't have helped.'

'We had his mother's permission, Mr Gwynne. He'd gone and barricaded himself inside the flat after certain callers tried to break the door down. He was in a panic, wouldn't even open the door to his mother. The mother was worried that he'd do something foolish, try to throw himself out of the window.'

'But DI Steadman said nothing about this when I saw him this morning.'

'No . . . that's right,' Montgomery said, with an odd, lingering emphasis. 'It was decided to keep my investigation off the record. For security reasons.'

'Since when are investigations off the record?'

'On the say-so of my guv'nor Chief Superintendent Clark. Here . . .' Montgomery reached into his inside breast pocket and, pulling out a card, handed it across. 'He's expecting you to call.'

It was Chief Superintendent Clark's business card, complete with embossed badge of the Avon and Somerset Constabulary.

Montgomery said, 'If you look on the back . . .'

On the reverse was written *Please feel free to call me, Tony Clark*, with a mobile phone number.

Hugh stared at the card for several seconds before saying quietly, 'Go on.'

Montgomery tried sitting back against the sofa cushions, but finding no comfort there sat forward with one elbow on the sofa arm. 'A few years back we had a corruption problem on our patch. Nothing major, but it had to be stamped out. I joined the special squad that was set up at the time. We nailed three officers for recycling seized drugs, then the squad was disbanded. But where there's drugs there's always going to be temptation. So you keep half an eye out for officers who've got new cars and plasma TVs and have a low arrest rate. But that's the careless ones. The clever ones keep their arrest rate up, even if they never manage to catch the top villain. And they can always account for their money. Like having a wife with a successful business. So when you see the handmade suits and the Audi and the new house, you think, lucky sod, to have a wife who brings in the money.' Montgomery's face took on a grim expression. 'I worked alongside Brian Steadman in the anti-corruption squad. Did a couple of big cases together after that. Never a whisper against him. Not so much as a murmur. His wife had a successful hairdressing salon, which accounted for the new house, the car, the holidays. Come the Jason Jackson murder, I was glad to have him on my team. Hard worker, good contacts. Thought we were quids in when he got a tip-off about Denzel Lewis within two hours of the killing. And when he led the raid on Lewis's flat and discovered the bloodstained jacket, well . . . Nothing to suggest it was anything but good detective work. Nothing to—'

'Who killed my wife?'

Montgomery said cautiously, 'I can't give you a categorical answer, Mr Gwynne. Not at this point in time.'

'But you can give me a good idea.'

Montgomery paused, as if coming to a decision. 'We're intending to make an arrest later this evening.'

'Who is it?'

Another pause. 'I must ask you to keep this in the strictest confidence, Mr Gwynne.'

'Yes.'

'We expect to arrest DI Steadman on suspicion of arson.'

It was like running into a wall, the shock and the anguish. Hugh felt as if the breath was knocked out of him; for a moment he could neither think nor see nor hear. Then, as he gasped for breath, a wave of anger came over him in a red-hot sea. The monumental arrogance of Steadman's deceit, his patronising dismissal of Hugh's worries, his pretended concern at the evidence of arson, his apology for getting it wrong: these thoughts tore into him first. Close behind came the images of the night itself: Steadman entering Meadowcroft, drugging Lizzie, carrying her upstairs, and – almost unendurable – the picture of him lying her on the bed and removing her clothes. It was then, with a shiver of terrible elation, that Hugh experienced the wish to kill another human being. He was barely aware of Montgomery speaking to Pertusio and Pertusio leaving the room, he heard nothing of what Montgomery was trying to tell him until the anger subsided almost as quickly as it had come, leaving him shaky and nauseous. 'What were you saying?'

'I said arson's just a start. We hope to charge him with more.'

Hugh closed his eyes.

'DC Pertusio's gone to make some tea. He won't be long.'

'You've got evidence?'

'We're working on it, Mr Gwynne.'

In a nudge of memory, Hugh said, 'You know a friend of my son saw a man carrying my wife upstairs? Elk – James Elkins? On the night of the fire? He saw him carrying her upstairs—'

'We know, yes.'

'He was there – he saw him – well, not his actual *face* – but he saw him carrying her up the stairs. He gave a statement . . .'

'Yes.'

'He gave a statement to *Steadman*. To *Steadman*.'

'Yes. We have the statement.'

'You do?'

'It's with Chief Superintendent Clark.'

'And you know Elk – James – saw a motorbike parked down the side of the house? It was too dark to get much of a look at it, but it was newish, shiny.'

'We do know, yes.'

'There's a CCTV camera in the village – you should look at that. You might see what time he arrived – what time he left—'

'Mr Gwynne—'

'It probably doesn't have any film in it, but you never know.'

'We'll cover all that, I can assure you.'

'There might be tyre tracks. The ground's quite soft

there – on the left-hand side of the house. And I don't think anyone's been there since.'

'We'll be carrying out another search first thing in the morning.'

Hugh whispered almost as an afterthought, 'He's got a motorbike, has he?'

'He has, yes.'

'What sort?'

'A BMW.'

The make wasn't important to Hugh, it was the sense that he was gaining knowledge of Steadman, as Steadman had gained knowledge of Lizzie, that somehow knowledge would begin to diminish the enormity of the man in his imagination. 'He did it on his own?'

'I can't say. My personal guess is yes.'

As Pertusio arrived with mugs of tea, Montgomery's phone rang and he left the room to answer it, leaving Hugh to Pertusio's diffident gaze.

'You followed me today,' Hugh said.

'I did, sir.'

'Thought you were the enemy. Thought of ramming you.'

Pertusio blinked. 'Right.'

'Why? Follow me, I mean?'

'The guv'nor's orders.'

He was only a detective constable; it was the only answer he was going to give. Hugh took a sip of tea, wishing it was whisky. Montgomery came back, apologising for the interruption, and sat down again.

As more realisations came to him, Hugh stated flatly, 'She would have let him into the house because he was a police officer.'

Montgomery nodded.

'She even offered him a drink . . .'

Montgomery was silent.

'He probably told her that *you'd* sent him.'

Montgomery's expression admitted to the possibility.

'Probably told her he'd arranged police protection. Tricked her into giving him Wesley's name.'

'There are things we may never know, Mr Gwynne. Things he'll never tell us.'

Even as Hugh rebelled against this idea, he realised it was true, that he might never have the consolation of certainty. 'Well, don't let me anywhere near him,' he growled.

'It might be an idea to turn off your phone, Mr Gwynne.'

'What?'

'In case he calls you.'

The thought of hearing Steadman's voice brought nausea back into Hugh's stomach. 'Why haven't you arrested him yet? Why wait?'

'A couple of things we need to tie up first. In the meantime we need to get Wesley to a safe place, Mr Gwynne.'

'How safe is safe?'

'This time it'll be round-the-clock protection somewhere away from here. It's been authorised.'

Hugh murmured, 'What sort of a life will that be?'

'Better than being targeted by the Forbes family.'

'He may not think so.'

'He'll get a new identity, a new life.'

'He's only a child.'

'He's eighteen. He can start again.'

Some association of ideas, youth perhaps, or fresh starts, brought Hugh another jog of alarm. 'Elk . . . my son – what about them?'

'Mr Elkins has made his statement. It's on file. But we're keeping an eye on him all the same, just till tomorrow.'

'You know where he is?'

'We do, yes.'

'You had them followed?'

'A safety precaution.'

In the strange new world into which Hugh had been plunged this seemed not only reasonable but logical. With hindsight his reaction to being followed by Pertusio seemed almost irrational. Coming to a decision, he said, 'I'll take you to Wesley. On one condition. That I get to speak to him before anyone else, to make sure he knows exactly what he's in for. Because it'll be months, won't it, before anything comes to trial. Before he can start a new life.'

'It could be a while,' Montgomery conceded.

'And another thing. He'll need a mentor, someone who's not police or family liaison, someone from the Citizens Advice. Someone he can trust. Someone like my wife.'

'I'm sure that can be arranged.'

'I need your assurance.'

'You have it,' Montgomery said.

*Have I missed anything, Lizzie? Have I done all I can?* Before he could decide, he heard the sound of the front door and, throwing a questioning glance at Montgomery, getting a blank look in return, got to his feet and went out into the hall.

It was Lou, with Charlie close behind.

'What about your film?'

Lou hugged him. 'Didn't want to see it anyway.'

Hugh turned to Charlie. 'What about Elk? You haven't left him on his own, have you?'

Charlie shook his head. 'He's with a mate from NA. He's gonna kip at his place.'

'He's all right then?'

'Yeah, he's cool.'

'He doesn't mind you leaving?'

'Got tired of having me around,' said Charlie, with one of his enigmatic shrugs.

Everything was all right then, yet in his jittery emotional state it seemed to Hugh that they had all been on the brink of some nameless catastrophe and only just managed to pull back in time. 'You shouldn't have . . .'

'But we wanted to come back. Didn't we, Charlie?'

'Yeah.'

'Didn't want you here on your own.' She stepped forward and laid a hand on his arm.

His throat tightened, his eyes pricked with tears. Putting an arm round her, he kissed her head, then, the tears hot on his cheeks, he reached out his other arm to Charlie and pulled him close. 'Thank you,' he managed to say. 'Thank you for everything.' Most of all, he thought, thank you for being safe.


Pertusio took the wheel while Hugh and Montgomery sat in the back. 'Into the city, is it, sir?' Pertusio asked.

Montgomery looked to Hugh for an answer.

'Into the city, yes,' Hugh said. 'Head for the Carstairs Estate.'

Before leaving, he had made two calls. First to the chief superintendent, a crisp dead-voiced man who confirmed that Montgomery's investigation was fully authorised, that a witness protection programme was agreed and ready to swing into action, and that every necessary resource would be employed to obtain a successful prosecution in the matter of Lizzie's death. Next Hugh had called John Emmanuel and heard the chatter of a TV and the roar of canned laughter. Wesley was fine, John reported when he had retreated to a quieter room. He had eaten well and seemed less jumpy. They agreed that John should say nothing to Wesley about the police coming, only that Lizzie's husband was on his way over to say hello and help find somewhere safe for Wesley to go. John wasn't sure if Wesley knew about Lizzie's death, so they agreed that this too was best not mentioned. Then, last thing before leaving, Hugh had taken Lou and Charlie into the kitchen and told them about Wesley and why he had to go with the police to find him. There wasn't time to tell them about Steadman even if he'd wanted to, which he didn't, not till he could explain properly. He gave them instructions not to open the door to anyone, or, if they had to, to say no one had been there that afternoon, even if those asking were police officers. Lou paled at this, casting him the same worried look she'd given him when he demanded she leave the house for the night. It was Charlie who calmly nodded and repeated the instructions back to him by way of confirmation.

Pertusio drove fast but smoothly. The day had been so long that Hugh had lost track of time, but from the amount of traffic on the main road he supposed it must still be rush-hour. Once, Pertusio put on the concealed siren to overtake a line of stationary cars, but otherwise they drove in silence broken only by the intermittent blare of the police radio and Montgomery's occasional murmured conversations into his phone.

Finally Hugh said distractedly, as if thinking aloud, 'We had a break-in not long ago. I don't suppose you'll ever know if it was connected to Steadman.'

Montgomery, illuminated by the oncoming headlights, gave a slow shake of his head. 'Hard to establish now.'

'Nothing was taken except a bit of cash and costume jewellery. But they knew how to get in without setting off the burglar alarm. At the time I thought my wife must have got it wrong . . .' Leaving the rest of this thought unspoken, Hugh looked out of the window and waited for the radio to stop one of its periodic bouts of jabbering before going on in the same unhurried tone, 'I hired a fire expert called Slater. He can prove the fire was arson. But how can you tie Steadman to the fire? How can you prove he was there?'

Perhaps it was the darkness, perhaps it was the tone Hugh had set, but Montgomery confided, 'We know he called your house from a mobile phone at 20.30 on the night of the fire.'

Hugh kept his gaze on the passing streets and the flicker of lights.

'Now we're waiting for the mobile phone company to come back to us with the location of the mobile, both then and later that evening. It's a lengthy job, but we're hoping to get something by morning.'

Hugh absorbed this silently. 'Is it going to be enough?'

'If there's more to find, we'll find it,' Montgomery declared in an intense way. 'Anything that fixes him to the house. DNA. A tyre print. We'll find it. He reckoned he'd covered everything, but the phone was his first mistake. He used a pay-as-you-go phone, the same one he used to contact the Forbes family, but he hung on to it too long, we obtained the number before he threw it away. Same with the money. He must have been on the take for at least four years. You can be clever with extra cash once or twice, lose it around the place, pretend a car's second-hand when it's new, say you got the new conservatory at a knock-down price, but you can't go on hiding it for ever. We'll get him for perverting the course of justice in the Jason Jackson murder. We'll get him on everything we can, Mr Gwynne. However long it takes.'

They had left the suburbs and were entering the city along a street of brightly lit shops and busy pavements.

'How did you find Wesley?' Hugh asked.

Wrapped in other thoughts, Montgomery took a moment to answer. 'Through your wife's client list at the Citizens Advice.'

'That was enough?'

'Along with her phone records, yes.'

Hugh's first instinct was to baulk at this invasion of Lizzie's privacy, but of course there was no right to privacy once you were dead. 'You contacted all her clients?'

'Not all, no. We matched key dates to her calls, and then it was a process of elimination. We knew he was young. Your wife had told me he was young.'

They were climbing the long hill towards the Carstairs Estate, where the lights of the tower blocks gleamed coldly against the night sky.

'Go right just before the church,' Hugh told Pertusio. Then, turning to Montgomery, he asked in the same mild, unhurried manner how Steadman had first got to know there was a witness, but either Montgomery didn't hear or he didn't feel like answering because he stared ahead, frowning absently, and made no reply. Then Pertusio was making the turn and Hugh was telling him to pull up in front of the second house on the left, which was one of a long terrace of squat geometric squares built of concrete with metal-framed windows and, going by the misted glass, a condensation problem.

'Any idea how long you'll be?' Montgomery asked.

'Twenty minutes, half an hour. How did Steadman get to know there was a witness?'

Montgomery gave a sharp nod, as if to acknowledge that he'd heard the question the first time, and, pushing his door open, swung his bulky frame round to climb out. When Hugh joined him on the pavement he was staring at the line of concrete houses, the streetlight casting a sulphurous light over his heavy features.

'He found out because I told him,' he said bleakly. 'I told him because I thought I could trust him.' He turned to Hugh, his mouth in a bitter down-turned arc. 'There's no way I can undo that, Mr Gwynne, much as I'd wish to. All I can do is nail him. Get the prosecutions. And that's what I'll do. However long it takes.'

They stood in silence for a moment, then Hugh walked up the path and rang the doorbell. When he looked back Montgomery was still there under the streetlight.

Then John Emmanuel was answering the door and Hugh was stepping inside to meet Lizzie's lost boy.

# TWELVE

The family courtroom was small and modern and arranged like a meeting room to make it seem less intimidating. The main participants sat on three sides of a rectangular table, Tom Deacon at the near end with Emma Deeds, Linda Deacon with her solicitor further up the table, with court and social services officials opposite. At the far end, behind the clerk, the district judge sat alone at a raised bench. She was a brisk, jolly woman who smiled easily, which Hugh took as a good omen.

She addressed Ainsley, who was sitting in a witness box which looked as if it had been set down at random on the carpeted floor. 'Dr Ainsley, in your report you state that Mr Deacon is capable of meeting all the children's emotional and physical needs. Are you saying his illness won't impact at all on his ability to care for the boys?'

'Even on his bad days I believe he'll be able to function perfectly adequately as a parent,' Ainsley replied easily. 'His motivation to do his best for the boys is extremely strong. If he has a sleepless night, for example, I've no doubt he'll be up in good time to make the boys' breakfast and get them off to school.'

'What about the depression? You say it's controlled

with medication and therapy, but could it recur under certain circumstances?'

From where Hugh was sitting at the side of the room Tom's bony face was in quarter profile, he could see the muscle in his jaw flickering its message of distress.

'It could, yes. But I wouldn't regard the risk of deterioration as high at the present time. His medication is reviewed regularly. And he seems to be responding well to a new therapy called neuro-linguistic programming. New to him, I mean.'

'New to me too,' said the judge. 'What does it involve?'

'It's not a technique I practise myself, but it involves – in the simplest terms – blocking and reframing negative thoughts and building on positive ones. It's not scientifically proven but anecdotal evidence suggests it has some success with phobias. Tom found out about it himself and signed up for a course of treatments. He's always on the lookout for ways to improve his condition.'

The judge made a note. 'And the alcohol abuse? You say he's able to keep it under control when he has charge of the children. Are we sure about that?'

'I would say so, yes. He tends to be honest about his alcohol consumption.'

The judge raised an eyebrow.

'He's primarily a binge drinker, ma'am. He's never proud of himself afterwards. He talks about it quite freely.'

'And when he's not bingeing, what's his consumption then?'

'As I understand it, a beer or two.'

Tom turned to Emma Deeds and whispered urgently.

The judge went on, 'You say he's anxious to overcome his dependency, but you don't state whether you think he's likely to succeed.'

'I can't say he'll succeed in abstaining altogether, no. But as I've stated, he seems to be capable of controlling his problem when he has the boys with him, and I have no reason to think that he won't be able to maintain that level of control in the future, particularly when the matter of the boys' residence is settled. He responds well to routine and certainty – and to having the boys with him, of course.'

The judge referred to another document. 'One report states that Mr Deacon seems to have problems with anger management. Would you agree with that?'

'He can have problems with anger management, yes, but it's almost exclusively directed at people or bodies he regards as frustrating his attempts to regain control of his life. It stems from the overwhelming feeling of powerlessness he experienced on witnessing the death of his daughter. But he recognises the problem, he understands it achieves nothing. He's working on it.'

'There's no suggestion that his anger is ever directed at the children?'

Tom's jaw muscle went into overtime.

'Absolutely not.'

'Thank you, Dr Ainsley. You may step down.'

Ainsley came back to his seat next to Hugh.

The judge said, 'Now, the last matter of concern was the housing. We have a development there. Is that right, Ms Deeds?'

'That's correct, ma'am. If I could call on my colleague Mr Gwynne?'

'Indeed. Mr Gwynne?'

Hugh stood up. 'I can report that in the matter of Mr Deacon's claim against the driver of the car that injured him and killed his daughter, a settlement has been reached whereby Mr Deacon will receive damages of six hundred and twenty thousand pounds, with an interim payment of two hundred and fifty thousand, to be paid within the month.'

'And this money is not ring-fenced in any way?'

'No.'

'Thank you, Mr Gwynne.' She turned her attention to Tom. 'And it's your intention to buy somewhere as soon as possible, is it, Mr Deacon?'

Tom straightened his back. 'Yes, ma'am. I've already seen one place I like for the right money.'

'Good.'

'And, ma'am, can I say something else?'

'By all means.'

'When I'm caring for the boys I can go for days without a drink. Days and days. I just don't feel the need.'

The judge was already nodding, as if to discourage Tom from overstating his case. 'Thank you,' she said. 'Is there anything more you'd like to say, Mrs Deacon?'

Linda, who had been silent throughout the proceedings, except to confirm that she was happy for the boys to live with their father, shook her head.

'Counsel?' Meeting a silence, the judge announced in a tone of decision, 'Taking into account the reports, and the wishes of Mrs Deacon and Mr Deacon, and of course those of Matt and Joe themselves, the Court makes a shared residence order in favour of both parents, the boys to spend term-time with their father plus half the holidays, the other half of the holidays to be available for the boys to go to their mother, should she feel able to have them.'

For several seconds Tom was completely immobile, as if the significance of the words hadn't sunk in. Then, as the judge went into detail on contact and visiting arrangements, he turned to Emma Deeds as if for confirmation, but she was writing busily so he turned the other way and sought out Ainsley's gaze. Only when Ainsley gave him a broad smile and a firm nod did his face slowly contort with agonised joy.

The judge said, 'And, Mr Deacon?'

Tom straightened again. 'Yes, ma'am.'

'The Court asks that you continue to visit your doctor on a regular basis, so he can monitor your health. Is that acceptable?'

'Yes, ma'am.'

'How often shall we say? Is monthly convenient?'

'Yes, ma'am.'

'Monthly it is, then.'

'You understand why I'm asking, Mr Deacon? We want to avoid any deterioration in your health going unnoticed and untreated.'

'Yes, ma'am.'

'And, Mr Deacon? No more persuading yourself you're better than you really are?'

'No, ma'am.'

'I appreciate your reasons for doing it, but it didn't help your case.'

'No, ma'am.'

When the court rose, Tom stood to attention, shoulders back, arms stiff as arrows at his sides, until the door closed behind the judge, when he fisted his hands and gave a small whoop of triumph before hurrying from the room to find his sons, who were waiting outside with Isabel.

'Lucky with the judge,' Ainsley commented.

Lucky was not usually a word Hugh associated with Tom, but for once he agreed.

'Let's hope Tom doesn't blow it,' Ainsley murmured as they watched Linda Deacon leaving the room.

'You think there's a risk?'

'As we both know, compromise isn't his strong point.'

'The judge has laid down some pretty clear rules.'

'But you know Tom – he'll bend the rules, and the ones he can't bend he'll challenge. He's a fighter. He needs a battle.'

'So long as he doesn't embark on any more legal battles.'

'I'll second that. Oh, and congratulations on negotiating a settlement. You must be relieved.'

'Tom feels he's been cheated, of course, because we had to take a drop of over two hundred thousand pounds on our claim.'

'He was never going to be happy, whatever happened.'

'Needless to say, I'm the villain of the piece. But it was settle or have the whole thing drag on for another year or more while everyone appealed and counterclaimed. It was the best deal in the circumstances, but nothing Desmond Riley or I could say was ever going to convince Tom of that.'

They went out into the hall where Tom was sitting in a tight huddle with his boys, talking earnestly, while the heavily pregnant Linda Deacon sat a few feet away, looking tired and dull-eyed.

'Oh, I almost forgot,' Hugh said, 'could I ask you to send your account to me personally?' He reached into his pocket for a card and a pen, and wrote the Meadowcroft address on the back. 'It's the old house, but it'll find me all right.'

Ainsley took the card. 'It'll just be a few expenses.'

'If you're sure? That's very kind.' Embarrassed, Hugh went on, 'That therapy Tom's trying – what was it called?'

'NLP. Neuro-linguistic programming.'

'Do you think it might work for agoraphobia?'

'They say it has quite a lot of success, yes.'

'Where would I find a local practitioner?'

'Tom mentioned the name of the man he's going to. I can't remember it off-hand, but I made a note, I can let you know.'

'There's this boy we need to get out and about again. He was a client – well, more of a young friend – of my wife's. But whoever takes him on, it'll have to be someone who likes a real challenge. The boy hasn't been outside for years. And he's needed as a key witness in a trial where the defence will do their best to tear him to shreds.'

'I'd like to say I could take him on myself, but . . .'

'You couldn't get down here often enough,' Hugh said, helping him out. 'And the funding's very limited.'

They looked towards Tom, waiting for their opportunity to say goodbye, but he was still talking to the children.

'And you, Hugh?' Ainsley asked. 'How are you managing?'

'Me? Oh, you know . . .'

Ainsley, trained in the art of listening, said nothing.

'As good as anyone who's useless at being on his own.'

'Your children not with you?'

'Charlie's back at college. Lou's in Sri Lanka on her gap year.'

'Must be hard for you.'

'No point in them hanging around. They've got to get on with their lives. And my son . . . he phones every day. He does the worrying about me, asks if I'm getting out of the house, tries to get me to go for bereavement counselling.'

'But you're not persuaded?'

'Call me old-fashioned, Doc, but therapy's not really my thing. Work's the nearest I get to therapy.'

'You're busy then?'

'I hope to be. I'm setting up on my own. High-street law. Everything and anything that comes through the door. Well, almost.'

And the work wouldn't come a moment too soon. In the immediate aftermath of Lizzie's death Hugh could see now that he'd been like Tom, carried along by a grand obsession for truth and justice. Then, once the funeral was over and the police investigation complete, he'd thrown himself into activities with the children. To avoid a traditional Christmas with all its associations he'd taken them skiing for two weeks. He'd involved them in decisions about wall colours and curtain fabrics as the restoration of Meadowcroft got under way. He'd helped them pack, and driven them to college and air-

port. Only when he came back to the empty house did
he feel the full force of Lizzie's absence. He missed her
all the time, but it was the loneliness that took him by
surprise, how gruelling it was, how quickly it reduced
him to self-pity. To keep himself occupied he'd set up a
fund in Lizzie's memory to provide sports equipment
for the kids on the Carstairs Estate, he'd gone to the fire
station and thanked the firemen who'd tried to save her,
he'd twice visited Charlie at college, he'd started taking
long walks and fewer bottles of wine. He told himself
it was getting easier all the time, and perhaps it was.

Ainsley said, 'Have you long to wait till this man
comes to trial?'

Hugh resented the reflexive tension that pulled at his
stomach when the trial was mentioned; it was like the
jerk of a string, a reminder of Steadman's hold over his
past. 'They think it could be May, but they're not sure.'

'He'll get life presumably?'

'In theory. But he could be out in ten years.'

Ainsley looked shocked. 'Why so soon?'

'They're not sure they can prove murder, only man-
slaughter. He could get more for the arson than the
killing.'

'Well, I hope it's a lot longer than ten years.'

'I'm trying to reach the point where I no longer
care.'

'Nothing wrong with wanting justice, though.'

'But look what happens when you can't let go. Look
at Tom. No winners there.'

As they watched, Tom urged the boys towards their
mother. As she embraced them Joe, the youngest,
butted his head against her shoulder and began to cry
in short, breathless sobs. Tom said something to his

ex-wife. She nodded and, letting go of the children, stood up. Joe clung to her leg, while Matt, face contorted, rubbed tears from his eyes. Tom dropped a hand on Matt's head and drew Joe gently away from his mother.

'No winners,' Ainsley echoed. 'But a fresh starting point.' He held out his hand. 'Well, I'll say goodbye, Hugh, and wish you the best of luck.' On his way out he paused by Tom to touch his arm in farewell.

Isabel came up and said, 'Poor kids.'

'They'll be all right. They know he loves them.'

'But they want their mum as well.'

They watched as Tom said something to the children which seemed to cheer them up. Matt gave a small, brave nod while Joe stopped crying and attached himself to Tom's hand. Linda spoke to Tom, and they both nodded as if settling on an arrangement.

'When's your train?' Hugh asked Isabel.

'There's one in about half an hour, I think.'

'I'll drop you at the station.'

'Thanks, because there's something I need to ask you,' she said determinedly.

'And the answer's going to be the same, Isabel.'

'But I promise I've never wanted to work in a large firm. Never. I've always wanted to work in a small one.'

'You've got to finish your training, and you can't do that with a one-man band. Besides, there won't be enough work for you.'

Her look of disappointment was also an acknowledgement of defeat. 'In a couple of years when you're overwhelmed with work, then.'

They were distracted by the sound of a child shouting

excitedly and looked round to see Tom and his boys making for the door. Joe, holding tight to his father's hand, gave a little skip, then as Tom held the door open for them Matt flung his father a bright grin.

Outside, the day was overcast with spitting rain, but it seemed to Hugh that the path ahead was brightening. He would drive up to see Charlie at the weekend, he would go with him to a group therapy session, they would have a quick meal. Then he would return to the rented house and work on his second case as an independent solicitor, a complex conveyance for one of his old clients. And in the moments when his mind wandered he would remember love and kindness, he would disallow the rest.

Visit **www.panmacmillan.com** to read more about all our books and to buy them. You will also find features, author interviews and news of any author events, and you can sign up for e-newsletters so that you're always first to hear about our new releases.

© 2005 PAN MACMILLAN    ACCESSIBILITY    HELP    TERMS & CONDITIONS    PRIVACY POLICY    SEND PAGE TO A FRIEND